W9-BCD-507

ELIMINATION NIGHT

ELIMINATION NIGHT

A NOVEL

Anonymous

NEW HARVEST
HOUGHTON MIFFLIN HARCOURT
2013 · BOSTON · NEW YORK

This edition published by special arrangement with Amazon Publishing

For information about permission to reproduce selections from this book, write to Permissions, Houghton Mifflin Harcourt Publishing Company, 215 Park Avenue South, New York, New York 10003.

www.hmhbooks.com

Library of Congress Cataloging-in-Publication is available.

ISBN 978-0-547-94207-0

Book design by Brian Moore

Printed in the United States of America
DOC 10 9 8 7 6 5 4 3 2 1

This is a work of fiction.
Any similarity to any persons living or dead—or to any real organizations and/or corporations—is coincidental.

The following document was recovered from a laptop computer left in a dumpster behind the offices of Zero Management in Los Angeles.

No one has yet claimed ownership.

The true identity of the author remains unknown.

CONTENTS

PROJECT ICON

SEASON THIRTEEN SCHEDULE

July–August

Preauditions

September

The Reveal

November–December

Auditions (with judges)

Early January

Las Vegas Week

Late January

Season Premier

February

Live episodes from Greenlit Studios

May

Season Finale

ELIMINATION NIGHT

1

Becoming Bill

September

"LOOK AT ME, Bill," said Len.

I looked.

"Now, tell me what you see."

I had no idea where he was going with this. I didn't really *want* to know, to be honest with you.

"I see . . . your face," I said.

"And tell me, Bill," Len went on, "is my face betraying any sign, any hint—any indication *whatsoever*—that I might actually care about the logistical difficulty of performing the task I delegated to you? Is my face telling you that, Bill? *Is that what you see?*"

"No," I sighed.

"Good. Now, *please* give the judges the run-through. And chop-bloody-chop. We're on in ten."

With that, Leonard Braithwaite—Supervising Producer of the Most-Watched Television Show on Earth—twirled on his heels like the backup dancer he used to be, and took his ridiculous English accent and even more ridiculous suit over to the other side of the room. Clotted cream and baby blue, that was today's color scheme—with pinstripes so wide they could have been rolled onto his pants by one of those lawn painting machines they have at Wimbledon.

Len is an asshole, in case you haven't figured that out already. I would go so far as to say that he's an *asshole's* asshole, such is his lifelong dedication to the craft of assholeness. Len also couldn't exist anywhere outside of reality TV. Take that faux bronze wet-look man-perm: "The Merm," as it's known here backstage. In the non-TV universe, such a hairstyle would be nearing the outer limits of credibility if its owner were merely approaching middle age. As it is, Len can't be a day under seventy-five. It's the *teeth* that give it away: an unnatural shade of white, with the lumpy, thick-grained texture of medieval church cabinetry.

I stared at the clipboard in my hand, as if that might somehow make the next ten minutes of my life any easier. Attached was the run-through Len had just mentioned: a twelve-page script for the eleven o'clock press conference, which would take place in the auditorium downstairs and would be streamed live on the Internet to a worldwide audience of two hundred million people (or so the Rabbit network was optimistically claiming). If you believed *ShowBiz* magazine—the holy text of industry gossip that lands on every desk in Hollywood once a week—an entire billion-dollar-a-year franchise depended on our not screwing this up. As, therefore, did all our jobs. So it was strange that Len wanted to put *me* in charge of the run-through. It wasn't unusual for him to over-delegate, of course: He did it all the time, usually so he could take one of his five-hour lunch breaks at Mr. Chang's. But today was different.

Today *mattered.*

I tried to calm myself. What was it my old meditation tutor used to say? "Imagine yourself as a *majestic mountain.*" I closed my eyes and pictured Everest, but my inner mountain wasn't cooperating. Besides, when I first moved to LA, I promised myself I'd never turn into the kind of person who would say "imagine yourself as a majestic mountain" unless in mockery. So instead I just stood there, watching as four crew guys carried a vast airbrushed banner—in colors that looked suspiciously like the branding of a certain global hamburger chain—through the pre-show lounge area. "*PROJECT ICON: THE DREAM REAWAKENS!*" it read.

Len had told me to fire the sign writer weeks ago. I had yet to find the right moment.

"Nine minutes until we're on!" a voice behind me yelled.

I had to do the run-through. If only I hadn't left my jar of little green pills in the bathroom cabinet at home. How else was I going to find the courage to address a room full of celebrities? Unless . . . unless I did what I'd been fantasizing about since my very first day at *Project Icon,* and quit. It wasn't like I owed anyone here anything. I could just walk out, right now. I'd be at the baggage carousel at Honolulu International before dinner. Then a fifteen-minute taxi ride to Waikiki Beach, and then—oh, yes!—one of my sweet, handsome Brock's frontal lobotomy mai tais, served under the hundred-year-old kiawe tree in the bar of the Huakuwali Hotel to the romantic, albeit slightly cheesy rhythm of hula music.

Only that wasn't the plan.

No, the plan was to keep working, keep saving, until I had enough in the bank to leave this place and never come back.

Only then could I get on that plane.

So my name isn't actually Bill, just FYI. It's Sasha. Bill was—sorry, *is*—the name of my immediate boss, Bill Redmond, whose duties as assistant producer of *Project Icon* are now mine, or at least until Bill gets out of the ER at Denver General Medical Center.

Long story.

Len calls me Bill because he didn't want there to be any confusion during the "transition of responsibilities." Which means to say: Len calls me Bill because he thinks of his employees as being basically interchangeable. "That's just how things are, Bill, when you work in live television," he once explained to me. But really that's just how things are when you work for Len, whose Repulsive Personality Field seems to have doubled in strength since he returned to the show for its thirteenth—and almost certainly final—season.

And so: Back in June, on the morning of that unfortunate incident in Denver, I, Sasha King—the pale, red-curled, non-girliest girl ever to work in live entertainment—became Bill. Or "acting assistant producer," to use my official title, which no one does. The "acting" bit means I get the double privilege of responsibilities—serious, one-hour-of-sleep, lifespan-shortening responsibilities—while still being relied on for menial tasks, such as procuring obscure fried meat products for homesick Southern contestants or collecting Len's eighteen-month-old adopted Congolese orphan from his nightly Bikram yoga class.

No, Mom *really* couldn't believe it when I took this job.

"Since when have you wanted anything to do with *show business?*" she asked, spitting vodka everywhere. "You've never cared about glam or glitz in your life! You don't even wear *makeup,* dear. I thought you wanted to be a writer, like that man—y'know, the one who wrote that depressing book you're always carrying around with you, *Never-ending Misery.*"

"It's *One Hundred Years of Solitude,* Mom," I sighed. "And it's not depressing. It's the greatest novel ever written. Dad gave it to me for my sixteenth birthday."

"This is just very . . . *unlike* you, dear. What about Brock? Is he going to LA, too?"

"No, Mom. Brock's not coming with me. He's moving to . . . look, it doesn't matter. This is a short-term thing. If I'm ever going to finish my novel, I need to take some time off. And for that, I need some money. The student loans are gone, Mom."

"What about your inheritance?"

"Jesus, Mom. Dad left me four dollars and half a pack of Camel Lights."

"I thought he left you his moose socks, too?"

"*And* the moose socks, yes."

Mom did have a point about all of this, of course: Growing up in the fishing hamlet of Babylon, Long Island—with its peeling paintwork, Babylicious Crab Cakes, and twice-weekly hurricanes—I mocked anyone with an interest in celebrities. Even as an infant (or so I've been told) I considered most forms of popular entertainment beneath me. Rattles? *Meh.* Stuffed animals? *Please.* Life was a serious business, as far as Baby Me was concerned, requiring deep thought and a frown at all times. Even a giggle was asking too much: If you tickled my belly, I would grunt and try my best to punch you in the face. (Dad found infinite amusement in this, judging by the camcorder footage.) Things didn't change much as I got older. I preferred the Discovery Channel to the Mickey Mouse Club, the spelling bee to the cheerleading squad, *The Times*' op-ed page to the sex quiz in *Seventeen.* Full-blown nerdism, in other words.

Nevertheless, by the time I got to high school—where I hung with the cooler of the uncool kids—my knowledge of early seventies Tom Waits albums and appreciation for Lou Reed's experimental period gave me a certain kind of credibility with a certain kind of boy . . . and of course it did no harm that by then I'd learned how to manage my inextinguishable wildfire of orange curls, or that I'd inherited Dad's nerves, which kept me on the bonier side of slim despite a lifelong pastry habit. (Unfortunately, this effect is no longer quite as reliable as it once was.)

As for college: Well, I was an okay student . . . but a little cocky. "Jesus, Sash, even your *irony* is ironic," as Dad used to say. A classic teenage self-defense mechanism, of course. But this was lost on the admissions officers of the prestigious schools to which I applied. They took it as detachment or over-confidence, maybe both. Hence my place at the J-School you won't have heard of, half the tuition paid for with loans, the other half by Mom, who had worked double-time shoveling meds as a Walgreens pharmacist for the best part of a decade to make sure her only child went to college. (Shockingly, Dad's "career" as a wedding trumpeter didn't contribute much in the higher education department, unless you count the time he sent me a plastic-wrapped tray of hallucinogenic cookies.)

Suffice it to say, I was turned down for internships at all our nation's great metropolitan newspapers, and quite a few of the not-so-great ones, too. Same story with the big magazines. And the TV news networks. Then Dad's Irish peasant genes went and gave him cancer, and shortly after that god-awful funeral in the church he'd been to only once before, I embarked on my Novel of Immense Profundity. Or rather, I spent a year living at home, staring tearfully at an empty Word document. I wanted my book to be epic. A generation-spanning masterpiece. Something Gabriel García Márquez himself might have written. The problem was, I couldn't decide where to set it. Long Island seemed too obvious. Aside from college, however, I'd never really *been* anywhere else before . . .

I was saved from this indecision by Brock—calm, funny, excitingly toned Brock Spencer Daniels—whose frat buddy worked at Rabbit News and was looking for a talent booker's assistant. Before I knew it, I'd been offered the job—if the word "job" can be used to describe a position whose salary consisted of a MetroCard and a daily canteen allowance. My first assignment: help organize a panel interview with the cast and crew of *Project Icon,* led by none other than Leonard Braithwaite.

A couple of months later, Len called my cell (I hadn't given him the number) to offer me a "dazzling opportunity in Hollywood, California."

"I bet they've got you working for free over there at Rabbit, haven't they?" he chuckled.

"Yes," I admitted (stupidly).

"Well, then—I think we can offer you a raise," he replied. "How does *more than nothing* sound?"

The line went fuzzy with laughter. To Len, the world's funniest joke is the one he's just told.

The money he offered wasn't good, but it was good enough for

Brock and me to hatch a plan: He'd move to Honolulu to focus on his "surfing career" (while making cocktails on the weekends and finding us a place to live), and I'd take the job at *Icon* until my savings account was refilled. Then I'd join him beachside to finish my novel. He'd win the MegaWave Super Crown. I'd win the Most Immensely Profound Novel of Our Generation Award.

We had it all worked out.

So off I went to LA.

"Another one of Len's Lovelies, huh?" sneered the vinegar-faced woman in *Icon*'s accounts department on my very first morning. "Funny – they're usually blondes, not redheads. His standards must be slipping."

I didn't know it at the time, but I had just met Len's wife.

2

A Horrible Farewell

I CHECKED THE TIME on my cell phone: Barely seven minutes to go now before the press conference—or "The Reveal" as Len insisted on calling it—was due to start.

The run-through.

Must do the run-through . . .

I began speed walking down a yellowing hallway, wondering vaguely if the exercise might spare me yet another depressing visit to the Starlight Gym on Hollywood Boulevard—which typically involved an hour of heavy breathing on an elliptical machine while staring at the absolute perfection of some cow town beauty queen's Lycra-encased buttocks. I could definitely have used *something* to burn the dumpster-sized box of sticky buns that I had emptied into my digestive system earlier, when I thought Len wasn't there. (No such luck. "Look, everyone, *here comes Miss Cinnabon!*" he'd boomed over the PA system during rehearsal.)

The corridor dead-ended.

Where the hell were the dressing rooms?

I wished for a moment we were on the more familiar territory of

Greenlit Studios. It would be *months* before we reached that stage of the competition, however. For now, *Project Icon* was still touring from city to city, prescreening potential contestants. This week, conveniently, we were in LA—but we needed a venue with a big enough parking lot for the "cattle call" of mostly delusional masochists who wanted to line up all day for the opportunity to be insulted on TV. That's why Len had rented The Roundhouse, a big old concrete arena down by the oil fields. The place had originally been designed to resemble a Roman coliseum, only they'd slathered the entire thing in cheap sixties stucco, so now it just looked like a giant overflowing porridge bowl.

"Six minutes!"

Shit.

Another corridor.

I broke into an undignified half-jog, half-run. At last, after turning a corner, there they were . . . two doors, side-by-side, a golden star on each. Pushing my hair back from my eyes, I tried to breathe deeply from my abdomen. "*You're a majestic mountain,*" I told myself. Then I knocked twice loudly, in an attempt to project confidence, before flicking through the sheaf of papers on my clipboard, one last time. Len's notes were underlined in the right-hand margin:

11AM: HOUSE LIGHTS DOWN

On time, please!

11.05AM: VIDEO PACKAGE

Slow motion clips of previous *Project Icon* winners/contestants, set to Carl Orff's "O Fortuna."

Bill—this isn't Carnegie fucking Hall.
Anything weepy and out of copyright will do.

11.07AM: INTRODUCTION

WAYNE SHORELINE (HOST)

Welcome, welcome everyone. This . . . [long pause] is *season thirteen* . . . [even longer pause] of *PROJECT ICON!* And I am your host, Wayne Shoreline, at your humble service. So, by now the whole world knows our incredible story: How the business genius Sir Harold Killoch discovered an obscure TV talent contest in Belgium — featuring a revolutionary system of telephone voting — and brought it here to the Rabbit network in America, where it shot to the top of the prime-time ratings and became a worldwide sensation.

[Audience goes wild. Close-up of Sir Harold smiling front of house.]

Bill — talk to the smile-coach again.
Need Sir H. to look more Cuddly Grandpa,
less Dark Lord of Evil.

And who could forget our original, *iconic* lineup of judges? America's favorite uncle, JD Coolz [applause]; the beautiful and dare I say sometimes a little *unpredictable* Pamela Crabtree *Wayne — double-check with legal for approved crack-head euphemisms.* and of course "Mr. Horrible" himself, our erect-nippled Scottish friend Nigel Crowther . . .

[Audience boos]

Bill — let this run a bit. . . . Erect-nippled — really?

Over the years our show has gone through lots of changes — most dramatically when Nigel sadly left the judging panel last year to pursue other opportunities at the Rabbit network. We wish him all the very best, of course, and we're sure he'll have many, many more successes. *Wayne — NO FUCKING SARCASM.* But one thing has remained a constant: Our NUMBER ONE ratings. So! [Tense music.] Back to the news that everyone has been waiting for. There has been *talk.* There have been *rumors.* We've all heard mention of many, *many* names. But now, finally, here in this room, we can reveal WHO will be sitting in the judges' chairs over the coming months, helping us find. . . . [another pause] the next winner . . . [pause again, spool-up title theme] of *PROJECT ICON!*

Wayne — new delivery ideas?
All these pauses are getting
a bit old, no? Food for thought . . .

I wondered how many people would know that most of this intro was bullshit. In particular the bit about the "business genius Sir Harold Killoch" having anything to do with *Icon*'s success. I mean, yes, Sir

Harold owned both the Rabbit network, and its parent company, The Big Corporation—so in that sense he was responsible for putting the show on the air. But as everyone who'd ever read *ShowBiz* knew, it was the mogul's younger brother George who'd seen the original Belgian format—while on a beer-tasting vacation in Antwerp—and suggested that Rabbit license it from its creator, Sven Svendsen, a reclusive Swedish talent agent.

"Who the hell wants to listen to a bunch of piss-poor wannabes who *can't* sing?" was Sir Harold's response, according to his unofficial biography, *Harold's Killing.* Nevertheless, he ordered Rabbit to buy the rights, and within a few weeks, a pilot had been commissioned. "Old Harry thinks it's the dumbest TV pitch he's ever heard," as *ShowBiz* reported at the time. "But his baby brother George—like all Killoch family members—is a voting shareholder in Big Corp, and therefore needs to be indulged. We predict a swift cancellation."

Rabbit aired the first episode at midnight on a Friday: "The hospice slot," as I've since learned it is known (due to the fact that ninety percent of viewers at such an hour reside in assisted living communities). That in itself might have been enough to kill *Project Icon,* if not for the fact that Sir Harold asked Sven Svendsen—a.k.a. "Two Svens"—to help run the show.

Two Svens' first move? Hiring his old friend Leonard Braithwaite as supervising producer.

I had no idea who Len was back then. No one in the US did. It was only later I found out he'd starred as a cruel-to-be-kind mentor in *From Arse End to the West End,* an acclaimed British TV documentary about the creation of a theater production using actors cast entirely from soup kitchens. That's how Len persuaded Two Svens to hire exactly the same kind of villain for the Rabbit version of *Project Icon.* He couldn't cast himself, though—the network wouldn't let him—so he found a doppelgänger, Nigel Crowther, and spent months coaching him on "sneer technique" and "insult metaphors."

Oh, America had *no idea* what was coming.

Pretty much everyone remembers the first time they saw Crowther on TV. Me? I was at my friend Maggie's house, pretending to study for a math exam. I'd actually wanted to watch a *NOVA* documentary about long-whiskered Peruvian owls (that's how hard I partied as a thirteen-year-old), but Maggie insisted on loading up *Icon* from her early-model TiVo. And thanks to Crowther, I couldn't stop watching: Here was this aging, pudding-bellied, apparently heterosexual Scotsman with a toilet-brush hairdo, who kept his shirt unbuttoned to several inches below the navel, and appeared to have doused himself repeatedly in some kind of fluorescent orange tanning solution. More extraordinary, however, was his willingness to insult contestants to their faces, even if they were deranged or sobbing with fear—or both, which was more often than not the case.

"When you reach for the high notes, David, you look like a brain damaged orangutan with a genital itch who's trying to lick poo off its nose," he informed one visibly quaking teenager, who promptly fell to his knees weeping.

Within a few days, "Mr. Horrible" was a national sensation. The Concerned Parents of Young Christian Patriots tried to sue to remove him from the airwaves. Several members of Congress petitioned. Even the president of the United States himself made a personal call to Sir Harold, which the mogul put on hold, then sent through to voicemail, before leaking the voicemail—out of habit—to the editor of one of his more prominent news websites.

"PREZ BLASTS MR. HORRIBLE FOR POO-LICKING RETARD JIBE," read the headline.

Everyone wanted to know: *Who the hell was this guy?*

It didn't take long for *ShowBiz* to dig up an answer: Before *Icon,* Crowther had been a talent scout in Glasgow, best known for discovering a pop duo named the Dreami Boyz, whose gimmick was to appear on stage wearing only pajama bottoms. They'd been a spectacular hit with both the grandma and gay demographics—hence the two million sales of their abominable first album, *Sweet Dreamz & Warm Cuddlez,* which received the first ever negative-starred review from *NME.*

Perhaps inevitably, Two Svens—three hundred pounds, ice-skating enthusiast, face like an exploded dumpling—couldn't stand Crowther. He swung a punch at him a couple of times, in fact. Even Len fell out with his protégé within a few days. But it didn't matter. By the end of *Project Icon*'s first season, "Mr. Horrible" had become one of the most famous men on earth. And by the second season, more votes were being cast by the show's viewers every week than it takes to win the keys to the White House. As a result, Crowther was able to negotiate a contract that made him the best-paid performer in TV history.

And now?

Well, as the script said—there wasn't any hiding it—Crowther had left. What the script *didn't* say was that Two Svens had turned almost homicidal with rage upon learning this news, especially given that he'd offered Crowther a "Triple Oprah"—i.e., *three times* the salary of the Queen of Daytime TV during her final season on network TV—to stay on for another year. Crowther's counteroffer? No salary. But one hundred percent ownership of everything.

Two Svens thought he was joking.

Another fact omitted from Wayne's script: Crowther had now started to work on his own rival TV franchise, *The Talent Machine,* which the Rabbit network had paid for and promised to air. Thankfully, *The Talent Machine* wouldn't be ready for another year. But when the show did finally make it onto Rabbit's prime-time schedule, it seemed obvious that only *one* singing competition could survive.

As Chaz Chipford, the newly-assigned *Project Icon* correspondent for *ShowBiz,* summed it up:

> Season thirteen is a live or die moment for *Project Icon*—a last chance for the Rabbit tentpole warblefest to prove that it's still viable without superstar Crowther. Odds don't look good, even with dancepants-wearing showrunner Leonard Braithwaite back in the supervising producer's seat (robo-host Wayne Shoreline also inked a new contract last week). After all, *The Talent Machine* is revving up like an eighteen-wheeler for its debut next year, and Madison Avenue expects it to spatter *Icon* like a bug on its windshield. Sure, *Icon* and *T-*

Machine won't air at the same time, but Rabbit insiders say Crowther will likely soak up all the audience for warblefests in the fall, leaving *Icon* to pick over the scraps come January. Besides, as Sir Harold already knows: *Icon*'s format is as stale as a week-old Pink's hot dog, and ratings have been tanking by TEN PERCENT a year for the last five seasons. Word is even going around The Lot of a top-secret plan at Big Corp to ax *Icon* THIS season if it loses its number-one position. Old Harry — who celebrates his eighty-second birthday next week at Skullhead, his private island in the South Pacific — wants to spare it (or perhaps himself) any future humiliation. What few hopes remain now rest on a cast of untested new judges, after Sir Harold ordered Braithwaite to "nuke the panel." JD Coolz remains — he's cheap — but dud celebrity chef Helen DeMendes has been ankled, as has sourpuss tunesmith Kat Patrigliano. Rumor has it, only two "stars" will be hired to fill the three empty seats. Trouble is, no matter who comes on board, there'll still be a gaping, Crowther-shaped hole.

Those two stars were now supposed to be in their dressing rooms, waiting for me to give them the run-through of the press conference, where in five minutes we'd reveal their names. But I'd knocked six or seven times now, and no one had answered.

Where the hell were they?

"Ahem. Hello?" I said, rapping on the first door again, hurting my knuckles. "Anybody there?"

Silence.

Another try, this time on the second door.

"This is Bill," I called out. "For the run-through. We're starting in two minutes."

Nothing.

Out of options, I turned the handle in front of me and pushed. The door swung open to reveal an untouched room. The red sofas I'd bought on the *Project Icon* credit card for five thousand dollars apiece showed no creases. Neither did the five hundred dollar red silk pillows. Likewise, the red candles were unlit, the red iPad on its red docking station next to the red roses was still playing *The Best of Enya*, and the seal on the room temperature Pellegrino (placed on the red table, next to the red vase) was unbroken. In spite of the *eight days* it had taken me to furnish this room to such precise specifications, no one appeared to have set foot in it.

Same deal: leather bean bags fluffed and perfect. Mongolian dream catcher untroubled by a breeze from the switched-off wind machine. Giant vat of drinking water (marked "Kangen" in black Sharpie) still full to the brim and gurgling quietly to itself. And under the Broadway-style vanity mirror, a foot-long roast beef sub, placed strategically next to a square-jawed Action Man figure, who for reasons not worth getting into right now was dressed in nothing but a frilly pink Barbie doll bra. Attached to the latter was a note from Len, which read, "Best we could manage, I'm afraid!"

Uh-oh—something's up, I thought.

And this was a problem. Because we were out of time.

3

Sanity Check

THINGS WERE PRETTY desperate at *Project Icon* after Nigel Crowther left. I mean, by most accounts, season twelve had been our worst ever. This was of course thanks largely to Crowther, who—in a blatant act of sabotage—had repeatedly told the audience to vote for Ernie Bucket, a cross-eyed Wisconsin tractor salesman with horrific facial warts and a single octave range (his debut album, *Ain't Pretty, But Sure Can Sing,* would go on to sell a hundred and twenty copies, mostly in the greater Milwaukee area). Predictions of our cancellation were all over the Internet, and the crew's morale was so low, I saw people—okay, *one* person—weeping at their desks.

As for me: Every morning, I woke up with a new plan to get on a plane to Honolulu.

That wasn't an option, of course. Not if I wanted enough money in the bank to take a year off and finish my Novel of Immense Profundity. In fact, I was starting to wonder if a year would be *enough,* given the lack of recent progress.

So far, this was all I had written:

> The old man's knobbled, weary arms pulled at the oars, as a lashing rain drenched his robes. With each hellish clap of thunder, he thought of what his grandfather had told him when he was a boy: "Let ye be warned, my child! Never go out on the Black Lake of Sorrow when the shutters of the Old House are closed!"

It was epic, for sure. And it spanned generations. (I was quite proud of the grandfather character.) But as you'd expect at such a preliminary stage of the creative process, a number of plot issues remained. Such as: Who the hell was this knobbled, weary old man? Why was he wearing a robe? What was he doing on a boat, on a lake? *Where* was the lake? Why hadn't he used a more convenient mode of transportation? Was the name "Black Lake of Sorrow" a little overwrought? (I'd already toned it down from the "Black Lake of Doom.") And how could the shutters of the Old House *possibly* have any effect on the local sailing conditions?

Still, I was confident the answers to all these questions would come—along with the rest of the chapter and the remaining twenty-nine *other* chapters I planned to write—just as soon as I got to Honolulu. All I had to do was keep my job at *Project Icon* for a few more months, so I could afford the ticket to get there.

It was tough in LA without Brock, though. I missed his stupid jokes, his refusal to think about anything too deeply. "He lightens you up," as Mom once said. "You *need* that, dear. Especially after what you've been through with your father."

In fact, Brock and I wouldn't have started dating if it hadn't been for Dad's funeral: He just happened to be working behind the bar at Billy McQuiffy's when we all piled in there after the service. (It's a King family traditional to get drunk after—or during—most significant occasions.) I already knew Brock Spencer Daniels from Babylon High, of course. He'd practically been a *celebrity* when I was there: too slight for football, but a huge track and field star. Oh, and his girlfriend was Jenny Baker—who kept having to take days off for modeling shoots in

Manhattan. Brock and Jenny were a couple of such impossible glamour, kids had posters of them pinned up on their bedroom walls.

Brock lost his way after senior year, though. He got into college—an athletic scholarship—but dropped out for some vague reason after a few months. Then Jenny dumped him for a police officer: a *female* police officer. He'd been in limbo ever since. Working for his dad during the week. Chasing waves in Montauk at the weekend. His plan, he told me, was to make surfing a career. He'd already won a few championships, and his next goal was to get an endorsement deal. That's why he wanted to go to Hawaii, where most of the board makers were based.

When I saw Brock that afternoon in Billy McQuiffy's, he was just as absurdly handsome as I remembered. Same shaggy dark hair. Same outdoorsy tan. Same blue-gray eyes. I wasn't exactly in the mood for romance after the funeral, of course. And maybe Brock wasn't interested, either. But he did make the first move.

"Hey, wanna go skydiving tomorrow?" he asked, pouring my fourth refill. (By then we'd already been through the don't-I-know-you-from-somewhere conversation, which basically established that no, he didn't remember me at all.)

"*Skydiving?*"

"I'm going with Pete Mitchell," Brock elaborated. "You remember Pete, doncha?"

"Crazy Pete who got a pencil sharpener stuck up his nose in seventh grade?"

"Yeah, Crazy Pete. A buddy of his has got a jump school down near the Keys. He's offered us some free rides, as long as we gas up the plane ourselves."

"Wow, Florida," I said, now even more surprised by the invitation. "How are you getting there?"

"My mom's SUV."

"Where are you staying?"

"My mom's SUV."

I laughed. "Thanks for the offer, Brock. I'd really love to. But I'm not going to be much fun. I'm going to be the *opposite* of fun, actually. Now isn't a good time."

"You kidding me?" said Brock. "The day after your dad's funeral is the *best* time."

Brock was right: I needed a distraction. And as I found out when we got to Florida, it was impossible to think about Dad—anything, really—while falling from a plane at 115 mph. Especially given that I was strapped to a man named Crazy Pete.

Nothing happened between Brock and me on that trip, I should add. Nothing physical, anyway. But when we went back to the Keys a few weeks later—this time, no Pete—we got through two bottles of wine on the first night and woke up in an embrace so close, it took a day for the circulation to return to my left arm.

All that was two years ago—and we barely spent a day apart until I left for LA.

Being separated from Brock wasn't the *only* difficult thing about living out West, of course: I was also broke—a result of trying to put at least half of every paycheck into my Hawaii fund. Hence my crappy Little Russia basement apartment, which received precisely three minutes of sunlight a day through its single half-pane window, and the fact that I commuted to work on a sit-up-and-beg bicycle, which had somehow become stuck permanently in seventh gear.

"I don't get it, Meess Sasha," as my Siberian super kept telling me. "You say you work with all these superstar people, but you live *here*. This place is total sheethole. I give you job cleaning toilets, and you afford nicer place. It crazy situation, Meess Sasha. You beautiful redheaded woman, even though you're pale as a ghost and dress like old man. Why not you find some rich celebrity boytoy, so you can have sweeming pool?"

"Actually, I've *got* a boyfriend," I protested.

"He invisible?"

"No, he lives in Hawaii. I'm moving out there to be with him next summer."

"Like I said: *Invisible.* Why not you try eCupidMatch.com? I help you write profile."

"I've gotta go, Mr. Zglagovvcini."

"On rusty bicycle? You *madwoman!* Why not you buy a car?"

"Because I'm saving money."

"Life too short to be so tight in the ass, Meess Sasha. You young. You should leeve a little."

Mr. Zglagovvcini went on like this pretty much every day—or at least until things got so crazy at work, I was getting home at one in the morning, only to leave again at dawn, when he was safely in bed and snoring with enough force to make the pipes in my bathroom vibrate.

I suppose it should have come as a relief to avoid his nagging.

And yet . . . I kind of *missed* it.

So: the first of the potential Crowther replacements to come in for an interview was none other than Joey Lovecraft. Yeah, *that* Joey Lovecraft. Not that Len allowed us to use the word "interview," of course. God, no. Officially, it was a "strategy session." In reality . . . it was neither of those things. It was a *sanity check.* Joey Lovecraft had a reputation, after all. And Sir Harold had already made it clear he didn't think Joey was mentally fit for the job—*any* job, not least as a celebrity judge on the world's most-watched TV show. (Given the recent YouTube clip of his "accident" in Houston—for God's sake don't Google on a full stomach—there wasn't much point in arguing.)

Nevertheless, the executives at Rabbit were convinced Joey could be managed. It was just going to take a little patience. That, and a full-time squad of Joey-minders.

Actually, the fact that Joey had been given *any* kind of meeting at all was pretty incredible. After all, when news first broke about Nigel Crowther leaving *Icon,* Len's cell phone turned so hot—1,438 missed calls in ten minutes—it literally began to melt. Every agent in Hollywood wanted to set up a meet and greet for their client. And it wasn't just the reality TV crowd who wanted in: It was some of the most famous people alive—people whose names come above Coca-Cola in global brand surveys. Did any of them give a crap about "finding the next Elvis" or whatever bullshit their reps came up with to explain their sudden interest in a singing competition? No. What they cared about—what they *really* cared about—was the Triple Oprah.

Joey was different, though. He didn't need the money. Maybe that's why Rabbit wanted him so bad, regardless of Sir Harold's very public misgivings.

Clearly, the job of vetting judges couldn't be done at Greenlit Studios: It was June, so the set was being dismantled, and we were getting ready to move out until the following year, when the live shows of season thirteen would begin. The meetings also couldn't be held at the offices of Two Svens' company, Zero Management, because the enormous Swede was still crippled with rage over the whole *Talent Machine* situation—that, and the hour-long "farewell ceremony" Nigel Crowther had bullied Rabbit into staging for him during *Icon*'s season twelve finale. In terms of pomp, the latter had been pitched somewhere between a papal death and the Beijing Olympics—and Crowther's fellow judges had to sit there for the duration, grinning and clapping, in the full knowledge that he was single-handedly responsible for getting them all fired. (Apart from JD Coolz, that is—but he didn't know it at the time.)

Hence Joey was told to go to The Lot, the walled minitropolis out in the San Fernando Valley where Rabbit Studios makes its movies and respectable, scripted TV shows. More specifically, he was booked to sit down with Ed "Big Guy" Rossitto, president of Rabbit's Mainstream Entertainment division, whose office is located about a half-mile north of the twin golden bunnies that sit atop The Lot's entrance on Sir Harold Killoch Drive. Len was also asked to come along—or maybe he invited himself, hard to tell—which meant I also needed to be there for moral support. Or to "look smart and fuckable" as Len put it helpfully, with a disapproving nod at my comfort-focused getup of jeans, hiking sneakers, and a pizza-stained halter top. (Note to self, I thought: *wear pants.*)

In truth, I was glad to at least be a part of the hiring process—even though my stomach had second thoughts when the morning of the interview finally came around. It took *three* green pills to halt the resulting panic attack before I climbed into the back of Len's dark green chauffeured Jaguar.

Then off we went. No turning back.

Rossitto's office turned out to be on the top floor of a tinted-glass tower overlooking an immaculate bunny-shaped lake.

At least the view would be good from up there, I told myself.

Boy, was I wrong.

We stepped out of the private, leather-upholstered elevator into darkness. Rugs and sheets hung over the windows. Incense sticks burned. Beyond the long, oak table for Rossitto's assistants was an inner lair, in which a grand piano stood next to a suit of armor, under an oil painting of some beardy guy from the Revolutionary War. We were shown to an ancient chesterfield in the far corner and invited to sit. Rossitto would be here in a minute, we were told, after he'd finished doing something else (something more important, being the hint). I'd been to enough Hollywood meetings to know the drill: He'd "arrive" seconds after Joey walked in the door—"Perfect timing!"—all man hugs and buddy slams.

"So, what d'you know about Joey Lovecraft?" Len semiwhispered, as we sat there in Rossitto's penthouse batcave, our eyes aching as they adjusted to the half-light.

"Oh, y'know . . . the headlines."

In fact, I had a binder of research in front of me. I'd spent most of the previous night reading it—even though it wasn't exactly necessary. I mean, this was *Joey Lovecraft* we were talking about. His life story had been turned into five movies. His leather pants had been sent into orbit aboard Apollo 16. He'd even been mentioned in a Rose Garden speech. ("Joey Dumbass," President Reagan had called him.)

"Coffee?" interrupted an assistant.

"Water," countered Len. "Not tap."

"Black, four sugars, please," I said.

Len looked at me with disgust. Then, when the assistant had left the room, he said, "Go on then."

"Huh?"

"Jesus Christ, Bill. *Give me the bloody headlines.*"

For a moment I thought this must be some kind of test. But then I realized: Len was too old for Joey's music. He must have been born in the late thirties, before the Second World War. Meaning he would have spent his later teenage years listening to Bill Haley and Elvis Presley, not the Rolling Stones and Honeyload. Or maybe Len was even *older* than that: a Tommy Dorsey and Frank Sinatra guy. Looking at him in that unflattering gloom, it wouldn't have surprised me to learn that Leonard Braithwaite predated the twentieth century altogether.

"Okay, the headlines," I said, glancing around to make sure no one was listening.

Then I recited from memory: "Joey Lovecraft, the world's least boring Canadian, and lead singer of hard rock band Honeyload, until their latest break-up, anyway . . . one half of the so-called Devil's Duo with his childhood best friend and Honeyload lead guitarist Blade Morgan . . . survivor of drunken parachute jump from a small aircraft over Manhattan *without a parachute* . . . longest-ever resident of the Betty Ford Center . . . he was there for every single day of the nineties, apart from the forty-eight hours when he attempted to murder the president of BeeBop Records . . . seven-times divorced, his last wife being the eighteen-year-old Pacific Island Princess Aleeya Khootna-Nmubbi . . . honorary doctor of chemistry at the University of Toronto . . . creator of his own strain of LSD . . . unbearable perfectionist . . . author of *My Fifty-Year Hangover: Worth Every Shot* . . . and of course defendant in that lawsuit a few years back about touring contracts, in particular a rider stipulating that after every show, a naked transsexual must prepare roast beef sandwiches for the band and its groupies, with the beef never to exceed a thickness of one-eighth of an inch. It's said Joey carries a ruler with him at all times to enforce this."

"Ah yes," said Len, wistfully. "I remember the beef. Anything else I should know?"

"That's about it, really."

Actually, I could have gone on for another hour or so, but I didn't want to come across as a fan. It's not cool, being a fan, when you work with celebrities. I mean, yes, you say, "I'm a fan," to every one of them you meet. But you don't actually *mean* it, because if you did, no one would trust you. Fans are civilians. And as such they are a liability.

In Joey's case, however, I am indeed a genuine fan. Somewhere in my old bedroom closet at Mom's house, I even have a collection of Honeyload T-shirts, each featuring the band's logo of a gleaming silver tool: wrench head at one end, penis head at the other — the latter glowing red and orange, as if reentering Earth's atmosphere at a great speed (while firing sperm-shaped bullets). In fact, I can still remember the very first time I ever heard Joey's voice on a warped cassette that I'd liberated from Mom's old boom box in the attic. I was seven years old. The song was from some bootlegged gig that Honeyload had played in Wichita Falls, back during the last days of legal acid and curable STDs. It was his tone, more than anything, that I fell in love with: like three singers in one, each slightly above or below the key, combining to form this aching, ragged noise that could jump between five or six octaves without ever losing power — a voice so clear, it sounded as though it had been recorded and mixed *inside the singer's lungs.*

Lucky for me, Honeyload had its first big comeback a few years after I discovered them. In fact, Joey was as big a star when I graduated from Babylon High as he'd been when Mom had done the same thing twenty years earlier. I remember him pouting down from my bedroom wall: shirt open, legs astride, flower protruding from between those enormous, never-quite-settled lips. To me, Joey was — will always be — The King of Sing, The Devil of Treble, The Holy Cow of Big Wow, and yes, The Wizz o' Jizz, as he'd so infamously christened himself during that 1998 *Hellraiser* magazine interview. (During the fifteen-page Q&A—no longer available online for legal reasons—Joey declared that he had never counted his conquests: "I only count the number of times they *scream,* man." He went on to claim responsibility for 1,028,981 female orgasms since Honeyload's first record deal.)

"So tell me something, Bill," asked Len. "If everything you say is true, why in God's name does a man like Joey Lovecraft need a show like *Project Icon?*"

I thought about this for a moment.

"He doesn't," I concluded.

Len gave a condescending snort. "Oh, c'mon," he said. "Even *you* know better than that."

"I mean, he doesn't need the *money,*" I clarified. "Honeyload sells ten million albums a year from its back catalog. And Joey does a lot of stuff on the side. His venture capital group just invented a marijuana-infused soft drink that's legal in twenty-three states. It's going to IPO next month."

"Nevertheless," said Len, impatiently. "There's a *reason* he's coming here today."

Before I could answer, I felt a vibration near my waist. Instinctively, I reached for my phone.

"Oh, I'm sorry," declared Len, with as much sarcasm as he could manage. "I didn't realize I was *disturbing* you. Would you like me to leave the room while you take that? Would you like me to tell Joey to come back another day?"

"I thought it was off," I protested, glancing at the screen while reaching for the power switch. A flurry of text messages had just arrived—all from a number I wouldn't have recognized, had I not programmed it into my address book a few hours earlier when the faucet in my apartment began delivering raw sewage instead of hot water. "Mr. Z," was how it came up.

I couldn't resist reading:

QUESTION FOR YOU, MEESS SASHA
WEBSITE NEED TO KNOW
ARE SUPER-LOGICAL GUYS ARE A TURN-ON?
OR YOU PREFER EXCITEMENT?
PLS ANSWER
PS: I FIX THE SHIT IN YOUR BATHTUB

I closed my eyes and shook my head. Mr. Zglagovvcini and I needed to have a very long talk.

"Is somebody *dying?*" asked Len.

"No," I replied, finally shutting down the phone. "It's nothing. Spam. Won't happen again."

"Good. Now tell me what Joey Lovecraft wants out of this deal. And hurry. He'll be here any minute, swinging that giant dick of his everywhere."

4

The M-Word

THE ANSWER TO LEN'S question was simple: Joey wanted to get Honeyload back together. Or more accurately, he wanted Blade Morgan to *beg him* to return as lead singer.

Without *Project Icon,* however, this wasn't likely to happen. After all, Joey hadn't spoken to Blade for three years. No phone calls. No e-mails. Not even a single text message. And the reason why Blade and Joey hadn't spoken was because Joey had gone back on the pills and the cognac during their last tour. Hardly a big deal in itself, of course: Joey had been high during every tour in the band's history. The big deal was this: On the night they played Houston, Joey walked on stage, dropped his pants, and proceeded to evacuate his bowels in front of Blade's amp stack, as punishment for Blade's refusal to turn down his reverb setting—which was allegedly interfering with Joey's ability to hear himself sing.

Now, again: Not such a biggie. Joey had been known to do worse. Much worse—especially when he was going through a pills-and-cognac period. But the evacuation had led to another issue—namely, that when Joey stood up after this toxic protest, he slipped and fell headfirst into the orchestra pit, breaking a leg and his collarbone in the process, which of course meant that the rest of the tour, all twenty-six dates of it, had to be cancelled. At first, the band wasn't particularly upset: This was precisely why they had bought a very expensive gig-cancellation insurance policy. But when they tried to make a claim, the underwriter—who'd watched "the Houston incident" unfold in graphic detail on YouTube—pointed out a clause in the policy that invalidated coverage in the event of "self-destruction." He argued, not unreasonably, that this included "broken limbs caused by slippage after a voluntary act of onstage defecation."

Joey was devastated. Unlike him, Blade and the other members of the band hadn't invested in the marijuana-soft drink industry. They *needed* the five million dollars they were due for those remaining gigs. And they didn't take it well, either. In fact, they cut Joey off completely, aside from a "Fuck You" card they sent to the hospital. Meanwhile, still tortured by guilt over what he'd done—and now on crutches—Joey headed to the only place he still felt welcome: the Betty Ford Center. But on the way there, he *disappeared.* It took a four-county manhunt and a worldwide vigil by fans before he was finally located, three days later, naked in a Kmart near La Quinta, California, singing "Psycho Sluts from Paradise" over the PA system. And when he finally cleaned himself up and tried to make good with the band, he discovered that in his absence, they'd been auditioning a new singer. As if that weren't humiliating enough, the singer was Billy Ray Cyrus.

He *hated* Billy Ray Cyrus.

Joey spent four days up a tree in his backyard, howling.

Then he took out an injunction against Honeyload to stop them touring without him and hired the nastiest managers he could find, Stanley Wojak and Mitch McDonald. "I need a fuckin' day job, man," he told them. "Go get me *Project Icon.*"

Like most of the other celebrities who'd applied for Nigel Crowther's position, Joey had never watched the show. Not a single episode. Neither had he shown any interest in watching it. He didn't even own a TV—it contradicted the teachings of his muse, the Tibetan high lama Yutog Gonpo. For Joey, *Icon* meant only one thing: leverage. He wanted to be able to say to Blade Morgan and his other ex-bandmates: *You can't fire me, I'm employable! I'm so hot, I'm worth a Triple Oprah!* And what better leverage could you possibly get than a twice-weekly gig in front of twenty million TV viewers? That was four times as many people than had bought *Deathray Juggernaut* in 1972, giving Honeyload their very first triple-diamond LP.

I'd just finished explaining all this to Len when a figure appeared in the doorway to Rossitto's office.

"Mitch!" said Len, getting up.

An uncomfortable half-handshake, half-hug followed.

"Bill, this is Mitch McDonald," Len announced. "Joey's manager. One of them, anyway, ha-ha."

"Only one that matters," declared Mitch. He didn't seem to be joking.

Mitch was short, pumped, entirely hairless—a human pool ball. Closing in on fifty, I guessed, and dressed as though for a funeral at an Apple Store: black jeans, black polo shirt, black sneakers. His face, meanwhile, was set into a frown that suggested the long-term expectation of disappointment.

"So who *is* this guy Ed Rossitto?" he growled, looking around the room skeptically.

"Oh, he's huge," said Len. "I mean, well . . . not *literally* huge. But a very big deal at Rabbit. A top decision maker. If Joey and Ed vibe"—in my entire time at *Project Icon,* I had never heard Len use this word before—"my guess is, this will be a go."

Mitch took a seat opposite us, crossed his legs, and said, "Save the bullshit for the teenagers, Len."

"Excuse me?"

"This isn't about Joey and Ed *vibing,*" sighed Mitch. "This is a sanity check. You want to make sure he's not crazy. You wanna look the guy in the eye, and not see cuckoos. Right?"

Len's face reddened slightly. Chuckling nervously, he said, "C'mon, Mitch."

Mitch just shrugged.

"There are *concerns,* yes," Len confirmed, delicately. "But it's not—"

"Truth is," Mitch interrupted, "we don't blame you. Joey's been in a bad place. But he's roaring back. *Roaring.*"

"Look, Mitch," said Len, leaning forward with a leathery squeak. "Given Joey's, y'know . . . *history,* and everything, there's something you should probably know. Just so it doesn't put anyone off balance. It's about Ed Rossitto. He's, uh . . ."

I wondered what the hell Len was about to say. Mitch was also clearly wondering: every sinew in his body seemed to have contracted. "What's the problem, Len?" he snapped. "Spit it out, man."

"Ed's . . . a wee guy—that's all. A bit on the short side. Just so you're prepared."

" . . . what the . . . ?"

"I know . . . I know. Not an issue. I just want you to have as much information as possible."

There was a long, baffled pause. I noticed Mitch begin to stare at Rossitto's suit of armor.

"*How* small, exactly?" he asked.

"Fucking tiny," blurted Len.

"Jesus, are we talking . . . *midget?*"

"No! Ssshh!" Len looked around. "He's not a *midget.* He's just, y'know—'wee,' as they say."

A troubling thought suddenly made itself visible on Mitch's brow. With a grunt of irritation, he stood up and began to pace. "Len," he said, "my client is *extremely* sensitive at the moment. He's stressed out, to be honest with you. Couldn't sleep last night. I got calls from him every hour, all through the night. He woke the baby up twice. Today means the world to him. The *world,* Len. And if you'd bothered to read the guy's autobiography—or do any kind of research whatsoever—you'd be aware of what happens to Joey when he gets all wound up like this."

Mitch stared at Len, as though awaiting an answer.

Len just stared back at him. I could tell by his expression that he was struggling to take this seriously.

"Flashbacks," Mitch resumed, angrily. "He gets flashbacks."

"Oh," said Len.

"He had a bad trip at a circus, Len. Summer of '63. And d'you know why the trip was so bad?"

Len's eyes were blank. I began to wonder how on earth I'd missed this in the file.

"*Do you know why?*" Mitch repeated, louder this time.

"No," said Len.

"BECAUSE HE GOT LOCKED IN A DRESSING ROOM FULL OF FUCKING MIDGETS."

Len and I looked urgently toward the reception area. Astonishingly, none of Rossitto's assistants seemed to have heard Mitch's potentially catastrophic deployment of the M-word. Or maybe they had, and were just ignoring it. Regardless, Mitch lowered his voice to a forced whisper, and continued: "And now you're telling me—with two minutes' notice—that the guy we're about to meet is gonna walk through that door *singing the Oompa-fucking-Loompa song?*"

Sweating now, Mitch reached for his briefcase, pulled out his phone and attempted to dial, before aborting the task to search for his reading glasses. "Gotta call Joey," he muttered, to no one in particular. "This is gonna be a shit show if we're not careful."

Len's face, which can bloom in many colors during moments of extreme pressure, had turned almost purple. "Mitch, *Mitch,* please," he said, standing up. "Ed's a great guy. I shouldn't have even mentioned this. Look, there's a piano in here. Why not suggest to Joey that he sit down and play a few bars of something, eh? That'll calm him down, right? And Ed will love that. He's all about bringing musical credibility back to the panel. And you don't get any more credible than Jo—"

Suddenly, a commotion outside.

Len and Mitch froze, then threw themselves simultaneously in the direction of the noise. I followed, to see what appeared to be a Native American chief striding out of Rossitto's elevator. Two absurdly hot girls flanked him, one of them wheeling a . . . a *tank of water?* "My Kangen water!" announced the chief. "Can't go anywhere without my Kangen water! It's got the yin and the yang, and the bim and the bam, and it soothes my aching soul, baby. *Yeah!*"

Joey Lovecraft.

The King of Sing.

My fingertips prickled with adrenaline, like I'd just had a near miss on the freeway. He was tall—seriously tall, like six five—and he wore a long bearskin coat over pants that might very well have been melted onto his legs with a blowtorch, they were so tight. No shirt, as you'd expect. Just a bone-deep tan, a lot of gold, and a stripe of crimson on either cheek. Not to forget the tusk of what appeared to be some kind of recently deceased ocean creature that hung from a rope around his neck. Oh my God, and the *hair:* a magnificent, walnut-hued mane, into which the plumes from several exotic birds had been intricately woven.

"Wassup, honey?" he said to me, with a smile wide enough to swallow the room.

"Hi, how are you?" I squeaked.

"Don't you mean—'*How high are ya?*'" he shot right back, with another sensational grin.

"I'm Bill," I managed.

"A lady named Bill, huh?" Joey bellowed. "Let me guess, Bill: When you order breakfast, you like to get the muffin *and* the sausage? *Right?*" With this, he proceeded to make a series of high-pitched yelping noises—accompanied by rapid wiggling of his enormous tongue—causing Mitch to flinch visibly. Len coughed so hard, I felt sure he must have done himself some permanent damage.

"Say, Bill," Joey went on. "Meet my lay-deez. Mu and Sue."

"*Moo?*" I said, confused.

One of the girls stepped forward.

"Em-you," she clarified. "A pleasure." She offered the kind of bony, pathetic handshake that only the most pornographic-looking of females can ever hope to get away with.

"And I'm Sue," added Sue, doing the same.

"Joey," interrupted Mitch, with urgency. "We've gotta talk. There's something you need to—"

"Where's my man Ed?" asked Joey, arms outstretched.

On cue, Ed emerged from a doorway to our left. Only no one noticed this development, because his face was at table level. I now began to understand why Len had decided to raise the height issue with Mitch. Ed "Big Guy" Rossitto was—without any doubt—one of the smallest human beings I'd ever set eyes on. He might not have been small enough to make a career out of it, but it was surely only a matter of a few inches. That, however, was only the beginning . . . indeed, it was almost as though Ed had decided to upstage his unusually limited stature with every other aspect of his appearance. His miniature knee-high cowboy boots (with spurs), for example. Or his child-sized Guns N' Roses T-shirt—on top of which was a tiny, silver-studded biker jacket, complete with S&M chains. Ed was also quite obviously wearing eyeliner and foundation, and when he walked toward us, this entire strange ensemble jangled, as though he were an approaching sleigh. It at least served to announce his presence.

When Joey saw him, he staggered backward in mock disbelief. "Who's the little fella, huh?" he cried, looking at Mitch. "Look! Someone shrunk Jon Bon Jovi!"

Joey's overwhelming human charisma—enough to warm a seventy-thousand seat football stadium on a rainy night in Philadelphia—had clearly long since stopped his worrying about the sensitivity of such comments. *He was Joey Lovecraft! He could say whatever the hell he wanted! Everyone would still laugh and say how much they loved him!* But Ed wasn't everyone. He was one of the most powerful men in television. He earned fifteen million dollars a year. And he looked seriously pissed.

"Joey," coughed Mitch. "This is—"

"Grumpy!" shouted Joey, doubling up and shrieking. "No, wait . . . I've got it. Nick Nack!"

"I'm Ed Rossitto," said Ed, sharply.

Joey fell silent.

An excruciating pause.

"Ed . . . ?" croaked Joey.

"Rossitto. From Rabbit. Shall we?" He motioned towards the Dickensian murk of his office.

Joey's expression was now one of horror. His eyes seemed to have turned black with panic. Mitch grabbed his arm, like a father leading his son across a busy street. "Is that a piano in your office, Ed?" he asked, desperately.

"Yeah," said Rossitto.

A few more awful moments passed. Then Rossitto seemed to make a decision. "Hey, Joey—wanna play?" he said, grudgingly. "It's a Bösendorfer. Epic bass, man. C'mon."

We all followed Rossitto into the batcave. I tried not to catch anyone's eye—it would only have made things worse. Mu and Sue remained outside with the assistants, their hot pants clashing with the antique furniture. Rossitto shut the door behind us, then walked over to the chesterfield to take a seat. The rest of us took his lead.

Not Joey, however.

No, Joey was very much still standing. "Gimme a second," he said, distractedly.

"C'mon, Joey," soothed Mitch.

It was too late: Joey groaned and fell to his knees in front of the piano. And then—still groaning—he began to crawl under it, until his entire six-foot-something frame was beneath the glossy black canopy of the enormous Austrian-made instrument.

"Interesting," murmured Ed.

Silence.

"Whatcha doin' down there, Joey?" asked Mitch, in a tone of upbeat curiosity, which suggested there might be an entirely practical reason for this behavior.

Joey said nothing. Instead, he began to hug one of the piano legs. Len and Mitch were now gesturing frantically at each other, each trying to get the other to intervene, to stop the madness. I noticed that

Rossitto's eyes hadn't left Joey for a moment, however. He seemed transfixed; fully entertained by the spectacle.

"When I was a kid, my momma had a piano just like this," Joey announced suddenly, his voice low and thick. "She was trained at the Royal Academy over there in Copenhagen, y'know. Quite a woman. She practiced six hours a day, every day—even when she was workin' full time as a school teacher. We had this tiny, *tiny* apartment, and this huge, this *epic* piano. When the movers brought that thing into our place, they must have had to take apart the laws of fuckin' physics to get it through the front door. Anyhow. Far back as I can remember, I would sit under it—like this—and close my eyes. She never showed me much love, my momma. Danish blood. Different generation. Saw affection as a sign of weakness. But I felt it, man, oh yeah. Under that piano, I felt it so strong, I'd curl up and sleep for hours, knowing that my momma was right there, making these beautiful tunes for me. And when I woke up, she'd still be playing. I'd be diggin' Mozart, man. Shosta-fuckin'-kovich. Shit by dudes with white fuckin' wigs. Like their souls were being poured right into mine."

No one said a word. I studied Rossitto: He was still entirely focused on Joey, only something wasn't quite right with his face. It was . . . his eyeliner. It had smeared.

There was movement now from under the piano: Joey was coming out from his hiding place. He stood up, wiped his eyes, and made his way to the keyboard stool. And then—I could hardly believe it—he began to play. Yes, right there in front of me: Joey Lovecraft, *performing live.* Hesitant at first. But then his foot came off the soft pedal. The notes became louder, more confident. The rhythm quickened. He started to sing. That incredible noise! It filled the room, making everything vibrate. I felt a sudden, almost violent elation build within my chest.

Now I was crying, too.

"Psycho Sluts from Paradise," I heard Rossitto say, as Joey reached the chorus. *"Greatest song . . . ever."*

5

Bibi and the Boy King of the Bronx

THERE WAS NEVER going to be any "sanity check" with Bibi Vasquez. Hell, no. Not even so such much as a phone conversation. If the executives at Rabbit wanted her—which they did, perhaps even more than they wanted Joey—they were going to have to beg.

Or rather, they were going to have to beg her manager, Teddy Midas.

Now, as I probably don't have to mention, Teddy isn't exactly known for his calm, rational demeanor. He's a hysterical narcissist. What's more, he has nothing to fear from being exposed as an Evil Diva From Hell, because no one expects anything less. While dining recently at Amuse Bouche in West Hollywood, for example, Teddy emptied his entire meal into the pants of the head waiter, due to an innocent misunderstanding over the phrase "courgette flower beignet." And that wasn't the end of the incident, if you believe the report by Chaz Chipford that appeared in the following week's *ShowBiz.* As Teddy left the restaurant, his bodyguard, Mr. Tiddles—seven one, four hundred pounds—"accidentally" fell on the manager, breaking his leg in three places. Teddy left a half-a-million dollar tip, so the matter never went any further.

No further than *ShowBiz,* anyway.

Exactly how Teddy and Bibi's friendship developed is something of a mystery. If I had to take a guess, however, I'd say Teddy saw a lot of himself in his future client when they first met in a TV studio a decade ago. Born to Chinese immigrant parents in rust belt Indiana (they owned a Laundromat), Teddy was a musical prodigy, but ended up on the street at the age of sixteen after his father caught him in bed with the eldest son of his business partner. Teddy never spoke to his family again. Instead he went to Nashville to work for BeeBop Records as a writer of country songs, of which his biggest hit was the Christian radio favorite, "I Love Ya, Honey (But Don't Git Between Me & Jesus)." After that, Teddy relocated a second time, to New York City, where he became a houseguest of his janitor uncle, with whom he lived for all of seventy-two hours—long enough for him to later create a TV drama series about the experience.

Boy King of the Bronx was the title.

Teddy was able to move out of his uncle's place so quickly because he got a job at Galactic Records, where he rose with similar speed to senior vice president, charged with overseeing the career of the nightclub owner/rapper/all-round hustler Bossman Toke—a.k.a. Bossy T. And it was Bossy T who introduced Teddy to Bibi: She was his girlfriend at the time, having just appeared as a thong-wearing, bare-nippled Queen Victoria in Bossy T's music video for the multiplatinum hit "Kneel for the King." In the extended ten-minute cut, which cost twenty-five million dollars to make, Bossy T plays a black English royal from the future who builds a time machine so he can sleep with every "smokin' hot bitch queen since history began." The video ends with him unzipping his fly in front of Cleopatra, allowing a solid gold asp to slither from his pants. It won Best Artistic Vision at that summer's Cool Beatz Video Awards.

And *why* did Teddy and Bibi have so much in common? Well, Bibi had also been thrown out on the street at the age of sixteen, after refusing to accept a place at hospitality school. The Vasquezes lived in

Middle Village, Queens: Bibi's mother, a Dominican baby nurse, had come to America to work for a wealthy family in Manhattan; her father was a French Canadian dishwasher. Bibi took her mother's surname on the advice of her manager: "Bibi Le Poupe" just didn't have much of a ring to it.

Bibi's parents yearned for their daughter to become a successful, independent American woman—and hospitality was something, the *only* thing, she seemed to be any good at. Or at least, when she waited tables at the French restaurant where her father worked, she earned more tips in a week than the manager made in a month . . . which she found out soon enough because she married him.

It lasted nine days. And still Bibi didn't want to go to hospitality school. No, she wanted to be a dancer, an actress, a model . . . a singer. So she moved into a squat on the Lower East Side and auditioned every day. Eventually she got a two-week gig as a bikini-wearing pole dancer on a late night music TV show and wound up giving an on-screen lapdance to Bossy T, who by then had been profiled in *Forbes* thanks to his unexpectedly successful diversification into the plus-size underwear market.

I didn't even need to Google the rest of this story when I was putting together my research file: Bibi's breakthrough casting in *Elsa,* a movie about the tragic life of the *narcocorrido* singer Elsa Melindez; her first single, "My Love Goes Bang-Bang," which spent four months at number one largely thanks to the publicity created when Bibi, Teddy, and Bossy T got into an argument in a Chelsea ice cream parlor, during which Mr. Tiddles let off three rounds from his gun. (Bibi and Bossy T were questioned but not charged. Mr. Tiddles spent the next three months on Rikers Island, saying nothing to nobody.)

The scandal was enough to end Bibi and Bossy T's romance—but Bibi stuck with Teddy, who became her manager, publicist, charisma coach, agent, and business partner, taking a separate percentage for each. He quickly consolidated her image as an unsmiling, imperious diva with a white fur wardrobe and a Queens-girl toughness. Every woman in

America wanted to be her. Every guy in America wanted to sleep with her. Black, white, Asian, Hispanic—it didn't matter. The great irony being that Bibi achieved all this without even being able to sing.

That was hardly the point, of course: Bibi was a brand, an idea, an *aspiration.*

I can hardly even begin to imagine how many millions Bibi and Teddy made together. They opened a chain of nail salons (Mani Bibi), launched a perfume brand (Bibi Beautiful), and created a line of personal massage wands (Bibi Naughty). As for Bibi's personal life: She became involved with her hairdresser, Tommy Stiles, who proposed within three weeks of their first date. Teddy was both the officiant at the wedding—he sang the vows—and the best man. He even joined the couple on their honeymoon at Bibi's villa in Italy, where the staff expressed surprise to an undercover *ShowBiz* reporter that the groom was spending more time with Teddy than he was with his bride.

When they all got back home to LA, Bibi hired two lawyers: One to annul her marriage; the other to sue Teddy. Not long after that, Bibi's new boyfriend, Logan Deckard—Oscar-winning actor, chairman of the Hollywood Actors Union, patron of multiple cancer charities, and presumed candidate for governor of California—had his people take a look at Bibi's books. Among the excesses uncovered: a full-time employee whose sole task was to switch on Teddy's iPhone. (Teddy had never quite mastered technology.) Meanwhile, Bibi and Logan made inevitable plans to wed. He bought her a ten million dollar ring and a Siberian tiger in a cage. She bought him a private island and helicopter by which to get there. Then she recorded a song, "Bibi from the Hood," the gist of the lyrics being: a) she was richer than God, and b) she was still a down-to-earth girl from Middle Village, Queens. Clearly, no one had thought to point out to her that writing a song expressing point a somewhat invalidated point b.

Then came Bibi and Logan's first movie together, *Jinky,* which one critic summed up by praising its ability to "take the sexiest, most closely watched celebrity couple in the universe, remove all their chemistry, and make you want to stab yourself in the neck with a rusty fork for no other reason than to relieve the boredom." *Jinky* made $400.25 on the Friday it opened in a few dozen theaters. Its costars had called off their wedding by the following weekend.

Thus began the most recent—and troubled—stage of Bibi's career, which this time I *did* have to Google, largely because of the press's waning interest in her affairs.

Her nail salons filed for bankruptcy. The company that Teddy had outsourced to manufacture her branded massage wands was found to be employing six-year-old girls in China. And try as she might, she just couldn't recover from *Jinky*. Her follow-up movies bombed. Her albums didn't sell. Even her fashion sense was mocked: "Bibi's acrylic bedsheet," was how the *Style* section of the *New York Chronicle* described her eccentrically dimensioned Oscars dress that year. (Teddy had previously selected all her outfits.) Exhausted, Bibi took a break to get married, again, this time to her teenage sweetheart Edouard Julius, the actor, trapeze artist, and former Olympic show jumper. To everyone's surprise, it lasted more than a week. They even had children together: quadruplets, in fact. Hence, Bibi became "Mama B." But her career was in worse shape than ever. A low point was duly reached when her comeback single, "I Wanna Rock (Any Diamond Will Do)," was released with spectacular insensitivity only a week after the Great Recession began, just as millions of her fans were being laid off and/or foreclosed upon. Worse: During a performance of the song at the Cool Beatz Video Awards, Bibi climbed up on the backs of twelve oiled and loin-clothed male dancers, broke a stiletto, and fell backward onto a giant projection screen.

"NEEDY DIVA WANTS A ROCK—BUT TAKES A KNOCK!" gloated *ShowBiz.*

A handwritten note from Teddy was delivered to Bibi's suite at the Four Seasons that same morning. (I discovered this among the exhibits in a lawsuit filed between them, along with transcripts of several emotional telephone conversations.)

It read:

B,
I am your family.
I am your best friend.
Let me adore *you*.
Forever,
T.

Ten minutes later, Teddy was once again getting ten percent of everything Bibi earned (expenses not included). His first piece of advice? "Take the call from Ed at Rabbit. Be a judge on *Project Icon*. Your fans will see your humanity, your tears, your compassion. Plus, it's a fuckload of money, with endorsements up the wazoo."

Bibi agreed.

But Teddy didn't go the easy route. Of course he didn't. Instead of calling Ed Rossitto, he leaked a story to *ShowBiz* "revealing" that Bibi was in talks with Nigel Crowther to join the judging panel of *The Talent Machine*. Then he quickly issued an official denial, saying, "At this time, Bibi Vasquez is focused only on her family." All this was enough to prompt a second call from Rossitto, who by now was wondering if things were going on at Rabbit that he didn't even know about. An increasingly strained back-and-forth ensued, culminating in one of Teddy's assistants finally delivering a list of "Artist Requirements" to The Lot:

- Artist to be paid sixty million dollars a year.
- Artist to be provided with customized, four-thousand-square-foot dressing compound to accommodate hair, make-up, and wardrobe personnel.
- Artist's body to be insured with one billion dollar policy in case of injury. (Breasts/buttocks to be valued at one hundred million dollars each.)
- No fewer than five promotional Artist videos to be broadcast by Network.

- Network to offer promotional-rate advertising deal to Bibi Beautiful Cosmetics.
- Crew to be forbidden to make eye contact with Artist (and Manager) AT ALL TIMES.
- Artist to be provided with chauffeur-driven limo for duration of season, available 24/7. Limo to be Rolls-Royce Phantom, white. Artist to select driver (male, under twenty-five) from head/torso shots.

There were seventy-eight pages of this in total—the last twenty devoted entirely to the requirements of Bibi's "dressing compound," including a lengthy addendum to promote "a deeper understanding of the tastes/preferences of the Artist, with regard to beverages and snack items."

When Ed Rossitto had finished reading the document, he slammed down the lid of his laptop, stabbed the case repeatedly with a letter opener, then threw it off his office balcony into the bunny-shaped lake below. (Or so I heard from Len.) Then he logged on to another computer, retrieved Teddy's list of demands from his e-mail, and forwarded it to Chaz Chipford, the *ShowBiz* reporter. Within minutes, the entire unedited file was available on the magazine's website as a downloadable PDF.

That afternoon, Bibi called Teddy while her assistant took notes.

"You're an *asshole,*" she told him.

"That's why you employ me," he replied.

"I *don't* employ you."

There, the transcript ends.

6

Sanity Check: The Sequel

I STOOD OUTSIDE JOEY'S dressing room in a hot panic. The run-through was so far behind schedule now, there was no conceivable way that the press conference could start on time.

This was ridiculous.

How the hell could I . . . *lose* the judges? They had to be around here somewhere. "Think, Sash, *think!*" I said to myself. But I could think of only one thing: Len's face when he realized the biggest news event in *Project Icon*'s history would have to be delayed because his assistant producer couldn't find the panel.

With no better ideas, I checked the catering area, the conference facility, the public bathrooms, the hallway that led to the parking lot, and then—in rising desperation—the janitor's storage closet. (You never know with Joey Lovecraft.) All empty. *Shit.* So I returned to the back-stage lounge area, where a couple of crew members in black T-shirts were standing around, looking confused.

"Hey—shouldn't this thing have started by now?" asked one of them, in an accusatory tone.

I offered him my very best shut-the-fuck-up face.

He was right, of course: The judges should have been on stage two minutes ago. A few more minutes' delay wouldn't be so bad, I kept telling myself. Even ten minutes—well, we could just about pull that off. Any longer, however, and we'd be charged an extra half-day for the venue and crew—not to mention all that wasted bandwidth for the live streaming—which would put us into overtime rates. It could add up to a few hundred thousand dollars, easy. Len had already been hospitalized twice since returning to *Icon,* due to a peptic ulcer and a burst appendix. A bill of that size could send him right back to the ER again.

Come to think of it, though . . . *why hadn't Len called me already?* It wasn't like him. Under normal circumstances, he would have threatened me with some kind of medieval torture at least three times by now. Unless . . . oh God, please no . . . *unless he was already front of house with Sir Harold,* waiting—and waiting—for "The Reveal" to begin. I could just picture him now: cheeks ablaze, nostrils flaring, the Merm quivering with fury. And in his eyes, two words, written in flames:

KILL BILL.

Sir Harold had blown twenty million dollars on the new *Project Icon* panel—and it all came down to this moment. Indeed, Big Corp's newly-issued "earnings guidance" for the next year depended heavily on Joey and Bibi (even JD Coolz, I suppose) keeping the show viable for one last season. Sir Harold had granted an interview to the Monster Cash Financial Network that very morning on the subject—I'd watched it with Mitch and a few others in the Roundhouse's canteen. Jesus, what a disaster. The anchor had started out with a long, ass-kissy intro about Sir Harold's upbringing in South Africa—all that stuff about his English merchant-banker father and Nguni housemaid mother, the national scandal of their marriage, and how the young Harry had *literally* inherited a gold mine at age seventeen, fought the apartheid-era government to hold on to it, then used the profits to build the world's largest media empire. Standard life story, basically. And then, just as Sir Harold was beginning to relax — or grow bored (hard to tell the difference) — out came the Gotcha Question: "Wouldn't you agree, Sir Harold: *Project Icon* without Nigel Crowther is a zombie franchise, with only three ways to go — down, down, and *down.*"

The anchor's smug attempt at humor was a bad idea. The mogul's great face trembled. His sun-spotted lips gathered into a sneer. Then he slapped down his hand with such force on the coffee table in front of him, it made the TV camera shake. For a few seconds, the studio looked like the deck of the *Starship Enterprise* under Klingon attack.

"Let me tell you something, boy," Sir Harold rumbled, adjusting his steel-rimmed glasses. "We could lose HALF our audience, and we'd still be number one. And who do you think owns *The Talent Machine,* eh? WE DO. So when it goes live next fall, we'll have ANOTHER number one show. Big Corp is *always* number one!"

The interview was over at that point. The anchor tried to ask a follow-up question about the German televised bingo market — apparently there'd been some major development over there recently — but Sir Harold stood up, unhooked the microphone from his ten thousand dollar suit, and peered directly into the camera, until the Big Corp CEO's unmistakable turret of white-silver hair filled the frame.

"*Number one!*" he reiterated, poking a bony finger into the lens. And with that, he shuffled off the set.

Sir Harold's confidence in *Project Icon* should have been reassuring, I suppose. But from what I'd seen over the last few months, it was practically a miracle that season thirteen had even gotten this far. And no matter how much money Sir Harold still hoped to wring out of the franchise, no one doubted for a second that he would pull us off the air if the ratings didn't hold up. One fuck-up, that's pretty much all it would take. One fuck-up, and the world's most popular TV show — a format that *ShowBiz* magazine once said had "revolutionized prime time, creating an entirely new genre of programming in its wake" — would be gone, never to return. Hence, it was of such vital importance that this morning's press conference go flawlessly, with no delays, budget overruns, or—God forbid—*missing judges.*

Yeah, it was all working out just perfectly.

There was nothing left for me to do. I had to call Len.

Oh, wow, this was going to be ugly. *"Oh, er, hi there, Len. No biggie—but you know how we were due to start fifteen minutes ago? And how the future of an entire billion dollar TV franchise depends on all this whole press conference thing going smoothly? Well, about that . . . Oh, Sir Harold's sitting next to you? Cool. Anyway, uh, just wanted to let you know: I've been running up and down hallways for, oh, at least twenty minutes now, and I can't seem to find the people we paid twenty million dollars to be here today."*

At least it wouldn't the first time the new judges had caused us any problems, I reassured myself. I mean, the entire hiring process had been one bang-your-skull-against-a-rock moment after another, each more outrageous—and exhausting—than the last.

And to think how *straightforward* everything had seemed when Rabbit first made the decision—after an eight-hour board meeting on The Lot—that Joey and Bibi were the only candidates famous and qualified enough to make up for the loss of Nigel Crowther. Ed made Bibi an offer that very same day, in fact. (By then, she'd reconciled with Teddy, who'd issued a statement to the press, saying, "It is a measure of Bibi's extraordinary humanity that she has offered me a second chance—I pledge to work tirelessly to help my client achieve her career goals of a billion record sales and the eradication of hate.") As for Joey: although Ed had found him to be "functionally stable" after his emotional monologue under the piano, Rabbit wanted to bring him in once more, just to make absolutely sure. So a week later, back to the batcave we went, for *Sanity Check: The Sequel,* as Joey himself described it. This time, there were two other executives in the room: Ed's boss, David Gent—another Brit, and so close to Killoch, he doesn't need a title—plus the gargoylesque, three-pack-a-day smoker Maria Herman-Bloch, CEO of Invasion Media, the production company that handles studio rental, crew logistics, and other tedious backstage aspects of the show.

"Make no mistake," Len warned everyone beforehand. "Gent can *take a shit* on Sir Harold's behalf. And chances are, that shit will land on one of our heads."

We all knew from reading *ShowBiz* that Gent's real job was to find a replacement for *Icon*—and that he'd personally signed off on Crowther's deal for *The Talent Machine.* So it was hard to know what to expect. If Gent loved Joey, would he steal him for Crowther? And what if he thought he was a liability? Would he let us hire him *anyway,* so the show could go out in a bonfire of its own negative PR?

No one knew.

The meeting began calmly enough. Joey turned up on time—in lederhosen and moon boots—and leaned down to greet Ed like one of his oldest friends. As for Gent, he seemed like an okay guy. I knew from his bio that he was ex-military (wing commander, Royal Air Force), but he was making an effort to disguise it, what with his herringbone shirt, navy blazer, and wispy brown college-professor hair. In fact, it was hard to believe this was a man who had penetrated the very highest levels of Big Corp and had a policy of automatically demoting employees if they asked for business cards—titles being a sign of complacency and (a far more serious offence at Big Corp) "box-inward thinking."

"So, Joey, tell me: *Why* do you think you can do this job?" was his opening question, after a round of handshakes. "You've never even watched our show, have you?"

In an instant, the temperature of the room seemed to drop ten degrees. I swear Mitch groaned.

"It's true . . . I've never seen it," Joey answered. "But, y'know, I've *heard* about it plenty."

A seriousness had descended over Joey's face that I'd never seen before. There was also a tone in his voice I didn't recognize. Not so much anger. More like petulance.

"I've *heard* that your ratings have been falling by ten percent a year," he went on. "And I've *heard* that you made a giant fuck-up with your panel last season, 'cause you hired a chick who can tell you how to bake a cake" — he was almost yelling now — "*but can't tell the Rolling Stones from her FAT TALK SHOW HOST ASS.*"

"Easy, Joey," urged Mitch.

Joey ignored him.

"I mean, if it were *me,*" he continued, "and *I* had a show about MUSIC that made a billion bucks a year, I think I'd be looking to hire someone who knew a little about *MUSIC.* Maybe someone whose mom was trained at the Royal fuckin' Academy, maybe someone who grew up under a grand piano, who plays five instruments, who taught his band everything they know, who can fuckin' *sing,* man. And I mean SING — not blow into a goddamn computer. But what do I know, huh? I'm just a rock star! I'm just someone who's sold one and a half billion records during my career! But if it were up to me — li'l old me, who doesn't know shit and belongs in the crazy house — I'd want to give the job to someone who actually KNOWS WHAT THE HELL HE'S TALKING ABOUT."

Joey sunk back in his chair. He looked spent. The rant had clearly been forming for some time.

Gent was smiling.

"I share your sentiment entirely, Mr. Lovecraft," he said. "Just so you know: We're also talking with Ms. Bibi Vasquez. How would you feel about working with her?"

For a moment, Joey looked bewildered — as though he were halfway through a gig and had just realized he was at the wrong venue, in the wrong city, playing with the wrong band. Then he showed the room his magnificent teeth.

"*Man,*" he said, pointing at Gent and drumming his feet. "You had me there! You *had* me, man!"

"So what about Bibi?" asked Gent again.

"Bibi?" Joey replied. "Just saw her in a movie. Mitch, what was that thing we saw on the plane?"

"*Nannyfornia,*" answered Mitch.

"There you have it," Joey confirmed. "*Nannyfornia.*"

"And how did you like it?"

"Can I be honest?"

Gent looked surprised. "Of course," he said.

"As long as I have a face," said Joey. "Bibi Vasquez will always—*always*—have a place to sit."

I thought we might have to call an ambulance for Len, he choked so hard. Mitch studied the carpet. Gent said nothing—he just stood up and offered Joey his hand. *Sanity Check: The Sequel* was over, and Joey had surely passed. Ignoring Gent's outstretched arm, he moved in for a hug, only to pull back in frustration: The Brit had tensed instinctively, unused to such man-on-man contact.

"Hey, don't fuckin' hug me like that, man!" Joey scolded, loudly. "Hug me like you hug your *wife.*"

They tried again.

I couldn't watch.

So that was that: Bibi and Joey were hired, terms to be agreed on. Which left only JD Coolz, who no one ever doubted would accept whatever scraps were thrown in his direction to stay on the show. "Coolz is well aware that he is the luckiest man alive—or at least the luckiest man to have ever been paid more than a million dollars a year to appear on TV," as Len once put it, after a record-breaking lunch at Mr. Chang's that lasted from 10:45 a.m. until early evening. "His talents, such as they are, amount to saying 'booya-ka-*ka!*' a thousand different ways."

Ed Rossitto hadn't been much more diplomatic.

"I like to think of Joey as the devil on this new panel," he told JD, during one of those early batcave sessions. "And Bibi—well, she's the angel, of course. And you? You're the American everyman, JD. Fat and ordinary. And I mean that as a compliment."

Poor old JD. Raised out in Bakersfield, California—a.k.a. The Most Boring City on Earth. White kid, black neighborhood. Subject of ridicule from an early age due to his fondness for the deep-fat fryer. By his twelfth birthday, losing weight meant getting back down to two hundred pounds. But with JD's size came a certain presence. He moved *slow,* wore a lot of jewelry, communicated only in fist bumps and monosyllabic slang. On the whole, people found him . . . reassuring. There was a calmness to JD. A Great Dane–like lovability. And so, when he turned eighteen and moved to LA—after teaching himself how to play bass guitar—he soon became a fixture in the weed-smoking rooms of all the major recording studios. "Oh, that's JD: He's cool, man," went the standard introduction. Which is how Jason Dee, son of a Bakersfield agricultural inspector, became JD Coolz, multiplatinum session player.

If I'd been JD, I would have picked up Rossitto by his tiny legs and dangled him out of the window until he apologized for the "fat and ordinary" comment. But JD is Mr. Nice. He just kept mumbling "yo" and "I get it" before asking plaintively if there was anything he could do to help with the recruitment of Joey. (JD had once toured with Honeyload, in the days before *Icon*'s success made earning a living from music unnecessary.) The meeting ended with Rabbit offering JD what it described as "a generous offer," which turned out to mean a fifty percent salary cut. He accepted right there in the room, no complaints.

If only Bibi and Joey's negotiations had been so easy.

With Bibi, the problem was Teddy. It was simply impossible to communicate with Bibi unless you did so via Teddy, and even then, you could never quite be sure if you were getting through. "It's like being at a fucking séance!" I once heard Rossitto yell into his speaker phone. And in spite of Teddy's claim to have changed his ways since the whole *ShowBiz* leak debacle, his original sixty million dollar demand for Bibi remained the same—minus the "dressing compound" that had been ridiculed so mercilessly on the late night talk show circuit.

So when Rabbit made its first offer to Bibi—a mere ten million—Teddy's response was . . . no response. He just ignored it. It was such a derisory sum, in Teddy's eyes, that it qualified as no sum at all.

Things didn't go much better with Joey—but only because he'd already read what Bibi was asking for. "You ever heard the phrase, 'most-favored nation'?" he asked Ed during a conference call. (I remember this largely because Joey insisted on the call starting at three a.m., West Coast time, as he'd just flown to Paris to buy shoes.) "International law, guys. United Nations: Look it up in your fuckin' dictionaries. Means whatever one cat gets, the other has to get. Not a cent more, not a cent less. I want *that* in my contract."

This was in fact impossible, because what Bibi wanted in addition to cash—breast insurance, for example, or the discounted advertising rate for Bibi Beautiful—Joey simply wasn't equipped to receive. The closest thing he had to a cosmetics company, *any* company, was a twenty percent share of a Colorado brewery, which had repeatedly offered to buy him out because of "urination issues" during shareholder meetings. While putting together Joey's offer, Rabbit had also been under the impression that Joey wasn't interested in the money. "I AIN'T FUCKIN' INTERESTED IN THE FUCKIN' MONEY!" as he'd screamed on many occasions. What Joey *really* wanted, Rabbit thought, was leverage against Honeyload. But things had changed during the week or so between the first sanity check and Rabbit's offer: Namely, Honeyload had reformed. They still weren't *speaking*. They had simply agreed to perform together. None of them had any choice in fact because when Joey had taken out his injunction against the band for allegedly considering Billy Ray Cyrus as his replacement, they countersued, arguing that if Joey was going to prevent their hiring a new singer, then he had to go back on tour immediately to allow them to continue earning a living. That's what Joey had wanted at the very beginning, of course, but everyone had forgotten about that by then—including Joey.

Fortunately, Mitch was able to remind him before yet another court date was set.

Meanwhile, Honeyload knew nothing about Joey's interviews for *Project Icon* (he'd denied all rumors)—and if they had, they would have almost certainly done everything possible to kill the deal. After all, Joey couldn't exactly appear on a twice-weekly TV show *and* play a gig with Honeyload in a different city every night. Being a judge on *Project Icon* would render all his promises about touring meaningless.

The day Rabbit finally approved Joey's appointment, Honeyload was booked to play a gig at the Freaky-Cola Amphitheater in San Bernardino. I was in the room when Len and Ed tried to make the call to Joey personally, but he was already on the road and wasn't answering. So instead they called Mitch, who was still in LA. He knew exactly what was coming, of course—thanks to the story that had gone up a few moments earlier on the *ShowBiz* website:

> **HOUSTON, WE HAVE AN OFFER!**
> *(A CHAZ CHIPFORD EXCLUSIVE)*
> BUNNY NET DANGLES FIVE-MILLION-DOLLAR CARROT IN FRONT OF YOUTUBE POOPER'S NOSE—
> SEEN AS LEVERAGE, REHABILITATION FOR TROUBLED HONEYLOAD FRONTMAN

"I'm going down to meet Joey at the show tonight—if the rest of the band haven't killed him before then," said Mitch. "I'll see what he thinks of the terms."

"Great," Len replied. "Bill will go with you."

Actually, I was supposed to be having a video chat with Brock at seven o'clock.

Not anymore.

Mitch didn't put up a fight—which was just as well, otherwise the three-hour Town Car ride that followed might have been a bit awkward. Maybe he wanted the company, I thought. Or a witness, in case things got nasty backstage.

When we finally got to the amphitheater, Blade Morgan was waiting just beyond the crew entrance, looking about as unhappy as it is possible for a human being to look. Holding up his BlackBerry—on which the headline from the *ShowBiz* website was displayed—he said, "Tell Joey to go fuck himself up the ass with a razor blade. Actually, don't: He'd probably enjoy that. Tell him I hope he drops dead, so I can skull-fuck his eye sockets."

"One word, Blade," Mitch replied, pushing the screen away from his face. "*Franjoopta.*"

"That was different," Blade steamed. "That was fuckin' *different,* you asshole!"

Mitch just raised his eyebrows and walked away. Franjoopta was of course the worst contestant in *Project Icon*'s history. Indeed, when he was voted into the season eight finale as a result of an ironic "Save Franjoopta" campaign, the nation was so outraged, questions were raised in Congress. The point being: Franjoopta's final song on the show (before Sir Harold ordered his elimination "by any means necessary") was a spectacularly misguided light reggae affair, supposedly based upon The Beatles' "Helter Skelter." And Len, in a desperate effort to add credibility to the proceedings, had invited a "rock 'n' roll icon" to play George Harrison's riff as a special guest. Unfortunately for Blade, that icon was him. He'd never heard of Franjoopta. This changed soon enough. The ridicule from Honeyload's fan base was so overwhelming, he couldn't go out in public again for a year.

For the next three hours, I sat on a giraffe-skin couch in Joey's trailer, listening to Mitch being subjected to a meandering, tearful lecture outlining the many, many ways in which he was a failure as a representative, and how, *if Joey Lovecraft were a manager*—"li'l old me, who doesn't know shit and belongs in the crazy house"—he would never, ever have allowed his client to be humiliated with such a pathetic, insulting sum as five million dollars. For a moment I wondered if all this were for my benefit: a negotiating tactic. But no. I doubted Joey could remember my name, never mind who I worked for.

"Did you even do any research on these Rabbit clowns?" he asked Mitch, loading up a DVD of an old episode of *Cannon Jump.* It was a TV show from the eighties about a nine-year-old kid who takes a job as a human cannonball, only to find that every time he gets shot up in the air, he goes back in time. "I mean, *hello?*" he yelled, waving at the image paused on his giant flatscreen. "The kid. *Ring any bells?*"

"Not really," shrugged Mitch.

"Look again."

Mitch studied the child. There was, in fact, something oddly familiar about the shape of his—

"Holy shit!"

"Yeah," nodded Joey. "Ed fuckin' Rossitto! Guess how old he was when he got this part?"

"Eleven?" guessed Mitch.

"Thirty fuckin' three!"

"Wow."

"You shoulda WARNED me about this guy, man. He's freakier than a cow who goes 'quack'! And have you seen the . . . the *shit* he put on TV before *Icon?*" He passed Mitch an entry from Wikipedia that Mu or Sue must have printed out for him earlier.

"*When Sharks Eat Babies,*" Mitch read.

"Yeah. Dude belongs at a fuckin' *circus.*"

Awkwardly, Mitch then had to reveal that JD Coolz and Maria Herman-Bloch were on their way to that night's show (Ed couldn't make it, thank God) to help convince him to sign the contract that Ed had just e-mailed over. "Ain't nothin' to discuss," Joey huffed. After another hour of complaining, he agreed to at least give them both backstage passes, so they could watch from the wings.

It wasn't until Blade dropped to his knees for the guitar solo in "Hell on Wheels"—while staying within the contractually mandated No Lead Singer Zone drawn around him in chalk—that Joey even acknowledged their presence. He did this by running over to Maria, grabbing her hand, dragging her out on to the stage, and forcing her to dance. When the music stopped, he bent her over backward until she was about to fall. "*More, s'il-vous plaît,*" he whispered.

It was the last thing he said to anyone all night.

Eventually, revised offers were made to both Bibi and Joey: Twenty million dollars combined. To keep Joey happy, the basic salaries were exactly the same, but Rabbit came up with all kinds of other tricks to guarantee millions of dollars' worth of publicity for Bibi's various enterprises. Everything was ready to go.

And then came the weeks and weeks and weeks of arguing over

every subclause and footnote, right down to the number of Balance Bars in the minibar of Bibi's trailer, versus the number of Ghirardelli chocolate squares in Joey's. Finally, when all this had been agreed in writing—it took July, August, and some of September—Mitch and Teddy were loaned private jets from Big Corp and told to go find Bibi and Joey, wherever they happened to be in the world, and get their signatures within twenty-four hours. But Teddy couldn't help himself: He leaked a story to *ShowBiz* bragging of how Bibi had gotten the better deal. Example: She'd been given a dressing room for The Reveal, when Joey had been told to show up "camera ready" with nowhere to sit but the backstage lounge area.

Mitch was so mad, he had to be strapped to a gurney and shot up with Xanax. By the time he'd calmed down, it looked like the whole thing was off. But then Ed got on the phone and convinced Mitch that Teddy had been bullshitting.

All the judges had to turn up camera ready.

"If it makes you feel any better, I'll give both of 'em *both* dressing rooms," he said. "How about that? We've got an assistant producer down at The Roundhouse—Len will get you her name—who can sort it out. Tell her exactly what you need."

Grudgingly, Mitch agreed. It didn't change the fact that Bibi and Joey wouldn't actually *need* the dressing rooms. But it was enough of a symbolic gesture to finally get some ink on the contracts. That's why I had to spend eight days and fifty thousand dollars making sure every last detail was taken care of, right down to Bibi's red iPads, which had to be custom-ordered from a store in Hong Kong. It never occurred to me the judges would never even see the result of all this work.

Clearly, when it came to celebrities, I still had a lot to learn.

7

The Run-Through

LEN'S PHONE WAS ringing now.

The tone was broken and distorted, probably due to interference from the microwave trucks outside.

Still ringing.

My panic had now mutated into a kind of existential doubt: Was this even the *right day* for the press conference? Had I somehow completely misunderstood Len's instructions? Was I about to wake up in my old bedroom at Mom's house, soaked and trembling, from some horrendous anxiety dream? Nothing about this situation made any sense whatsoever. How could Bibi, Joey, and JD—even Wayne Shoreline—just *disappear,* at the exact moment they were all due on stage? And where the hell were Teddy and Mitch when I actually needed them?

I thought I might throw up. But then a strange kind of anger came over me. This job was taking decades off my life. And for what? My salary was a joke. My colleagues were psychotic. I'd never even wanted to work in TV. Certainly not *this kind* of TV. If it hadn't been for that random call from Len, with this "dazzling opportunity," I would never have come all the way out here to LA. And, who knows, maybe I'd have found another way to write my novel, like I promised Dad I would.

Great: Now I was thinking about Dad. Or rather, I was thinking about our final conversation in that greasy-walled diner he used to like, the one so close to the Long Island Expressway, everything would rattle when an eighteen-wheeler drove past.

"I'm not gonna be around forever, Sash," he'd announced, halfway through his standard midafternoon breakfast of coffee and buttered toast. Dad was skinny as hell. It was nerves, he said. Toast was the heaviest thing he could get into his stomach before a show—and he played two shows a night, every night of the week. That's what it takes to make a living when you're splitting the money among a fourteen-piece wedding band.

I'm pretty sure Dad knew about the cancer by then. No one else did, though. Not even Mom. I mean, how could she have? Dad was away most of the time, and he didn't want her to worry. It took her months to find out that his "tour of Louisiana" was nothing of the kind. He'd booked himself in a hospice on Staten Island.

"I'm sorry I never had much money to give you," he said, between gulps of weak, sugary coffee. "But at least your old man did what he loved, right? I mean, look at Stevie, Jimbo . . . Fitz. You think those guys wake up every morning, happy to put on their shirts and ties and get in their goddamn *cars* and drive to an office? No way. They're always calling me up, wanting to know how it's going on the road. They want me to tell 'em how *hard* it is, that I've grown out of it. But I haven't, Sash. I still love this life. *It's who I am.* I made my choice, and I've never regretted it."

"Jesus, Dad," I said. "Enough with the obituary already. You're only forty-three."

"I just wanna prepare you, Sash. You've got some big choices ahead. You finish college this year. And I know you wanna write that novel of yours, whatever it ends up being about. But that's not gonna be easy. There'll be bills to pay. Mom's gonna want you to get a *real* job. You might even want to take a real job yourself, when you see your friends buying apartments and cars and clothes and all that bullshit they think they need. But write your book, Sash. Find a way—'cause if you don't, you'll never forgive yourself. Trust me. *Do what you love.*"

Back then, of course, I hadn't written a word. The knobbled, weary old man of my imagination had yet to set off on his unwise journey across the Black Lake of Sorrow on a night when the shutters of the Old House were closed.

Next time I saw Dad, it was in Mom's living room. They'd put him in his favorite tux, trumpet by his side. Open casket. The cancer had been genetic, apparently—no avoiding it. Everyone got drunk, then the band played him out: *A Taste of Honey,* of all things. The Herb Alpert version. I was a mess. Angry, too: why hadn't he gone to a doctor earlier? *Why hadn't he told any of us?* Stevie, Jimbo, and Fitz were there, all in shirts and ties, all still very much alive. My God, the stories they told.

Of course, if I'd known that Dad was giving me his last words in the diner, I would have stayed for dessert. Or at least some coffee. I would also have taken the opportunity to ask for some clarification: Like, how can you do what you love if the thing you love isn't a job that anyone will pay you to do? What then, Dad? *What then?*

I tried calling Len a second time.

Stabbing at the digits on the screen, I noticed three unplayed voicemails from a number with a Honolulu area code. Brock. What with the chaos of the press conference, I still hadn't gotten around to calling him back. I hadn't spoken to him since . . . wow, last week. But he'd understand. He always did. I liked that about Brock: His laid-back personality. The fact that he let me do my own thing.

Now Len's phone was ringing again in long, ragged tones.

Ringing.

Ringing.

Hang on a minute . . . it was actually *ringing.* As in: Ringing here in the room, somewhere behind—

I turned, and there was Len, walking toward me, his face so paralyzed by preshow Botox injections, he might as well have spent the night in a cryogenic chamber. Behind him: Bibi, Joey, JD, and Wayne—four across, like a slo-mo credits sequence. Teddy and Mitch lingered behind, each trying not to acknowledge the other's presence, but failing conspicuously. I felt light-headed with relief.

Oh, thank you, God. *Thank you.*

Joey had out-crazied himself this time: He was barefoot, with a feathered scarf around his neck and what appeared to be a shark's tooth lodged in his hair. Still, he had nothing on Bibi. For this important occasion, Teddy had selected for her a golden chain mail dress, crotch-high plastic boots, and detachable cape. She looked like a visiting extraterrestrial queen from the forty-second century. As for JD and Wayne, they'd both chosen dark gray business suits, in two very different sizes.

"You ready now?" asked Len, pointing in my direction.

I was aware of some kind of movement in my jaw, but no sound was coming out.

Sensing my confusion, Len said, "Oh, these guys all had a little breakfast together at Wayne's place—a camaraderie-building exercise. Then we decided to do some prerecorded press stuff outside before we got going. New start time is 11:30 a.m. Doesn't give you long for the run-through, so chop-bloody-chop, Bill. Take them up to conference room five. I'll meet you back here when you're done."

Classic Len: I was too unimportant to be told about the change of plan, so he'd let me flap around up here, questioning my own sanity, until I figured it out for myself. What an ass—

"C'mon, Bill, cock-a-doodle-doo!" yelled Len, clapping his hands. "We're on in ten."

Unbelievable.

"Okay, everyone," I announced as loudly as I could, to disguise the fear in my voice. "I'm going to give you the run-through, so follow me, please. Conference room five."

I led the way confidently, phone in one hand, clipboard in the other. No one followed me. So I returned to the lounge area, repeated my instructions, and tried again. Still no luck. Then I noticed the reason for the distraction: Mitch had cornered Len before he could leave the room and was chewing him out about something. "You'd better not fuck us today," I heard him threaten. "I mean it. Joey still hasn't forgotten about that dressing room bullshit you tried to pull on us."

"No one's fucking *anyone*, okay?" Len hissed, impatiently. "As we explained to you before, Mitch, the dressing room situation was all in Teddy's imagination."

Mitch didn't look convinced—and for a moment, I found myself sharing Len's frustration. Why did these celebrity managers have to be so . . . *angry* all the time? Couldn't they put their trust in human nature for one second? I couldn't imagine what it must be like to view the world through such a dark vortex of cynicism.

Like I said before: I still had a lot to learn.

As Len finally broke away (where the hell was he going, anyhow?) I tried yet again to marshal the panel. This time, they fell in line behind me. Conference room five turned out to be on the floor above, with a U-shaped table in the middle, some cheap plastic chairs, and an overhead projector that probably hadn't been switched on since the Clinton administration. The place smelled vaguely of beer and ashtrays. Or maybe it was urine and ashtrays, it was hard to tell. Whatever the case: Joey couldn't have looked more at home if he'd just been returned to his mother's womb. Bibi, on the other hand, seemed disgusted. Fortunately, one of Teddy's assistants had brought some plastic wrap for her to sit on.

"So, uh, hi everyone," I began, excruciatingly. "How was breakfast?"

"We all held hands and sang *Kumbaya*," replied Wayne, nastily. "Now can you give us the run-through—or is there something else you'd like to know? We had eggs, if that helps."

Suddenly, heat in my face. "Okay, yes, right," I said, between shallow breaths.

"She's *sorry*," Wayne snorted. "My God, where do they get 'em? Producer school?"

Titters.

Joey wasn't laughing, though. He lifted his bare feet onto the table and said, "Take your time, Bungalow Bill. Ain't no hurry. Don't listen to HAL fuckin' 9000 over there."

That's the big joke about Wayne Shoreline, of course: That he's not actually human. It's a compliment, of sorts—an acknowledgment that his ability to host a live one-hour broadcast with such ruthless calm is beyond the realm of mere flesh and blood. But there's another reason for Wayne's heart-of-silicon reputation: The fact he's never had any kind of public relationship—male or female—during his entire twenty-year show business career. Indeed, when he's photographed at dinner, it's usually with his mother. "The press thinks he's gay," as Mitch once told me. "But I doubt it. I don't think he's *anything.* If you pulled down the guy's pants, the only thing swinging between his legs would be a USB stick."

Everyone was now waiting for me to continue. So I cleared my throat and started again.

"Okay, so Wayne's up first," I said, consulting the script on my clipboard. "He's going to do the intro, recap *Project Icon*'s backstory, et cetera, et cetera . . . then we'll introduce JD. Lights will go down, there'll be a two-minute video package—a kind of 'best of' thing, lots of booya-ka-*kas*—and then Wayne will invite JD on stage, there'll be cheering, flashbulbs, a bit of music, Wayne and JD will do a very short Q&A, thirty seconds maximum, lights will go back down, JD will leave the stage, and we'll move on to Joey. Everyone good with that?"

"You mean Joey's not *last?*" replied Mitch, as if this were some kind of huge, deal-breaking surprise.

Clearly, Bibi would be last. Mitch surely knew this already.

"We're not thinking of it in terms of 'first' and 'last,' Mitch," I said, surprised at my ability to bullshit without hesitation or shame when the occasion called for it.

"Don't fucking bullshit me, Bill. You're no good at it."

"Look, the running order is JD, Joey, then Bibi," I said. "It's in the script. Sorry, Mitch."

"Why can't Joey and Bibi come out on stage at the same time?"

Mitch wasn't letting this one go.

"*Mitch,* we're running a video package and a separate Q&A for each panel member. We can't do them *all* at the same time. It's a 'reveal.' It's supposed to be dramatic."

"Okay, so why not do Bibi second? Ladies before gentlemen."

"THAT'S AN OUTRAGE!" yelled Joey, so loud it almost made me lose my balance. Then, with a shriek of hilarity: *"Don't ever accuse me of being a gentleman!"*

Everyone laughed—anything to relieve the horrible tension in the room—but not Mitch. He crossed his arms and stared at me, eyes gleaming. Behind him, Teddy grinned.

I flipped through the pages of the script, noticing that Len had replaced the final section—this much was obvious from the spelling errors and formatting. He'd typed it himself, it seemed, and at speed. I wondered why he hadn't mentioned that.

"So anyway," I went on, shakily. "Next up: Joey. Same deal as JD, basically. First the video package, then Wayne will invite Joey on stage, there'll be a Q&A, cheering, flashbulbs, bit of music—et cetera, et cetera—lights down again, then on to Bibi."

"Ooh, me?" Bibi squealed.

Teddy's smile grew wider.

I turned the page.

"Okay: so the lights will go down once more," I read. "The darkness will last for ninety seconds. We'll hear distant thunder. Then the thunder will get louder. Smoke will gather . . ."

"OH, FOR FUCK'S SAKE!" Mitch screamed.

" . . . and then, in a blinding flash, lightning will strike the stage . . ."

I had to take a breath. Len hadn't warned me about any of this. This was exactly what Mitch had feared. *They'd fucked him.* There was simply no other way of putting it. Joey had been reduced to a sideshow, a supporting act—no more important than JD. Len and Teddy must have cut a deal, without telling anyone. And now *I* was the one having to deliver the news. No wonder Len hadn't told me about the script changes. No wonder he'd been so insistent that I do the run-through, even though *he* was supposed to be in charge.

" . . . at this point we'll hear the first few bars of Bibi's new single, 'Gotta Disco,' and as the music gets louder, images of Bibi Beautiful cosmetics products will be projected on to the auditorium walls . . ." — I found myself speaking faster, trying to get it over with — " . . . then fade out as we cut to Bibi's fifteen-minute video package. When the package is over, Wayne will move to the wings. All lights out. More thunder. More lightning. Then a trapdoor in the stage floor will open, and Bibi will rise on a mechanical arm over the audience, as Wayne says, 'Ladies and gentlemen: The legend, the movie star, the multiplatinum-selling, Grammy-winning artist, also known to the residents of Planet Earth as a mother, thinker, philanthropist, businesswoman, dancer, style icon, and best-selling author . . . BIBI VASQUEZ. Then lights up, 'Gotta Disco' will resume, Bibi's dancing troupe will run up the center aisle, and Bibi will perform a three-song set. Then cut to the prerecorded *Rabbit News Special* with Bibi featuring Sir Paul McCartney, the Dalai Lama, and the First Lady of the United States."

Finally. It was over.

The only sound in the room now was Teddy giving his own heartfelt personal round of applause.

Mitch was under the table, making a noise I'd never heard anyone make before.

Then it began. Joey stood up, loosened his belt, and began to adjust his leather chaps.

"Get the pee cup, Mitch," he ordered.

A few seconds earlier, I wouldn't have believed it possible for Mitch to sound any unhappier.

He was now proving me wrong.

"The pee cup," Joey repeated. "It's in the contract, right? These guys want me to take a pee test every week, to make sure I ain't gonna do any crazy shit on prime-time TV?"

A muffled voice from under the table: "Joey . . . please . . . this isn't the time or the — "

"Mitch: SHUT UP. I need the pee cup, and I need it now, 'cause trust me, I'm gonna take so many pills and drink so much booze, my pee ain't gonna be clean again for a thousand fuckin' years. You promised me equal treatment, you motherfuckers. And now Little Miss Perfect over there is getting a royal coronation? Mitch, you suck. Teddy, you suck *cock.* That's cool, but you fuckin' ain't."

He turned to me. "And *you,* girl-called-Bill," he said. "I thought you were okay, man. What happened? You're all the same, you people. You've all got the same poison in your soul. Fuckin' TV producers. And to think I fell for it. Well, I hope you're happy now, 'cause I ain't doing this bullshit anymore. Show over. Go fuck yourselves."

"Joey," I said. "This is isn't how it— "

Too late. He was out of the door. "*Th- Th- Th- That's all, folks!*" he yelled, as it jerked shut behind him.

8

Six Things

I AWOKE IN MY clothes—again—to the sound of knocking. With great effort, I opened my eyes. It was almost noon, judging by the patterns of sunlight on the ceiling.

God, my head hurt.

Surveying the floor by my bed, I glimpsed the silver foil of a half-eaten chicken shawarma, three tubes of lip balm, my college-era laptop, and a pair of white earbuds (of the please-go-right-ahead-and-mug-me variety), still vibrating to the tinny frequencies of a Nick Cave album that had seemed a lot more profound at three o'clock in the morning. What had I *done* last night? Whatever it was, I suspected it had involved breaking my promise to never smoke another cigarette for as long as I lived. Every time I swallowed, I could taste the ash. *Disgusting.*

There it was again—that awful noise. And a voice. "*Meesash,*" it seemed to be saying.

More knocking.

Ah, *now* I could make out the words: "*Meess Sasha? Meess Sasha?*"

I buried my head in the pillow. Then my cell phone began to ring.

Well, not *ring* exactly—before Brock left for Hawaii, he'd set it to play the opening riff of "Hell on Wheels" whenever it received a call. This had seemed pretty funny at the time. It didn't now.

Dn.

Dn-nn-nah.

Dn-nn-*nah*-nh! Bleeeowww-neow-newo . . .

"*Meess Sasha? Hello? Meess Sasha?*"

"Please . . . make it stop," I moaned, yanking the comforter up and over my head.

Unfortunately, "Hell on Wheels" reminded me why my brain felt as though it had been removed from my skull, beaten repeatedly with a nine iron, then reinserted upside down: *Joey Lovecraft.* The very thought of his name was enough to make me curl up and cover my ears, as if that might shut out the memory of the previous day.

Bursting into tears after Joey's little speech in conference room five certainly hadn't been a good idea. I mean, sure, I'd made it into the ladies' room before the snot storm began—thus saving myself from *abject* humiliation—but it's not exactly hard to tell when a redhead has just given a box of Kleenex the workout of its life. When I finally emerged from the bathroom with a face like a thousand bee stings, Len had already returned from wherever the hell it was he'd been, and was trying to save The Reveal from a disaster of show-destroying proportions. To that end, he'd located Joey (who'd mercifully been unable to find an open bar anywhere in the building), sat him down with Mitch in the judges' lounge—Mu and Sue providing additional comfort—and was busy explaining that there'd been a *horrible* misunderstanding. Or rather, that I had failed to give him the "full context" of the last-minute changes to the run-through, thus creating the *absurd* impression that he had been relegated to Bibi Vasquez's supporting act.

"What Bill should have told you, Joey—and I don't for the life of me know *why* she didn't—is that Bibi's entrance, with the mechanical arm and the dancers and so on, is designed to, well . . . *poke fun* at her," he said. "She's a diva, Joey. *You* know that. We were just trying to make some mischief, without crossing a line. To be honest with you, Joey—and this goes no further, I hope—we were worried about *Bibi's* reaction. I mean, Teddy's been trying very hard to position her as 'recession-sensitive' lately, what with the ad for the Chevy Frugal and everything."

The Frugal ad, by the way, was another disaster—largely due to Bibi's refusal to visit downtown Detroit for the filming. A body double was therefore hired in her place, this fact being leaked to the press by a furious Madison Avenue executive a few hours before the commercial aired. Things only got worse when a viewer noticed that the green-screened interior shots of Bibi in the Frugal featured a suede-upholstered steering wheel that clearly didn't fit in a seven-thousand-dollar car. After some cursory Internet research, it was discovered that the wheel in fact belonged to Bibi's Bentley Mulsanne. Not only had Bibi refused to go to Detroit for the filming, she'd also declined to *sit in the car.*

"It's all about dramatic narrative, Joey," Len pressed on. "And we get that with *contrast.* I mean, look: there's JD, everyone's friendly uncle; Bibi, the stuck-up, out-of-control ego; and you, the musical genius . . . the, uh . . . the icon of a generation."

Joey nodded seriously. "Makes sense," he said, sniffing.

"It does, Joey," agreed Len, gripping Joey's arm. (What an unbelievable toad.) "It really, *really* does."

That was when I emerged, only half recomposed, from my sob session. Joey's comment had really gotten to me. I mean, maybe I *was* "poison," as he'd suggested. Maybe all this—Len, Sir Harold Killoch, the whole Two Svens-versus-Crowther thing going on between *Project Icon* and *The Talent Machine*—had already damaged my soul in some profound yet intangible way. Maybe I'd become one of those "Hollywood people" you hear about. After all, I was only there for the money, wasn't I? Okay, not a *lot* of money—barely more than I could have made serving eggs at Mel's Diner on the Sunset Strip—but my job was still a means to an end. Which made me a phony: a fact that Joey had recognized so clearly.

I could barely look at him. Not that I had much choice. As I approached, he stood up and walked straight at me. "Come here, babe, let's cuddle through this muddle," he rapped, with a concerned frown. "Let's face the embrace, let's *seize* the squeeze, honey."

And then his arms formed a wall of crazy around me. I tried not to choke on his cologne.

"We'll be better next time, okay?" Joey whispered, as my eyes began to water.

His eyes were watering, too.

Not from the smell, though.

"Okay," I nodded, too busy withholding a cough of lung-exploding force to be irritated by Joey's use of the word "we" and its implicit suggestion that I was somehow *jointly* to blame for Len changing the format of the script, prompting a grown man to act like a toddler who'd just discovered the unfairness of gravity.

Joey clapped his hands as he pulled away from me.

"Showtime!" he announced, with another sniff. "Let's get this baby on the air." Then he ambled off, jewelry clanking, in the direction of his Kangen machine.

Mu and Sue followed.

There were more complications to come, naturally. As it turned out, someone on Team Bibi had been listening in to Len's conversation with Joey (could it have been Teddy? Had he been hiding under the sofa?) and had informed Bibi that her Messiah-like entrance during the press conference was in fact a form of mockery, not celebration. Within minutes, the Beverly Hills attorney Karl Hurt—managing partner at Dammock, Hurt & Richardson (known in the industry as Damage, Hurt, and Retaliation)—had called Len, threatening a lawsuit for breach of contract. There was a "ridicule clause" in Bibi's agreement with *Project Icon,* apparently. While Len dealt with the atomic-tempered lawyer, he shooed me back to the front line of conference room five to calm Bibi.

"*Don't* fuck it up this time," he mouthed.

Bibi was actually in the hallway, encircled by Teddy, Teddy's four assistants, and five stylists.

I straightened my back (I'm five eight, so taller than Bibi by five inches) and exhaled.

"Ahem. Miss Vasquez?" I attempted.

"Miss Vasquez is busy," said Teddy, appearing center frame. "Very busy."

This was quite obviously untrue. Bibi wasn't busy at all. The people *around her* were busy. One stylist was using a miniature spray bottle to apply toning liquid to her calves, giving them a warm, buttery texture. Another was using some kind of air gun to apply perfect distress to individual strands of hair. Meanwhile, an assistant held out an iPad upon which Bibi's horoscope from a supermarket tabloid was displayed on the maximum zoom setting. Bibi was reading it with great interest. She'd clearly noted my arrival, yet nevertheless had enough plausible deniability to ignore me without risking any awkwardness.

"Look, Teddy," I began, emotionally. "I just need you to know . . . we all *love* Bibi."

"Everyone loves Bibi," snipped Teddy, now distracted by an e-mail on his phone. As with Bibi, an assistant was holding it out for him. *Couldn't these people do anything for themselves?*

"Of course!" I fawned. "But we think she's, y'know, really, *really* amazing. And, er, I just want to, er— "

"Hasn't Len fucked you enough for one day, Bill?" Teddy interrupted, without looking up (the e-mail he was reading had come from Bibi, I could see, with Karl Hurt copied). "You really wanna get fucked again? Why not let the grown-ups handle this."

Grown-ups? Oh, that was rich.

"I mean, Len sent you over here, right?" Teddy continued, now offering me a full twenty-five percent of his attention. "And he thought you could talk to my client?" He laughed. "Len thought YOU could talk to one of the most famous, successful women alive today? *You?* With your . . . *boyfriend jeans* and *hiking shoes?* Oh, hilarious."

That was it: screw these assholes. I was all set to give up and walk away when suddenly, the stylists around Bibi parted, giving me a direct view of the star herself.

Eye contact.

Holy crap: *Bibi Vasquez was looking at me.*

"Honey," she said, in a tone that suggested an attempt at warmth. "What is it you wanna talk to me about?"

Silence.

A crippling panic. Then irritation. What is *wrong* with wearing hiking shoes when you spend sixteen hours a day running around a set under hot studio lighting, especially if you have an abnormal big toe, like I do? Then I made a decision. If Len could bullshit Joey, *then I could bullshit Bibi.* When in hell, do as the devil does, as they say. Okay, so no one actually says that. But you know what I mean.

"Look, Bibi," I began. "I just want to say, as both a producer *and* a fan"—yes, I was going all the way on this—"you're the biggest thing that has ever happened to this show. Everyone at *Icon* feels that way, Bibi. And I know for a fact that Joey does, too. But he also feels . . . well, threatened. You've got to remember, he's an alpha male, Bibi. A rock star. And that makes him want to compete with everyone—even when he's not even in the same game. He just doesn't know how to respond to your level of fame and success, Bibi. Or the fact that you're a woman, a mother . . . an *icon.* That's why we sometimes have to talk him down from the ledge. I mean, you saw what happened today, right? But he's okay now. He's ready to go. And all I want to say is—if you're ready, so are we. We're ready to go out there and *own* prime time, Bibi. This is so . . . amazingly . . . awesome."

My bullshit generator had reached maximum capacity. If I didn't stop talking immediately, it was gonna blow. So I wrapped up my speech with a fake little shudder of excitement, then looked over at Teddy, hoping for some support.

His lower jaw hung open.

"Okay, honey," said Bibi, as a stylist dabbed at her face with a microscopic lip gloss wand. "You didn't have to say all that, but you're sweet. I'm glad Joey is feeling better. He shouldn't feel threatened. But I understand. Let's get this over with."

Back to my hangover:

My head felt like a busy market square after a car-bomb attack. Broken glass everywhere. A high-pitched ringing noise. Smoke damage. At least my phone had stopped playing that Blade Morgan riff. Instead it told me with two dying shudders that a voicemail had been left. Brock, probably. *I really needed to be better about returning his calls.*

I released a long, tobacco-infused sigh—had I *eaten* the damn cigarette?—and stared up at the cracked stucco on the ceiling. Must tell Mr. Zglagovvcini about that, I thought.

Speaking of whom.

"*Meess Sasha?" Are you there, Meess Sasha?"*

More knocking.

"Jesus Christ!" I yelled, rolling out of bed furiously. "I'm coming!"

At least I didn't have to bother getting dressed—one of the few yet undeniable benefits of falling asleep in your clothes. Another blessing: It took only three and a half paces to reach the front door. My apartment—if it deserved such a title—was basically one room, with a sink and microwave at one end, my bed at the other, and a folding door in the middle that led to a bathroom with no actual bath and a towel rack that forced me to lean forward at a forty-five degree angle while doing whatever it was that I had to do. Such luxurious accommodation came with a price tag of eleven hundred dollars a month. The sympathetic real estate broker had told me this was cheap for Hollywood.

"I thought we were in Little Russia?" I'd replied, dumbly.

"Little Russia is in Hollywood, dear," she'd said.

"But—"

"I know, dear, I know. It's not like it is on television, is it? You'll get over that. Eventually."

I'd taken the place largely because it was close to Greenlit Studios, allowing me to cycle to work. The rent seemed more reasonable if it meant I didn't have to buy a car.

"*Meess Sash—*"

To the sound of splintering plywood, I yanked open the termite-infested front door. "What *is* it, Mr. Zglagovvcini?" I demanded, with more anger than I'd intended.

"Ah, Meess Sasha, you alive, good, good. Two things . . ."

It occurred to me that I'd never seen Mr. Zglagovvcini wearing anything other than tennis shorts, flip-flops (in lifeguard yellow), and an obviously counterfeited blue Ralph Lauren T-shirt (obvious because the horseman on the breast pocket is holding up an AK-47, not a polo stick). Presumably the favorable contrast between the LA weather and his native Siberian climate had convinced him to remain as close to naked as possible—within the local decency laws—at all times. I didn't exactly blame him. Dad, who was raised on the drenched shore of the Irish Sea, had been exactly the same way when he'd taken me to LA as a kid. Except he hadn't worn any kind of shirt. Just jeans and his old running shoes.

"Mr. Zglagovvcini," I pleaded. "Can we do this some other—"

He raised both palms.

"Very quick," he promised. "What would you say are the six things you could never live without?

I closed my eyes. *Please tell me I hadn't gotten out of bed for this.*

"Look, I—"

"Six things. Answer carefully."

"What are you talking about, Mr. Zglagovvcini?"

"It's question for eCupidMatch.com."

I began massaging my temples, which seemed only to make my head feel even worse. "Mr. Zglagovvcini," I began, "are you *seriously* creating a profile for me on a dating website?"

"Noooo! Mrs. Zglagovvcini say I not allowed to go on such thing. She think I might run off with stripper. Me! With wrinkly old dick! So she taking care of it, only I have to get information from you, as she very shy." With a shaking hand, he lifted up his reading glasses and studied a list. "Which you say describes you best: dreamer or schemer? If you eaten by cannibal, how you most like to be prepared?"

"Mr. Zglagovvcini, I really, *really* don't want you to — "

A car horn sounded outside.

"Oh, that reminds me," said Mr. Zglagovvcini. "The other thing I need to tell you: Your car has arrived. Driver says he was sent here by Meess, er . . . Gee Gee? Dee Dee? Maybe *Zee Zee?* Anyhow, whatever her name is, she didn't want you turning up to her house on bicycle. She obviously knows you crazy woman."

I couldn't process what he was saying. My brain, like the CPU of an aging computer, had maxed out with the stress of running other applications (talking, standing up, keeping my eyes open) leaving me with a spinning wheel-of-death where thoughts should have been. "*Whose car? Where? What?*" I said, uselessly.

"Your car," he repeated. "It's here."

He pointed to the window of the lobby, beyond which a white Rolls-Royce was waiting. It was gleaming in the sun. The driver waved as I squinted at him.

I thought I might black out.

9

"I Hope You Like Celery"

TEN MINUTES LATER, I was in a teak and leather capsule, being swept along the 101 freeway in total silence at eighty-five miles per hour. Yes, that's correct: *Teak.* Being inside that car was like being aboard a transatlantic steamship from an alternative, retro-futuristic universe. There was even a pull-down picnic table in front of me, the clasp as heavy and stiff as the stops on a cathedral organ. When I pushed open the sliding lid on the surface, it revealed a tiny computer keyboard in matte steel. Tapping on a key activated the iPad embedded in the headrest in front of me. There was another screen in the door pillar to my left: This served as a vanity mirror—a camera was hidden in the frame—with honey-toned backlighting that gave even my reflection the luster of good health. Impressive, given how close I felt to *death.* Or at least as close to death as it was possible to feel in the embrace of such a ludicrously overstuffed chair, beneath the constellation of fiber optic stars that had been woven into the padded suede above me.

"Hey—you comfortable?" asked the driver (twentyish, stubbled, his jaw so perfectly set that I had been forced to swallow an involuntary gasp upon first sight).

"Well, if I'm not comfortable now," I replied, cheesily, "then I don't think I ever will be. Ha!"

I swear I could win gold at the Nerd Olympics.

"Alright," he said, nodding slowly in a way that involved his entire upper body, as athletic, overconfident young American men often do. "If you need anything . . ."

The car surged on, without effort.

It had taken me all of seven minutes to change out of the previous night's clothes, shower, apply makeup (and by that I mean lipstick), and locate my least-unimpressive dress. I was actually surprised by how little thought it required to select the outfit. I mean, what are you *supposed* to wear when going over to Bibi Vasquez's house for a lunch appointment? It's not like I owned any velvet Dior jumpsuits or feathered Alexander McQueen stilettos. So my only black dress, purchased at a chain store whose name I am too ashamed to reveal, would have to suffice, as would my leopard print kitten heels, which had seemed like a good idea on the slightly tipsy (okay, totally wasted) afternoon when I'd bought them. Unsurprisingly, they weren't standing up very well to examination in the illuminated shag pile footwell of a half-a-million-dollar automobile.

In all honesty, I couldn't even remember Bibi inviting me over to her house. It was possible, I suppose, that the message hadn't directly come from her. Perhaps Teddy had passed it on. Or (more likely) one of his many assistants. There was, however, another explanation: That my hangover — or rather, the alcohol that caused it — had erased a crucial section of my memory between the end of The Reveal and whenever it was that I had made it back to Little Russia.

I hadn't planned to get wasted, FYI. I was just so relieved when the day was over, I agreed to go for a postwork drink with the crew. And the crew being the crew, they wanted to go to Timmy Dergen's, a poorly lit, sticky-floored Irish dive over on Fairfax and Wilshire. That was fine by me: Dad pretty much raised me in sticky-floored Irish dives. Indeed, one of my first memories — I must have been five or six — is of his taking me to Billy McQuiffy's in Long Island City for one of his wedding gigs, and then sending me out, across an eight-lane highway, *at night,* to buy him a pack of smokes from a gas station half a mile away. (We lived in a high-rise a few blocks away at the time.) Mom gave Dad a black eye when she found out. As far as I was concerned, of course, it had all been an incredible adventure. Dad was a hero. Mom was a bore. Parenting can be unfair like that sometimes.

Which made me think: If only Dad could see me now. He'd go nuts. Lunch at the house of Bibi Vasquez, a multi-Grammy-winning recording artist? In a white Rolls-Royce?

So anyway: Timmy Dergen's. Me, plus ten big dudes in black T-shirts and dusty jeans. Naturally, the after-work drink soon turned into an after-work let's-all-get-hammered. Now don't get me wrong: I can hold my drink. Dad used to joke that the most valuable thing he ever gave me was a liver of truly prodigious capacity. I've seen men twice my size (that's you, Brock) collapse into a puddle of drool *hours* before I've reached my limit. But there *is* a limit. And I reached it. The evening faded to black at some point while I was dancing with a valet in the Mel's Diner parking lot, a borrowed cigarette fizzing in my hand.

And now . . . here I was, barely recovered, speeding my way to the home of Bibi Vasquez, a woman so famous, you could hike for weeks through the Liberian jungle, meet a one-hundred-year-old tribal elder, and he'd be able to recite to you the lyrics of "I Wanna Rock" without a moment's hesitation. Shamefully, a part of me wanted to crow about where I was going. A casual, single-line Facebook posting, perhaps, in the obligatory format of the humblebrag: "Bibi's for lunch — how weird is that??" But you can't humblebrag in this job, let alone brag-brag. It's like working for Homeland Security. They monitor you. One indiscretion — one blog post, one Twitpic, one status update — and you're out.

I wondered if Len was coming today, too. I hoped not. Then again, it seemed unlikely — no, impossible — that Bibi had invited me over for a private get-together. The very thought of me and Bibi, *alone,* was enough to induce panic, and before I knew it, I'd cracked open the window and was gulping air, trying not to vomit.

"You okay?" asked my handsome driver, glancing back.

"Fine," I said, pulling out my phone and dialing Brock's number. This was long overdue.

"Yo!" said Brock, after barely half a ring.

"Hey, babe," I began, trying to keep my voice down. "So, you'll never guess—"

"This is Brock," he interrupted. "I'm either busy right now, or a robot from the future has vaporized me and is impersonating my voice, hoping to lure you into a deadly trap."

"Brock?"

"If you're planning to meet me someplace, BRING WEAPONS. Otherwise, wait for the—"

Beeeep.

"Arrrgh! Jesus, Brock, how *old* are you?"

I hung up. Brock had no doubt been watching *The Terminator* again with Crazy Pete, his old high school buddy. Pete smokes weed like most people chew gum. I wouldn't have cared, but Brock is annoying on weed. It makes him giggle. Men shouldn't giggle.

About forty minutes had passed when the Rolls-Royce took a ramp off the freeway, crossed a bridge, wafted down a side street, crossed another bridge, then arrived at a gatehouse. The barrier opened automatically as we pulled up to it, and a uniformed attendant waved us in. "Welcome to Secret Mountain," read a woodsy-looking sign on the other side. I knew the name from *ShowBiz:* This was a private town, with its own private supermarket, private cinema, private church, and private school, where celebrities could live beyond the lenses of the paparazzi. Or at least that was the theory. Unfortunately, the paparazzi had discovered an invention known as the helicopter.

After turning up a steep driveway, we at last reached Bibi's house. Well, I say "house" . . . but the place was big enough to hold its own on the international palace circuit.

The Rolls came to halt in a circular motor court. The driver got out and opened my door. Stepping out of the car, I took in the view: Ranchland in every direction. Not a road, not a rooftop, not a single transmission tower. (I've since learned that Teddy paid to have all the electrical cables buried within a twenty-mile radius.) We were only a few miles from LA, yet we might as well have been out in Montana.

"Please," said the driver—my God, he was hot—gesturing toward the entranceway.

A maid ushered me inside calmly. Russian or Polish, I guessed. Her manner was somehow both deferential and unfriendly. It occurred to me that I'd never been inside a celebrity's home before. Not that the usual rules of domesticity apply, I guess, when it comes to the likes of Bibi Vasquez. No, for someone like her, a home isn't so much a *home* as a private hotel, built and operated for the needs of a single guest. As such, they tell you little about their owners, aside from their choice of interior decorator, and the manner in which they manage their staff. In Bibi's case, however, both of these tasks had been outsourced to Teddy, presumably in return for yet another percentage point or two on her income.

I was led down a gnarled-oak hallway. Along the way, we must have passed a dozen other household employees—not explicitly uniformed, but identifiable by their ironed polo shirts and creased khakis—attending unobtrusively to various chores. In one room, a woman was bathing five pit bull puppies. In another, a giant popcorn machine was being recalibrated. And then of course there were the cleaners, odd-jobbers, security guards, and landscapers outside (using rakes, I noticed, not blowers, to avoid disturbing the peace). Finally, we emerged into a kitchen with a floating central countertop that was more continent than island. Beyond it was a table of UN Security Council dimensions, a clutter of wooden chairs, and perhaps two dozen people, none of whom I recognized. Judging by the mix in ages, they were family, not friends. All were focused exclusively on a tiny woman in a white and gold jumpsuit, pacing the floor under a wall-mounted television while brandishing a highly complicated-looking remote. "Wait, *wait,*" she was saying. "You gotta fuckin' see this shit. This shit is fuckin' unreal. How do I unpause this motherfucker? Oh, here." She jabbed at the device and the image on the screen became unstuck.

"OH! MY! GOD!" she exclaimed, hand over mouth.

The real Bibi was now looking at the celebrity Bibi on the screen. I recognized the footage instantly: It was from the press conference at The Roundhouse – the last few seconds, when all three judges were on stage together, locking arms. This wasn't the raw video feed, though. It was a clip, repackaged for an episode of *The Dish,* the sarcastic nightly entertainment show hosted by Jordan Wade, one of Wayne Shoreline's less successful friends. From what I could gather, Jordan was making a joke of the improbably large fish tooth that dangled from Joey Lovecraft's blown-out mane. "Dude, where d'you get that?" Jordan was asking the camera, holding up a rubber shark. "How did it *get* up there? Were you, like, cutting your hair with a hammerhead – and it *just fell out?*"

Bibi screeched with pleasure.

"D'oh!" mimicked Jordan. "*Happens to me all the time!* Damn those hammerheads and their shitty-assed dentistry! Still, give the fish some credit: It didn't eat your head, right?"

"Goddamn, he's a fuckin' funny motherfucker!" wailed Bibi, catching my eye for a moment, but ignoring me nevertheless. It was though she were on stage, midperformance.

"Did Teddy write that?" someone yelled, struggling to be heard over the television.

"Of course!" snorted Bibi. "Well, not Teddy *personally.* It was that scriptwriter guy he hired. Y'know, the one who won that Oscar for that . . . war thing."

"Teddy can get *Jordan fuckin' Wade* to talk shit about Joey on his show?" asked someone else.

Bibi tapped her nose theatrically, as though this were some big trade secret.

Delighted laughter.

Not quite knowing what to do, I sat down. The guy next to me – European accent, expensively dressed, and seemingly desperate for Bibi to notice him laughing and slapping the table after everything she said – nodded an acknowledgment of my presence, then passed me a bowl of celery sticks. Unfortunately for my hangover, this appeared to be the extent of the lunch. I began to wonder why Bibi had brought me here for . . . *this.* It didn't make any sense.

And it wasn't about to get any clearer.

After *The Dish,* Bibi went through her DVR playlist, selecting all the other shows that had featured the *Project Icon* press conference. Seven in total. Then it was time for a screening of the unedited footage of the event, which I noticed featured my left foot (complete with hiking shoe) protruding briefly from one of the wings.

"Wayne Shoreline is *such* a douche nozzle," Bibi kept saying during the introductions.

The room jeered in agreement.

Due to the frequent pausing, all of this went on for perhaps two or three hours.

"She curses more in real life, don't she?" said a voice to my left, near the end. I turned to see an Afro-Caribbean woman, perhaps late sixties, wearing bejeweled jeans and a purple leather blazer. Was this . . . *Bibi's mom?* I didn't have the nerve to ask.

"Hmm," I nodded, diplomatically.

"Such a perfect face. And such a dirty, *dirty* mouth. You know what we call her?"

I shrugged.

"Ghetto Barbie. It's worse when Edouard and the kids aren't here."

I smiled, not sure if it was safe to agree.

"It's hard for her though, poor baby," the woman continued, as if for her own benefit. "Everyone wantin' her for her money. Y'know, in my own way, I know how she feels . . . when I came here from the islands, I worked as a baby nurse for a rich white lady in Manhattan. And oh—*the men who chased me!* Everyone wanted themselves a baby nurse for a girlfriend. Cash income. Woman away all the time, working nights, so they could play around. Ha! I learned the hard way how it worked. That's why I wanted my Bibi to get herself an education, find a man with a college degree, so he could take care of *her.* But it didn't work out like that, I guess." Chuckling sadly, she continued: "I worry about that boy Teddy she got managing her things, y'know. Odd fellow. Gives me the heebie-jeebies. I'm not even sure about Edouard, sometimes. He's a *man,* even if he don't act like it half the time. And real men don't like to earn less than their wives."

So this *was* Bibi's mom.

I could hardly believe what I'd just heard. It wasn't much of a surprise that she didn't trust Teddy, of course—I mean, who *did?* But Edouard? *Her own son-in-law?*

As much as I wanted to ask her for an explanation (was Edouard jealous of Bibi's success?) it didn't exactly seem like the place or the time. Instead I opted for some generic expression of sympathy. By the time I opened my mouth to speak, however, Bibi's mom had already wandered off, gin and tonic in hand.

It must have been seven o'clock before I found the courage to leave. Not that I really knew *how* to leave: I'd arrived in Bibi's Rolls-Royce, after all. And it didn't seem right, either. I mean, there I was, at Bibi Vasquez's house, in her inner-inner circle, doing what presumably millions of her fans would love nothing more to do. And yet I was, well, bored. Bibi wasn't exactly a terrific conversationalist. She just made statements, with which everyone agreed. And they weren't even interesting statements. In fact, her commentary on the *ShowBiz* coverage of *Project Icon* made me yearn to be home, in bed, reading a long essay in *The New Yorker.* I felt like one of those foreign military generals you see on the news, pretending to be amused by the latest interminable speech from their beloved dictator. And I suppose that wasn't too far from the truth. For as long as I worked at *Project Icon,* Bibi's power over me would be absolute. Without her—or Joey, for that matter—the show didn't stand a chance of holding on to last season's twenty million viewers. And without those twenty million viewers, the advertisers wouldn't pay to air their commercials during the breaks. And without the commercials . . . well, the whole thing would fall apart. No show. No job. No chance of me going to Hawaii. No mai tais with Brock. Bibi's mom was right: *Everyone wanted her daughter for the money.* Depressingly enough, that included me.

Nevertheless, as it got dark, I *had* to go home. My hangover had entered the must-sleep phase, and I was no longer able to contain my yawns. Bibi had by now disappeared somewhere, so I found the maid who'd shown me in, and asked her for the address of the house, so I could call for a cab. "Oh, you don't need to do *that,* Miss Bill," she said — she knew my name! — "David is waiting for you outside in the car."

"David?"

"Your driver."

I'd be lying to you if I said I wasn't delighted by this news.

In the kitchen, I said my good-byes — no one seemed particularly interested — and made my way back to the front door. It troubled me that I hadn't spoken to Bibi. Had this been my fault? Had I failed some kind of test? And then, in the hallway, a hand grabbed my arm. I turned, and felt a cold trickle of fear; the sensation of a teacher waking you from a classroom daydream with a difficult question to which you don't know the answer. It was *Bibi,* wearing pajamas.

"I'm glad you could come over," she said. Then, laughing: "I hope you like celery. Blame my new nutritionist. She says it's okay to be famous for a big butt, but not a *fat* butt. So the cheeseburgers are on hold for now, along with all the other fun stuff."

"I love celery," I blurted. "I'd be totally happy as a Wonder Pet."

I couldn't believe that I'd just made a Wonder Pet joke. Only teenage stoners with nothing to do all day are familiar with children's TV shows like *Wonder Pets,* and therefore know that Linny, the caped Guinea Pig, likes celery. What a hopeless dork.

"Right," said Bibi, absently. "Anyway: I just wanted to tell you, honey: It's not true."

What the hell was she talking about?

"I'm sorry?" I said.

"About *you,* honey. About you being 'poison.' All that stuff that Joey said when he was being mean."

"Oh, that . . ."

"It's pretty rich, coming from him, y'know," she continued. "I mean, he's says he's not in this for the money or anything, but that's, like, total fuckin' bullshit. Trust me: He's more into the money than Sir Harold Killoch. Don't fall for the act."

I didn't know what to say.

"At least I'm honest about what I want," Bibi went on. "With Joey, it's all this, 'Hey, I'm just diggin' the High Lama Yuti *whatever-the-fuck-his-name-is.* He's the fake, not you."

I nodded dumbly.

"Whatever," she concluded. "Enjoy the Rolls, honey. Just stay away from David. He's all *mine.*" Then she gave me a smile—the very same smile that had been framed in lights and hung from skyscrapers in every major world city—and walked away.

I watched as she padded barefoot up the hallway.

When the maid spoke, it made me jump. "Shall I let David know you're ready now?" she asked.

"I'm ready," I confirmed, with relief. "Very ready."

I tried to sleep in the Rolls, but couldn't. The day had been just too strange. Besides, the toxic fog of my hangover was now finally beginning to lift, making me feel suddenly energized. So I folded down the picnic table in front of me, tore a sheet of paper from the "BV" monogrammed notepad in the armrest, and began writing, pausing to think carefully between each line. And when we finally got back to Little Russia, I slipped the result of my work under Mr. Zglagovvcini's door.

It read:

Hey there, Mr. Z:

Okay . . . so I'm not including "oxygen" or any smartass bullshit like that. That said, here goes:

SIX THINGS I CAN'T LIVE WIHTOUT

1. Brock (my BOYFRIEND).
2. Mom (tied with No. 1).
3. *One Hundred Years of Solitude* (first edition hardback, gift from my dad).
4. Maker's Mark on ice.

5. Sweet potato fries (or horseradish—tough call).
6. Blue (the color, not Apt. 23-A's goldfish, though he's adorable).

This DOES NOT mean I want you to create that profile, Mr. Z!!! I'm leaving for Hawaii to see "Mr. Invisible" very soon. If you want something to do, send me your own list.

Later,

"Crazy Woman" (Apt. 7-B)

10

N for Yes

November

OKAY, SO IT SOUNDS ridiculous, I know—but I could hardly resist asking myself the question: Had I *made friends* with Bibi Vasquez? Had our conversation in the hallway of her Secret Mountain home marked the beginning of one of those fairytale, princess-and-the-pauper-style relationships—like the ones you see in those corny English movies, which always seem to end with some poofy-dressed royal making an unexpected visit for tea to a humble, chintz-stacked, semi-detached house in Olde Yorkminster (as the gawping, woolly-hatted neighbors peer on)?

Don't get me wrong. I didn't actually *want* Bibi to make an unexpected visit to my apartment. There was nowhere for her to sit, for a start. And the only thing I could offer her, foodwise, was old cheese. And then of course there was the issue of Mr. Zglagovvcini, with his incessant coughing and lethal bouts of flatulence . . .

If I was being honest with myself, however, I knew that friendship with Bibi was out of the question. Even if she wasn't worth half a billion dollars, even if the LAPD didn't close the street whenever she went to a restaurant, even if she wasn't so busy, she had to schedule time with her kids via a global network of childcare logistics coordinators. *Even ignoring all that,* we'd still have nothing in common.

I like to deflect attention; Bibi wants as much of it as she can get. In high school I was Little Miss Bookworm (or "the freckled dorkworm" as one of the more talented bullies put it); Bibi was named Most Likely to Marry a Movie Star. And then of course there's the age difference. Bibi is *twenty years* my senior: old enough to be my mother! Not that anyone would know this by looking at us. Indeed, like most females of a certain wealth level, Bibi has essentially been freeze-framed by cosmetic technology—and will almost certainly remain that way for the rest of her professional life, or at least until the next major upgrade, from which she might very well emerge having lost another half decade.

So *why* had she sent the Rolls-Royce to collect me? Just to give me her opinion of Joey? It was hard to think of any other reason. Unless . . . unless Bibi was so lonely and insecure—as her mom had suggested—that she needed to fill her house with anyone willing to give her their uninterrupted attention for *seven hours.* What a depressing thought. Still, it would have explained the presence of all those random, grinning sycophants, even if they *were* all distant cousins.

Whatever the case, any fantasy that I'd indulged in regarding my "special relationship" with Bibi came to an end a few weeks later, when it was time to start taping the city-to-city audition episodes of *Project Icon.* Our first stop, according to the calendar e-mailed to all members of staff, would be Creamywhip Megacheese Stadium in Houston. Now, this was of course the very first stage of the competition, to air in late January. And although no one expected it to get the ratings of the live shows at Greenlit Studios later in the season—they're always more exciting because of the much narrower field of contestants, the telephone voting, plus the number of things that can go wrong while on air—it would be crucial in terms of establishing the relationships between the new judges.

"It's all about *camaraderie,*" as Len kept telling me, as if I were one of those zoo keepers you see on the news, whose job is to make two depressed, morbidly obese pandas from China have sex with each other. "If those guys don't loosen up on camera, we're gonna end up with no ad-libs. And it's ad-libs that make great TV, Billy the Kiddo." (Yes, Len had now started to call me "Billy the Kiddo.") I restrained myself from pointing out to him that his previous effort to get Bibi and Joey to comingle—the "judges' lounge" at The Roundhouse—had done nothing but provide the crew with a better quality of sandwich to steal.

My first task toward achieving this let's-all-pretend-to-be-friends goal: reserving the entire first-class cabin of an early morning American Airlines flight from LAX to Houston, due to leave the following Monday. I had even been loaned a cubicle at Zero Management on Sunset Boulevard—complete with workstation, headset, and telephone—to get it done. My plan was to put Joey and Bibi in seats 1A and 1F (the windows on either side), with their highest-tier assistants next to them, and Len, Ed Rossitto, Maria Herman-Bloch (along with a few other Rabbit executives) filling the row behind. Special nonalcoholic champagne would be arranged—I didn't want Joey failing his pee test—as would a pair of former *Icon* runners-up to act as singing flight attendants. Cheesy, sure. But the panda-wrangler inside of me figured it might help to improve the mood. Meanwhile, I would be in the rear, behind the Curtain of Shame, my back against the bathroom wall. At least *my* champagne would be of the alcoholic variety.

None of this seemed particularly difficult. An easy way to start the season.

But, no. Nothing is ever easy on *Project Icon.*

When I called Bibi to confirm the arrangements—I had stupidly assumed that she might actually pick up the phone—I was put through to Teddy, who screamed with such force down the line, the receiver was practically vaporized in my hands. "BIBI VASQUEZ HASN'T FLOWN COMMERCIAL IN FIFTEEN YEARS, YOU DUMB FUCKING INTERN!" he began (impressively, his rage needed no time whatsoever to gain momentum). "WHAT ELSE DO YOU WANT HER TO

DO, SHITHEAD? MOVE BACK TO THE GHETTO? GIVE BLOW JOBS TO GUYS ON TENTH AVENUE?"

After the sound of plastic being forced to confront the most extreme laws of physics (did he actually keep a *hammer* by his desk?), the line hissed and went dead. "If you'd like to make a call," said a disembodied female voice, "please hang up and try again. If you'd like to make a call, please hang up and try again . . ."

I stared at the phone.

Intern? Teddy really was a piece of work.

Bibi, I was informed via follow-up e-mail, would be taking her own jet to Houston. All by herself.

Cue a Joey problem.

"Look, Bill—Joey wants to go private, too," huffed Mitch, barely five minutes later.

"Okay, Mitch," I sighed. "Joey can take his jet. He can ride a camel to Houston for all I care. But we're only paying expenses that are equal to the price of the first-class ticket." This had been an order from Len, even though he'd already worked out a deal with Bibi to pay for her jet fuel, crew, and take-off/landing fees. Clearly this was unfair to Joey, but among the world's many injustices, it ranked fairly low on my list of Things To Get Upset About.

"Joey doesn't own a jet," coughed Mitch.

"Well that settles it, then," I laughed (a little condescendingly). "He'll have to go first class."

Now it was Mitch's turn to detonate. "No, Bill: You'll GET him a jet. Rent one. Borrow one. Steal one. Whatever it is you've gotta do, *he gets the same as Bibi.*"

Second hang-up of the day.

And that was the end of the negotiations. Bibi went on her own plane; Joey went on a chartered one. If they'd looked out of their windows at thirty-seven thousand feet, they could have waved to each other. So much for camaraderie. As for the executives, they flew American Airlines, as planned. Meanwhile, me and rest of the staff were rebooked on cheaper tickets, the kind with multiple layovers—Las Vegas, Phoenix, Albuquerque—to at least give the appearance of trying to stay within budget. It took us fourteen hours to get there, at a cost to the Rabbit network of $103.47 each.

The tab for Bibi and Joey's flights? $734,677.27.

That, I swear, is no exaggeration.

I should probably explain that Houston wasn't going to be a normal casting call, largely because of the long delay in signing the judges' contracts. In fact, to keep production on schedule, the entire *Project Icon* crew had already been to Houston over the summer, to get pretty much everything in the can apart from the scenes involving the panel. Not that the viewers at home would ever know the difference. After the credits sequence, there'd be a long, swooping shot from a helicopter over Creamywhip Megacheese Stadium, revealing ten thousand or so screaming teenagers in the parking lot outside, waving and jostling their signs (all this taped back in August); and then, after a few zany interviews, tearful backstories, and scene-setters from inside the grounds (also taped in August), the screen would cut seamlessly to contestants entering the judges' audition suite, one by one—as if it were all happening on the *very same day*—to do their thing.

In reality, of course, the auditions in front of the judges would be taking place *months* after the original cattle call. What's more, of the ten thousand contestants who'd originally showed up, only a hundred or so now remained, because most of the vetting had already been done by yours truly, along with a hastily assembled team of my fellow junior producers/office punching bags from Rabbit, Zero Management, and Invasion Media. Again, this wouldn't be clear from watching the show. It would look as though the panel had sat through *the entire thing*—what troupers!—when in fact they'd skipped the whole seething-mass-of-humanity part of the competition altogether. In fact, they wouldn't even have to go near Creamywhip Megacheese Stadium, because their scenes would be shot twenty miles north, in the penthouse suite of an eight-star downtown hotel. (The only issue with this being continuity: Some of the ditzier contestants would inevitably forget to wear the same clothes for both shoots, meaning I'd have to take them shopping for the closest match possible. Which I knew from experience could be infuriating, especially if they'd turned up to the first audition in costume—try finding an inflatable banana suit in a Houston mall at eight a.m.)

As for the original cattle call: *Hell.*

It goes like this: Day One, you get to the stadium at five a.m., and there are twice as many people lined up in the parking lot than can actually fit inside. That's because those ten thousand contestants bring another sixty thousand friends, pets, and family members. Most have camped out all night, making the place look like a postapocalypse refugee camp. And only about—oh—a *dozen* of them are talented. As in, could-be-famous talented. The rest are either delusional, in it for a laugh, or willing to do anything for attention. Hence the stripping Benjamin Franklin on a unicycle, and the woman who turned up to sing a duet with her parrot. And of course a few are genuinely deranged. It's scary, actually, when you think about the dozen or so *Project Icon* suicides, including that guy who broke into Nigel Crowther's house, left a demo of his album on the kitchen table, then hung himself from the upstairs balcony using a microphone cord.

Day One is the easiest, though, because all the contestants really have to do is line up for wristbands—in return for which they must show some ID and sign a wad of paperwork, promising they won't post any YouTube videos, tweets, blog entries, et cetera, or even *tell* anyone if they make it through to the next round, as this would destroy all the tension when the show finally airs. Day Two is when things get seriously intense. In total there are probably twenty prejudges, and we sit behind long tables positioned in the center of the arena, separated by black curtains. You feel like some exotic creature in a cage on display at the county fair. And what with the background noise—a stadium full of kids reciting lyrics, trying to find their pitch, strumming guitars—it's a struggle to hear your own voice, nevermind the finer qualities of the four thousandth rendition you've heard in one morning of *Don't*

Worry, Be Happy. (If I am ever given the option to erase a song permanently from history, this will be my choice.)

The first round of auditions is done in bulk—six contestants at a time. They line up in front of you, looking generally terrified and desperate, and take it in turns to sing. You're allowed to give them thirty seconds each, maximum. A lot of them refuse to stop, thinking that the more they go on, the better their opportunity for convincing you. Others are only too happy to give up and forget it ever happened, as if they're doing it just to *say* they've done it; to tick it off a list—the problem being that if you don't commit, you don't stand a chance, as with most things in life. When they're all done, you ask each one to approach the table, and you either cut off their wristband, which means they're out and have to be escorted immediately from the premises, or you give them a bright orange ticket, which grants them entry to the "Talent Lounge" where they await the next stage.

If it wasn't for the security team hired by *Icon,* I'm pretty sure the prejudges wouldn't make it out alive. You're spat at, punched, kissed, bribed, threatened, flashed . . . and nearly crushed by the hugs of those who make it through. All the while, Len is yelling orders into your earpiece. "Guy in yellow shirt, Bill. Three o'clock. Yes, him. That's a non-sponsored drink he's holding. GET IT OUT OF HERE. He's . . . sorry, what's that?—It's a, oh, it's a *medical* drink? Well, for the love of God, Bill, POUR IT INTO A SPONSORED CUP, JUST GET THE LEPROSY JUICE OR WHATEVER IT IS HE NEEDS TO STOP HIS BALLS FALLING OFF AWAY FROM THE CAMERA, DO YOU HAVE *ANY* IDEA HOW MUCH MONEY OUR DEAL WITH FREAKY-COLA IS WORTH? JESUS CHRIST ALIVE, BILL, GET A FUCKING GRIP."

(Five minutes after this particular rant, I saw Len hold an impromptu prayer gathering with a group of auditioning choristers from a Baptist church in Biloxi, Mississippi.)

I probably don't even have to point out that the contestants who make it into the Talent Lounge aren't necessarily any good. That's why their tickets are stamped with a secret code, almost impossible to find unless you know where to look.

"Think of when you book a flight somewhere and try to change the time at the last minute," as Len explained to me. "The first thing the call-center operator will say to you is, 'Oh, you've got the wrong *code* for that.' Only you didn't know the code *existed* when you bought the ticket—and even if you had done, you wouldn't have known what it meant. The idea, Bill, *is to confuse you.* And we do the same. That's why I need you to give a code to everyone who gets through. This week, we're going to use N for a definite 'yes, they'll go on to Hollywood'; X for a 'maybe'; and Y for a categorical 'no, but the kid looks like a crier or a psycho, so roll the cameras.' And remember: NEVER explain this to anyone."

I nodded, wondering how much longer my soul had left to live.

"Another thing," Len went on, breezily. "If someone has a good gimmick—y'know, dying kid, mom in prison, amusing facial tic—put a star in the top right corner."

11

The Loneliest Place on Earth

IT WAS ALMOST THANKSGIVING when *Project Icon* arrived in Houston again—this time *with* the judges. Unusually, all of us were put up in the same hotel, which would double as the venue for the shoot. Bibi was in the presidential suite; Joey in an inferior suite on the same floor that had also been named "presidential suite" for the occasion. (The hotel charged us a thousand dollars for the plaque, but Len figured it was worth it.) JD and Wayne were somewhere in between. The rest of us were on the lower floors, but I couldn't have cared less. I was just grateful that we hadn't been booked in a motel by the freeway and told to take a bus to the set, as was often the case when we were on the road—especially during one of Len's austerity drives (in which he never seemed to take part). Not that the king-size bed in my room helped me get any sleep. I can *never* sleep before filming.

First item on the schedule for the next morning: "Prepare for judges' arrival at hotel." Now, this might sound confusing, given that the panel was already *staying* at the hotel. But for the sake of the cameras, they couldn't just step out of the elevators and roll into the audition suite. That would be boring. Instead, they had to pull up outside in limos, work a line of screaming fans, raise their arms in the air, wipe away tears, say "oh, my God!" a lot, and . . . well, you get the idea. We also had to make it look as though they were turning up to a stadium, not a hotel. All of which was going to take a lot of work, hence an early "call time" (by celebrity standards) of eight a.m. This didn't actually mean eight a.m., though, because we were all fully aware that Joey would be late. And however late Joey would be, Bibi would be later by a fixed ratio of time calculated by Teddy, who is said to have invented his very own mathematical formula for such etiquette. So the *real* call time, as the crew named it privately between themselves, was WTFBIR—"whenever the fuck Bibi is ready."

WTFBIR turned out to be noon.

Even Len, who had never displayed anything but total obsequiousness to Bibi, couldn't disguise the pinkish flare of irritation in his cheeks. "Right, good. Let's go, shall we?" he said, grabbing her arm, when she eventually stepped out of the private, bellhop-operated elevator from her room (I noticed Joey looking at it quizzically, but I couldn't decide if he was wondering why *his* presidential suite didn't have its own elevator, or if he was simply ogling Bibi's ass). Then we were off, following Len and Bibi down a hidden service corridor that led to the hotel's underground parking lot, accessible only by valets and VIPs. Three black Jaguar XJs were waiting: one for Bibi; one for Joey; and another for JD, Len, Maria, and Ed. (In case you're wondering, Ed was wearing a cowboy hat and checked shirt, which made him look like an actual-size Woody from the *Toy Story* movie.) When everyone had climbed in, the Jags pulled expensively out of the garage, circled the block in near-silence three times, then headed back to where they'd started, only this time at the public entrance on the opposite side of the building. There, about two hundred rent-a-fans were waiting. They cheered while brandishing signs and banners ("Bibi, I LUV YOU!") that looked homemade, but had in fact been manufactured by Steve, our props guy, and handed out that morning, along with free coffee and donuts.

Anything for a bigger crowd.

And then, with a bump of adrenaline that took me by surprise, we had climbed a flight of thick-carpeted stairs to the audition suite, and it was *on.*

Season thirteen of *Project Icon* was underway.

I stood with my trusty clipboard at the side of the room, amid a heap of cables that resembled the corpse of some multitentacled sea creature, taking in the scene. It was hard to think of anywhere outside a foreign interrogation cell that could be so intimidating. The judges' table was positioned in front of a tinted wall-to-ceiling window offering a giddy view of Houston's downtown oil company skyscrapers. On the other side of the room was a massive piece of wheeled scenery, covered entirely with sponsors' logos. And halfway between the two was the Loneliest Place on Earth: A circular podium, about a foot off the ground, upon which each contestant would have to stand while trying to win the panel's approval. Above, two dozen or so microphones hung, ready to capture and amplify every mangled lyric, bad note, and mistimed breath. Cameras peered intrusively from every possible angle. And the lights, wow, *the lights.* Each one like an oncoming train —and hot enough to fry a steak. Meanwhile, an "X" made from duct tape let the specimen know exactly where to stand, and an arrow—directed off-puttingly to the left of the judges' line of sight (this was deliberate)—indicated where they should look, assuming their eyes were open when they sang. Underneath, in marker, Len had written, "ARE YOU REALLY GOOD ENOUGH?"

So . . . the auditions. One by one, the contestants arrive. Bug-eyed, way tall nerdy guy. Plump, almost pretty aw-shucks girl. The Deep Voice. The Squeaky Voice. The Whisperer. The desperate, weeping, borderline talented but possibly crack-addicted waitress. Clean-cut brothers who hug each other too much and sing in falsetto. The inevitable underage pageant veteran (impressive fake birth certificate) whose first appointment after leaving her mom's birth canal was probably an audition for a diaper commercial. Hipster chick with tattoos and flapper outfit who sounds exactly like *every other* hipster chick with tattoos and a flapper outfit (about three per season, mainly because they tend to show a lot of flesh, of which Len approves). Here they come, every size, shape, race, musical genre, dress style, and personality you can think of. Sweet hula girl from Pacific military base with nice voice but nothing to say. Mouthy rocker chick with beer breath and ashtray complexion. Rapping ex-Amish kid. Chinese American football player who's big into Johnny Cash. Acrobat from the Houston circus who can perform any physical feat *except sing on key.* Beauty queen from Idaho —just turned eighteen yesterday!—with a hot pink T-shirt that reads, "I Da Hoe."

There's a twist to all this, however. Before any contestant is allowed into the room, they must first be screened one last time by Len, Maria, and Ed, who form a kind of decoy panel, a psych-ops team, whose aim is to confuse and demoralize. The strategy might not be complex, but it's effective: They tell the singer the *very opposite* of the truth. The bad ones are informed of their greatness, their limitless potential, and, yes, their *Gift* ("Darling, you're a tonic for our weary, cynical ears!") And the good ones? They're torn into a thousand bloody pieces, informed with a concerned, ever-so-sorry frown, of their obvious, multiple failings, and the *unusually high quality of the competition this year.* If they don't want to go any further, Len tells them, that's okay. No shame in quitting. He understands.

The purpose of all this? Drama, of course.

Take contestant number three: A terrible, terrible singer. As pleasing to the ears as a rock stuck in a vacuum cleaner—but he's been told by Len & Co. of the great talent he possesses. His "instrument" is truly a Gift from nature, they enthuse. *He must respect its power.* So in he goes to the audition suite to torture the panel with twelve bars of *River Deep—Mountain High.* It's atrocious. A musical homicide.

When it's over, JD shakes his head and goes into one of his "oh, *man,*" routines.

Bibi can't even look at the podium because Teddy has ordered her never, *ever* to sneer. "Oh, sweetie," she coos, trying to sound maternal.

A difficult silence.

Then—

"THAT FUCKIN' SUCKED ASS!" blasts Joey, who for reasons known only to himself has taken the desecration of Ike and Tina Turner as a personal insult. "Seriously. You should be fuckin' . . . [sighs] just get the hell outta here, man. This ain't for you."

In the contestant's eyes: disbelief. Only three minutes ago, he had been compared favorably to Otis Redding; he had been asked to give "serious thought" as to who might produce his first album. He had been told to *respect his Gift.*

"No, no . . . this can't be right!" he says, remembering that he's signed a contract agreeing never to disclose any "private discussions with the producers," especially not on the podium. "I *know* I'm good. They told me! Let me sing you another—"

"Duuuuude," says JD. "Joey's right. This ain't for you."

"But it . . . *is!*"

Bibi: "It isn't, sweetie."

"But . . . but . . . [beginning to whimper] my *instrument!*"

Close-up on face. Len's voice in my earpiece: "Are you getting the tears? *Are you getting the tears?*"

The contestant throws his orange ticket on the floor, stomps petulantly, then storms out in a rage. Only we've directed him to the wrong door, and it won't open. He rattles the handle. He's burning with shame. Humiliation on humiliation. A handheld cam in his face, pushing closer, pushing closer. He swats it away, finds the right door—this takes some time—and practically throws himself through it, anything to get away from this horror, this travesty. But there, on the other side, is none other than the Evil HostBot himself, Wayne Shoreline.

"This must be the worst day of your life, right?" asks Wayne, chirpily. "Wanna tell me about it? It'll feel *good* to get it off your chest. *Tell me why you feel so betrayed.*"

Now the contestant falls to his knees. He's forgotten all about Len & Co. now. He simply *knows* the truth. His Gift is a fact established beyond any question. It has nothing whatsoever to do with what was fed to him a few minutes ago by a trio of manipulative television producers. But this Gift, with its great power, and the great responsibility that comes with it, *has not been recognized.* Why?! Why would the judges so deliberately ignore it? Are they jealous? Is this . . . a case of *professional jealousy?* How else could they not see what was so *obvious?* But he can't get any of this out because he's wailing, gnashing, beating his fists repeatedly on the floor. "It's j-j-just so, uh, uh . . . j-j-just so . . . *unfaarirgh!*"

At this point we've got what we needed.

"All right, cut," someone yells. Security intervenes.

And then it's time for the *good* singer to come in, and we go through this all again, only in reverse.

12

Snake Break!

I SUPPOSE THERE'S AT least one thing to be said for filming a TV show this way: *It's quick.* Len makes drama as efficiently as General Motors makes cars. In fact, it takes just three and a half minutes to "process" a contestant in the judges' audition suite. Enter. Sing. A few words from the judges. Yes or no. Then on to the next. (The yeses are told, "You're going to Vegas, baby!" referring to the last round of the prerecorded shows, held in Las Vegas, where the contestants are filtered yet again before the live episodes finally air. The nos are given any number of euphemisms for "you suck," including the JD classic "you're not ready yet.")

And how did Joey and Bibi do?

Well, they were cordial, at least. And if they were bored, they at least disguised it, unlike Nigel Crowther during season twelve, when he barely kept his eyes open during the auditions—on the few occasions he bothered to show up at all.

Len's fears about *camaraderie* proved well-founded, though. It wasn't so much bad as just nonexistent. Sure, every so often Joey would get mad about the vandalism of a beloved song—thus providing the highlight of the day's filming—but for the most part he was uncharacteristically inoffensive and uncritical. What had happened to the piano-hugging Joey from the sanity checks? As for Bibi, she was an even bigger disappointment. She didn't even seem to be *looking* at the podium half the time. In fact, if one person held it all together during that first afternoon, it was JD, with his reassuring "booya-ka-*kas*" and genuine efforts to offer musicianly advice. Without him, the footage would have been a write-off.

The biggest problem, as far as I could tell, was the stop-start nature of the takes, which meant the panel never gained momentum. The interruptions came in three forms. First: Bibi's makeup. It seemed that every other minute, she halted production to call in the so-called Glam Squad—i.e., her five stylists, who formed a silent, diligent circle around her, like surgeons preparing to remove an organ. And every time Bibi called in the Glam Squad, Joey felt obligated to do the same—only he had the Mojo Squad, which consisted basically of Mitch and a powder puff. The second cause of delays: Wardrobe changes. Bibi went through three in a day, a number exceeded only by Teddy, whose suits changed by the hour. Fortunately, Joey didn't feel the need to compete in this regard. But Joey disrupted the proceedings in another, more serious way: Snake breaks.

As in, "Okay, folks, gotta shake the snake!"

I swear, Joey took a snake break between every contestant. Either his prostrate was shot, I concluded, or his bladder was the size of a peanut. And of course it didn't help that he was getting through a gallon of Kangen water every other minute.

No one on the crew dared complain. After all, Bibi and Joey were saving all our jobs—or that was the idea, anyway. In reality, I can't have been the only one to wonder how long it would take for Sir Harold to cancel the show when he saw our first day's work.

It was Day Two when Len finally lost his patience. We were four hours behind schedule thanks to snake breaks, outfit changes, and the Glam/Mojo Squads, the contestants had been uniformly boring, and it was time for the judges to deliver their opinions on yet another depressingly average rendition of "Rolling in the Deep." Only Bibi wasn't concentrating. *Again.* She was just staring blankly into the middle distance — which meant that if we ever used the footage, some poor editor in a darkened bunker would have to make sure she was cut out of the shot. Not an easy task, given her regal position at the center of the judges' table.

"Bill," said Len, over the headset. "Follow Bibi's line of sight. Find out what the *fuck* she's looking at. This is *ridiculous.* I've seen zombies make more eye contact."

Len's order wasn't as straightforward as it sounded. To see where Bibi was looking meant standing directly behind her, but this was impossible because: a) there was barely any room between the back of her chair and the window, and b) I couldn't appear on camera. So I crouched down and waddled along on my haunches to the far edge of the judges' table, then backed up as much as I could — making sure I was well out of the shot — to see if I could approximate her viewing angle.

My leg muscles felt as though they were about to snap.

"Dude, for *me,* that was just okay for you," JD was saying. "It's wasn't the full booya-ka-*ka.*"

"Please," the contestant begged. "I *know* I can do this."

"I thought it was all right, man," countered Joey. "Good job. Over to you, Bibi. Your call."

"Thank you, thank you, Mr. Lovecraft," the contestant wept. "Ms. Vasquez — please! Oh, *please!*"

"NOW!!!" screamed Len into my headset, making me almost fall backward into a light reflector. "WHAT THE FUCK IS SHE LOOKING AT, BILL?"

I tried to follow Bibi's gaze, but a light was blocking the way.

"Hold on," I hissed.

"Now, Bill, *now.*"

"There's something in the — "

"Jesus Christ. Can't you do *anything?*"

"Arrgh!" I'd knelt awkwardly on something hard and spiked, and pain was now coursing through my knee and into my leg, which was already sore from walking on my haunches. And then, in my agony, I glimpsed it: a clear path from Bibi's eyes in the direction they were currently pointing. If I could just move . . . my other leg . . . yes, yes . . . watch out for the . . . good, good . . . a little more . . .

"I've got a lock," I whispered. "Repeat, I've got a . . ."

"TELL ME WHAT SHE'S LOOKING AT."

Bibi cleared her throat to deliver her verdict. Then — as always — she paused.

That blank stare again.

Now I was seeing *exactly* what she was seeing: the contestant trembling on the podium; the vast, glossy billboard of the sponsors' wall behind him; the dense, tangled thicket of cameras, lights, mic stands, and monitors that loomed to either side; the black-T-shirted crew members, crouched down like me or flattened against the walls. *What the hell was she focused on?* I adjusted my angle by a tenth of a degree. Another tenth. C'mon, Bill, look. *Look harder.* There! Was that . . . ? Yes, in the blackness beyond the cameras. Just to the left of the sponsors' wall. A glint from a pair of eyeglasses. A figure on tiptoe. A man. Standing there, motionless. No . . . not motionless. Holding something up. He was holding up a —

"*Oh my God,*" I said, but I was drowned out by Bibi.

"It's a no from me, honey," she blurted, at last. "I'm sorry. You're just not ready."

"You'll never believe this," I hissed into the headset. "*Teddy is holding up cue cards.*"

We broke for lunch in an adjoining room, where the hotel staff had set up a temporary canteen. I'd learned the previous day that these lunches were like the first day of high school all over again, with a rigid hierarchy of seating. The popular kids were the judges, who were allocated a table all of their own. Of secondary coolness was the table for Len and his "Lovelies," which included two blonde Rabbit publicists, and some of the better-looking assistants. Then there were the groupings of assistant producers and the like—i.e., me and my fellow underlings—followed by hair and makeup, lighting and sound, and then the rest of the crew.

Today, however, was different: Joey, Mitch, and Len were sitting together, and when I walked in the room, they called me over and invited me to join them.

This can't be good news, I thought.

"Before you ask, yes, I'm hungry," said Joey, by way of explaining the spread in front of him. It included a dozen oysters, half a cheeseburger, some fries, a bento box of sushi, and a whole grilled salmon. At Joey's table, I soon discovered, there was no menu. You just asked for whatever came to mind when you sat down.

"Where on earth do you *put* it all, Joey?" asked Len. "You've got a ten-inch waist."

"Overactive thyroid," Joey mumbled, through a mouthful of bun. "Plus ADD. I can eat *anything.*"

"Incredible," Len marveled.

"You should have seen him on cocaine," offered Mitch, glumly.

Joey stood up. "Don't let them clear this," he instructed, gesturing to his plate with one hand while using the other to push half a roll of sushi into his still bun-filled mouth. "I'm sooo fuckin' hungry, man. But I gotta siphon the python. I'll be right back."

With that, he rose from the table and stumbled off in the direction of the bathroom, his twelfth visit of the day. (I knew this because the crew was now keeping an official tally.)

"That man has the smallest bladder of anyone I've ever met," Len declared. "Can't you get him a new one, Mitch? We have to stop every three fucking minutes for it."

"Ha-ha," sneered Mitch. "I think you've got a more urgent problem to deal with, don't you?"

I looked at Len. He took a swig of water. "It's okay," he said, when he was done. "*Mitch knows.*"

"So what are we going to do?" I asked.

"*We?*" said Len, feigning shock. "Shouldn't the question be 'what are *you* going to do?'"

"Me?"

"Forgive me," said Len, in his most condescending tone. "I must have mistaken you for Bibi's newest little friend. You know, the one she sends for by dispatching the very lovely David in a white Rolls-Royce Phantom to her crappy little apartment in Little Russia. I could have sworn that was *you,* Bill. Clearly I was wrong."

"How did you—"

"I know everything."

"But it wasn't *like* that. We're not fri—"

"You need to talk to her," said Len, pointing his fork at me. "I don't care how you do it, just do it quick. And don't fucking *upset* her, okay? But I want Teddy off the set, no excuses, and this bullshit with the cue cards has got to stop. I'll be amazed if we can use a single contestant from Houston, based on what I saw today. It's a joke. She's your *mate* —have a quiet word. Oh, and this didn't come from me. If you so much as mention my name, I'll deny all knowledge. Understood?"

I stared back at Len numbly. I had no more appetite. I wanted to leave the room and never come back. Before I could mount any kind of protest, however, there was a commotion outside in the lobby. Loud male voices—possibly security guards. Sobbing. A walkie-talkie hissed and crackled. And then one of Len's Lovelies—a publicist named Dana —entered the room in a state of obvious distress. Flushed from walking at top speed in heels, she made her way directly to our table. Sensing trouble, Len wiped his mouth and began to get to his feet.

Now I could hear sirens. Distant, but unmistakable.

Holy sh—

"It's Joey," announced Dana, breathlessly. "We just found him in the bathroom . . . with, uh . . ."

"SHIT!" yelled Mitch, jumping up with enough force to make his chair topple backward. "Did he have the crack pipe? That piece of—I *told* him, dammit, I *told* him!"

"He didn't have a crack pipe," said Dana, firmly.

The sirens were getting closer.

"Huh?" Mitch looked bewildered.

Pandemonium in the lobby.

"It's worse than that, Mitch," said Dana.

The sirens were right outside the hotel now. Car doors slamming. More walkie-talkies.

"He *didn't* have the crack pipe?" Mitch had turned gray. He didn't understand.

"No."

"Then *what?*"

"He had . . ."

"*WHAT?*"

"He had Miss Idaho."

Mitch doubled over, winded—as though he'd just been punched in the gut—and then tried to make a run for the door. With considerable effort, Len held him back.

"You mean . . . the contestant?" I asked. "The girl with the 'I Da Hoe' T-shirt?"

"Well, it turns out she is," Dana confirmed. "Unfortunately, her dad doesn't quite see it that way. He says she's his little angel. There's . . . there's a lot of blood."

13

Coach Andy

ONE WEEK LATER . . .

"How's he doing?" I asked.

"Let me tell you something," Mitch replied, his nose dotted with the foam of a triple-shot cappuccino. "Joey Lovecraft's moods are like Martian weather. Little understood. Spectacular from afar. And basically unsurvivable by humankind."

"Ah." I tilted my head to catch more of the early afternoon sun. "So not good, then?"

"I'd say he was a nine today. Borderline ten."

I stared blankly across the table.

"No one told you?" said Mitch, surprised. "We track Joey's moods with a numbering system. Ten is the worst; one is the best. Mu sends out an e-mail to the staff every morning. Just a number in the subject line—that's it. She's never reported a one, as far as I'm aware. If you believe some of the older roadies, he came close during the summer of 1983, before that stupid fucking parachute jump. Typically, though, four is as good as it gets. Five means Mu and Sue go home in tears. Higher than a six, and Joey's bodyguard has the okay to call his doctor for a medical-marijuana prescription. An eight usually means hospital or incarceration."

"And a ten?"

"Imagine an asteroid the size of Manhattan landing on Manhattan."

We were back on The Lot in the San Fernando Valley. Only this time, we hadn't gone anywhere near Ed Rossitto's batcave in the sky. Instead we were seated in Rabbit's garden commissary, which serves eggless-egg scrambles and meatless-meat burritos to ageless movie executives with mortgaged dental work and two-rounds-of-golf-per-day tans. They seem so much slicker than the likes of Len and Ed, these movie people. But I guess when you strip away the gloss of their A-list casts and seven-figure budgets, they're basically selling the same thing: stories of human conflict, with their highs and lows, tears and laughter, heroes and villains . . . only our stories cost a lot less to tell. Not that season thirteen of *Project Icon* was in any way *cheap,* of course. In fact, I'd seen our budget, and it had pretty much doubled since the previous season. That didn't bode well, given everything that had gone down, both literally and figuratively, in Houston. *ShowBiz* was already printing vague rumors of "trouble in Texas." Its latest story quoted David Gent as saying Rabbit was "ironing out issues with the new panel" but that the network still had "confidence in the show."

Not *total* confidence, I noted. Just confidence—quantity unspecified.

"D'you think we'll get cancelled before we even get to air?" I wondered aloud.

"Jesus Christ, Bill, keep it down," Mitch hissed. "Never—*ever*—mention the C-word on The Lot."

With that, his phone began to squirm its way across the metal table in a fit of groans and yelps, as if there were a small animal inside trying to break loose. He glanced at its screen and said, "Right, he's *here.*" We both stood up. Mitch wiped his nose—at last—but only half-caught the foam, and there didn't seem like a good moment to bring up the subject as we made our way to the narrow pathway outside. A long-wheelbase golf cart—green canvas sunshade pitched over the three rows of seats—was waiting. The driver, who looked barely old enough for sixth grade, proceeded to transport us at the maximum velocity allowed by the vehicle's tiny electric motor through fake Brooklyn backstreets, a miniature Sahara desert, and the scene of a crashed Boeing 747 filled with half-melted alien corpses.

"Imagine coming to work here every day," mused Mitch. "No wonder these people are so twisted."

Eventually, we jerked to a halt outside a beige conference hall at the other end of the property. Beyond the jungle-landscaped entrance: a beige lobby with beige walls, beige carpet, and an air-conditioning system so powerful, the place felt like an industrial meat locker. It couldn't have been more than forty degrees in there. Ahead of us was a set of double doors, upon which someone had taped a sheet of laser-printed paper. "*Project Icon:* Fraternization Seminar," it read. "Attendance COMPULSORY for all cast/producers. Starts: 3:30 p.m."

The clock on the wall read 3:29 p.m.

Mitch and I looked at each other with here-goes-nothing faces, then pushed our way inside.

We emerged into a small yet plush auditorium with a low stage at the far end of the room and a dozen or so rows of fold-up seats, arranged in tiers. Suspended from the ceiling was a digital projector, and embedded in the walls were the yellow Kevlar cones of audiophile-quality Bowers & Wilkins loudspeakers (blame Dad for my knowledge of such things). Behind us, meanwhile, was a generously stocked drinks and snack counter, the kind you might find in a business-class airline lounge. Knowing what was to come, I was tempted to pour myself a Maker's Mark on ice. No one else was drinking, though, so I resisted.

Joey was already in a front-row aisle seat, next to Mu and Sue, both of whom had dressed for the occasion like soft-porn librarians. He was wearing high-top sneakers and a tweed suit with one pant leg cut off at the knee, all the better to display an actual-size tattoo of a tartan sock on his right calf. (He did this one himself while in London's Pentonville prison for urinating on Buckingham Palace, because it made him smile every morning in his cell.) The novelty sock tattoo wasn't the first thing to catch my attention about Joey, however. Instead my eyes were drawn to his fly-goggle sunglasses, the kind that Manhattan Project scientists might have worn during atomic bomb testing in the New Mexico desert. They served to only partially disguise a black eye of such severity, its purple-yellow tendrils crept all the way out to his middle cheek. This had been a gift from Miss "I Da Hoe"'s father, an ex-U.S. Marine and, as it turned out, committed member of the Coeur D'Alene chapter of the Aryan Nations. Indeed, if it hadn't been for *Icon*'s security detail, Joey's record company might have already been enjoying the spoils of a posthumous album release.

By inflicting such a dramatic injury on Joey, however, the Idaho Klansman had actually done *Icon* a huge favor. Without the assault, the show would have been looking at a shut-up-and-go-away settlement on the scale of Bibi's salary. But now they had leverage: the attempted murder of a celebrity judge. Plus, Miss "I Da Ho" herself—she had in fact only ever won a minor village pageant—apparently didn't share her father's politics, and had no interest in punishing Joey.

The matter was resolved privately, in a matter of days.

That wasn't the end of Joey's issues with young female contestants, however.

Oh, no.

It quickly emerged that Joey's indiscretions hadn't been limited to Miss "I Da Ho." He had also been exchanging direct messages on Twitter with several other female contestants (had he *searched* for their accounts, or had they followed him first?), providing them with both his cell phone number and Twitpics of his bulging underwear, taken from under the judges' desk. All had responded in kind, so Joey had scheduled each of them to visit his room, at fifteen-minute intervals, that very same night. It was hard not to be impressed by the man's ambition. It was also hard not to wonder how he could manage such a back-to-back operation at the age of sixty-two, without either surgical or chemical assistance. This question was never answered, however, because someone in Rabbit's human resources department (a.k.a. Team

Joeysitter) noticed what was going on—they were already in crisis mode after the whole beauty queen affair—and dispatched an emergency task force to the scene. Joey's phone was confiscated, his Twitter account deleted, and he was ordered by Sir Harold Killoch to attend today's "fraternization seminar" at The Lot. For good measure, the other judges and key members of *Icon*'s staff were ordered to go, too.

And now . . . well, *here we were.*

Being the last to arrive, Mitch and I took seats at the rear. Bibi was to our left, a few rows forward, obscured partially by Teddy, and engrossed in her phone. Looking closely, I noticed that she had the FaceTime app running, and was actually examining herself in the screen. Len was visible only via his Merm, which was wobbling around somewhere near the front, next to Maria and Ed (or that's what I assumed, as Ed's head didn't reach the top of his chair).

We waited.

And waited.

And—

At last, the house lights dimmed, the stage lights brightened, and in an unmistakable glow of smugness, our "fraternization coach" appeared. "My name's Andy," he announced unnecessarily (it was written in blue marker on his circular name tag). "And I know what y'all are thinking: I'm here to *judge.* Well, bad news, folks"—cheesy smile—"the only judges in this room are sitting right in front of me here. I'm here to inform. To guide. Think of me as a resource."

Andy was unbearable, this much was already clear.

He went on: "Now, what I'm going to talk about today is what we at Rabbit call *fraternization.*"

"You mean screwin'?" interrupted Joey.

Oh, God. I closed my eyes.

"Ha-ha," said Andy, nervously running a fleshy hand through his overly product-enhanced hair.

"Call it what it fuckin' *is,* man," said Joey, disgust in his voice. "I fuckin' hate—"

"We *call* it fraternization," Andy reiterated, a little testily. "Now, what does fraternization mean, exactly?"

Joey snorted with contempt and began to shuffle boisterously in his seat.

"Well, folks, if you look it up in the ol' dictionary," Andy continued, reaching behind him to pick up a heavy black volume from the table behind him. "It says, 'To associate or mingle as brothers with a hostile group, especially when directly against military orders.'"

Andy made a hokey face to illustrate confusion.

"Now, we're not all brothers here, are we?" he continued, in the tone of a preschool teacher breaking up a fight over a jigsaw puzzle. "And we sure as heck ain't running an '*army*'! Also, I wouldn't suggest for one second that the wonderful, talented contestants on *Project Icon* are your enemy. No, sir! Nevertheless, you have to understand, if ANYTHING that could be deemed 'inappropriate' goes on between any of YOU and any of your subordinates—i.e., *the contestants*—then you're putting both yourself and the Rabbit network in DIRE JEOPARDY."

Andy went on like this for three hours. He passed around leaflets featuring stock photographs of men and women in "uncomfortable" workplace situations. He used the digital protector to a show a graph of recent legal settlements in key sexual harassment cases. He even distributed Rabbit-branded key rings and notebooks featuring the slogan "Professionalism, Respect, Boundaries."

Bibi didn't look up once from her phone. Joey, on the other hand, seemed transfixed.

"Any questions?" asked Andy, when he was finally done.

At last, it was over.

Only it wasn't.

"Yeah, actually," declared Joey, to groans from the row behind him. "Let's pretend for a moment, Andy, that you're a *winner.* Let's pretend that you don't spend your life giving pious lectures to other people about their own private goddamn business. Let's pretend that the no-fun-sized miniwiener in your sad-assed, beige fuckin' kill-me-now slacks has ever seen half a *second* of action—which, by the way, I personally guarantee it fuckin' hasn't. But let's pretend all that, anyway . . ."

Mitch's head was now in his hands.

" . . . so you're a hot dude," Joey went on. "Rockin' your shit as a judge on *Project Icon.* And you've gotta drain the dragon. *Snake break.* So off you go to the bathroom, and on your way—BLAM!—you run straight into Little Miss Over Easy, Sunny-Side-Up Beauty Queen. Now, this chick ain't no nun. She's more into the Holy Molys than the Hail Marys, if you get my vibe. She's wearing a fuckin' T-shirt that says 'I Da Ho' *for the love of sweet Jesus Christ!* So this little smokin' firecracker of a pageant princess says to you, 'Hey, my best friend says you'd never let me blow you in the *Icon* bathroom. Wanna help me win a hundred bucks?' "

Joey was now standing, leaning over the edge of the stage, inches from Andy, who was gripped with either panic or anger, it was hard to tell which. "What was I supposed to DO, huh?" Joey yelled, before turning incredulously to his audience. "Send the girl home, empty-mouthed and a hundred bucks poorer?"

He grinned to prove his point. So many teeth. Such ludicrously proportioned lips.

Silence.

Beside me, Mitch looked as though he were in physical pain.

"HUH??" repeated Joey.

Then Andy spoke.

"*Yes,*" he began, quietly. "That's what you were supposed to do, Joey. Send her home, without putting your sixty-two-year-old *dick* in her goddamn eighteen-year-old *mouth,* okay? Now is that too much to ask, to save yourself and your employer from years of depositions, a public trial, jail, and/or possible financial ruin? Is it really?"

Andy's face now had the hot, lumpy texture of rage.

"Jesus," said Joey, throwing up his hands. "Shoot me. Just fuckin' shoot me, okay? I had some fun. This is America. You guys should go work for Tali-Qaeda."

"You mean the Taliban," Andy corrected.

"Whatever, man."

"Or al-Qaeda."

"Jesus, okay, Mr. Dictionary."

"Not Tali-Qaeda."

"Suck on it, fat boy."

Ignoring this, Andy leaned down and got closer to Joey, until their faces were almost touching. "Now answer my question, Mr. Lovecraft," he snarled. "Will you restrain yourself? Or do you want to lose this lucrative day job of yours?"

Joey crossed his arms and tried to outstare his adversary. But Andy wasn't intimidated. He'd clearly been given orders by Sir Harold to deliver an unambiguous message.

"Well?" demanded Andy.

"Okay—you fuckin' win!" Joey huffed, sitting back down heavily. "Now why don't you give me your goddamn address, so I can FedEx my fuckin' balls to you overnight."

14

Little Green Pills

December

AS IF JOEY'S LIBIDO weren't enough to contend with, there was still the unresolved matter of Bibi and her cue cards—a problem that was apparently all mine to handle, thanks to Len's shameless ass-covering. I suppose it shouldn't have come as a surprise that Len had pulled such a weasel move on me, given his long history of weaseldom. And yet . . . it kind of did. How did he expect me to take Bibi aside and have a "quiet word" when even Teddy often had to make appointments to speak to her? More to the point: How did Len think this notoriously imperious businesswoman—*worth half a billion dollars!*—was going to react when the most junior producer on *Icon* accused her of behavior that amounted to cheating?

My first tactic—inspired by Dad's tried-and-true approach to conflict resolution—was to simply ignore the issue and hope it went away by itself.

And in this, I had a useful ally: Joey. After all, his unhappy encounter with Miss "I Da Ho"'s father had left Len with no option but to halt the filming in Houston. The thirty or so contestants who had yet to audition were given flight and hotel vouchers and told to come to Milwaukee, the next stop on our tour—which of course had to be delayed by a week to give Joey some additional recovery time. His black eye wouldn't have entirely disappeared by then, but we figured the Mojo Squad could disguise its severity, and that he could invent an excuse that wouldn't make the press think he'd suffered another major drug relapse.

All this bought me some valuable time on the Bibi front, which was great—while it lasted. But Milwaukee came around soon enough, as inevitably did the problem with the cue cards. My only lucky break was that Len had to remain in Los Angeles for meetings (which I suspected meant an urgent Merm-maintenance appointment), giving me yet more time to come up with a plan, which I did on the second day of filming. And if I may say so myself, it was a pretty genius idea: Instead of confronting Bibi directly, with all the unpleasantness that that would involve, I would simply notify the crew of Teddy's presence at the back of the room and tell them to keep "accidentally" bumping into him with heavy (or better yet, greasy) equipment, until it become impossible for him to remain on the set without lodging a complaint, *which of course he wouldn't do.*

And guess what?

It worked. It worked *perfectly* . . . until Edouard turned up and took Teddy's place.

Awesome. Now I had an even bigger problem.

To his credit, Edouard was at least more subtle about his signals to Bibi (as I suppose you'd expect from an Oscar-nominated actor), moving constantly around the set, never looking directly at his wife, and relaying his yeses and nos via a system of casually handsome facial gestures that took me a few minutes to decode, primarily because of the unlit cigarette in his mouth. Basically, a one-finger rub of the nose was positive. Two fingers meant the opposite. The effect on Bibi was the same, regardless, however: She became noticeably distracted while peering beyond the set for her cues. It threw off the rhythm of the show completely. Where there should have been drama, there was just . . . Bibi squinting, followed by a half-hearted verdict, followed by more squinting to make sure she'd translated the code correctly. Heightening the problem: We had only a single take for the judges' decisions — otherwise, the contestant would know what was coming, ruining everything — so whatever footage we got, we were stuck with.

I couldn't understand why Bibi was so unsure of herself. I mean, there she was, this fantastically wealthy, exquisitely beautiful, world-famous megacelebrity — and yet she needed the approval of her husband before voting a contestant on or off *Project Icon.* I couldn't imagine ever taking instructions from Brock when it came to my job, or anything else, for that matter. I wondered if Edouard had the same influence over all the decisions in Bibi's life. Was their marriage basically a father-child relationship? It just didn't add up. I wanted to grab Bibi by the shoulders and say, "Who cares if Edouard is jealous of your career? *He's* not the reason you're here. *You* are! *Don't let him control you!*"

Joey, meanwhile, was pretty much the exact opposite. Having loosened up since Houston, his decisions were now as instantaneous as they were emphatic. One contestant, upon reaching the third bar of a 1968 Honeyload classic, found himself interrupted by Joey's airborne soda bucket, which exploded upon contact with the sponsors' wall behind him. "THAT'S LIMPER THAN MY DICK IN A ROOM FULL OF FAT CHICKS!" he screamed. Another contestant opened his eyes at the end of "Bridge Over Troubled Water" to find Joey on his knees in front of him, literally worshipping his feet. Joey needed no cues. All he needed was his gut.

"That feelin' in ma' belly is the reason why I've sold enough records to buy two live-in hookers and put fifty million dollars' worth of blow up my nose," as he explained — in complete earnestness — to a sixteen-year-old member of the Lake Jackson Pentecostal Baptist Church, who had wept during her spirited rendition of "My Jesus, I Love Thee."

I was beginning to suspect, however, that Joey often confused his gut with the area directly below it — namely his penis. Hence the yeses he delivered so predictably to the females wearing the fewest items of clothing. Often, these contestants also triggered within him an inexplicable urge to improvise obscene-sounding ditties, many of which, thank God, made no actual sense upon a closer listening.

Example:

JOEY: A-whop-bop-a-loo/I'd like to goo on your chew!

GIRL IN STRING BIKINI (Wrinkling nose adorably): Eew. What's my *chew?*

JOEY: Why, it's right there in your . . . OOOH! (Violent thrust of crotch)

But here was the thing with Joey: No matter how badly behaved he was—and as time went on, he became more and more like the Joey we'd seen in the sanity checks—we knew he could be tamed in the editing suite. Bleeping out a word or pixelating a finger is easy, unlike trying to hide the fact that a judge *isn't even looking at the podium.* And Joey trusted us to take care of him in postproduction. With Bibi, it was as though she were convinced the edits would be used against her. Why else would she be so reluctant to offer her spontaneous thoughts? Unless, of course, it was Teddy or Edouard who didn't trust us and had persuaded Bibi that she needed to double-check every decision.

Whatever the case, something had to be done before Len got back on set. And I got my opportunity sooner than I'd expected, near the end of the first day of filming in Milwaukee, when I walked into the bathroom just off the hotel lobby to find Bibi there alone, rinsing her hands in front of the mirror. The moment I saw her, I knew what had to happen. *This was my moment.* My one and only chance to confront her in private, without Teddy or Edouard standing guard.

"Oh, hey there, Bibi," I said, as casually as I could manage. Aside from my nerves, I needed to pee—urgently—but if I used one of the stalls, I'd lose my opportunity. So I held it in and stood next to her, pretending to fix my makeup . . . the main problem being that I wasn't wearing any. I *did* have some lipstick in my purse, however, so I pulled out the tube and began to apply it. My hands were shaking. At this rate, I thought, most of it would end up on my teeth . . .

"Going anywhere?" asked Bibi, with a semicurious glance.

"Oh—er—yeah," I lied. "Date tonight."

Bibi gave a little squeak of excitement. "Okay, tell me everything," she demanded.

"An Internet thing," I said, suddenly picturing Mr. Zglagovvcini in his yellow flip-flops, with his eCupidMatch.com questionnaire. "A friend's been trying to set me up for a while."

"Weren't you going out with that surf guy? Mr. Hawaii?"

How did she know this? "Long-distance relationship," I shrugged. "Too much trouble."

Bibi laughed with more sincerity than I'd expected. "I hear you, sister," she said. *"I hear you."*

This was my chance.

Now.

Ask the question. *Ask the question, Sash!*

"Oh, er, Bibi?" I began, in a tone that suggested I'd just remembered something.

"Hmm?"

"About Teddy. And Edouard."

The towel in Bibi's hands stopped moving. "What about them?" she asked, the warmth suddenly gone from her voice.

Too late to back down. "Do you think that maybe they're, y'know . . . *distracting* you?" I ventured, as the blood in my entire upper body diverted toward my face. "I've noticed that you look at them . . . a lot. Especially when you're making a decision, y'know? Maybe it would be better if they weren't on the set?"

Bibi said nothing as the towel began moving again, slower than before. Worried I might not have made myself absolutely clear, I added, "I think Edouard might even be allergic to something. He's always seems to be rubbing his n—"

"So you take those little green pills, too, huh?" interrupted Bibi, peering into my purse. My orange-tinted pill bottle was there for all to see, with the name and address of my doctor's office and "Sasha King, take as needed" printed on the side.

I hesitated, not quite knowing what to say. Was Bibi simply *changing the subject?*

"You have . . . panic attacks?" I asked.

"Not often, sweetie," she said, throwing the towel into a basket under the sink and reaching for her bag. "Sometimes." She no longer seemed interested in our conversation.

I wondered if I should risk bringing up the subject of Teddy and Edouard again. What if she just ignored my question entirely and walked out now? *What would I tell Len?*

"So . . . about Teddy and Edouard," I said. "What do you think?"

"Oh, um, yeah . . ." Bibi nodded, lowering her head slightly to make eye contact with her reflection. "Well . . . here's what I think about what you've just said to me . . ."

I relaxed slightly, expecting her to make a joke of the whole thing. I'd given her—very skillfully, I thought—an out. This would go no further. Just between us. *As friends.*

"I think that you've been getting prescriptions filled for Joey," she said, abruptly. "Everyone knows he has a problem with those green pills, and that they're the only drug that won't show up on the pee test if you drink enough of that stoopid . . . *kangaroo* water, or whatever the hell it's called. So what a coincidence you're carrying them around with you, huh? That's what I think, *Bill,* since you've been thoughtful enough to ask. I think you've been selling those pills, making a little money on the side, because they certainly ain't payin' you much here. Are you even a *real* assistant producer? Or are you still filling in for that other guy, the one on life support in Denver? Isn't that why they call you 'Bill'—so you can be *replaced,* if he ever gets over his head injury and comes back to the show? But don't worry, dear. It's none of my business how you pay the rent. Your issue. For you alone. Just like *my* issues are for me to deal with, on my own. Without interference. Are you understanding me yet, Bill? Are you clear with what I think now?"

I felt numb and cold. All I could do was nod.

"Good," said Bibi. She smiled and gave my arm a little squeeze. "I'm glad you get it."

Then with a clatter of heels she was gone. Her fingernails, I noticed, had left white marks on my skin.

15

The Moment

I MUST HAVE CALLED Brock ten times when I got home. But he had an all-night shift at the bar of the Hua-Kuwali and wasn't answering. He probably couldn't even hear the phone. For the first time since I'd arrived in LA, I felt a shudder of uncertainty about him. Could this *really* work — one of us in California, the other on a rock in the Pacific, halfway to Japan? Why hadn't I just gone with him and taken a job as a waitress, as he'd once suggested? Wouldn't that have been easier? But, no . . . I had to take Len up on his "dazzling opportunity," mix with the celebrities, be the hotshot producer, and try to stash away enough money to *take an entire year off.*

It was beginning to seem like an almost delusional plan — especially given the current status of my Novel of Immense Profundity, which had recently undergone some significant revisions, mostly to the grandfather character's dialogue. I'd deleted it, basically. So now my manuscript was one sentence long. As for those unresolved plot issues, they remained very much unresolved — I'd finally had an idea about where the Black Lake of Sorrow might be located.

"Hey, it's me," I told Brock's voicemail, sounding croaky as hell. "I know I haven't been calling you back . . . I'm sorry. And I know I've been bad on e-mail and Facebook and pretty much everything else. It's just . . . things are crazy. I've had a bad day, babe. I'm not sure I can do this. Call me, okay? Just call me."

Click.

I wondered if he'd get my message tonight. I had to talk to someone, tell them about Bibi, the whole situation. I mean, *what an unbelievable bitch!* I didn't doubt for a second that she could get me fired by saying I'd given pills to Joey—or more likely, relaying the accusation via Teddy. I wondered if anyone at Rabbit would even bother to ask Joey if it was true. Probably not. An addict's word can never be trusted. And besides, for someone like Ed Rossitto or David Gent—Bibi would definitely go that high, if not all the way to the top—it would be more trouble than it was worth. Better to just fire the stand-in producer (*what was her name again?*), keep Bibi happy, and forget it ever happened. And Len wouldn't object. Better me than him. That's why he'd put me up to this in the first place—just like he'd had me take the fall for Joey's treatment during The Reveal. The whole thing was crazy, like my worst day at high school squared. I also felt a bizarre kind of shame—as if this were all my fault, as if only a world-class loser could make an enemy of a woman so admired and so powerful.

I debated calling Mitch. He'd understand. He'd tell me what I wanted to hear. But he'd also tell Joey everything, which would be a disaster. That left only one other person whose number I could dial: Mom. But it was past midnight on the East Coast. And she'd worry. Or rather, she'd lecture me about how I should have never gone to "Hollyweird" to begin with, and then she'd start checking in with me every day, asking questions, making me paranoid, getting herself into a state. Which meant calling Mom was an option best left for *real* emergencies. Like if I was fired. Or if *Icon* was cancelled, which basically meant the same thing.

Slumping down on the bed, I allowed myself a fantasy of escape; of not going to San Diego—the next stop on the *Icon* audition tour—and instead taking the morning flight to Honolulu. If I could find a ticket for less than a thousand bucks, I still had enough credit left on my Visa card. No more Bibi. No more Len. No more clipboards and swollen toes. Just white sand and flip-flops . . . and Brock making me breakfast. Ah, yes . . . lovely, blue-eyed Brock, muscular and bare-chested, holding up a tray of . . . ooh, yes, Danish pastries . . . as the Tom Waits version of "Ol' '55" plays on the radio . . . and our pet sea turtle—*all* my Hawaiian daydreams involve a pet sea turtle—rests in his shell on the rocks beyond the lanai . . .

I closed my eyes.

That was more like it.

"Hey—me again."

I was back on the line with Brock's voicemail, sitting upright, the hoarseness now gone from my throat. "What if I get on a plane tomorrow? Seriously. Screw *Icon.* I can find a job—whatever. I can write on the weekends. Call me, call me, *call me.*"

But he didn't.

When I awoke the next day—still in my clothes (I know, *I know*)—my phone showed no new messages, no missed calls. Not even an e-mail or a Facebook message. WTF. Usually, Brock was the one chasing *me.* Had he just had a busy night at work? Had he left his phone on the beach? Or did I no longer have a boyfriend? (If I'd been having doubts, maybe *he'd* been having doubts, too.)

What a perfectly shitty end to a perfectly shitty week.

So.

I made myself coffee. I ate a week-old bun. I took a shower. I found some clean clothes and put them on. I decided to buy cigarettes. I walked to the 7-Eleven up the street. I decided against buying cigarettes. I walked home again. I changed my mind. I walked back to the 7-Eleven up the street. I changed my mind again. The guy behind the counter asked me if I was okay. Uh-oh—sobbing redhead! He gave me a soda on the house. I reassured him that I was okay. I reassured him again that I was okay. I told him that, no, seriously, I did *not* need his cell number.

Then I walked to Plummer Park and spent ten minutes on a bench, watching old men play chess, and feeling pathetically sorry for myself. But here's the thing with self-pity: *It's boring.* I just don't have the patience for it. So I walked back home, and when I got to my front door — a surprise. Wedged into the jamb was a white envelope. I pulled it out and ripped it open.

On ruled notebook paper, this:

Crazy Woman!

You have date next Tuesday night, eight o'clock, with Boris, nice boy from. He meet you here and take you for dinner. And don't worry your head — I watching out for you.

Mr. Z.

PS: Nothing I can't live without (apart from Mrs. Z).

PS: Mrs. Z make me write that.

Oh boy, I thought.

This should be interesting.

Another day passed, and still no word from Brock. Judging by his Twitter feed, he was still alive — he just wasn't returning my calls. Maybe he was trying to teach me a lesson by doing what I'd done so many times to him for the past few weeks. Or maybe I really *was* dumped. I guessed I'd find out soon enough. In the meantime, I sucked it up and took the early morning Amtrak to San Diego, ready for the next round of auditions. It was going to be awkward, being on set with Bibi, that was for sure. But whatever. As long as I still had a job, why should I care?

As usual, the venue was a downtown hotel, all thick-veined marble and smoked glass, glittering over the marina. But this time, no one was staying there apart from the judges. The rest of us had been booked in a dive so far across town it was practically in Mexico, and told to get to work using public transportation. This wasn't a big deal, apart from the fact we had to be at work by 4:30 a.m., when there *wasn't* any public transportation. Which meant we had to get taxis at our own expense. In a mass e-mail to staff, Len explained that Zero Management and Invasion Media had implemented a "rigorous cost-control program" to meet "significantly lowered expectations" from Rabbit's advertising sales department. This was almost certainly bullshit. The real explanation, I guessed, was that Sir Harold had finally gotten around to watching the footage from Houston and Milwaukee, and had issued another cancellation threat. Cutting the budget was probably Len's way of trying to buy us some more time.

I wished there was something I could do, other than talk to Bibi again, which wasn't even worth thinking about. Not that Len knew what had happened between us, of course. As far as he was concerned, I'd at least managed to get rid of Teddy from the set, which was an achievement of sorts. He'd even slapped me on the back and done that pointy-clicky-winky thing that bosses do when they're pleased. But with Edouard now on the scene—a.k.a. The Man With The Very Itchy Nose—it would only be a matter of time before he figured things out.

And then?

Hello again, Square One. *Great to be back.*

At least the routine of the auditions was now becoming comfortably familiar: the judges faking their arrival at the hotel where they were already staying; the contestants doing their thing, first for the decoy panel, then the real one; Joey consulting his "golden gut"; Bibi consulting Edouard's facial signals; JD saying "booya-ka-*ka*" interminably; and then, finally, the verdicts being reached, followed by Wayne Shoreline's ambush and interrogation of the winner/loser beyond the deliberately hard-to-find exit. Not to forget the countless delays for the Glam and Mojo Squads, plus snake breaks and outfit changes . . . all of which left us behind schedule on Day One by two and a half hours, even before lunch.

Still, there was a sense that something was different in San Diego. The stakes had now changed: We needed to have a *moment,* as Nigel Crowther used to say, or just pack up and go home. And sure enough, that moment came toward the end of the first afternoon, just as I was beginning to think that another day had been lost. Daylight was fading, the judges were tired and cranky (I'd caught Joey yawning at least four times), we'd failed to get back on schedule, and—aside from a couple of exceptions—the contestants had been a bore.

Then at five o'clock, Len called my cell. "Okay, Billy the Kiddo," he announced, "something a bit different next. Tell everyone to hold tight, I'm on my way."

This was unusual, to say the least. When Len wasn't busy messing with contestants' heads on the decoy panel, he tended to watch the auditions from a mobile control room, located in the back of an eighteen-wheeler parked outside the hotel entrance. This allowed him to issue orders to the judges through me—then deny all knowledge if something went wrong. So the fact he was coming upstairs to take *personal responsibility* for a segment was nothing short of a Major Event.

I looked down at my clipboard. It told me that the next contestant due to audition was "Bonnie Donovan—*with husband Mikey.*" I groaned internally. That's all we needed: another husband-wife duo, thus giving Len the opportunity to send one of them home, just to see what would happen to their marriage. (That very scenario had already led to three *Project Icon* divorces and one very expensive lawsuit—which, admittedly, had improved season five's ratings.)

But wouldn't I have *remembered* a married double act from our first visit to San Diego back in August? Maybe not . . . I was one of twenty prejudges, after all. Still, these things tended to be discussed at production meetings. And I hadn't heard a word about it.

Seconds later, Len strode into the room in his usual manner—i.e., with an impatience that suggested his time was more valuable than everyone else's. "Listen up, everyone," he commanded, smoothing his tie and adjusting his cuffs. "It's time for our last audition of the day. But there's a twist to this one. Here's the deal: Two people, a man and a woman, are gonna come through that door"—he pointed to the entrance—"but only one of them's gonna sing. Now, be warned: It's a heartbreaker. He's a U.S. Marine, back from Afghanistan. She's a public-school teacher. Childhood sweethearts—they met in eighth grade. I'll say no more."

A groan of protest went up at the unnecessary suspense.

"C'mon, Len, what's so *heartbreaking?*" complained Bibi, her chin tilted at a strange angle so the Glam Squad could perform some microadjustment to her foundation.

"You'll see."

Bibi rolled her eyes.

As Len left the room, the Glam Squad packed up its cases and brushes, the set was cleared, and the crew hunkered down behind the scenes. With a shout of "action!" from the director of the day (Len went through so many, I'd given up keeping track), in they came: a man and a woman, just as Len had promised.

But they weren't *at all* what I had expected. For a start, Bonnie was pushing Staff Sergeant Mike "Mikey" Donovan in a wheelchair, her tiny arms straining with effort to move the two-hundred-pound Marine. They were also *young.* Like, not even out of their teens. And yet Mikey's life—such as it was—was over in any conventional way. His right leg below the thigh was missing. His left arm was gone completely. And the skin covering his face, neck, and hands glistened like translucent plastic—a result, I assumed, of reconstructive surgery. A roadside bomb had inflicted this terrible damage. Mikey was the only member of his unit to survive, if *survive* was the right word: His injuries had left him with brain damage so severe, he'd never talk again. Indeed, he had lost control of nearly every muscle. But he could still understand spoken words. And after months of therapy, he was slowly learning to communicate using a system of coded blinks.

Mikey had proposed to Bonnie a week before the explosion. And when he finally got home after the first stage of his recovery on a German military base, Bonnie insisted they go through with their wedding plans—against the advice of both families, who said that at her age, she should feel no obligation to spend the rest of her life as a full-time caregiver. Her response? *She loved her Mikey. She wanted to be with him—forever, no matter what.* And now Bonnie, as blonde and tan and hard-bodied as only a military wife can be, had entered *Project Icon* to help raise awareness for veterans' charities. "I'm no Aretha Franklin," she told the panel. "But I like to sing, and it's for a cause I believe in. Besides, nothin' can happen to me up here that's worse than what my Mikey's been through."

By the second line of "I'll Stand By You," most of the room was unashamedly weeping. And by the last chorus, even Teddy's bodyguard, Mr. Tiddles—all four hundred pounds of him—was sobbing in thick, gulpy barks, like the cry of a mortally wounded elephant seal. It wasn't that Bonnie was a great singer. She had a narrow range and limited power. But she was on key, and what she lacked in talent, she made up for with sincerity. It was a truly devastating performance. So devastating, in fact, that for the first time since I'd taken my job on the show, I stopped feeling ashamed of it. So what if *Project Icon* was mass entertainment? If we could find and help people like Bonnie, then maybe it all had a greater purpose, *maybe we were actually doing some good in the world.*

When Bonnie was finished singing, however, I immediately began to worry about the judges. How would they react? Did any of them have the depth or composure required to honor Mikey, this national hero—not to mention his incredible, selfless wife—in a way that could do any justice at all to what we had just seen and heard?

The answer was no, if the expression on Bibi's face was any indication. She was immobilized. It was as though she knew she was expected to do something—something *real*—but didn't have the first idea what that might be. As for JD: "Booya-ka-*ka*" wasn't exactly an appropriate response. So he just sat there, saying nothing.

And then . . . oh, Lord, there was Joey.

But Joey didn't hesitate.

When "I'll Stand By You" was over, he got up from his chair, walked around the judges' table to the podium, and threw open his arms for Bonnie. They wept as they hugged. They hugged as they wept. It was tender, fatherly . . . beautiful. And then Joey pulled back, moved over to Staff Sergeant Mike Donovan, and knelt down beside his wheelchair. He took hold of the wounded soldier's only remaining arm. He looked him right in the eye. And then he swung around his other arm to lock him in a muscular embrace. "You're a hero, buddy," rasped Joey. "We all know what you did for us. Don't ever think that we don't. Every one of us here, *everyone in this room,* and all the people out there in America"—he motioned to the cameras—"we know you went through this for the sake of our freedom. And look"—he reached out for Bonnie's hand—"God has sent you one of his very own angels. That voice of hers; *that's the voice of an angel, buddy.* She's been sent from above to look out for you, man. I swear that's true."

Mikey tensed, his body gripped with some passing spasm. Then he blinked. Once. Twice. Then five or six more times. "What's that?" asked Joey. "You *tellin'* me somethin'?"

Now Bonnie was in tears. "Yes, he is," she nodded, swallowing heavily. "He's telling you—"

"Yes?"

Bonnie tried to go on but couldn't, so Mikey's mom spoke up from the corner of the room. (Len had waived the rules to let her in, along with a few other family members.)

"He's saying . . ."

Now an unfamiliar shudder in my chest. Wow, Mikey's story was *really* getting to me.

Mikey's mom gulped and started again. "He's telling you . . ."

Another shudder. I took a long, deep breath. I needed a drink of water. I needed some air.

" . . . when he first went to Afghanistan . . ."

Jesus, what was wrong with—

SHIT, it was my phone! It was ringing—or vibrating, rather. Right there in my breast pocket, where I'd put it a few minutes ago, because my belt clip had broken. I'd totally forgotten it was there. Worse, *I hadn't switched the damn thing off.* Hands shaking, I yanked the warm plastic casing from my jacket pocket. Any second now, it would break into "Hell on Wheels." Fuck! Len would kill me! *He would literally throw me out of the window, headfirst.* Manic fumbling. Find the red button. *Find the red button.* At last, the rings stopped. I looked around for any witnesses of this near disaster. None. Slowly, I released the oxygen from my lungs and glanced down at the now-muted device. "Brock, missed calls (3)," it told me.

Perfect timing, Brock. *Perfect timing.*

When I looked up again, Mikey's mom had finished speaking. Everyone was howling, even Len.

I hadn't heard a word that she'd said.

16

When They Were Young

BONNIE DIDN'T STAND a chance.

This wasn't because of her voice—far worse singers had thrived in the competition—but because she represented a triumph for Joey Lovecraft. And a triumph for Joey Lovecraft was by definition a failure for Bibi Vasquez. You could see the look of horror cross Bibi's face the very moment Joey got down on his knees in front of Staff Sergeant Mike Donovan in that San Diego hotel suite. Until then, Bibi had been convinced that *she* was the real star of the show. She was paid more than Joey—a lot more. She got better treatment (in spite of Mitch's best efforts). She had quadruple the number of assistants and stylists. Sir Harold Killoch called her personally every other day to make sure she was doing okay. And the reporters and paparazzi who thronged outside every *Icon* audition venue were interested only in *her,* not some crusty old relic from . . . whatever the hell his loser band was called. As far as Bibi was concerned, Joey was a B-list (if that) sidekick, a provider of occasional moments of comic relief.

But when Bonnie and her husband walked into that room, everything changed.

For Bibi, the irony must have been excruciating. *She was the one who was supposed to be revealing her humanity, tears, and compassion!* Teddy had promised her this, over and over. Ridding herself of the shallow, bragging, pre-Recession Ice Diva legacy of "I Wanna Rock (Any Diamond Will Do)" was the *whole point* of her being on the show. And yet when confronted with Staff Sergeant Mike Donovan, she had reacted in precisely the way an Ice Diva would: *She had frozen.* And who could really blame her? Nothing in Bibi's life until that moment had prepared her to interact with such a human tragedy, at such an uncomfortably close range—a man with limbs blown off and half of his face missing, who was rocking violently back and forth, making some god-awful gurgling noise, while producing a steady ooze of greenish-yellow fluid from his lower jaw.

But *Joey* hadn't flinched! His first instinct as a Child of the Earth, brimful of Kangen water, channeling the teachings of the great High Lama Yutog Gonpo, was to embrace.

There's more to it than that, of course. For all Joey's many faults—his compulsive libido, his terminal addictions, his lecturing of others on their every perceived failure—the man has a preacher's gift for connecting with strangers. And not just strangers who also happen to be teenage beauty queens. Grandmas. Toddlers. Truck drivers. Bankers. *Anyone.* Joey loves people, and people love him right back . . . which makes Joey love people even more, because Joey needs to be loved above everything else. This much was obvious from his behavior while on the road with *Icon.* Morning and night, he would greet fans outside each venue, signing autographs, nuzzling babies, posing for photographs, answering questions—the very things Bibi took immense care to avoid. And at lunch, Joey rarely made use of the judges' table, instead making sure to sit with the lowliest members of the crew, even if he'd just been humiliating them over some insignificant grievance a few moments earlier. Bibi? She ate only in her two-story trailer—sometimes with Teddy, at other times with Edouard and the four kids.

Mostly, though, Bibi dined alone.

Now, I should state for the record that I have no *proof* there was any plot against Bonnie. Perhaps it was simply my encounter with Bibi in the bathroom of that Milwaukee hotel that made me immediately assume the worst. All I can say is this: It was obvious to everyone after Bonnie's appearance that Joey had become the undisputed star of season thirteen. Nigel Crowther might have defined *Icon* once with his "Mr. Horrible" routine, but it was now possible to glimpse an alternative future for the show: A kinder, softer, tearier *Icon*—and all because of the actions of a sixty-two-year-old drug addict and serial philanderer who had once been declared "the enemy of America's children" by the U.S. Congress.

Len couldn't have been more delighted. Hence the impromptu announcement he made over the crew's headsets while Joey was still down on his knees in front of the injured US Marine. "In case anyone's still wondering," he'd croaked, between sobs of triumph, "*this is why we hired him.* Now listen up, all of you—I want ten moments like this EVERY SINGLE EPISODE."

Bibi of course had no choice but to fight back—to launch (as it were), a countercaring offensive. Either that, or she had to find a way to recover the Bonnie situation at a later date. Joey was already both the wit of the show and its resident musical genius. If he also became its heart and soul, *then what was Bibi for?* Clearly, she and Teddy had to come up with a plan—and quick, as there were only four more stops left on the audition tour before so-called Las Vegas Week, where the finalists from each city (about a hundred and twenty in total) would be whittled down yet again to the "Final Fifteen." After that: Too late! The episodes would have started to air, the critics would have delivered their verdicts ("A triumph for Lovecraft!"), and Bibi would have started the live shows at an unrecoverable disadvantage. Assuming Sir Harold hadn't switched off the lights by then.

By the second day of filming in San Diego, it was already clear we were playing by new rules. For a start, Edouard was gone. Bibi said he'd been called away urgently to visit a sick relative in France and had taken the kids with him, along with the family Gulfstream (actually, *one* of the family Gulfstreams). No one believed this for a second. The previous night, there'd been reports of screaming coming from Bibi's suite. Guests had complained; a room service tray had been dropped from the balcony; maintenance staff had been seen carrying away broken furniture. I wondered if Teddy had been involved, or if it was Bibi who'd asked her husband to leave. (I could never quite tell how the power was distributed among the three of them.) Whatever the case: Edouard had vanished, and Teddy hadn't taken his place, which meant no more cues from behind the scenes.

It was like making a whole new show. Bibi might not have been as confident as Joey in her decisions—who could be?—but she was at least now *looking in the right direction* when she made them. And while she was for the most part nauseatingly positive ("You have a beautiful instrument, sweetie, and your dedication moves me"), there were times when traces of the real Bibi Vasquez leaked through. Typically, this happened when she was asked to judge a younger, better-looking female ("Honey you're cute . . . but y'know, cute is a dime a dozen these days")—or, even more noticeably, when a male contestant was unwise enough to say something like, "*Man, I was totally obsessed with you when I was a kid.*"

Oh, this riled Bibi like nothing else.

"When you were a *kid,* huh?" she spat, on the second occasion it happened. "Was that when the world was still in black and white? You sure know how to make a girl feel good."

He blushed. "I didn't mean it like—"

"So how did you mean it?"

"I meant—"

"That I'm older than your mom?"

"No! It's just that . . . y'know . . . when I was growing up—"

"You need to learn some *manners,* douche nozzle. Get outta here. You ain't going to Vegas. The only place you're going is home. And don't expect to see this on TV. Hey Len—we're cutting this guy, okay?

Where's makeup? I'm upset now. I don't wanna look upset. Jesus—MAKEUP! My day is ruined. Disrespectful motherfucker."

As requested, the contestant was cut from the final edit. Nevertheless, I was fully expecting an order from Len for me to have another "quiet word" with Bibi, to make sure it never happened again. I should have known better, of course. Len had a far more evil plan. He told the staff in the waiting room to whisper in every male contestant's ear that what Bibi really loved to hear, *what really flattered her,* was how much her fans used to lust after her when they were young. So, one by one, the men walked into the room, stood on the podium, and delivered this unwitting insult, causing Bibi to seethe and curse and single-handedly eliminate at least another two male singers, both of whom were actually pretty good. Eventually, however, she had little choice but to take the comments with a smile; or at least a curl of the lips that approximated a reaction of humble amusement.

I doubt she suspected for an instant that her torture was entirely manufactured, that she was just another performing animal in the *Project Icon* circus.

After San Diego, the remaining cities on our list were Newark, Chicago, and Los Angeles. It took us three weeks to get to them all, and with each new location, my mood improved. Some of this was no doubt relief at finally getting in touch with Brock. He hadn't dumped me, it turned out. He'd just left his phone on the beach while surfing (as I'd first suspected) and forgotten about the tide. It was now either halfway to Papua New Guinea, or in the belly of a passing whale. And without the phone, of course, Brock didn't have my numbers, and because he was smoking so much weed (this seriously had to stop when I got to Honolulu), it took him forty-eight hours to figure out that he could simply borrow Pete's computer and get all the details from my Facebook page. That's why it took him so long to call. Or at least that was his explanation, and I was happy to go along with it. It had once taken me a week to get back to *him,* after all.

Anyway: By the time we finally reconnected, my late-night plan to quit *Project Icon* and get on the next flight to Hawaii had long since been abandoned. Bonnie's audition had changed all that. Besides, I'd come this far. *Might as well get to the end of the season.*

Another reason to stay at *Icon:* Finally, season thirteen seemed to be gaining momentum. Aside from the rising confidence of the judges (JD had actually started to use real words, in addition to variations on "booya-ka-*ka,*" including "Takin' it to the Ka!", "Yaka-yaka-yaka!", and "Ka-booya-boom-*ka!*"), the contestants had gotten stronger with every city. This was no accident, of course: When we'd done our pre-audition tour in August, we'd become better at our jobs with every city. More to the point, we'd started to cheat by using talent scouts, who found us promising young singers on the local club circuits and offered them VIP treatment if they came in for auditions. And by VIP treatment, I mean bribes. Phones, concert tickets, T-shirts. That kind of thing. Oh, yeah, and cash.

Thanks to all this, Bonnie wasn't the only early standout who seemed guaranteed a place in the Final Fifteen. Another was Jimmy Nugget, an eighteen-year-old country yodeler, with the wide-legged stance and apple-cheeked complexion of a 1950s farm boy. "It's like Roy Rogers made love to a Bee Gee!" as Len enthused. The only problem, as far as I could tell, was Jimmy's promiscuity, which in terms of sheer turnover made Joey seem practically abstemious. Not that Jimmy was in any way *competing* with Joey. Oh, no. His emphatic preference wasn't for *Icon*'s female contestants, but for members of his own sex: hotel waiters, judges' assistants, his fellow contestants, even a couple of passing construction workers. You could tell when he'd just emerged from a particularly invigorating encounter by his lopsided belt buckle and the V-shaped flush of crimson under his open woodcutter shirt.

Jimmy achieved these feats in spite of the near-constant presence of his father, a gigantic Nebraskan cattle rancher who insisted on being addressed as "Big Nugg." From what I could tell, Big Nugg wasn't so much in a state of denial regarding his son's sexual orientation as living in an entirely different universe. At every opportunity he spoke about Little Nugg's love of "our Lord and savior," his devotion to the Holy Temple Faith and Deliverance Center in Scottsbluff, Nebraska, and his high-school courtship of "sweet li'l Annie, my beautiful future daughter-in-law." Whether or not sweet li'l Annie actually existed was anyone's guess, but Big Nugg's commitment to the fiction was unwavering, almost as unwavering as his commitment to the advancement of his son in *Project Icon.* With respect to the latter, Big Nugg had brought with him a yodel coach, who took Little Nugg away for "private sessions" at every opportunity.

As for the other front-runners: Near the top of list was Mia Pelosi, former member of the children's chorus at the Metropolitan Opera, speaker of six languages, wearer of sweeping ball gowns and diamond neckwear, and in pretty much every other respect a foul-mouthed tramp from the mean streets of Newark. Mia's vocabulary made Bibi Vasquez sound like a mother superior at Mass on a Sunday morning—an effect heightened by her thirty-a-day cigarette habit, strict diet of fast-food cheeseburgers, and frequently deployed party trick of belching and talking at the same time. And yet by some unfathomable accident of genetics, Mia had been appointed custodian of a larynx that produced a noise as rich and nuanced as any eighteenth-century Stradivarius—a fact noted early on by her public-school music teacher. He was the one who'd sent her to the Met, causing the visiting Czech conductor Milos Dzbirichzijec to literally sob with ecstasy from the orchestra pit. A scholarship at Juilliard followed, interrupted briefly by a stint in a juvenile-detention facility for drunken brawling in public. Mia graduated with distinction in spite of this, and soon became a professional mezzo-soprano, earning tens of thousands of dollars per month, most of which she invested in a burgeoning methamphetamine habit. Fortunately, Mia was eventually able to clean herself up, largely thanks to a year-long recuperation at the Bedford Hills Correctional Facility for Women in upstate New York. And when she emerged at the age of twenty-three, with renewed focus, a supportive parole officer, and a battle scene from the Book of Revelations tattooed across her buttocks, she returned to the audition circuit, only this time for *Icon.* Her rendition of "The Prayer" caused a studio-wide outbreak of goose bumps, and the panel's verdict was an instant and unanimous yes.

Which left one other contestant who seemed destined to become a season thirteen finalist: Cassie Turner, the defiantly unwashed Pennsylvanian folkstress who performed her audition while sitting cross-legged on the podium, strumming on a beat-up guitar. Cassie was older than the others by at least five years, she was a single mother of three kids, and she resided in one of Pittsburgh's less desirable trailer parks. But her voice . . . oh, my Lord, her voice: a harrowing, broken sound, at times a roar of almost beast-like rage, at others a falsetto of such sweetness and vulnerability, you wanted to pick her up and cradle her like a child. More than that, she *meant* every word.

Like the others, however, Cassie had her issues. Chief among them: As a purveyor of songs about the struggle and dignity of the working class, it didn't help that her father was the owner of a Boston private equity firm. Yes, Cassie's noble life of poverty *was entirely a matter of choice*—and not just because of the generously endowed trust fund that had been established in her name when she was two years old. At the insistence of her parents, she had also graduated *summa cum laude* from Harvard Law School. If Cassie's musical career didn't work out, there was a job already lined up for her in the litigation department of Dammock, Hurt & Richardson (Karl Hurt being one of her father's oldest friends).

None of this would matter during Las Vegas Week, of course: The press didn't usually develop an interest in *Icon* contestants until much later in the season—and even then, it didn't necessarily mean the details of their personal lives would become public. Two Svens was unusually protective (or just old-fashioned) in this regard. "I want my finalists *alive* at the end of the season, dammit!" I once overheard him screaming at Nigel Crowther through a closed office door. "How can they sell any records for us if they keep hanging themselves from your balcony?"

Crowther had laughed for a long time at this. "C'mon, Sven, old boy," he crooned. "How many of them"—he had to cough and blow his nose—"*sell* any records?"

Two Svens named two ex-contestants whose albums had been certified platinum. This only made Crowther even laugh harder. "Two people!" he squealed. "*Two people* in the history of this show! What about the other others, eh? There are fifteen finalists every season, you daft old Swede, and we've been doing this for twelve years."

"Some are very successful."

"Yeah—in the cruise ship and wedding industries."

"No, you fat-nippled *arsehole,* on Broadway."

"They make us more money in the *tabloids* than on Broadway! *Think,* man. Reality deals. Advertweets. Doctor-sponsored cosmetic implants. Those kids could be out there getting photographed without their underwear, or spending time in celebrity rehab. They could be *productive.* Instead, what? Forty-second Street? Oh, please."

That was when the office door had opened, prompting me to dive for cover as Two Svens emerged, still in a fury. Crowther was gone from the show a few weeks later—he'd signed his deal for *The Talent Machine.* I remember wondering if he'd actually *tell* any of his future contestants what he had planned for them.

Maybe they wouldn't care.

17

Lion's Den

January

LAS VEGAS WEEK WAS a relatively new thing for *Project Icon.* Until season ten, the Final Fifteen had always been selected at Greenlit Studios in Los Angeles, a week before the live shows began. And then . . . well, Len had bought a house in Las Vegas. Or rather, he'd bought a sixteen-bedroom mansion with its own golf course, moat, drawbridge, and private volcano, ten minutes from the Strip. I have no idea how much he paid for the place, but it hardly mattered: Four months later, the Great Recession began, and the market for dictator-grade real estate featuring simulated lava eruptions became somewhat less attractive. For a few difficult weeks, Len spent a lot of time on the phone, using phrases like "negative amortization" and "complete fucking obliteration." And that's when Vegas Week was born—with Len declaring his *extraordinary foresight* in purchasing a residence near the chosen location, large enough to accommodate both himself and "key members of the staff" (i.e., Len's Lovelies), while also allowing him to exploit the considerable advantages of a business-use tax write-off.

I could hardly believe he'd pulled it off—until I found out that Sir Harold Killoch, Two Svens, and Ed Rossitto also owned properties in the same bankrupt development.

The cost of Las Vegas Week to Rabbit must have been immense: a hundred and twenty airfares and hotel rooms for the contestants alone, plus food and other transportation, not including those very same costs for the crew, and on top of all that the rental charge for the venue—a hangar-like conference facility at the back of the Bikini Atoll Resort & Casino (known for detonating a "replica fifteen-megaton hydrogen bomb" in its glass-domed, hyperoxygenated lobby at forty-minute intervals throughout the day, as waiters dressed as Pacific Islanders handed out Chain Reaction Martinis from the Crater Lagoon Bar & Grill).

Expenses aside, however, our annual trip to Las Vegas marked a crucial point in the season. The circus was over. The real competition had begun. Take the set, for example: The contestants performed on an actual stage, with the judges' table placed on a dais behind the orchestra pit—just like the arrangement at Greenlit Studios (only without the studio audience). In addition, there was a separate location —known officially as The Decision Room—into which each contestant was ushered on the last day of filming and informed whether or not they'd made it through to the live shows in Hollywood. This obviously didn't end well for most them: With only fifteen places available, the success rate was barely twelve percent—a fact Wayne Shoreline took great pleasure in repeating at every opportunity, especially when a contestant seemed close to breaking down.

The Decision Room was actually nothing of the sort: It was a giant steel cage, borrowed from the Paradise Bros. Circus—they used it for transporting lions—suspended via hooks from the ceiling. The only way to get inside was via a custom-made staircase, barely visible through the green-tinted fog that billowed from a rack of theatrical smoke machines. (Len had wanted the set to look "futuristic, like something from one of those Schwarzenegger movies," by which I presumed he meant *The Running Man,* in which a sadistic game-show host presides over the hunting and killing of his contestants.) Adding to the general science-fiction theme, the cage was equipped with a white, egg-shaped sofa, several transparent blobs of plastic (of no obvious purpose) and a lonely, straight-backed chair, which appeared to have been sprayed with glue, then dipped in glitter. The latter was of course for the potential finalists, and had been modified under Len's orders to make one leg two inches shorter than the others. The idea was to ensure as much discomfort as possible—although I suspected Len also secretly wanted the chair to break, ideally with one of the more obese contestants sitting in it. Such moments of shame were Len's favorite kind of ad-lib.

The format of Las Vegas Week was fairly straightforward: Each contestant would perform an Elvis classic—in keeping with the location—followed by a song of their own choosing. At the end of the second song, the judges would whisper to each other and take notes, but make no official comments—these would come later in The Decision Room. Or as the crew had renamed it, The Lion's Den.

Bonnie was one of the very first on stage. Although it had now been a month since San Diego, no one had forgotten that epic audition—or how it had transformed Joey into the *de facto* star of season thirteen. *Bibi* certainly hadn't forgotten. That's why she'd been trying to out-care Joey whenever possible. After Cassie Turner's performance of "The Internationale," for example, she'd spoken at length, in a tremulous whisper, about how *she too* wanted to unite the human race—the effect being only slightly undermined by her apparent belief that Bruce Springsteen had written the song. In the same vein, she had wept for a minute and a half over Mia Pelosi's rendition of "I'd Do Anything for Love (But I Won't Do That)," and had climbed up on stage to embrace Little Nugg after his yodel-based interpretation of "Imagine," declaring that "Isaac Hayes would be incredibly proud of how you honored his legacy."

Bibi wasn't done yet with Operation Sensitive, however.

Oh, no. Not even close.

I knew something was up when Bonnie's Elvis number was switched at the last minute. She was supposed to be singing "Can't Help Falling in Love"—another heartbreaker—but Len somehow convinced her that "Suspicious Minds" was a "better fit." This clearly wasn't true. Plus, Bonnie couldn't remember the words. As a result, her performance was borderline unwatchable. She missed her cues. She improvised the verses. She searched for, but never quite located, the key. And it shook her confidence so badly, she could barely make it through her own choice of song, a reprieve of "I'll Stand by You." When the ordeal was finally over, you could feel relief coursing through the room like a shot of post-op morphine. As instructed, however, the judges didn't say a word. They just made vague *hmm* noises and hung their heads, unable to pretend even to talk among themselves or jot in their *Project Icon* notepads.

Being one of the first to sing, Bonnie was also one of the first to enter The Lion's Den at the end of the week. Now, at this point I didn't think there was any serious doubt she would make it into the Final Fifteen. Len's meddling with her song choice had seemed like an obvious ploy to create drama, to convince the audience that *the very best contestant* of the auditions round might be eliminated before the live shows began. But I wasn't fooled: Why would *Project Icon* get rid of a performer almost guaranteed to bring in higher ratings (most of the supermarket tabloids had already featured her on their covers), thus allowing Rabbit to charge more for its advertising? Also—Bibi would clearly never let this happen. Her job now was to *out-care* Joey, a mission that wouldn't exactly be helped if she voted to send home the beautiful and talented wife of an injured American serviceman.

Still, something didn't feel right.

I could tell.

Moments before Bonnie was due to enter The Lion's Den, I saw Teddy, Len, and Bibi huddling by the lighting desk. They were discussing something in great detail. Teddy was upset. Len was pointing. Bibi walked away, arms folded, then returned, scowling. More talk. Then whatever it was they'd been haggling over seemed to be resolved. Bibi took her place in the cage, Teddy disappeared, and Len made a long, whispered phone call.

Five minutes passed . . . Len was still on the phone. Another five minutes. Snorts of impatience now from the crew. *This was getting ridiculous.* Finally, Len hung up. Instead of getting back to the shoot, however, he called Joey over. They had a short but violently animated conversation. Joey seemed pissed. Len seemed pissed, too. Then Joey called over Mitch, who seemed even more pissed. Mitch ended up doing that whispery-shouty thing, arms flying about all over the place. And then—at last—some kind of peace was reached.

Mitch huffed off somewhere. Joey returned to The Lion's Den with his fellow judges.

Lights down.

Mic check.

Positions.

And-a-three. And-a-two. And-a—

Now: Bonnie climbing the stairs to the cage. Anxious music. Close-up as Bonnie reaches the top. She looks sensational: red shoes, gray pencil dress, hair in a layered ponytail. Extraordinary to think she's just nineteen years old, *that she has willingly dedicated the rest of her life to a man who will never walk or talk again.* She gives a little wave to the judges—it's too awkward for kisses or hugs in The Lion's Den. Then she sits. Rebalances herself. Tips back. Tips forward. Looks down at the chair, laughs nervously, and then, with leg muscles pulled tight, she holds herself steady.

"It wasn't your strongest performance, babe," begins Joey. "But like I said the other day—you're an angel. And whatever happens here, I don't want you to stop singing. Okay?"

Bonnie nods, gulps. "It was that song," she explains. "I shouldn't have let them—"

"It's all about song choice, man," JD interrupts, pointlessly. "You *gotta* pick the right song."

"But I didn—"

"Dude, you had the Boo, but not the *Ka.*"

"We love ya, Bonnie," adds Joey. "Just remember that. Always remember that, please. Some things in life—as you know—are just out of our hands. And you gotta let 'em be."

A bluff is coming: This much is obvious to anyone who's ever watched *Icon* before. The strongest contestant gets negative signals. The judges look weary, depressed. They shake their heads a lot. They smile like it's all for the best. And then—*how could this be happening?*—the awful sentence begins: "I'm so sorry, honey, but . . ." Cut to the break. Everything seems lost. But it's not. *It's just a bluff.* When the commercials are done, it's back to the studio, and the verdict resumes: "I'm sorry, honey, but . . . YOU'RE GOING TO HAVE TO SEE US AGAIN IN HOLLYWOOD! YOU'RE THROUGH TO THE NEXT ROUND!"

So predictable.

In the monitors, Joey and JD look weary, depressed—just as expected. Now JD is shaking his head, as if preparing for the worst. Here it comes. *Here it comes.*

"I'm so sorry, honey," says Bibi, attempting to smile like it's all-for-the-best. "But . . ."

Bonnie whimpers.

The bluff is coming.

Wait.

Wait . . .

"But . . . you're out," says Bibi, her face revealing no emotion whatsoever. "I'm sorry."

I'm choking. Everyone's choking. The room is clean out of oxygen. This surely isn't real.

Why would they be doing this?

"You're going home," Bibi confirms, almost like she doesn't even believe it herself. "This is the end."

A photograph of Staff Sergeant Mike Donovan now fills the monitors. He's looking strong and handsome before his injury. Then another photograph, this time of Bonnie and her husband on their wedding day: Bonnie is kneeling beside the wheelchair, clutching her husband's only remaining arm. Mikey isn't here today, thank God—

his condition means he can't fly. So he'll have to watch this scene in February, with the rest of America. If he can bear it, of course. Now music is playing in the studio: "Last Post" bugle call. "He's injured, not *dead,* you morons," I'm thinking. Then back to Bonnie in The Lion's Den. She's holding it together. She stands up, thanks the judges in turn—each gets a lipless nudge on the cheek—and then she leaves the cage, managing a smile as she goes.

Wayne Shoreline is waiting: "Tell me why you feel like you've failed your brutally injured husband."

"I don't—"

"It's okay, Bonnie," he says. "It's all over. Let it out. This is a tragedy for you, right? How does this compare to the day you heard the news from Afghanistan?"

She begins to respond, but up in The Lion's Den, something is happening.

What on earth is that . . . *noise?*

Bonnie stops talking.

Bibi, who had seemed so composed a few moments earlier, is making a terrible, pitiful sound, her blue dress crumpling around her like a punctured birthday balloon. Her hands are shaking. Her face is a flash flood of tears and mascara. A robotic-arm camera nosedives overhead for a better angle. If Bibi's faking this, she's doing a phenomenal job. Now her whole body is convulsing. She covers her face. Joey looks at her in bafflement, then turns to JD. They both shrug. Bibi's wailing intensifies, so Joey tries to comfort her, but the effort is wary, half-hearted.

"She's so brave!" Bibi is protesting. *"She doesn't, uh, uh, DESERVE this!"* JD is edging into the action now: With some trepidation, his left arm creeps across Bibi's shoulder.

Meanwhile: The sobs are getting louder, thicker, faster . . . wetter. "This wasn't my decision!" she yelps, hugging a pillow. "I can't believe we did this! I can't . . . uh, uh . . . *go on.*"

She goes limp. Literally—WHUMP!—*face down.*

Another camera swings overhead.

"Er, guys?" says JD, looking at the camera. Everyone's thinking the same thing: What the hell's he doing? First rule of television, *never acknowledge the camera.*

"Jesus!" yells Joey, also breaking the rule. "Can we get some help here? We got a screamer!"

KLUNK.

Houselights come on. Everything stops. Then a blast of cool air as the emergency doors swing open. From behind them come loud, confident voices. *"Where is she?"* Boots on metal. A uniformed ambulance crew is now climbing the stairs to the suspended cage. I glimpse an oxygen tank, a stretcher, a survival blanket. Joey and JD are told to stand aside. Then a thick palm over the camera. For a moment: Nothing in the monitors but calloused flesh and a dirty wedding ring. Another camera ducks into the fray, almost cracking Joey in the temple. Len tries to stop it—*"SWITCH THOSE BLOODY THINGS OFF!"*—but he's too late: Joey has already drop-kicked the telescoping lens, cracking the glass.

Now sirens outside, as the fire department arrives—all of it, judging by the noise. The Las Vegas Police Department isn't far behind. I no longer feel as though I'm on the set of a TV show. I feel as though I'm at the scene of a natural disaster. A steady beat of rotors above is making the walls vibrate. More sirens, at hearing-loss volume. As for Bibi—she's no longer visible amid the uniformed personnel. They've picked her up and are carrying her down the stairs in a well-rehearsed sixteen-legged shuffle. People are yelling, pointing, running in all directions—with the exception of one man, who's standing right across from me, surveying the chaos while talking calmly into his phone.

It's . . . Teddy. Is he *dictating* something? I move closer but he hangs up, passes the phone to an assistant, and with a tiny smirk, thrusts his hands deep in his pockets.

He seems amused. No, *satisfied.*

I look around for Bonnie, but she's gone.

18

Vengeance Enough

THE SEASON THIRTEEN premier of *Project Icon* was due to go out at eight o'clock on a Wednesday evening, near the end of the month. It was hard to believe it was *actually happening*—but with every day that passed, it seemed less and less likely that Sir Harold Killoch would order the preemptive cancellation that *ShowBiz* magazine kept predicting so confidently on its front page. Billboards went up. Listings were printed. And then the very first sneak-peeks began to air during Rabbit prime time—most of them featuring Joey being either pixelated or bleeped.

Seven months it had taken us to get this far—thanks to the sanity checks, the contract negotiations, the audition tours, and then Las Vegas Week. It felt more like seven years.

My plan was to watch the show at home in my pajamas—a luxury I obviously wouldn't have when the live episodes began. I'd even bought my very first TV for the purpose. Yeah, I know: How very nineties of me. But the show wasn't going out live on the Internet, so I didn't have any choice, and as much as I wasn't exactly looking forward to seeing how the auditions had been edited together, there was no way I was going to miss it. I had the whole evening all mapped out, in fact. At around seven, I'd open a bottle of wine from my super-special reserve—i.e., the stuff that cost more than two dollars a bottle—then I'd order a chicken tikka masala from The Gates of Eternal Destiny (Full Bar & Restaurant) on Sunset, and then, when my one-woman feast arrived, I'd sit on my bed with my plastic glass and disposable cutlery and cringe alone at Bibi's distracted gazing, JD's booya-ka-*kas,* and Joey's . . . well, his general offensiveness. ("That performance was almost as crazy-ass hot as your daughter," he remarked to one of the older contestants during the early auditions, apparently unaware that the girl in question had only just celebrated her twelfth birthday.)

My fantasy night in never happened, of course. Len wanted the judges and "a few key members of staff" to watch the season premier *together*—yet another effort to promote camaraderie. In reality, the only thing it promoted was an argument between Bibi and Joey over where the screening should be held. Joey, who was booked to play a gig with Honeyload in Kuala Lumpur the night before, said it should be at his house, because he was a sixty-two-year-old man, and he'd be exhausted from all the traveling. Bibi countered by saying that because she was looking after quadruplets (or rather, she and her *twelve nannies* were looking after quadruplets) the gathering should take place at her place. Joey then pointed out that he lived at the top of Sunset Plaza Drive in the Hollywood Hills, a more convenient location for pretty much all the executives and producers who'd been invited. Bibi responded with the observation that her house was bigger, more expensive, and had twice been featured prominently in *Architectural Digest* magazine. Plus, she had her own private movie theater.

And so it went on.

Bibi won, naturally. Which meant I had to take the hour-long journey to Secret Mountain, and then the hour-long journey back home again. Only this time—no surprise—Bibi didn't send David to Little Russia in the Rolls-Royce to pick me up. Instead, I had to take a cab, which charged me four hundred dollars (thanks to an obviously rigged meter) for the ride. Worse luck: The cab wasn't allowed beyond the military-grade checkpoint at Secret Mountain's entrance.

"That's prohibitive, ma'am," said the spectacularly obese woman who filled (quite literally) the gatehouse. "No taxicabs, buses, coaches, minicoaches, or multipassenger vans."

"Prohibitive?"

"It's on the sign, ma'am."

"Don't you mean *prohibit-ed?*"

"Read the sign, ma'am."

This wasn't going anywhere. "Okay," I said, changing tactics. "I'm here for the Vasquez residence."

"Name?"

"Sasha King."

" . . . I only have a Bill King, ma'am."

"Yeah, that's me."

"You just said your name was Sasha, ma'am."

We went back and forth like this for—oh, forever. Eventually, it was established that, *yes,* I was indeed Bill King, and *no,* this did not mean an exception to the no-cabs rule could be made. So my unshaven driver with his jerry-rigged meter performed a U-turn in the fire lane and declared that I now owed him an extra eighty-five dollars for waiting time. I paid him and climbed out onto the street. There was no alternative: I was going to have to walk to Bibi's. Uphill, in the dark. With no sidewalks. The woman in the gatehouse told me it was "probably less than a mile" but given that she looked as though she'd never walked farther than a few yards in her life, I wasn't about to take her word for it. In fact, the Google Maps app on my phone informed me that it was *two* miles.

At least I'd worn jeans and flats.

This no longer seemed like such a good thing when I reached the house, however. I'd underestimated—by some degree—the grandness of the occasion. This wasn't going to be a bunch of us sitting around in wearable blankets, chugging domestic beer, and laughing at inside jokes, as the e-mailed invitation had suggested. Oh, no. By the looks of things, it was going to be something more closely resembling an awards-season aftershow party. Bibi's driveway already resembled a Concours d'Elegance, what with the vintage gull-wing Mercedes, next to three black Range Rovers, next to a glowering Aston Martin. And more cars were arriving by the minute, greeted by a line of valets in red "BV" monogrammed jumpsuits. They ignored me as I crunched wearily through the gravel between them.

At the door, I was met by the same housekeeper as before. If she knew who I was, she didn't acknowledge it. This time, she led me in the opposite direction to the kitchen, to a separate wing of the house. We walked all the way through it to the other side, exited into an rose garden, and followed a stone pathway to an outhouse, which I assumed from the vintage *Gone with the Wind* billboard at the entrance was Bibi's private movie theater. Tuxedoed waiters greeted me there, holding aloft trays of champagne and mini lobster rolls. I inhaled three of the latter before getting through the door. And then . . . well, there I was, feeling catastrophically underdressed. Bibi was wearing some kind of orange-plumed minidress with matching plastic go-go boots and a necklace with enough diamonds on it to fund a minor African civil war. Edouard was in a three-piece suit, as were the couple's five pit bull puppies. Len had turned up in his chalk-stripes. Joey sported a kilt. And just when I thought things couldn't get any more uncomfortable, I noticed a terrifyingly familiar outline across the room: a jagged edge, almost like a royal crown. White-silver in color. Yes, there was only one man on earth who could be identified with such ease by the mere *shape* of his hair.

Sir Harold Killoch.

I felt as though my soul had just frozen over.

Surprisingly, however, the evening turned out to be a relaxing affair—at first, anyway. The wide red armchairs in the theater were the softest things I had ever sat on. The champagne was delicious. And after the lobster rolls, we were each presented with a single, luxuriously battered french fry, followed by a buffet of candy served in little paper bags. And the show? Well, it was better than expected. I even teared up for a moment during the bit when Mia Pelosi walked onto the podium in a purple ball gown and sang "The Prayer." The editors had earned their wages, that was for sure. Especially when it came to Bibi. One or two moments notwithstanding, they'd managed to cut the tape in a way that made her seem entirely focused on the contestants throughout, rather than gazing beyond the set at Teddy's cue cards, as she'd done throughout most of the Houston and Milwaukee auditions. What surprised me more, however, was her *presence.* You didn't feel it in person, when she was just this tiny, glittery . . . *pain in the ass.* But up there on screen, no matter *where* she was in the frame, it was extraordinary. She was — for want of a better way of putting it — a *star.* When the cameras were on her, *Icon* wasn't a reality show any more: It was a blockbuster. Amazingly, Joey didn't have this same effect. He was more entertaining, no doubt whatsoever. But he wasn't an event in his own right.

When the hour was over, the lights came on to the double-*ting* of silver on glass. The screen went black. And then Sir Harold appeared in front of it — spoon and champagne flute in hand — grinning in a way that could have been taken as either sinister or paternal. I decided on the latter. It might have been the booze.

"Well, well, well," he began. "And to think they said you'd never make it this far."

Nervous laughter.

Sir Harold looked slowly around the room, as if mentally identifying each employee in turn, calculating their value, their cost . . . their *usefuless* to the whole Big Corp operation.

"Seriously, everyone," he continued. "Very well done. Really, I really mean that." With his hands still full, he mimed applause. "I know you've all been reading about yourselves a lot in the press lately. And if you believe *ShowBiz* magazine, which I don't, by the way" — this prompted more laughter, and mutters of "Chaz fucking Chipford" — "you guys are facing an either/or situation with *The Talent Machine.* Nonsense! I truly believe that *both* shows can thrive."

Silence.

"Well, don't *you?*"

A desperate cheer filled the room, led by Len, who sounded almost hysterical.

"And the proof of that I'm certain will come tomorrow morning," Sir Harold went on, his tone unexpectedly hardening. "With all the hype around season thirteen, and our greatly increased budget to attract the very best in talent"—he pointed in turn at Joey and Bibi—"I'm very, *very* excited to see where the ratings come in. Even a *modest* ten percent gain in the metrics will really prove to the world the ongoing strength of this franchise. And anything more than that—well, that's just *gravy!*" He paused for a moment, resuming in a more contemplative tone. "Y'know" he said, "In the village of Nbdala, South Africa, where my dear mother was born, they have a saying, and it translates something like this: 'For the wise farmer, a good harvest is vengeance enough.' So here's to silencing our critics with a good harvest, eh? And to some *gravy* on the top, heh-heh-heh."

Up went his glass.

This time, no cheering. Just a roomful of sweaty, quickly sobering faces. A *modest* ten percent gain? *Was the man out of his fucking mind?* We'd be lucky if the ratings didn't fall by that much! What the hell was he talking about? *Was he thinking of a different show?*

"Hmm," said Sir Harold, answering the silence. "Well, it's late, and I've got to be on a plane to Germany tomorrow morning—a few local difficulties. So a good night to you all."

Then he left through the wrong door, tripping Bibi's fire alarm.

In spite of the noise and the flashing lights, no one spoke or moved for a very long time.

19

Fallen Icon

THE NEXT MORNING, I avoided the news: no Twitter, no Facebook, no TV . . . nothing. I didn't even switch on my phone. If *Project Icon* had made the morning headlines for any other reason than an unprecedented jump in the ratings (*Breaking:* "Every Man, Woman, and Child in America Watches Season Premiere of Singing Competition!"), I didn't want to know. I mean, what good would it do? The number of people who'd tuned in the previous night was now beyond anyone's control.

In reality, of course, the curiosity was just about killing me. After all, my future life with Brock—not to mention my writing career—depended on the show's success.

A new season of *Icon* wouldn't make the news all by itself, of course. (Other than on Rabbit News, which had been running shameless puff pieces since early December.) But if the daily network rankings published overnight by the Jefferson Metrics Organization moved in any way that could support *ShowBiz* magazine's predictions about the show's imminent death, no TV anchor in the country would be able to resist the opportunity to run a clip of Bibi Vasquez and Joey Lovecraft instead of reading aloud the latest minutes from the Federal Reserve.

I suppose it was the unreasonable pressure from Sir Harold—a.k.a. Mr. "Modest Ten Percent Gain"—that made me want to pretend the Jefferson Metrics Organization didn't even exist. There was just no plausible reason to believe we could hold on to twenty million viewers *and then add another two million*—as he'd suggested—and all in the first night of the season. And if missing the numbers was a certainty, then why bother going through the whole demoralizing process of hearing it on the news, along with all the inevitable talk about our cancellation?

So, that morning, with a champagne hangover, I took my usual shower, drank my usual three cups of coffee, left my apartment at the usual time of just after nine o'clock, but in a total information vacuum. NASA could have accidentally blown up Canada a few hours earlier, and I wouldn't have known any better.

I was off the grid.

I'd gone dark.

Dark or not, however, I was still expected to report to my borrowed cubicle at the global headquarters of Zero Management on Sunset, where I was going to be working until the live shows began, assuming season thirteen ever got that far. So I unlocked my bicycle from the rack outside, and ten minutes later, I was at the office.

And guess what? *Everything seemed normal.* The lobby was empty aside from Reza, the security guard, who was reading the latest issue of *Uzi Enthusiast* magazine. The TV was muted and tuned to a finance channel. And from the speakers embedded in the ceiling came the unmistakable chorus of Ernie Bucket's "Ain't Pretty, But Sure Can Sing." I marveled at how it sounded even worse than the first time I'd ever heard it.

Ping.

The elevator arrived.

I stepped inside and hit "PH."

Ping.

Now I was surging upward to the whine of a distant pulley mechanism. Seconds later, the doors opened with a knock and a clang. I took a breath. I *always* take a breath when emerging into the Zero Management lobby. I swear, the view is better from up there that it must be from space: San Gabriel Mountains to the north, sunlight mirrored from the snow on the peaks; the giant shards of glass that made up downtown to the east; a great slab of ocean to the west; and of course La Brea Avenue, a glowing lava stream of hot metal, cutting south over the horizon.

But something wasn't right. It was Stacey, the receptionist. She was nose deep in a tissue. By the looks of things, it wasn't the first tissue she'd used that morning, nor would it be the last. She was so distraught, in fact, that she didn't even notice me. So I walked quickly past, hoping this was a romantic problem (her Belgian boyfriend, Fufu, seemed obviously gay to everyone who'd met him) and *not* related to the Jefferson Metrics Organization. There was something else amiss, though. The cubicles to either side of my own were empty. As were all the others.

Where the hell was everybody?

I tapped awake my computer and reached for my phone—I couldn't keep it switched off forever. And that's when I saw it: my browser homepage, which was set (as a matter of company policy) to the *ShowBiz* magazine website. Below the masthead, there were no stories—just two words, in the biggest, boldest, *blackest* typeface I'd ever seen:

FALLEN
ICON!

Oh . . . *fuck.*

I clicked on the link, hoping the story wasn't what I feared.

It wasn't. *It was worse.*

At the top of the page was a screenshot from the previous night's broadcast: Bibi with her hand over her mouth, and Joey in the background, slightly out of focus, grimacing—like they'd both just heard shocking news. *ShowBiz* must have trawled through every last frame of the first episode to capture that moment.

Assholes.

Below was a story by that annoying little scumbag Chaz Chipford, whose title had been upgraded (I couldn't help but notice) to "Executive News Editor." They'd even given him a byline picture, in which he smirked chubbily from under a reddish mullet.

He had written:

> Bloodbath for revamped Rabbit warblefest!!! Ratings CRATERED during season thirteen premiere—down THIRTY percent overall; TWENTY-EIGHT percent in the target demo. Worse: It lost its number-one position to *Bet You Can't Juggle That!*—the most dramatic upset the nets have seen in more than a decade. Sources tell *ShowBiz* that ex-backup dancer/*Icon* showrunner Leonard Braithwaite has been summoned to The Lot this morning by irate Big Corp honcho Sir Harold Killoch, who plans to "tear him thirty new assholes." Is this The End for the *Icon*-ic show? Nigel Crowther certainly thinks so. And unless the impossible happens over the next few days, *ShowBiz* has to agree . . .

I sank into my chair and watched as the operating system of my phone finished loading. The screen flashed from black to white a few times before the default icons finally appeared. Then—after a lengthy search for a network—it informed me of all the things that had happened, phonewise, since I'd gone off-line the previous evening: "Missed calls (518). Text messages (164). Voicemails (107)."

This was it. *Armageddon.*

Before I had a chance to do anything: a barely recognizable voice from the other end of the room.

"STACEY! SWITCH ON THE BLOODY TVS!"

No response.

"STAAACEY!!"

Nothing but a muffled sob from the direction of the reception desk. Stacey was still a mess.

"STAAAAACEY!!!"

Len was moving closer now, at speed, kicking away chairs and wastebaskets as he went.

"STACEY, ARE YOU STILL FUCKING ALIVE? SWITCH ON THE TVS."

He staggered into view. Holy crap, he looked bad. His tie was askew, his pants were creased, his fly was open, and . . . wow, *his face* . . . it had broken out into a tramp-like, whiteish-gray stubble, the color spectacularly at odds with the golden sheen of his recently upgraded Merm. He couldn't have looked any worse if he'd spent the night in prison. I actually wondered briefly if he *had* spent the night in prison.

"FOR THE LOVE OF GOD!" he yelled, right in Stacey's face. "DID YOU HEAR WHAT I— "

With another sob, the dozen or so flatscreens that hung from the office ceiling came to life. All were now displaying the same image: Nigel Crowther, shirt open almost from the waist, sunglasses on, makeup applied, his toilet brush of a hairdo practically quivering with smugness and indignation. He was standing beside a lime-colored Lamborghini while several aggressively branded network news microphones bobbed around in front of him like demented sock puppets.

A live-impromptu press conference was underway.

"Of course it's all over," Crowther was saying. "Why do you think I left? Any reality franchise that can't get—oh—*at least* twenty million viewers on a weekly basis should be put out of its misery, if you ask me . . . which, obviously, everyone is."

Those twinkly eyes.

That self-satisfied grin.

I wanted to throw something at the screen.

Now the TV reporters behind the camera were shouting over each other. To an inaudible question, Crowther responded, "Bibi and Joey? I have no opinion."

More shouting. As before, it was impossible to hear exactly *what* he was being asked. "Isn't it obvious?" Crowther laughed. "Like the rest of America, *I wasn't watching.*"

He tried to walk away, but the news people weren't done yet.

"Look, I'll say one last thing," announced Crowther, turning back to the camera and raising both palms. "*Project Icon* is the past. *The Talent Machine* is the future. *I* know that. *You're* all smart enough to know that. The American public knows that. And I would hope that Sir Harold Killoch and the Rabbit network now realize that after the frankly embarrassing numbers we've seen today. Now, if you'll please — "

"Mr. Crowther! Mr. Crowther!"

"*Please* . . . I have to . . . *seriously* . . . excuse me."

Still more shouting, but the vertically hinged door of the former *Icon* star's million-dollar ride had now powered open, and he was already climbing inside. Once seated, he gripped the thick, animal-skinned wheel and gave a final pout to the cameras. It was obvious he was loving this. Indeed, his expression suggested a kind of furtive sexual pleasure. The car's engine blarped and wheezed. Then Crowther winked — oh, the *smugness* — before disappearing behind a slab of green as the door hissed back into place, locking automatically. A caption appeared over it: "CROWTHER — '*Icon* is past, *Talent Machine* future.' " The car made a noise like a dinosaur being slaughtered inside a volcano, then flattened itself against the pavement. In the next instant, only dust and vapor remained.

Len spent the rest of the day in the hospital. "An allergic reaction to something," said his assistant, vaguely. I suspected it had more to do with him not wanting to become the proud owner of thirty new assholes, courtesy of Sir Harold Killoch. As for Stacey, she went home before lunch. No one else dared to come to work, leaving me alone in the office. I didn't even have my little green pills for comfort: they weren't in my bag, which meant I must have left them in the bathroom at home — again.

Of all the days to forget . . .

So I just sat there and tortured myself by searching for "*Icon*" and "cancellation" in Google News. We were the biggest story of the day, that was for sure — and I suppose there was a perverse reassurance to be found in that. I mean, at least people *cared.* But the fact we'd lost the number-one slot to *Bet You Can't Juggle That!*—the appeal of which mostly derived from the likelihood of a fatal accident each week—was surely the end, as far as the show was concerned. Sir Harold might have put up with a thirty percent viewership decline for a while, but he'd made it clear that on no account whatsoever would he tolerate a number-two position.

This was about pride, not economics.

"I don't believe in 'managed decline,'" *ShowBiz* had quoted him saying just a few days earlier. "If an asset isn't performing for Big Corp, I believe in *elimination.* And y'know what? I'm pretty sure Len Braithwaite and his team wouldn't have it any other way. I mean, these are the guys who've been doing exactly the same thing to their contestants every week for the past twelve years! They even invented a name for it: 'elimination night.' So I think it's perfectly reasonable for me to say to them, 'Look, if you can't hold on to your audience—well, then I'm afraid you'll have to face an elimination night of your own.'"

I wondered if the very first episode of season thirteen had been our elimination night, or if this was a humiliation yet to come. Not that it really mattered at this point. There were another six prerecorded shows left to air—two per week, for the next three weeks—so even if the cancellation order came later than expected, it was still pretty much a certainty that we'd never make it to Greenlit Studios.

Essentially, my job was over. It was just a question of turning up every day until the inevitable happened. Meanwhile . . . all I had in the bank was five hundred dollars. *Five hundred lousy bucks.* That wouldn't even pay for a *one-way* ticket to Honolulu, never mind a year of meals, rent, and beachside mai tais at the Hua-Kuwali Hotel.

I was so depressed by all this, I almost forgot to check the actual *reviews* of our first night with the new judges. The ratings had been so bad, it seemed irrelevant what the critics had to say. But curiosity eventually got the better of me, so I tapped "*Icon*" and "reviews" into Google, and then . . . yes, I laughed. I sat there at my desk, alone in the global headquarters of Zero Management, and I laughed my ass off.

The reviews were . . . well, see for yourself. Tripp Snuggins in the *New York Chronicle:*

> Joey Lovecraft has all the makings of an unlikely new American sweetheart. Sure, the White House might once have declared war on him as a toxic substance in his own right—with none other than President Reagan nicknaming him "Joey Dumbass" for that ill-advised parachute jump over Manhattan—but as season thirteen's natural protagonist, he brings wit and warmth and humanity to the circus; a welcome relief from Mr. Crowther's well-worn horrible-isms.

There was more like this. A lot more. And while Joey was overwhelmingly the critics' favorite, he wasn't the only recipient of praise. The *Dallas Morning Bugle* said Bibi "lent a new sense of occasion to the proceedings," while the *Los Angeles Mercury* even found a compliment for JD, noting that, "the man is obviously so in fear of his job, his vocabulary has finally moved beyond the inane, maddening cry of 'Booya-ka-*ka!*' Please, Mr. Coolz, keep this up!" Even the contestants seemed to have gained some fans. On YouTube, for example, 198,234 people had rewatched Mia Pelosi singing "The Prayer." Without a doubt, season thirteen had been as much of a critical triumph as it had been a commercial failure. So did that mean a word-of-mouth campaign could save us? Perhaps a #savejoey hashtag on Twitter? Not likely, unfortunately. As Len had once explained to me at great length, the season premiere of any show is nearly always the highest-rated episode until the finale. Hence the term "natural falloff," which describes the second and third week declines in audience that networks expect as a matter of course. And the usual falloff is about ten percent—which in our case would mean losing another million and a half viewers.

Even if a comeback managed to offset some of that, we were still screwed.

There was no point staying in the office any longer: might as well go home, order that long-overdue takeout from The Gates of Eternal Destiny, get the two-dollar wine flowing, turn on my new TV, and pretend that everything was going to be absolutely fine. But my day hadn't stopped getting worse just yet: As I waited for the elevator, I felt a buzz inside my purse. Pulling out my phone, I learned that my one hundred sixty-eighth text message of the day had just arrived. So far, I'd ignored them all. Not this one, though. Don't ask me why, but I tapped the screen to read it.

Bad move.

With a thud, my head fell against the wall.

Please, no—not now, not today.

Groaning, I checked the screen again. In a cheerful little green speech bubble:

> "REMEMBER! DATE WITH BORIS TONIGHT. SEVEN O'CLOCK—NO BE LATE! (HE WAIT FOR YOU UNDER PALM TREE OUTSIDE.)"

I'd totally forgotten that Mr. Zglagovvcini had *actually gone through* with his ridiculous plan to set me up on an Internet date. I'd meant to cancel, days ago. But I hadn't. There'd been too much going on. And now it was almost 6:45. Boris—whoever he was—would be arriving at my apartment in the next fifteen minutes, and Mr. Zglagovvcini would be watching from behind his heavy red curtains.

He'd become like a grandpa to me, Mr. Zglagovvcini. Always bringing me cookies that Mrs. Zglagovvcini had made, asking me how I was, showing me photographs of his sons, who now lived in Berlin. He'd be upset if I just didn't show up: It would be an insult. I should have cancelled in advance, like I'd planned to. But I hadn't.

There was no getting out of it.

20

Maison Chelsea

"LOOK, BORIS," I BEGAN, awkwardly, as I climbed off my bicycle, lost my balance, and clattered into the sidewalk with a startled ring from the handlebar bell. "There's been a—uh, *oof,* dah, grrr—misunderstanding. This whole, y'know, this Internet *thing*—"

Boris reached out to grab my hand.

I motioned to him—as best I could, given that I was on the floor with my feet in the air and a bicycle on top of me—that I could manage on my own, thank you very much.

"As I was saying," I resumed, now upright, dusting myself off. "This whole—"

"You speak English," said Boris, with surprise.

"*What?*"

"Oh, nothing. Just from your e-mails. I thought . . . y'know, you write with an accent." He laughed. Boris didn't seem nervous. He was also . . . dammit, I didn't even want to admit this . . . *not bad-looking*—by the standards of an Internet date, anyway. Or that's what I assumed, having never been on an Internet date before. Hair longish and brown. A couple of days' stubble. Hazel eyes. *Not short.* I mean, okay, the suit was a bit odd—who the hell wears a suit in LA?—but it was at least in a tan color and went very nicely with the fitted white shirt underneath.

"Look, about those e-mails, Boris," I said. "I didn't actually—"

"You like Japanese?" he asked, suddenly.

"The food?"

"No, the trains."

"Huh?"

Boris laughed again and play-punched me on the arm. "Messin' with ya," he said. "Yeah, the food."

This Boris was quite a character. I liked him already. More to the point: I needed a drink, and I was hungry. Would it really be so bad if I had some company for once? I mean, Brock would understand. Or maybe I didn't have to tell him.

"Ooh, how about some *balls,*" I blurted, excitedly.

"Excuse me?"

"Tempura rice balls," I clarified. "At Soba Kitchen on Third and Melrose. Let's go there. Oh, and yes, I like Japanese. Food, trains, people. Whatever."

"Well, let's do it."

"Okay!"

Then an awkward pause as the issue of *how* exactly we'd get there arose. Boris spoke first: "I'd suggest we take your bicycle, but I'm not sure I could fit into that"—he pointed to the wicker basket—"besides, I was kinda planning on being alive later tonight. No offence or anything. I'm sure you don't always fall off when you brake."

"That was the first time, actually," I protested.

"I totally believe that," said Boris.

"So?"

Boris coughed. "Oh, right. My car. It's over there. What were you saying about your e-mails?"

"Wasn't important," I shrugged, as we started to walk.

"It *sounded* important."

"It wasn't."

Okay, so a word about Boris's car. It had once been a fairly standard,

Asian-manufactured sedan. No longer. Take the airfoil on the trunk, for example. It wouldn't have looked out of place on a commercial jet. And that was among the less radical modifications, which included inch-high suspension, plastic bucket seats ("carbon fiber," Boris clarified), and a paint color I'd describe as radioactive carrot.

"Sorry about . . . y'know," mumbled Boris, as I attached my three-way racing harness, after searching without success for a normal seat belt. "It's kind of a hobby."

Boris, I now suspected, was some kind of major geek, albeit one who dressed against stereotype. And my theory was confirmed beyond any doubt when we got to the restaurant, which was just as I remembered, aside from one detail: The menu was in Japanese—with no translation. Now, this wouldn't have been so much of a problem, if any of the waiters had spoken English. But they didn't. Soba Kitchen is authentic like that. The best you can do as a non-Japanese speaker is point vaguely at the menu and hope they don't bring you their house specialty, the Fugu ("river pig")—which, if served with even a minor error in preparation, will kill you with a dose of tetrodotoxin, to which there is no antidote. (I'd once recommended the dish enthusiastically to Len.) "I forgot about the language thing," I told Boris, by way of an apology. "Last time I came here was with my friend Adam. He's Japanese. And Jewish, actually. Not as uncommon as you might think. I fell in love with the place when I tasted his balls."

Boris looked up from his menu.

"How many more testicle-based jokes are you gonna make this evening, Sasha?"

"Depends how the conversation goes."

Suddenly, Boris reached over the table. "Hey—gimme your phone for a second," he said.

I gave it to him. He tapped on the screen a few times—he seemed to be entering a password—waited a few seconds, then handed it back to me. "There," he said. "It's an app that a friend of mine from MIT has been working on. It's coming out next month. You're gonna love playing with this. Hit that icon—the red one."

I did as he said, and my phone switched to camera mode.

"Now take a picture of the menu."

Cha-chick.

Boris smiled. "Hold on," he said. "Seriously, this is so cool."

A moment later, the phone played a little jingle. "Language detected," said an automated voice.

"Check out the picture." Boris was grinning.

I did as he said. The image was just as I expected: the restaurant logo not quite in focus; too much glare from the flash; my finger in the bottom left corner of the frame.

"And?" I said.

Boris raised his eyebrows and nodded at my phone. I looked at the picture again. *What was so special about it?* It was just the *menu,* with the descriptions of each . . . oh . . . my God . . . *they were in English!* The app had recognized each Japanese character, translated it, and doctored the image accordingly.

"That's incredible," I said. "I mean . . . I say 'that's incredible' a lot. But this is actually *incredible.*"

"I know," said Boris, leaning over to take a look. "It can understand all the major languages, and they're adding more all the time. Soon they'll be moving on to the really obscure African and Middle Eastern . . . whoa—what the bejesus is *'river pig?'* "

Before I had a chance to explain, seven text messages arrived simultaneously, causing the phone to almost shake itself apart with excitement. This wasn't unusual, of course—Brock often sent me dozens of texts at once—but these messages hadn't come from Brock. They'd come from a number I'd used only once before. Mitch had given it to me, during the sanity checks.

I tapped the screen to read:

"GET YOUR GINGER MINGE OVER HERE, BUNGALOW BILL."

"MITCH SAYS IT'S AN ORDER!"

"SO DO I."

"OH—*HERE* IS CHELSEA HOUSE."

"LAST SUPPER!!"

"BAD NEWS COMING."

"DAH-DAH-DAHHH!!"

Boris was still looking over my shoulder. "Hey, I don't mean to pry," he said, raising his palms and moving back to his side of the table. "But is that . . . *the* Joey—"

"Yeah," I sighed. "It's him."

"Wow."

"Not really. Look, I'm sorry, Boris, but I'm gonna have to get my balls to go. It's a work thing."

"I'll drive you."

"That's very sweet, thank you."

"One condition, though."

"What?"

"We try this again next week."

I'd never been to Maison Chelsea before, but I knew what was it—a private club, owned by a mysterious Frenchman, located on the penthouse level of Fortune Plaza, one of the few high-rise buildings to cast a shadow over Hollywood Boulevard.

Pretty much every Big Name in town is a member of Maison Chelsea, and it's not hard to understand why: Paparazzi can't get anywhere near the place (the entrance is on the twenty-eighth floor); the commitment to privacy is such that all electronic devices are banned, and regardless of how famous you are, you can take a maximum of only three guests. The latter ensures that membership of Maison Chelsea is vital to anyone with even the vaguest of social aspirations. Marriages have failed because one partner's application to the club was accepted while the other's was declined. Similarly, lifelong friendships have been severed.

I asked Boris to drop me off outside, only to discover after fifteen minutes of wandering aimlessly between illuminated palms in the courtyard that the elevator to the penthouse level was located in the underground garage. So down the steep driveway I went, ducking under the traffic barrier by the ticket machine, and ignoring the sign that read, "THIS IS NOT — REPEAT, NOT! — A PEDESTRIAN WALKWAY." On the other side I encountered an amused-looking valet, who pointed me toward an unmarked glass doorway, barely visible between two black Maseratis. Beyond it was a small, dark lobby with two banks of elevators, an angular sofa—clearly designed for minimum comfort and maximum aesthetic value—and a reception desk. Downtempo electronica pulsed in the background.

"*Bonjour* and welcome to Maison Chelsea," said one of the male receptionists. He was dressed like a Depression-era newsboy and didn't sound the least bit French. He sounded British, in fact. (Just what I needed in my life: *another Brit.*)

"I'm meeting someone," I offered. The way it came out sounded like an apology for my very presence. I was annoyed with myself for being so easily intimidated.

"And the member's name?"

I had no idea if Mitch was the member, or Joey. Somehow, using Joey's name seemed ridiculous.

"Mitch," I said, my face now a boiling cauldron of shame.

"Last name?"

"McDonald."

"No."

"No?"

"No."

Several legitimate club members were now in line behind me. I could feel their pity.

" . . . what do you mean, *no?*" I asked.

"There's no 'Mitch McDonald.'"

"Can you try under Joey? *Joey Lovecraft.*"

The receptionist's concentration intensified. Skepticism had also made itself plainly visible on his brow. He moved the nib of his fountain pen quickly down a list in the leather-bound signature book in front of him while making a diligent-sounding clucking noise. "*Hmm,*" he said to himself. "Well, I see that Mr. Lovecraft *is* expecting someone this evening. But I'm afraid . . . *hmm,* I'm only seeing a . . . Bill."

"That's me," I said, relieved. "I'm Bill."

"Oh, so *you're* Bill?" said the receptionist, with only barely disguised sarcasm.

"Yes."

"ID, *please.*"

The "please" was delivered with such contempt, "fuck you" might have sounded a bit friendlier.

I produced my wallet. Then I realized the problem.

"Well, my ID says, 'Sasha,'" I began to explain. "But he calls me Bill."

"Fascinating," came the reply. "I'm sure there's an absolutely hilarious backstory. You should tell me all about it another time. Take a seat. I'll have someone look into this."

"But—"

The receptionist gestured to the unwelcoming slab of foam in the corner.

Sighing, I sat down. Five minutes passed. My back started to hurt. *Another five minutes.* I stood up and walked around. At least a dozen other Maison Chelsea members came and went, each displaying or otherwise confirming their credentials with no effort whatsoever. They were from another world, these people: a taller, better-dressed, more beautiful world, in which everyone looks a bit like Wayne Shoreline. I sat down again. Okay, so this was getting miserable. I would have called Mitch and Joey, but all communication devices were banned. Then, at last—thank God—I overheard the receptionist discussing my case on the phone with an assistant manager upstairs. "If you get a moment," he was saying, "could you ask Mr. Lovecraft to describe, 'Bill'? *Thanks.*"

I'd been here—what?—forty minutes now.

The receptionist raised his eyebrows at me as he waited for the callback. "Yes?" he said, when the phone finally rang. "A redhead. Very pale, you say. No makeup? Oohhkay . . . it *is* a she, then. Jeans. Plain top. Plain *everything.* Right."

Click.

"Please make your way upstairs," he ordered. "Mr. Lovecraft is in The Blue Room. You can ask the hostess on the penthouse level for directions when you get lost."

"*When?*"

"Oh, I'm sorry, I didn't realize you'd been here before."

"I haven't."

"I didn't think so. *Enjoy your night.*"

The Blue Room was indeed virtually impossible to find. Although Maison Chelsea is located atop Fortune Plaza for the views, the hallways that join the bar, restaurant, bathrooms, cinema, and private rooms are entirely windowless. I felt as though I were inside a tenth-century château, what with the narrow, wood-paneled walls, oppressive ceilings, and low-watt fixtures. It must have taken an interior design budget in the tens of millions to turn what had originally been a modern, open-plan office space into something so gloomy and unnavigable.

None of the doors were marked. Some were locked; others weren't. As for the staff, they didn't wear uniforms or make eye contact, so unless you caught them directly in the act of a service-oriented task, it was difficult to know who they were. Even then, they weren't exactly very helpful. "Honestly, *madam,* the only way I could tell you how to get to The Blue Room would be to take you there myself," as one waiter explained, as though he were describing a physical impossibility.

I found it by myself in the end, using a system of trial and error. The very instant I pushed open those gigantic double doors, there was no doubt I was in the right place. Aside from its size—I've walked through more intimate hotel atriums—it was . . . well, it was very blue. The ceiling was blue. The floor was blue. Even the view through the thirty-foot-high panoramic windows was blue, given that it was comprised mostly of early-evening California sky. The rest of the blueness, meanwhile, came from light reflected through water, which was possible because the room—and I appreciate how crazy this sounds—was *inside a swimming pool.* Or to put it another way: The ceiling was the glass-bottomed floor of the pool's upper deck, while in several places throughout the room, the water deepened to fill transparent cylinders that served as kind of Roman columns, which were in turn linked to more water under the opaque floor.

"What the hell took you so long?"

I turned to see Joey, alone on a king-size recliner. He was wearing nothing but a fluffy white gown, his wrinkled, skinny legs—along with that enormous, fading sock tattoo on his right calf—poking out from underneath. Not even Joey's tan could make those legs look any healthier. They were as mangled and gnarled as rotting timber—a result of forty years spent doing airborne splits while singing "Hell on Wheels." No wonder he'd fallen off the stage that time in Houston. No wonder he snacked on painkillers like they were M&M'S. It was incredible his legs could support a grown man's body weight, nevermind comply with the acrobatic demands of a world tour with Honeyload.

"Where is everyone?" I asked.

"Gone," he replied, sadly. He was surrounded by at least two dozen trays of half-eaten food—I caught sight of spring rolls, steak au poivre, lobster tails, steamed vegetables, a Cobb salad, three doughnuts, and a banana pudding—and as many empty champagne flutes. I hoped it had been non-alcoholic champagne. "They were all here," Joey continued, not quite sounding himself. "Mitch, Len, Bibi, JD, the ex-human cannonball Ed Rossitto—who still creeps me the hell out, just FYI. Oh, and that nasty little fuckhead Teddy. But they all went home."

"So soon?"

"Oh, y'know. Bibi got upset about the view."

He pointed to the aquarium-like glass above us. Now I noticed there were swimmers in the pool. Three or four women. Young. In exceptional physical shape. And all completely naked. They appeared to be performing some kind of water aerobics for Joey's benefit. One of them was now underwater, thrusting herself deep into one of the see-through Roman columns in front of us, leaving a trail of bubbles as she went. She righted herself and waved, treading water. Then she flipped over and performed a split, holding the gynecologically detailed pose for as long as the air in her lungs would allow.

Joey applauded.

"Um-*hmm,*" he said, as if tasting a vintage port. "LA strippers, man. Fuckin' outstanding. No wonder Mötley Crüe wrote a song about 'em." He began to sing the chorus of "Girls, Girls, Girls," humming the parts where he'd forgotten the words.

"I should leave you alone," I said.

"Here," said Joey, handing me a champagne glass.

"Does this have alcohol in it, Joey?"

"Chillax, *Mom.* Yours does. Mine doesn't."

He lit up a cigar and patted the space next him, beckoning me to sit. I couldn't stop looking at his legs. Those poor, mangled limbs! He might as well have fallen into a wood chipper, they were in such a state. And his toes . . . he didn't even have toes—he had *toe,* in the singular. A fused mass of bone, cartilage, and skin, located at the end of each twisted foot. How did the man even manage to *walk?*

I lowered myself onto the recliner, leaving as much room between us as possible. Then I drank the champagne. All of it, in one gulp. It had been that kind of day.

"The numbers, huh?" said Joey, nodding at my empty glass. "Not good."

"You said there was bad news coming," I replied, pouring myself another.

"Sure there is. We're gettin' nuked. They're giving us one last episode. No ratings, no more show."

"Our elimination night."

"Ha! Ironic, ain't it? God, I could graze on that ass for a month." He was looking again at one of the swimmers, who was performing an underwater handstand. Then he turned to me quickly, as if not wanting to cause any offence. "I fuck dudes, too, by the way," he said. "Just in case you're thinkin' I'm some kinda *sexist* or something. Size is a factor, though. More than seven inches and it feels like—"

"I get the idea, Joey."

"She blushes again!" he roared, pointing at my face. "Shit, man—the traffic lights on Sunset Boulevard turn red less often than you do. It's cute, Bill. Very cute."

"Do you ever *care* what happens to *Icon,* Joey?" I asked, with more bluntness than I'd planned. "I mean, if I were you, with your—y'know, the back catalog and everything—I wouldn't want the hassle. Taking orders from Len Braithwaite. Dealing with Bibi. Or worse, *Teddy Midas.* C'mon, Joey. Wouldn't you rather be sitting on a beach somewhere in Hawaii, writing your memoirs, sipping mai tais—"

"Whoah!" Joey interrupted, with an eruption of partially chewed spring roll from his mouth. "You got me ALL wrong, sugar. Holy crap-a-doodle-doo, *have you got me wrong.* Lemme tell you a story about how much I care, Little Ms. Bungalow Bill, about how much I *invest* in the shit I do. You remember the summer of '83?"

I blanked. It was the year *Swordfishtrombones* by Tom Waits came out. That was all I knew.

"Yeah, like shit you do," Joey went on, not waiting for a reply. "You weren't even a sperm in your daddy's dick! So let me remind you: It was the middle of Honeyload's third world tour. Me and Blade, we were banging ten chicks a night, drinking, fighting, playing, using. We'd gone deep into Crazy Land, man. And I lost my shit a few times, that I admit. But that summer, Blade went psycho-fuckin'-killer on me. Said he wanted to put a bullet in my head, 'cause the band was driving him insane. Accused me of not *caring*—just like you did a moment ago. He even got it into his head that I was gonna fuck everyone over and go solo. He'd seen how well Ozzy was doing after Black Sabbath, and he was shitting his pants. Big time paranoia, like you wouldn't even believe.

"So, it's the last night in July," he continued, "and we're booked to play Yankee Stadium. And our manager—may the devil roast his soul over the hot coals of hell for all fuckin' eternity—has this far-out idea for starting the show: He'll give us all some parachutes, take us up in his Learjet, fly over the stadium, and at just the right moment we'll jump out the back, pull our rip cords, and float down to the stage. And when our feet touch the ground—DNN, DNN, BLAM!—we'll launch into 'Duckin' and Fuckin,' the first track on our new album. Genius idea, credit where it's due. Only me and Blade were still fightin' so much, taking us up in an airplane was pretty much the dumbest thing anyone coulda done.

"It was a bad scene, man. In that tiny plane. Bumping around all over the place. It's dark. The door's open. Wind screaming in our ears. Me and Blade screaming at *each other,* swinging punches, arguing over . . . reverb settings, would you believe—*at twenty thousand feet!* And I just go off. I fuckin' *blow,* man. I unclip my 'chute right there in the plane, and throw it out the hatch. It's gone—a dot, a tiny dot, falling toward Manhattan. Some homeless dude in Central Park probably thought it was a sleeping bag from heaven. And I say to Blade, over the engines, I say to him, 'It's your lucky day, motherfucker, 'cause I'm gonna jump out this plane, *right now,* and you don't have to do a thing. Just let me fall, let me die, and all your problems are solved. You got enough dough from royalties, you'll never have to work another day again in your life; that's how much I care about you, *asshole.* But if you wanna trust me, if you wanna *COMMIT* to this band as much as I do, then jump out after me, and catch me, man. Just catch me. And we'll land together and do the gig. Your choice. Farewell, my friend.' "

I'd never heard this story before. I mean, I knew about the jump, of course. Everyone knew about the jump. After the Beatles playing *The Ed Sullivan Show,* it was the most famous event in rock 'n' roll history. But I thought it had been some kind of prank gone wrong, an accident with a very lucky ending.

"And?" I said, when I found my voice. "What happened?"

"*What happened?* Dude caught me. We played the show. Best night of my fuckin' life."

"He just . . . 'caught' you?"

"Blade's been skydiving since he was in the womb. Literally—his mom was some kinda champ, did jumps when she was pregnant. Dude can pull midair moves like an F-18. In fact, he messed with my head before saving my life. He flew right past me, showed me the birdie, and told me to aim for the spike on the roof of the Empire State Building. I thought I was pink slime, man. I was crying, praying, wishing I hadn't thrown away the 'chute, then — WOOOMPH — he's right there behind me, arm around my waist. Next thing I know, he's hooked me onto him, and we land together, best buddies again. It made me rock hard, man."

"That's . . . *amazing* — I mean, that he caught you."

"Well, the president didn't think so. He called me 'Joey Dumbass' the next day in the Rose Garden."

"Must have hurt," I said.

"You kidding? It was like a billion bucks of free advertising. Not that I was thinkin' about that at the time. Honestly, I just wanted Blade to believe me when I said I cared more about the band than my own life. By jumpin' out of that plane, I proved it to him. And believe it or not, Bungalow Bill, I feel the same way about *Project Icon.* I'm gettin' older. Look at my legs. I can't jump around on stage every night of the week. My doc gives me two years max before I start rollin' in a wheelchair, Johnny Cash–style. So I need a regular job. And no, by the way, I don't wanna sit on a beach. You think *that's* fun? Honey, you ain't never done it. I retired to Hawaii in 1984, after I got my first hundred million in the bank. Six days, it lasted. And I'm surprised I held out that long. I was hitting myself in the face with fuckin' rocks, I was so bored. Beautiful place, man, don't get me wrong. But live there? Try it, I dare ya. Relaxation is stagnation. Fuck that shit. Besides, at *Project Icon,* I can help give some cow town kid like Jimmy Nugget a shot at doin' what I did. That means the world to me, Bungalow Bill. Where else is the next generation gonna come from, huh? Without *Icon,* there'd be no music shows on prime time. There'd be no *audience.* Shit, if you're unknown, you can't even get a gig these days, 'cause the venues make you guarantee the takings at the door in advance. What kind of young kid can afford to do that?"

I didn't get a chance to answer this question—because without warning, Joey lunged. I guess I must have leaned in closer while he was speaking, or maybe it was the nude Olympics going on in the background that had triggered some sex impulse in his head. Whatever—I couldn't get out of the way fast enough. And by that I mean, *I couldn't actually get out of the way fast enough.* So there I was, pinned on the recliner, with the tongue of a sixty-two-year-old man trying to push its way between my clenched jaw and into my mouth. It lasted, oh, five seconds. The moment I struggled against him, Joey broke away, surprised at my reluctance. He'd miscalculated. He'd mistaken my interest for attraction. But as he retreated, something light and hollow fell out of his gown pocket and rolled across the floor. I looked down—and Joey made a dive for it. But it was too late.

I'd seen them.

I'd seen my jar of little green pills, with "Sasha King, take as needed" on the side.

"How the *hell*—!" I screamed, in a rage that took hold of me with a sudden, almost frightening force. The lunge had been bad enough: But this? He'd *stolen* from me, too?

"You left 'em right there!" Joey yelled, now slurring his words. It was now so horribly obvious what had happened. He must have taken a pill—or *pills*—right before I arrived, and they were only just beginning to enter his bloodstream. *He was high.*

"*Where?*" I demanded.

"My trailer. In Las Vegas. Shit, Bill, I'm sorry. But you left 'em, you left 'em right there, man."

It was a lie. *It had to be a lie.* I'd never been near his trailer, not in Las Vegas, not anywhere.

"Joey—*how could you?*" I said, the rage beginning to pass. Now I just felt confused. Depressed and confused. "And I thought you were one of the good guys. I really did, Joey."

I stared at him, still trying to process what had just happened.

He said nothing.

"Dammit, Joey," I sighed. "I liked you from that first moment in Ed's office—even when you weren't even being *likable.* And after all the shit we've been through with Bibi—what she did to Bonnie—I thought you were better. Jesus, what a sucker I am."

Joey's entire body stiffened. " . . . you think *Bibi* was the reason Bonnie left the show?" he said.

An awful silence. "Yeah. Why?"

"Oh, man. I'm a terrible person. A terrible, *terrible* person." He stood up and walked over to the balcony. I hoped he wasn't about to cry. Tonight had been bad enough already.

"What *happened,* Joey?" I asked, anger still in my voice. "Just tell me what happened."

" . . . I didn't mean to," came the forlorn reply. "I just . . . I'm just built that way, Bill. And that's what people want, isn't it? The whole rock star thing. Ain't that why they pay me all that money to be on the show? It was a *kiss,* goddamnit."

"*You KISSED Bonnie?*"

"Yeah."

"Oh, Joey . . . oh . . ."

"They made a whole big fuckin' *thing* out of it." Wiping his eyes, he stared out at the groaning, howling city below. "Guess they were just mad at me," he sighed. "Y'know . . . for making her *pregnant* and all."

21

Bingo-Bitte!

February

WAYNE SHORELINE WAS standing in complete darkness. Or rather, it would have been complete darkness, if not for the single, tiny uplight attached to the microphone in his hand: It shone against his lower jaw, casting shadows across his blandly androgynous features.

To Wayne, it must have seemed for a moment as though he were alone on soundstage three of Greenlit Studios—as though the only noise in the room were coming from his lungs, as they rose and fell in their machinelike rhythm.

But of course he was not alone.

Out in the blackness, a few yards beyond the stage, was a long table at which Joey, Bibi, and JD were seated. And beyond *them* was a live studio audience—only two or three hundred people in total, but the wall-to-wall mirrors made it seem as though there were more. Facing Wayne, meanwhile, was the cloaked hulk of a pedestal-mounted TV camera, its giant monocle of a lens taking in every last detail of his semi-illuminated face, and rendering it a high-definition video signal.

Then a voice.

My voice.

"New York, can you hear me?" I asked.

A rush of static over the studio monitors.

"Hello, LA," came the reply. "This is New York. We can hear you. Thirty seconds."

A long, fuzzy tone.

Soon, the digitized image of Wayne's face would be funneled through a heavy-gauge cable to a dish of Kennedy Space Center proportions on the roof, and from there beamed up to an orbiting satellite, before ricocheting back down to Earth—only this time in the direction of Manhattan, where it would be processed and distributed to approximately one and a half billion homes throughout the world.

One and a half billion homes.

Barely a single percentage of this theoretical "maximum reach" audience would be watching, of course—or at least by the definition of the Jefferson Metrics Organization, which doesn't count viewers outside the US, on account of their being "nonmonetizable." Still, you could take the largest venue in America—Michigan Stadium, with its 109,901 capacity—build nine identical replicas, put them side by side out in the Nevada desert, and you still wouldn't have a seat for every person about to watch the first live episode of *Project Icon*'s thirteenth season. And this in spite of its being the least-watched season in the show's history.

The pressure didn't seem to affect Wayne. Up there on stage, he was focused, yes, but calm. That's the thing with Wayne—his unshakable calm. Some take it as niceness. Professionalism, even. These people have got it all wrong.

Wayne is a functioning psychopath.

Watching him from my position in the wings, I marveled at his unbreakable confidence. Over the course of the next hour—not a second more, not a second less—he would conduct the cruel ballet of *Project Icon* with inhuman precision.

Not a bead of sweat. Not a syllable misspoken.

I've often wondered if the rise of the show in the early days was really more about Wayne's ability to make a live broadcast seem edited —while retaining just the right amount of unpredictability—than Nigel Crowther's "Mr. Horrible" routine. Or perhaps it was the obvious hatred between Wayne and Crowther that gave *Project Icon* its edge: Crowther the archmanipulator, Wayne the unmanipulatable.

A crazy fact: Before the show launched, Wayne *auditioned* for Crowther's job. He was twenty-two at the time, a warm-up guy for *Guess the Price.* He'd lost a lot of weight since leaving his hometown of Columbus, Ohio, where he'd dropped out of high school. He'd gotten his eyes fixed, too—dispensing with the goldfish-bowl spectacles that had caused him so much grief at school. The audition was his big chance. His moment to break out. But he was a terrible, lifeless judge. He felt *nothing* for anyone—not even contempt—and it showed. So Len tried him out as host and couldn't believe what he saw. Wayne read from the teleprompter with such control, he could time his sentences to within a sixteenth of a second. He could play the thing like a musical instrument. What's more: It was impossible to tell when his scripted lines ended and his ad-libs began. And his ad-libs—well, they were something else. Breathtakingly mean, and yet delivered with a bland pseudofriendliness that somehow made them seem okay. *"Hey buddy, come here, gimme a hug. Good job. Now, your mom's in the hospital, right? Very sick. And do you worry that if you get voted off the show tonight, she might take a turn for the worse? You could actually be singing for her life, right? Tell everyone how you feel about that."*

Like I said: *Functioning psychopath.* In another era, Wayne would have emceed hangings and public disembowelments. *"Hey buddy, come here, gimme a hug. Now, tell me what's going through your mind as this masked butcher behind me sharpens his knives?"*

Another thing about Wayne: He's always moonlighting. Red-carpet shows. Charity specials. Afternoon drive time on Megahitz FM. Which means he's on the clock, eighteen hours a day, seven days a week. He works so hard, he doesn't even have a chair in his office—if he wants to sit down, he uses an exercise bicycle. I saw him in there once, pedaling away while reading his e-mails and eating with chopsticks from some kind of prepackaged meal. I was struck by the *bareness* of the place. No plants. No photographs. Nothing. Just an enormous poster of Nigel Crowther, on which he had drawn crosshairs in red marker pen . . .

Another fuzzy tone over the monitors.

"Stand by, New York," I said.

A few seconds passed. Then a red light above the camera, flashing in sequence.

I began counting down.

"Ten . . . nine . . . eight . . . seven . . ."

The light was flashing quicker now, like a bomb ready to detonate.

" . . . six . . . five . . . four . . ."

Wayne's expression changed. He looked poised and deadly: a killer with cornered prey.

" . . . three . . . two . . ."

"*THEY SAID WE'D NEVER MAKE IT,*" began Wayne, his face still in almost total darkness. "*They said it was . . . impossible. Well, they say a lot of things, don't they? And sometimes they're wrong. Very wrong. Because here we are, back again for our thirteenth year of live broadcasts from Greenlit Studios, right here in Hollywood—with some of the most outstanding talent not just in the history of our show . . . but in an ENTIRE GENERATION. Mia Pelosi. Jimmy Nugget. Cassie Turner. These are already household names, folks. But who knows if any of them will make it over the weeks and months to come. We are in uncharted territory, my friends—in oh-so-many ways. It's gonna be quite a ride. Who will survive? Who will face ELIMINATION? And will our new judges be able to handle the pressure of sending home these talented girls and guys when they just don't make the grade. Well, if you want answers to these questions: Stay tuned—because THIS . . .*"

A pause, lasting precisely two-point-six seconds.

"Is *PROJECT . . .*"

Blinding whiteness as the lights came on.

" . . . *ICON!*"

It was nothing short of an act of God that we'd made it onto the air. I mean, Sir Harold had practically announced our cancellation during an interview on the Monster Cash Financial Network just a few days earlier. "The Jefferson numbers stink so bad, I gotta light a bloody match every time I walk in the studio," he'd raged, with his usual thumping of the table. "Nigel Crowther is absolutely bloody right: A prime-time franchise that can't give us twenty million eyeballs a week needs to be *put down.*"

A few people at Zero Management—including Stacey, the emotional receptionist—never showed up to work again after that. They just assumed it was all over.

But then . . . well, some extraordinary luck. Sir Harold became distracted. The entire executive board of Big Corp became distracted, in fact. The problem was Rabbit's German division. Those "local difficulties" it had been experiencing for the last month or so? They'd suddenly become a lot more urgent.

As I learned from the reports in *ShowBiz,* Rabbit had for years been producing a live Saturday night "bingocast" for one of Germany's largest broadcasters. But now the show, *Bingo-Bitte!,* had been exposed as a huge scam. Basically, a handful of employees of Rabbit Deutschland had figured out a way to hack into the *Bingo-Bitte!* computer (operated on air by two fulsome-breasted teenagers in Bavarian-maid outfits), which meant they could predict the numbers called with a hundred percent accuracy. This wouldn't have been of much use, of course, unless the hackers had also been able to make their own bingo cards . . . or unless, say, the largest printer and distributor of *Bingo-Bitte!* cards happened to be a daily tabloid newspaper, *Schnelle Lesen,* which was yet another subsidiary of . . .

Yeah: Big Corp.

Having already broken into the *Bingo-Bitte!* computer, it wasn't much of a leap for these algorithm-savvy Teutons to start meddling with *Schnelle Lesen's* presses—and before long, they'd fixed the entire game, allowing them to collect several million euros per week in winnings, via the generously bribed friends and family members who played on their behalf. As a criminal enterprise, it was brilliant. And like all brilliant criminal enterprises, it couldn't last forever. Eventually, one of the players got nervous and turned himself in, worried that someone else would do it first. One plea bargain later, and the Berlin Fraud Squad knew everything.

At first, they thought the scheme had gone on for a few months, making the "Bingo Betrügers" some ten or twelve million euros each. (The whistle-blower had been one of the last to get involved.) But then more evidence emerged: The *Bingo-Bitte!* hacking had in fact gone on for *years*—which meant the illegal winnings weren't in the millions at all. *They were in the billions.* Worse: An official at one of Berlin's most-respected auditing firms appeared to be in on the ruse. As a result, Rabbit's broadcasting license had been temporarily revoked, and Sir Harold, along with his most senior Big Corp lieutenants, had been called to give evidence to the Bundestag. Suddenly, the company was having to contemplate the possibility of arrests, bail conditions, and extradition demands—not to mention dual investigations by European Union officials and US financial regulators. Sir Harold had made a lot of powerful enemies since using the cash from his father's gold mine to buy his very first newspaper in Cape Town.

Now it was their payback time.

Given all this, it was hardly surprising that the ratings of a televised singing competition were no longer at the top of Big Corp's agenda. And thank God for that, because the first live episode of season thirteen was terrible. Not can't-take-your-eyes-off-the-TV terrible. More like switch-off-the-TV terrible. Something about it just didn't work. It seemed dull, spent; an exhausted, obsolete franchise. Which meant we had to find the cause of the problem, quickly, and put it right before the Big Corp Gulfstream got back to LAX. A week of interrogation by angry Germans wasn't exactly going to put Sir Harold in a very patient mood.

Here was the big surprise, though: *Bibi* wasn't the issue.

In fact, Bibi's performance during the first show at Greenlit Studios had been the strongest of all three judges. For a start, she'd been allowed (as per the contract that Teddy had negotiated) to stage a "live performance" of her latest single during the halftime break. Or as Len explained it to Ed Rossitto, "live in the sense that she'll be alive when we fucking prerecord it." In fairness to Bibi, the song was a good deal more entertaining than the usual lip-synched affair. This was due in large part to the choreography, which involved a break-dancing mariachi band, a troupe of eighteen mostly naked construction workers, six lions, several high-wire aerial stunts, an indoor explosion, and—the masterstroke, in my opinion—a choir of Nepalese lentil-famine refugees. It lasted two and half minutes, at a cost of approximately ten thousand dollars per second.

Bibi paid for it herself.

She had some help in another department, too: her lines. These were mostly the work of the Oscar-winning screenwriter Tad Dunkel, who'd been hired by Teddy to sit through the afternoon rehearsals and compose emotional monologues for Bibi inspired by the contestants' performances. (Which meant that no matter how much they improved in time for the live broadcast, it made no difference to what Bibi said.) At first, I was surprised Tad had even taken the job. I mean, the man had an *Oscar* on his mantelpiece. But then I discovered that since winning his sole Academy Award nearly two decades ago, Tad had sold only one other screenplay, the infamous animated comedy, *Terrence the Turkey*, released over the Thanksgiving weekend of 1995. It was infamous because it took in a grand total of $64.38 cents at the box office—a record that stands to this day. Tad never completed another full-length feature, although he did find work as a script consultant, becoming known in the business as "The Cry Guy" for his unfailing ability to make test audiences weep. His secret, went the Hollywood joke, was that he simply channeled the pain of *Terrence the Turkey*'s opening weekend.

And now Bibi had him on retainer.

It was, I had to admit, a brilliant move. Every time Bibi opened her mouth, it felt like the third act of a major motion picture. After a contestant's performance of "Stayin' Alive," for example, Bibi embarked upon a lengthy soliloquy about how the lyrics brought to mind her tragic childhood dachshund, Frankie, who had died in her arms when she was just six years old. We learned about Frankie's playful disposition. We learned about the time Frankie saved the family goldfish from an evil neighborhood cat. We learned about Frankie's love of meatball sandwiches. And by the time Bibi reached the part about Frankie licking her six-year-old face *one last time* before snuggling up to her chest and drawing his final doggie breath—and how she'd wrapped him in a blanket from her own bed and wrote a note to the angels reminding them to feed him a meatball hero every Sunday—the audience had experienced what amounted to a collective nervous breakdown. People were sobbing so hard, Len had to switch off the studio mics. The Cry Guy had done his job. Bibi had shown her passion, her tears . . . her *humanity.* As for the contestant: He stood there motionless and somewhat confused, wondering what *precisely* it had been about his rendition of a 1970s Bee Gees classic that had triggered such an epic canine obituary.

(It probably goes without saying, of course, that Frankie was a work of fiction.)

So, anyway: Bibi wasn't the problem. All of the caution she'd exercised during the audition rounds—her fear of being made to look stupid in the editing room—had vanished. Suddenly, Bibi was in her element. She was an actress, after all. She liked memorizing lines—it was so much easier than having to think of what to say. Which begged the question: If Bibi wasn't ruining the show . . . *then who was?*

It was Joey.

Something had changed in him since that night at Maison Chelsea. His eyes were bloody hollows. His hair was a rodent's nest. Even his mouth, with those spectacular, ever-shifting lips, looked somehow less luxurious than usual. He seemed to be . . . disintegrating. At first, I thought it was the Bonnie situation. But the more I found out about the circumstances of her pregnancy, the more I suspected that it had nothing whatsoever to do with Joey's malaise. Bonnie, it transpired, had always wanted a child. And after her husband's injury, not to mention the slaughter of his twenty-three comrades, the act of creating and nurturing a new human life seemed essential to her, a way of proving that the universe—God, I suppose—was still capable of love. But Staff Sergeant Mike Donovan was of course no longer able to father a child. And unlike many of his fellow soldiers, he hadn't visited a sperm bank before leaving for Afghanistan: It was the *married* guys who jerked off into test tubes before their tours of duty, not the likes of Mikey, who was still technically a bachelor at the time he was ambushed.

Now it was too late. Half of Mikey's groin had been taken out by shrapnel, leaving him infertile. Nevertheless, he was determined to give Bonnie a baby, one way or another, even if the child wasn't biologically his. It was the *very least* he could do, he told his wife (via coded eyeblinks), given all that she had sacrificed for him. So Bonnie signed up to a donor service, and was busy reviewing anonymous candidates online, purchasing every last piece of information she could about each one of them—voice recordings, handwriting samples, medical histories, *anything*—when she came in for her *Project Icon* audition.

It didn't take long for one of the research interns to find out about her plans to conceive. And it took even less time for word to reach Joey, who immediately stepped in to "offer my schlong in the name of God and country." Bonnie, who had grown up listening to Honeyload with Mikey, couldn't have been more delighted. And after consulting with her husband, she accepted his offer. Nevertheless, there was a small *misunderstanding* about how the . . . uh, transaction would take place. Hence the whole issue of the kiss. Or more accurately, the lunge. Still, Joey handled the rejection well, and although he confessed some disappointment about the means of extraction, he stuck by his promise, disappeared into the bathroom, and emerged approximately thirty-eight seconds later with a plastic beaker practically overflowing with what he called his "love spunk number nine." To Joey, who is thought to have at least forty-three illegitimate sons and daughters across the globe—along with his seventeen official children and thirty-five grandchildren (with another half-dozen grandchildren pending)—the idea of fathering an infant he would almost certainly never meet wasn't exactly a new one. And while he wasn't getting any "oopy-goopy" (his phrase) out of the conception, at least it wouldn't involve the usual paternity suit.

Not everyone shared Bonnie and Joey's enthusiasm for the artificial insemination idea, however. Len, for example, was especially unmoved by Joey's generosity with regards to the distribution of his semen. In fact, when he found out about it, he called Joey into his office, printed out a copy of the Nonfraternization Agreement that each judge had signed only a few weeks earlier, and informed him that he was now in official breach of his *Project Icon* contract. Not only could Rabbit fire him, said Len, but it could also sue him—as could Zero Management. Then Maria Herman-Bloch walked into the room with David Gent, Ed Rossitto, and five Big Corp lawyers. In Maria's yellow-tinged fingers was another contract, which outlined the terms of a payment from Big Corp to Bonnie of one million dollars in return for her immediate removal from the show and a promise never to take legal action over the "private incident involving Mr. Lovecraft's supply of biological fluids," nor discuss any aspect of it with anyone, *especially not the press.* The settlement included an agreement by Joey to forgo three months' salary as a disciplinary measure. He signed without protest.

That was what had caused the terrible scene in Las Vegas. In spite of her awkwardness around Bonnie initially, Bibi had in fact been genuinely touched by her story. It had made her go home, dismiss the nannies for the evening, and hold her young sons tighter than she ever had before. She'd even tried again to make up with Edouard, who was still upset about being fired as her cue-card holder back in San Diego. So when she was ordered to send Bonnie home with no explanation other than "it's the producers' wishes"—Len hadn't wanted to tell her the real story, because of what Teddy might do—she threatened to resign.

By this point, however, Len was operating on his special reserve tank of patience. So he called her bluff. He knew Bibi liked her new job too much to leave. Bibi's breakdown in Las Vegas was therefore only partially anguish over what she had been forced to do. It was also a tantrum over not getting her own way. And Joey? Well, he felt bad, of course. But the way he saw it, he had given Bonnie a gift more precious than winning *Icon.* Besides, there was nothing to stop her following a singing career after leaving the show. Nothing other than the baby's arrival in nine months' time, anyway.

So the question remained: Why had Joey become so . . . *boring* on camera suddenly? It didn't make any sense. He was supposed to be the King of Sing, the Devil of Treble . . . the Holy Cow of Big Wow!

My guess was the drugs. Although I'd reclaimed my jar of green pills (by then almost empty), Joey could easily have found another supply. He was an addict, after all. And an addict will do anything to get his fix, especially if the addict in question is a multimillionaire rock star with his own private staff. I'd alerted Mitch to the issue, of course—but there was only so much he could do without drawing Rabbit's attention to the matter, and that was the last thing he wanted after the whole Bonnie fiasco. "Let me handle it, Bill," he told me over the phone after the Maison Chelsea incident. "I'll call his sponsor. We'll get him fixed, don't worry."

Meanwhile, I couldn't help but think back to Las Vegas Week. Was there *any* way I could have left my pills in his trailer? Was there a chance, no matter how infinitesimal, that he was telling the truth, and that he hadn't actually *stolen* from me?

It just didn't seem possible. I couldn't even remember what Joey's trailer looked like, to be honest with you. I certainly hadn't been inside it. Which meant Joey must have seen the jar in my purse—just as Bibi had done in that Milwaukee bathroom—and then waited for his opportunity. It wouldn't exactly have taken a criminal mastermind to pull it off. The only flaw in his plan being that once his addiction was reactivated, he got through most of the jar in twenty-four hours. And then he needed more. So what did he do? He invited me over to his private club, on the pretence of a "last supper" with Mitch and the others, in hopes that by then I'd refilled my prescription. Better to steal from me (again) than call up one of his old dealers, with all the risk that involved. Only he was so wasted by the time I got there—and so driven into a frenzy of lust by the nude aerobics in the pool—that he made that desperate, fumbled pass at me instead.

Strangely enough, however, I still had enough faith in Joey to believe that he hadn't gotten hold of any more pills after I busted him. In fact, I suspected that he'd done exactly what Mitch had told him to and called his sponsor. When you're an addict, relapses happen: I'd learned that growing up from one of Dad's alcoholic friends. In rehab you're taught to prepare for them, recognize them, shut them down. *Pray for potatoes, but grab a hoe,* as they say. The reason for Joey's recent behavior, therefore, was probably more a combination of justified anxiety at the live shows coming up—during which he was expected to *talk,* not sing—and postrelapse shame. After all, he had another pee test due before the next live episode (they were scheduled every six weeks now) and he'd taken so many of my pills—at least forty, by my estimates—that not even an ocean full of Kangen water could flush all traces of the drug from his system. Which meant Joey was probably facing yet another self-inflicted career disaster. I doubted Len would fire him, even so. Way too much hassle. But that wasn't the issue. The issue was Joey's pride. If he failed the pee test, there was a good chance the story would get into *Showbiz,* thus proving Blade Morgan and the rest of Honeyload right about the shit they'd said about him over the years—i.e., that he was the biggest junkie in the band, a terminal fuck-up, and essentially unemployable.

The whole point of Joey taking the job on *Icon* had been "to stick a middle finger up to those fuckin' hypocrites." To say, "Screw you guys, I'm fine." And now . . . it might do the very opposite. Hence Joey sinking lower and lower into a private, croc-filled swamp of despair. His confidence, his swagger . . . his showbiz sheen—it had all gone. Just as Bibi had been afraid of *Icon*'s editors during the prerecorded episodes, Joey was now afraid of himself. *He was paralyzed.* He simply no longer trusted what might come out of his mouth on live TV. The King of Sing had become the Duke of Dull. The best he could manage after a contestant's performance was, "Yeah, that was *nice,* man. You did great."

He said it to everyone.

"That was *nice,* man."

Over and over.

"You did great."

Here was the problem, though: Self-censorship wasn't keeping Joey out of trouble. It was getting him into more trouble, just of a different kind. The Rabbit network wasn't handing over a million dollars per month to the man who had once urinated on Buckingham Palace, eaten a snake during a gig in Tel Aviv, and driven a Lamborghini Countach over Niagara Falls, to have him turn into another JD Coolz. No, they wanted a *rock star*—a lunatic who'd bang and crash around the place, making headlines and offending people. And yet they'd somehow ended up with the very opposite of that. Back at The Lot on Sir Harold Killoch Drive, David Gent was furious. So were Ed Rossitto and Maria Herman-Bloch. If Joey wasn't careful, he was about to become the first celebrity in the history of show business to be fired for not misbehaving enough.

22

Don't Say We Didn't Warn You

March

"ARE YOU READY YET?" I asked the brass telephone.

"Hold on," came the muffled reply.

"What's *taking* so long?"

"Is this gonna be on TV?"

"No."

"So there are no cameras out there?"

"No cameras. You're a contestant in a *singing* competition, remember—not a makeover show."

"You're promising me this isn't going to be on TV?"

"Mia," I said, heavily. "For the ten thousandth time: This is *not* going to be on TV. Please, let's get this over with. It's uncomfortable in here, and hot as hell. Can you open the hatch?"

Finally, Mia Pelosi hung up the receiver. Then a heavy scraping noise, as a bolt slid out of its metal casing.

The hatch opened.

"*Ooooh . . .*" I said, peering through the latticed grille. "That's, uh . . . wow. That's kinda . . ."

We were in a confessional booth—a *real* confession booth, fashioned from carved oak, the panels so distressed by age they had turned almost black. It had been salvaged from the burnt wreckage of a church up in Santa Barbara (or so went the story), shipped down to West Hollywood, and then converted into a novelty dressing room by the owners of Les Couilles En Mer, an erotic-themed boutique on Melrose and Crescent Heights. I'd brought Mia down here between rehearsals—Len had lent us his chauffeur-driven Jaguar for the occasion—to shop for new stage outfits. After Mia, I would do the same for Cassie Turner (more of a challenge, given her preference for dreads and general hobo-wear) and then Jimmy Nugget, and so on.

Under normal circumstances, of course, the contestants' two hundred dollar per episode clothing allowance wouldn't have been enough to buy so much as a single vagina-print T-shirt from this place. (The vaginas are tiny and pink, making them appear at first glance to be a vintage floral pattern.) Today was different, however. Today, as a reward for surviving three elimination nights since the live shows began, the dozen singers who remained in the competition had been presented with a two-thousand-dollar Les Couilles En Mer gift certificate.

The real reason for this? Len had been appalled by their fashion choices to date. "These kids are supposed to be *pop stars,* not sales assistants at Best-bloody-Buy!" he'd yelled, during a staff meeting. The vouchers were therefore designed to encourage more daring outfits, especially for the girls—the best looking of whom by far was the pale yet delicate Mia Pelosi, with her shiny black, just-out-of-bed bangs, and those sad, brown, sorry-about-last-night eyes. For all her hotness, however, Mia had a dress sense that was unusually conservative—a result, I assumed, of her years in the Metropolitan Opera. Len was determined to change that. He wanted some *flesh.* Yes . . . with the ratings still at all-time lows, and Sir Harold due back any moment, things were getting seriously desperate.

So there I was . . . behind the curtain in a former box of repentance, on the sinner's side. In the priest's compartment, meanwhile, was Mia, twirling in front of the open hatch. (When the grille was covered, the booth's oak panels were thick enough to make conversation impossible, hence the antique two-way telephone system.)

"Tell me," said Mia, her right arm rising defensively over her chest. "Is it too . . . *slutty?*"

"Nooo," I reassured, unconvincingly. "It's just . . ." I looked again at the purple sleeveless dress, split to within a millimeter of the crotch to reveal a long, milky (and slightly bruised) left leg. The split was provocative, that was for sure. And yet it was nothing compared with the suicidal free fall of the neckline, which left enough of Mia's surprisingly large breasts on display to put the average male imagination out of business for the duration of "The Power of Love," her first song choice of the night.

"It's funny," said Mia, looking down at herself. "In the opera, I was the trash from New Jersey. Those snooty fucks were always trying to improve me, turn me into one of them—like I was Eliza Doolittle or somethin'. Guess it must have worked. I've never worn anything like this in my life. I mean, it's beautiful, but—"

"Look, Mia," I said. "The dress is . . ."

"*What?*"

Now I noticed the transparent platform heels that completed the outfit. *Oh, what the hell,* I thought.

Exhaling loudly: "It's perfect."

All right, yes . . . *I know* . . . but what else could I say? Len had appointed me chaperone for the "wardrobe-enhancement" trips to Les Couilles En Mer on the sole condition that I *encourage* sluttiness. Or as he'd instructed: "I want every single guy who's watching the show tonight to have a T-Rex vertebra of a boner in his pants when those girls walk on stage. I swear to God, Bill, if you bring me back any of them wearing boyfriend jeans and/or hiking boots, you'll be out of a job faster than you can fix yourself another bowl of organic granola."

"I don't *like* granola," I protested.

"Oh, that's right, I forgot," he sneered. "You're the reason why I tried to buy stock in Cinnabon."

Asshole.

As for the men: Len didn't seem to care what they wore—the exception being Jimmy Nugget. "Make sure he stays more John Wayne, less Jack Twist," he'd ordered. "The dumbest dad in Cow Town might not realize his boy is yodeling for the other team, so to speak, but the last thing we want is a million preteen girls suddenly realizing that their First Big Crush is more into Justin Bieber than they are."

"C'mon, Len," I said. "Just because he's gay doesn't mean he's going to start shopping for . . . *tutus.*"

"You're not seriously going to give me this speech are you, Bill?" sighed Len, wearily.

"I'm just saying that—"

"We're not talking about a gay *librarian* here, Little Miss NPR. We're talking about an unusually promiscuous young fellow who likes to strut around on stage wearing leather chaps while yodeling. I think my concerns are perfectly justified."

"But—"

"JUST KEEP AN EYE ON HIM."

The "wardrobe-enhancement" trips to Les Couilles En Mer weren't my only chaperoning duties, now that season thirteen was fully underway. Not by a long shot. Every week, for example, I had to take the contestants back and forth to the so-called Icon Mansion, billed as the "luxury residence in the Hollywood Hills where our finalists live during their time on the show." It was nothing of the sort, of course: The Icon Mansion was an advertiser-sponsored set over at The Lot, filled with aspirational products. As for the exterior shots, which showed a French Normandy-style château (fish-eye view from the driveway, speeded-up walking tour through the hallways and garden, aerial swoop over the rooftop spires), these were taken from stock footage, supplied by a local real-estate company. In truth, the contestants lived in a Motel 6 between Highland and the 101 Freeway.

Icon Mansion aside, I was also responsible for taking the Final Twelve to their mandatory consultations with various lawyers, accountants, and shrinks on the Zero Management payroll—this being one of Two Svens' more paternalistic initiatives, although it also served another purpose, in that it fulfilled Zero Management's legal obligation to disclose and explain the hundreds, if not thousands, of ways in which the contestants were being reamed from every direction. The meetings were known as the Don't-Say-We-Didn't-Warn-You sessions.

The worst of these was the "contract workshop" with Zero Management's legal team. One by one, the contestants walked into that room with their lives ahead of them . . . and one by them, they emerged, silent and trembling, their lives now wholly owned subsidiaries of the Big Corporation. Escorting those clueless teenagers into that room was like throwing newborn bunnies into a tiger reserve. Still, I soon learned that it was the *smart* ones who shut up and went along with everything, because they understood the politics of the situation. They were unknown. They hadn't sold a single record, music download, concert ticket, or T-shirt. And without *Project Icon,* they had no means of achieving fame beyond the near-impossible odds of going viral on YouTube. Negotiation wasn't even a factor. To negotiate, you need something the other side wants, that it can't get cheaper someplace else. Contestants don't have that in their favor.

It's the whole point of them.

Of all the Final Twelve, only Jimmy Nugget put up any serious resistance. Not that he did any of the complaining himself, of course. No, that was taken care of by his not-actually-so-dumb dad, Big Nugg, who had already shouldered his way into pretty much every meeting involving his son. (You'd glance behind you, and there he'd be, sweating and fussing, putting up his hand every other minute to ask a question.) Big Nugg described reading through his son's ninety-three page contract as "like feelin' all the flames in hell a-lickin' at ma' face"—which of course the lawyers took as a huge compliment. The document in question began as follows:

I, *PRINT NAME HERE*, grant Zero Management unconditional and irrevocable ownership, in perpetuity, throughout all possible universes, in the future and in the past, the sole and exclusive rights to my voice, image, name, likeness, traits, personality, life story, other biographical information, words, actions, original thoughts, catchphrases, facial expressions, clothing, dance moves, *sequences* of dance moves, or any dancelike physical activity . . .

[thirty-eight pages later]

. . . and I agree that the during the making of *Project Icon,* the producers may inflict libel, slander, or any other emotional and/or physical and/or monetary distress upon me, based upon reality or entirely fictitious events . . .

[another twenty-four pages later]

. . . and that if I should disclose the terms of this agreement to anyone for <u>any reason other than court-ordered subpoena</u> it will constitute an act of massive and irreparable injury to Zero Management, Invasion Media, and the Rabbit Network, and I shall be liable for repayment of damages of up to a sum of five hundred million dollars . . .

[another thirty-one pages later]

. . . signed *SIGN AND PRINT NAME HERE*

The first time I read one of these contracts, I was disgusted — even though I'd had to sign a similarly worded nondisclosure agreement before taking my job on the show. I actually remember being pretty mad with Two Svens, who otherwise seemed like an okay-ish guy. It was Mitch, of all people, who later tried to explain to me why it was necessary to take eternal ownership of *Icon*'s annual cast of wannabes — who wanted fame more than they cared about getting a fair deal. "Look, Bill, every season, without fail, one of these kids gets their first whiff of success, some lawyer with hair plugs and a Porsche convinces them they've been screwed, and they file a lawsuit," he said. "That's why the contract is so tough. I've had my own clients sign the exact same kind of agreements. It lets you take more risks—invest more time and money in the talent, without always having to look over his shoulder. In a way, it protects those kids from *themselves*."

"You don't actually *believe* that bullshit, do you?" I laughed.

"Have you ever been sued?"

"No."

"Well, let's talk about this again when you have."

End of discussion.

If Mitch had a point, Big Nugg didn't see it. He just kept shaking his head, muttering to himself, and jiggling his legs with pent-up frustration. It was a clause on page sixty-four, regarding payment (or lack thereof) for Jimmy's services while he was on the show that finally seemed to break his will to keep the peace. "Says here, ma' boy gets paid nothin'—*nothin'!*—unless he wins the whole darn thing!" he exploded, after rising with a tremendous grunt from his chair. "What the heck kind of a scam you folks runnin' here? He'd earn more as a goddamn fruit picker!"

I wondered if Big Nugg had missed the part which said that if even in the event Jimmy *did* win, his prize would be five hundred dollars as "full and final consideration," set against expenses for flights, accommodation, food, and clothing throughout the season, which meant he would actually end up with nothing. Actually, *less* than nothing: Whatever negative balance remained would be taken out of his earnings, assuming there *were* any. That's why only two contestants in *Project Icon*'s history, both winners, had ever received any kind of paycheck.

The attorneys (seven in total) looked at one another carefully, faking concern. Then one of them spoke: "We completely understand if Jimmy doesn't want to sign."

This took the fight out of Big Nugg almost instantly.

" . . . you do?" he said.

"Oh, *of course!*" the lawyer soothed. "He should never sign *anything* he's not comfortable with." Then, with a quick glance at his colleagues: "This conversation is being recorded, right? Just in case any of us need to refresh our memories in future."

The others nodded.

"Okay," said Big Nugg, calmer now. "So what you offerin'?"

"Just let us know by the end of the day if Jimmy wants to leave the show."

"Huh?"

"If Jimmy doesn't like the contract."

"What you sayin'?"

"If Jimmy doesn't want to sign, Mr. Nugget, you need to let us know as soon as possible, because we'll need to find a replacement for him. I believe we eliminated a country-western singer a few weeks ago. We'll need to call him back. Make arrangements."

"You mean . . . ?"

"I really don't know how to make this any clearer."

"So it's *this*"—Big Nugg shook the contract in his hand—"or ma' boy's *off the show?*"

"I think you've finally captured the essence of the situation, yes."

The muscles in Big Nugg's neck were so tight now, I half expected them to pop through the skin. Clearly, the cattle ranching business in Nebraska had never taught him the concept of leverage. Or maybe it had, but he simply hadn't expected it to apply to the business of talent, which seemed so much more . . . *artistic* than that.

"C'mon, Little Nugg," he said, gesturing to his son. "This just ain't goddamn *right.*"

Little Nugg stood up and put on his cowboy hat. And with that, the pair of them left the room.

The lawyers checked their watches and didn't move.

One minute eighteen seconds later, Jimmy came back and asked where to sign.

The contract had already been laid out neatly on the desk.

23

Whatta Man

SO LEN JUST ABOUT gave me a raise when he saw Mia's dress. "Oh, Mamma Mia, you look delightful!" he exclaimed, his untrustworthy green eyes fixed on her nonexistent neckline. "Such elegance! Such class!" Then, grinning: *"Mes couilles dansent de joie!"*

I had no idea what the hell he was talking about. Mia, on the other hand, seemed to understand very well (all those operas had made her fluent in six languages, as I might have already mentioned). When Len pranced away, Merm shivering with pleasure, she looked at me with disgust and spat, "You promised me it wasn't slutty! I don't want some . . . *old guy* telling me his *balls are dancing for joy.*"

"That's what he said?" I coughed. The depth of Len's creepiness never lost its ability to shock me.

"And now I've got nothin' else to wear, you *bitch,*" Mia went on, with a nasal sob.

She was due on stage in five minutes. Too late for any wardrobe changes.

I guess I should have been mad at Mia for calling me a bitch—but part of me thought she had a point. I mean, the dress wasn't exactly to my taste. Then again, "The Power of Love" wasn't exactly to my taste, either. (Nor were any of the other songs she'd performed on *Project Icon.*) But for the show, for what Len *wanted,* the dress was perfect. So what was I supposed to have told her back there in the confession booth—that she should buy something else, something Len would hate?

Besides, it wasn't like I'd chosen it for her: She'd taken it off the rack herself.

"Look, Mia, I'm just doing my job here," I explained, without much conviction (if my eighteen-year-old self could have heard me say that, she would have vomited). "Len loves the dress. And he might be old and a bit of a pervert, but he's the boss, so be happy that he's happy. Oh, and if people think it's too revealing—*so what?* You're beautiful, you've got an incredible body, and you'll get a ton of attention . . . and attention means votes. It can only help your career."

"You people," she muttered. "You're so full of it."

"In case you've forgotten, Mia," I said, irritated now, "*you're* the one who picked out the damn—"

I'd become distracted.

"What is it?" demanded Mia, reddening.

"Your, um . . . your left side."

"What d'you mean, my left—?"

"The . . . your, um . . . you might want to—"

She looked down.

"OH MY GOD."

"Wow," I said, "the *whole thing* just popped out like that, huh? Can't you use sticky tape or something?"

"Fuck you, Bill. FUCK YOU." Mia teetered angrily for a moment on her plastic heels—almost falling into me—then clattered away to the nearest mirror.

She was right, of course: I *was* full of it. Or a lot more full of it than I used to be, anyway. It was the only way to survive in this place. I'd even started to *believe* some of my bullshit—especially when it came to the day-to-day management of the judges' egos. Nevertheless, it was true what I'd said about the importance of being noticed on the show. In fact, Two Svens had made the same point in a mass e-mail to contestants a few days after the Don't-Say-We-Didn't-Warn-You sessions. Len had printed it out and stuck it to the green room wall.

It read:

From: Svendsen, Sven [Zero Management]
To: All Talent
Subject: YOU!

Some advice before we head into these final live episodes. As a finalist on *Project Icon,* you will experience your career in reverse. Why? Because from now until the end of the season, you will have America's *undivided attention* for an entire hour of prime-time TV, twice a week. No matter how successful you later become, you will never, ever get this kind of exposure again in your lives! Which means you must seize the audience while you have the opportunity; convert as many viewers into fans as you possibly can. When the season wraps, you will ALL find yourselves moving backward. A few of you will get through it, and go on to sell many, many records. *Most of you will not.* Just remember this: You are the Benjamin Buttons of show business — you are starting your careers at a point where most successful artists end them. So don't just walk out on stage every night and sing. DEMAND to be seen and heard!
T.S.

And guess what? By this measure, *any measure,* Mia's dress was a triumph during that night's broadcast. And not because of any malfunctions, thank God. (Taking my advice, she'd borrowed some adhesive strips from the Glam Squad, so nothing short of a magnitude 9.2 quake under the studio could have shaken loose the two ounces of fabric that stood between her and a public indecency fine.) No, the dress was enough on its own to turn Mia into an instant phenomenon.

"At Last! (But Too Late?) — *Icon* Finds the Power of Glamour, Buzz," read the headline above Chaz Chipford's as-it-happens blog on the *ShowBiz* website — next to a picture of Mia, taken from the balcony, looking down. It was the probably the nicest thing *ShowBiz* had written about the show all season. But that wasn't even the best part. No, the best part was the spontaneous Twitter meme that developed while Mia was still on stage, under the hashtag #mammarymia. I mean, okay, a lot of it was obscene. Really quite shockingly obscene. But still, by the time we cut to the second break, she was "trending."

Or her boobs were, anyway.

Len was so happy, he high-fived me backstage — my first nonironic high five since fifth grade.

And Mia?

Still furious.

"Thanks to *you,* I'm a national fuckin' punchline," she raged, after hunting me down when the show was over. By then I was sitting cross-legged on a flightcase in the green room, wearing my super-ugly, emergency-backup pair of glasses — my right contact lens had fallen out earlier — and preparing scripts for the contestants to read during Michael Bolton Week. (Those quirky little backstories they tell about the songs they're about to sing? *Always ghostwritten.* They're also usually about as true as Tad Dunkel's tale of Frankie the tragic dachshund.)

"You're kidding, right?" I said, with genuine surprise. "You're *trending* on Twitter."

"You think I care about *Twitter?*" she yelled. She was livid. "If I'm *trending,* I want it to be for my work — not 'cause I'm 'Mammary Mia.' I'm an *artist,* not some . . . reality star."

"Mia, I hate to break this to you," I said, delicately. "But *Project Icon* is a reality show. And you're one of its stars. As of tonight, in fact, I'd say you're its biggest star."

"No — I'm its biggest fuckin' *joke.*" She was about to cry.

"Oh, c'mon, Mia. You're taking this way too — "

"You don't give a shit about any of us, do you?" she yelped, now shivering from cold or misery, I couldn't quite tell which. "We're all just *expendable* to you. All you care about is kissing Len's ass. Anything for the ratings, and your goddamn precious 'career.' God, it must really suck to be such a heartless bitch. Well, I guess you got what you wanted tonight. I hope it makes you happy."

She almost broke the door on the way out.

For a moment, I felt horrible. Worse than horrible. As much as Mia was becoming a pain in the ass of Bibi-esque proportions, it wasn't a good feeling, being accused of deliberately turning someone into a walking punchline. (I knew from my years as the "freckled dorkworm" at Babylon High how painful it was to be the butt of everyone's jokes.) At the same time, my patience with Mia was rapidly approaching its limit. I mean, was it just me, or was #mammarymia kind of brilliant —and funny? And surely it was ridiculous to suggest that caring about the ratings made me a "heartless bitch." *Of course I cared about the ratings.* It wasn't just about saving my job. It was about keeping the entire franchise on the air! Hadn't Mia been reading *ShowBiz?* Didn't she understand that if our numbers didn't improve before Sir Harold's return from Germany, *Project Icon* would be gone, for good?

The ratings were as much about *her* career as they were mine.

I must have sat there in the green room for ten minutes, going through all this in my head while sipping on a cup of instant coffee that managed to smell—and taste—like burning plastic. Still, at least it was keeping me awake, and it was the best I could get in the studio without having to bribe one of Teddy's assistants to sneak into the invitation-only judges' lounge and smuggle out a nonfat cappuccino made by Nico DeLuca, *Icon*'s implausibly accented in-house barista ("Dude sounds like a Euro retard, but *shit,* his coffee's Grade A," as Joey had announced a few days earlier. "One sip is like mainlining an eightball of coke into both fuckin' eyeballs . . . and I say that as a guy who once mainlined an eightball of coke into both fuckin' eyeballs.")

I was just about to get back to work when a voice made me jump. "Hey, why so glum? You okay?"

Looking up, I saw Mitch in the doorway, a nerdy little backpack in one hand, a stack of binders in the other. "No," I replied, not bothering to lie. "I'm not okay."

"What's up? Is it the *coffee?* You didn't use that instant crap, did you? It's about ten years out of date. I can ask Joey to get you some of the good stuff if you want."

"It's not the coffee," I sighed. "It's the contestants."

"Listen," said Mitch. "Don't worry about the contestants. They're expendable. Oh, and it looks like we'll get a big pickup in the ratings tonight. *Finally,* huh? Amazing what you can do with a slutty dress and all those filthy minds on Twitter."

"Yeah, amazing." I managed half a smile.

"See ya tomorrow. And, Bill?"

"Uh-huh?"

"Make sure to buy yourself a copy of *Cheer the Fuck Up* magazine on your way out."

With that, he was gone for the night.

I couldn't help but feel pleased about the ratings. Mia had no idea how lucky she was. Len would protect her now. *She was a star.* That dress had pretty much guaranteed her a place in the Final Three—if the season lasted that long. Better than that, of course, was the fact that I'd been partly responsible for it, and by extension, all the free publicity. Maybe this was leverage. Maybe I could use it to get a raise out of Len . . . *Jesus, Sash, listen to yourself,* I thought, *you're becoming one of them.*

There was no denying it: I'd changed so much since joining *Project Icon,* I sometimes hardly recognized the words that came out of my own mouth. Was I becoming a cynic? Or was I just seeing things a lot more clearly now? Another possibility: I was simply getting better at my job. Whatever the case, it was making me think about everything in a different way—even Hawaii. What Joey told me in Maison Chelsea had put doubt in my mind. It wasn't that I no longer wanted to write. No, I wanted to write more than anything else—especially now, with all this *material* everywhere—but what if Joey had a point, what if I'd ruin paradise by making it my home? *What was it he'd said exactly?* "Beautiful place, man, don't get me wrong. But live there? Try it, I dare ya. Relaxation is stagnation."

Also — I didn't even want to admit this — I was getting tired of Brock. Every time he called, he was high. Giggling pathetically. Then he'd start telling me some circular, thirty-minute anecdote about a practical joke he'd played on Pete that was, like, *so awesome,* and I'd have to invent an excuse to get off the phone. Then he'd call me again, and I'd put him through to voicemail. *What kind of person puts their boyfriend through to voicemail all the time?* His most recent message:

> "Hey, sexy! [*Cue ten seconds of giggling.*] Look, Sash, I've been thinking. I've been thinking you should just quit *Project Icon.* I mean, you hate it in LA, right? Man, I can't even believe you've lasted this long. And this is bullshit, us not being together. Come to Honolulu, Sash. Get on the next plane, like you said you were gonna do that one time. We'll figure it out. I got some money from my dad. I got a place here. I mean, Pete is sleeping on the sofa, but you're cool with that, right? He says hi, by the way. You're gonna love this Afghan resin his buddy got him from the Navy. The other day, we spent all afternoon just sitting on the beach, smoking that stuff and looking for dick-shaped clouds. [*A full minute of giggling.*] I wish you could have been there, Sash. Some funny shit. Anyhow, call me, okay? No more *Project Icon. Call me back.* Love ya, babe."

Why couldn't I listen to this without cringing? Maybe it was because he was so high, he probably wouldn't even remember having left the message by the time he woke up. And if all this was irritating me so much *now,* was it really such a great idea to go live with him on a distant tropical island? I didn't know the answer to that question any more. I wasn't sure of *anything.*

It was getting late. Although *Project Icon* went out at five o'clock, local time (which meant eight on the East Coast) there'd been so many logistical issues this week — missing caterers, broken mixing desk, outbreak of the flu — I hadn't been able to start work on Michael Bolton Week until seven. And now, thanks to Mia's outburst, it was almost eight thirty. I was hungry and tired. And, I had to admit, a little depressed.

Sighing, I snapped my laptop shut. There was no way I could concentrate on work right now. I needed to go home. Have a glass of wine. Sleep.

I drained my coffee and threw the cup at the trash, missing by about twelve feet. Pathetic. I was about to try again when my phone broke into the chorus of "Whatta Man."

I stared at the vibrating plastic for a moment, baffled.

What the . . . ?

Then I looked at the screen, and burst out laughing. "BORIS" said the caller ID. He must have put his name into my contacts book—and programmed that ringtone—while he was showing me his friend's translation app at Soba Kitchen.

"You're *unbelievable,*" I said, accepting the call.

"I had a feeling you might be a Salt-N-Pepa girl," he replied. "I mean, I know you *say* you're into all that 'smart-people' music—like that growly voiced dude Tim Watts or whatever—but I'm not buying it. I think you have some hidden shallows, Sasha King."

It was hard to believe I hadn't seen him since the night of Maison Chelsea, which was—what?—a month ago now. He'd tried to rearrange our date several times, of course, but things had just been too crazy. Besides, I had a boyfriend.

"So hey," Boris went on. "I got your message on eCupidMatch."

I was confused: I hadn't sent him a message. Then a terrible image came to mind: *Mrs. Zglagovvcini.* Or rather, Mrs. Zglagovvcini—half-blind even with her reading glasses on—bent over the yellowing keys of her ancient, wheezing PC. Oh, no.

"You didn't need to be so hard on yourself," said Boris, as I crouched down and bit into my fist.

"What do you mean?" I groaned, eyes closed. *Oh, what did you say, Mrs. Zglagovvcini?*

"Look, I admire that level of . . . honesty," Boris continued. "But you've gotta give yourself a break."

"Thank you, Boris," I said, deciding not to probe any further. I just didn't want to know.

"No—thank *you,*" he said.

" . . . for what?"

"For what you said about me. I mean, heh-heh—it's not every day a girl calls you—"

"Please don't mention it."

"I mean—"

"Seriously, Boris. Whatever it was. *Don't mention it.*"

Boris coughed, awkwardly.

"So, anyway," I said, ending the brief silence on the line. "I tried out your friend's new phone app the other day. I had no idea the Russian dry cleaner around the corner from me was offering happy-ending massages in its alterations department."

"Guess most cops don't speak Russian."

"Guess."

"By the way," said Boris. "I meant to say I'm sorry about what happened with your boyfriend."

I wanted to throw the phone on the floor and jump on it.

"I mean, what a *douche,*" he went on. "He gets a cushy bar job at some tiny hotel *in Hawaii* and you're the one who has to save up all the money, working day and night, only ever coming home to eat take-out food alone in front of the TV, even though what you *really* want is just to find a good guy, settle down in the country, and have kids. Wow, Sash. That dude sucks ass. And he's never even been over to visit you? *Not once?* Some guys have no idea how lucky . . . anyway, I'm glad you dumped him. I'm sorry. But I'm glad."

"I don't know what to say, Boris."

"You don't always have to contact me through eCupidMatch, y'know," he replied. "You've got my e-mail, right? And you can call. Anytime. My number's in your phone."

"I'm actually gonna shut down that eCupidMatch account," I said, my voice hardening. "As soon as I get home, trust me. I'm going to talk to my, uh, service provider, and I'm going to tell her to *mind her own goddamn business* from now on. I mean, uh, I'm going to, y'know, terminate my profile. I'm over it, to be honest with you."

"Hey," said Boris, "how'd you like to come over this Saturday and taste my granddad's — "

"Don't say it."

"*Meatballs.* He was Polish: left me some great recipes. I'm having some friends over at noon."

"I'd love that, Boris. But I gotta go. Sorry. My boss is calling me over. Speak later."

"Okay, talk to you — "

Click.

Truth was, Len wasn't anywhere to be seen. I was just out of breath.

I *liked* Boris.

Way too much.

24

The Talent and the Glory

IT WAS DARK BY the time I left Greenlit Studios. One of those surprisingly cold LA nights—with a huge, bright moon, the kind that follows you around so much, you feel like taking out a restraining order. The coyotes would be out later, I suspected, howling down from the hills. I wondered if Joey would do what he usually did on such occasions, and climb onto the roof of his house to howl right back at them.

Not likely. It had been weeks now since Joey's relapse, but he still hadn't returned to his former self. He was clean, at least: Mitch had established this beyond any reasonable doubt—with Mu and Sue acting as round-the-clock enforcers.

But Joey's funk hadn't lifted. Which meant he was still—I swear—the most boring judge on the panel. "Yeah, that was *nice,* man," went his tediously predictable nightly criticisms. "You did great." If *Project Icon* hadn't been in mortal danger, Ed Rossitto would almost certainly have fired him by now. Ironically, it was the show's weakness that had convinced Ed against such a radical move. *Project Icon* couldn't afford to make itself look vulnerable, not now. A midseason panel rethink would do exactly that. To the likes of Chaz Chipford at *ShowBiz,* it would be like seeing blood in the water. Instead, the show had to pretend it was still invincible. Hence Wayne's repeated claim that season thirteen had generated "more votes than any previous season in the HISTORY of our show"—without any acknowledgment that this was possible only because Rabbit had started to count the results of spam surveys and pop-up ads on third-party websites. In reality, the number of *telephone votes* was down by eighty percent . . .

I checked the time on my cell phone as I walked out into the parking lot: almost nine o'clock. The place was empty. Just Two Svens' Bugatti convertible, some crew vehicles, and my bicycle—its frame and front wheel chained to the fence. It was so cold, I had to pull my cardigan sweater tight around me and readjust the belt. Then a rush of air behind me. Turning, I saw Len's dark green Jaguar, which had come to a halt noiselessly about five feet away. The window was down, framing Len's Merm between the chrome pillars. Beside him was his wife, the scowling woman from accounts. I remembered her from my first day.

"Good work with that dress," said Len. "At last, *you're learning.* Now let's hope those tits translate into to some fucking ratings tomorrow. From what I hear, Sir Harold is due back first thing. We need all the help we can get, Billy the Kiddo."

"Here's hoping," I said, feeling dirtied by the compliment.

"Well, good night. Sleep well in Siberia."

Len's grin disappeared behind privacy glass as the Jaguar pulled away. After a few yards, however, the car stopped again. The window reopened. Len had forgotten something.

"Oh, and Bill," he called out. "I don't know if you're going for some kind of ironic dweeb look or something, but I think those glasses are the worst thing I've seen you wear to date. And frankly they're up against some pretty impressive competition."

"They're my *emergency* backup pair," I protested.

"They're an emergency in their own right, Bill," said Len. "For God's sake, buy some new ones."

"Is that all?"

"I guess we can discuss those pants another day. That's a ketchup stain, right?"

I looked down. He was wrong: It was in fact *two* ketchup stains, but one had annexed the other to form a larger, more influential federation of residue. When I raised my head to explain this, however, Len was no longer there. The Jaguar was already at the studio gate, tail lights on, turn signal flashing.

"Asshole," I muttered, returned to the task of putting on my helmet. No sooner had I got it on than I became aware of something else behind me. A voice, getting closer.

Couldn't everyone just leave me alone?

"Bill? Is that you, Bill?"

I turned wearily. The owner of the voice had now almost reached me. "Hey—it *is* Bill, right?"

"*David?*" I gasped, my face changing color instantly. It was Bibi's chauffeur. The hot one. He was dressed in skinny jeans and a puffy, dark-colored sleeveless vest, with a pair of headphones—or maybe they were earmuffs—around his neck. He reminded me of a life-size action figure. Only somehow more perfect.

"How did you know my name?" he replied, confused. Then he remembered. Snapping his fingers: "The ride to Bibi's, right? In the Rolls. Well, you certainly have a lot of powerful folk chasing after you, Bill. We're waiting for you on the roof."

"*We?* . . . what are you talking ab—"

"Follow me."

"But my bicycle."

"You can bring it with you if you want. But I don't recommend it. Heh, not where *we're* going."

I took David's advice and locked it up again, only this time without removing the wheel. Then I allowed him to lead the way, wondering what Bibi could possibly want from me this evening. We traversed the parking lot, left the studio grounds through a side gate, crossed Gower

Street, then entered the lower floor of a high-rise parking structure opposite. Two elevators gaped open in front of us. We took the first, with David tapping a button marked "H," whatever that stood for.

A giddy sensation as we rose.

"Are we going to Bibi's again?" I asked.

David smiled. "Bibi isn't my *only* client, y'know," he said. "I'm in the general transportation business. Celebrities. Politicians. High net worth individuals."

"So this isn't about Bibi?"

"You'll see."

The doors opened to reveal the top-floor level of the parking structure, the moon hanging there in front of us, huge and solemn. But I wasn't looking at the moon. I was looking at the large white H-shape in front of me—on top of which was resting a sleek white helicopter, its windshield shaped like the visor of motorcycle helmet. The rotors were spinning. "Here, you might want to wear these," shouted David over the noise, taking off his ear muffs and handing them to me. "If you wanna talk, plug 'em into the outlet next to you, there's a mic built into the cord. You'll figure it out." Then he pulled open the rear door and helped me inside.

This was insanity.

I'd never been in a helicopter. Then again, this machine didn't resemble any helicopter I'd ever seen before—not on the TV, not the movies, not *anywhere.* The cabin, for example, was even more unsparingly appointed than Bibi's Rolls-Royce—a feat I wouldn't have thought possible if I hadn't seen it for myself. Seating was provided by six retrocontoured armchairs in white leather. Under foot: floors made from some exotic timber. And between the chairs was a glowing console, outlined in blue LEDs, which served as both an armrest and a glass-topped champagne cooler. An open bottle was locked in place, next to a single tethered flute.

I was now alone, harness in place, looking out of the vast, bulbous window. David, meanwhile, had climbed in through the co-pilot's door and was also seated, checking instruments, making hand signals. He still hadn't told me where we were going, what we were doing, who had organized all this. And by the time I'd plugged in my headset to ask him once more, we were already in the air.

It felt as though we were barely moving.

"Have some champagne," said David, his voice in my ear. "He bought it especially for you."

"*He?* Who's he? Where are we *going?* This is crazy, David, you have to tell me now."

"Relax. You'll find out soon enough. Drink the champagne."

I did as he said. It was a midnineties Dom Pérignon, according to the label. Still, I couldn't exactly savor the taste when I didn't know what this was all about. Of all the people I knew, *who* had the means to send for me in a helicopter—*this* helicopter? Certainly not Len. David seemed to have ruled out Bibi, pretty much. Two Svens? Unlikely, given that he could see me whenever he wanted to at work. Joey? No, he *hated* helicopters—they made him nervous. And it couldn't be Sir Harold Killoch, because he was still in Germany. Besides, what possible reason could the Big Corp CEO have for this kind of ego display?

It took perhaps five or six minutes for us to reach the ocean. The aircraft banked. For a moment, I felt suddenly light-headed. Then we turned up the coast—ocean to one side, the lights of Highway 1 to the other. For the first time, I felt wind buffet the cabin. We seemed to be descending, somewhere near Malibu.

Static in my headset.

"Can you see it yet?" asked David.

I looked out of my window. Ocean everywhere now—the color of poured concrete in the moonlight. We must have been a mile or two offshore. Then spots of white in the gray vastness, gleaming brighter as we lost altitude. Was it an island? *A boat?*

More static.

"He named it *The Talent and the Glory,*" announced David, answering my question. "Took delivery last week. If you believe *ShowBiz* magazine—which I don't, personally—it cost fifty million bucks. The guys I work for say it was more like twice that."

"Damnit, David, *tell me who he is,*" I said. By now, I had a pretty good idea, of course.

"Four hundred and four feet long," he continued, ignoring me. "Forty-eight thousand horsepower. Maximum speed: twenty-eight knots. What we're about to land on is the basketball court, which he installed especially for his good friend, the president of the United States. Prez was out here on Monday, actually. Amazing the kind of company you can keep when you own a boy's toy like this."

The deck was right below us now. Any moment . . . any moment . . . bab-da-*bump.*

We were down.

David climbed out.

My door slid open.

Slowing rotors. Floodlights. Salt in the breeze.

It took me a second to recognize the figure standing there, waiting. Dark sweater, canvas pants . . . sockless feet in tasseled loafers. Not the usual open-shirted attire. Even the *hair* threw me off: It was loose and floppy, entirely devoid of product, like he'd just come out of the hot tub or shower. The voice, however — well, the voice was unmistakable. Somehow both oily and hoarse. It brought to mind gin cocktails, duty-free cigarettes, and carpeted bedrooms from 1985.

"Well, this isn't quite Hawaii," it crooned. "But we could sail there in a week or two from here."

"*Nigel Crowther,*" I said, dumbly.

"Oh, the pleasure's all mine."

25
El Woofaleah

I WAS SURPRISED AT HOW tiny and ancient Nigel Crowther appeared when he wasn't on camera. He couldn't have been much younger than Len, in fact. There was also an unsettling . . . *femininity* about him. Something to do with the tone of his skin—as though the outer layer had been peeled away—plus of course those infamous twin protrusions from under his sweater. It was extraordinary that Crowther's nipples were visible at all, given the thickness of the fabric that covered them—which made you wonder if it were somehow deliberate. The breasts, too, were unavoidable: great swollen mounds, not quite of Mia Pelosi dimensions, but large enough to make his belly seem almost modest in comparison.

"I, uh . . . I like your helicopter," I said, not sure of the etiquette in such a situation.

"You're quite an awkward girl, aren't you, Sasha?" replied Crowther, who'd noticed me staring at his chest. I hadn't meant to be so obvious. "That is your real name, isn't it: *Sasha?* I never approved of the way Len turned you into Bill. How dehumanizing. Then again, it's the only way Len knows. They gave him a terrible time at school, y'know, especially when he took up tap dancing. Imagine that: Chiswick Technical School, west London, just after the war—and there was Len, a sickly kid with curly hair and a passion for musical theater. There were toilet plungers in Chiswick which spent less time in the bowl than he did. Created a monster, if you ask me. And yet not a very *effective* monster, judging by those abysmal ratings. Anyway, come on inside."

He paused.

"Oh," he added, handing me an iPad with a stylus attached. "And if you wouldn't mind signing this. Standard nondisclosure agreement. Can't have you telling anyone about this little meeting, I'm afraid. But I think you'll want to hear what I've got to say."

Squinting, I tried to read the words on the display, but there was too much glare from the floodlights on my glasses. I gave up and signed anyway. I mean, what was I going to do—refuse, get back on the helicopter, and go home? Maybe Crowther wouldn't even let me *use* the helicopter. Maybe I'd have to swim.

"Jolly good," he said, as I handed the device back to him. "This way, my dear."

I followed him into the yacht's relentlessly modern entertaining area: a white box, essentially, with sharp-angled sofas, a circular fire pit, and brushed steel fixtures. It was an obsessive-compulsive's fantasy in there, a clean-room laboratory masquerading as a living room. The only vaguely organic-looking matter was supplied by the tall women with tiny waists draped everywhere—on the sofas, by the bar, inside the bubble chair that hung from the ceiling. In fact, I could see only one male: He was older than me, smirking, with a reddish mullet. He looked uncomfortably familiar. Was he from Rabbit? Invasion Media? Or perhaps the New York office of Zero Management? Then it came to me, and my fists balled involuntarily. It was . . . I couldn't even *believe* I was in the same room . . . it was that asshole reporter, Chaz Chipford, from *ShowBiz* magazine.

"You *know* him?" I hissed to Crowther, trying not to glare at the man who'd made a career out of running front-page "exclusives" predicting *Project Icon*'s demise.

"Who? *Chaz?* Oh, yeah."

"He's your friend?"

"God, no. Can't stand him. Dreadful little man."

"Then . . . why is he here?"

Crowther stopped walking and turned to me. We were in the middle of the room. Chaz was about ten feet away—too far to hear us over the nondescript Latin-themed lounge music. "They really don't teach you very much at *Project Icon,* do they?" he said. "Rule number one, Sasha: *Always look after the press.* That means lots of hot girls, otherwise known as publicists. It also means free booze, finger buffets, gifts, upgrades, whatever you can throw at them. Cash, if you must."

"You're kidding."

"Absolutely not. Chaz writes whatever I ask him to, more or less. Oh, and see those lights over there?" He pointed out of the window: Beyond it, I could just about trace the illuminated outline of a smaller vessel. I was surprised I hadn't noticed it from the air.

"Paparazzi," he said. "I invited them here myself. I even chartered the boat for them. And you know what that means? It means I know exactly what they're up to, all hours of the day. It also means they keep *other* paparazzi away, to protect their turf. It gives me control, Sasha. I get to be photographed at my best, when I'm not eating. No one looks good when they're eating, Sasha. Remember that. It's important."

"But . . . don't these journalists have . . . *ethics?*"

"C'mon, Sasha. Chaz Chipford isn't exactly a contender for any literary prizes. Look at him: He's pathetic. Entertainment reporters have all the sophistication of single-cell amoebas. Have you ever been to a junket before? My God, it's depressing. Full of broke, ugly, desperate morons. You don't even have to pay them for a good review most of the time. A free drink and two minutes with a celebrity is enough. It's incredible that the likes of Len Braithwaite hasn't figured that out yet. He won't even provide an open bar for the press at *Project Icon,* never mind a massage room. No wonder the trades have been so hostile. Well, it's too late now."

Suddenly, Crowther stood back, grinned, and opened his arms.

Someone he knew was approaching from behind me. I turned—and felt blood drain from my face.

Then I almost lost my balance.

"Hello, Sasha," said my former boss. "It's been a while."

"*Bill,*" I croaked.

"The one and only," he replied, "Although thanks to you, that's not exactly true any more, is it? I hear you stole my identity. Just don't take out any credit cards in my name!"

"But I thought you—?"

"All faked," interrupted Crowther. "The accident, the light falling from the rig—the blood, the ambulance. That's why we did it in Denver. We knew no one would ever go visit him."

"But . . . *why?*" I could barely move my jaw.

"Bill had a contract he couldn't get out of, and I needed his help. It's not easy setting up a franchise like *The Talent Machine* in eighteen months, y'know. I wanted the best of the best. And Bill here was at the top of my list."

"Sorry, Sash," offered Bill, sheepishly. "He made it worth my while."

"Len is gonna freak out!" I blurted.

"Len will *never know,*" said Crowther, firmly. "Remember our little agreement?"

"Oh, the nondisclosure thing, right . . . look, I don't mean to be rude, Nigel, *but why am I here?* What was the whole deal with the helicopter? Why am I in Malibu, on a yacht with a basketball court for the president, at ten o'clock at night? I don't understand."

"We should talk in private," he said. "Come to my room."

"Nigel," I said, raising my hands in protest. "I really don't think—"

"Relax, for God's sake, I'm not Joey Lovecraft. This is strictly business. This way."

He escorted me out of the room, through a door with a raised threshold, and down a narrow hallway.

"You *like* Joey, don't you?" said Crowther, when we reached the master suite.

"I'm mad at him, actually," I replied.

Now we were inside. The room looked pretty much the same as the entertainment area, only with a low, Japanese-style (i.e., hard) bed in the center, covered with monochromatic throw pillows. The entire yacht was such a heterosexual bachelor cliché, I couldn't help but wonder if its owner was trying to prove something.

"Yeah, but you *like* him," Crowther continued, pulling out a chair for me by his desk. "Even though I can tell from the look on your face that he's already made some kind of awful pass at you. God, how predictable. I bet he tried to win you over with the parachute story. That's his masterpiece, the parachute story. Such a shame it isn't true."

"What do you mean, *it isn't true?*" I said, feeling unexpectedly defensive. "Of course it's true! A hundred thousand people were at that gig. They all saw it happen. *It was on TV.*"

"Trust me: He didn't jump out of that plane."

"But that's . . . ridiculous."

"He didn't *jump,* Sasha. Blade Morgan *pushed* him."

"Oh, c'mon."

"Believe what you want. The truth is, Joey screwed Blade's wife. Knocked her up. And while he was screwing her *in Blade's own bed,* he also took the liberty of stealing his drugs—even more of a betrayal, in those days. He's a very twisted man, Joey Lovecraft. All the fault of his Danish mother, apparently—she used to throw boiling water at him when he sat under her piano. Anyway, in the plane, Joey gave Blade that whole speech about jumping—how the band was worth more to him than his own life, et cetera, et cetera—and before he could finish it, Blade just pushed him out. He figured that if Joey was going to die anyway, he might as well have the satisfaction of being the one who killed him. Then obviously he changed his mind, and went out and caught him."

"How can you be so *sure?*"

"Blade is a good friend. He regrets saving Joey to this day—wakes up in the night screaming about it. He says that if he'd let Joey die, Honeyload would have hired a new singer, and the last thirty-five years might have actually been fun."

"*He* sounds like the twisted one."

"Joey's not the *worst* of your colleagues, of course," Nigel went on, ignoring me. "God, no. I mean, who could ever hope to compete with Wayne Shoreline? He's a functioning psychopath, y'know. Len showed me the medical file that Rabbit had to send to the insurance company when he joined the show. Absolutely terrifying."

"Yeah," I said. "I know about Wayne."

I wished Crowther would get to the point. This was getting exhausting. But he seemed to be relishing this opportunity to speak ill of his former coworkers.

"Let me tell you something about Wayne, Sasha," he said. "The morning of the first ever 'results show'—in the days when *Project Icon* had only one voting line, because no one thought we'd make it past the midnight time slot in August—he called me at home. Told me he had a plane waiting, and we needed to go somewhere special for a late breakfast. Of course I was intrigued, so I went along for the ride. We flew down past San Diego, across Baja California, and over to some godforsaken island in the Gulf of California. Must have taken an hour and fifteen minutes to get there, maybe a bit longer. Anyway, so we land on this island—which is part of Mexico—and go to its only restaurant. Wayne insists on ordering for both us: some kind of thick—almost black—very spicy stew. It's the last thing I want to eat for breakfast, frankly. I can get only two or three spoonfuls down. But Wayne, he practically licks his plate clean, grinning the whole time. Then he gets the chef to come out and explain to us what it is we've just eaten.

"You know what the chef did? He just *whistled*—and all these dogs came running out of the backyard. Young dogs. Puppies. Very cute. Then he points to them and makes a throat-slitting motion. That's what was in the stew: *Puppy.* 'El Woofaleah,' the dish was called. Some ancient Mayan recipe, apparently. Or maybe it was Aztec. Whatever. Obviously, I was terribly upset. I happen to like puppies very much. But then Wayne got very serious. He told me that when he looked in the contestants' eyes that evening, he wanted to be utterly without mercy. El Woofaleah had been his mental preparation—like he was Muhammad Ali, getting ready for a fight. *'I don't want to feel like a human being,'* he said. And in truth, I think it helped him during the broadcast. He single-handedly delivered the most exquisite cruelty that Americans had ever witnessed on live TV. Back then, remember, we'd all seen kids get voted off reality shows before. But what Wayne did . . . oh, it was very different. I mean, here was a guy who walked on stage knowing that he'd just eaten a *puppy* for breakfast. No one ever called it a 'results show' again after that. God, no—it was an *elimination night.*"

"This is a joke, right?" I said, wanting to throw up.

"Ask Wayne," shrugged Crowther, as the intercom on his desk lit up. Crowther reached for the handset. "Okay, I'll be right there, captain," he said. Then, to me: "One moment. I'm needed on the bridge." When he left the room, I put my head in my hands. So much information to process. Bill Redmond wasn't on life support. *ShowBiz* reporters took bribes in exchange for positive coverage. Joey hadn't jumped out of that plane. *Wayne Shoreline ate puppies for breakfast.*

I needed a drink of water. Looking around, I noticed an unopened bottle on Crowther's desk, so I reached over to get it, glancing at his laptop as I did so. The e-mail program was running, with a message in the center of the screen. I tried not to look . . . but couldn't resist. The "From" line was familiar enough, but the rest was in some unintelligible font. I peered closer—I couldn't make out a single word—and then almost fell off my chair with fright when something moved against my right leg. False alarm: It was my phone, vibrating. Composing myself, I pulled it out of the buttoned cargo pocket on my thigh.

A text from Mitch:

"IT'S JOEY. COME QUICK. CYPRESS."

I'd barely reached the word "Cypress"—which presumably meant Mount Cypress Medical Center in Beverly Hills—when Crowther returned. He seemed impatient now, colder.

"Okay," he said. "Down to business. I want you to come and work for

The Talent Machine. Bill's been monitoring your progress at *Icon,* and thinks you'd make an excellent deputy. I can offer you a car—my assistant will coordinate between you and Aston Martin of Beverly Hills—plus the use of a penthouse at Seventy-eight La Brea. Salary: Two hundred thousand dollars, details to be agreed between my office and your representative. Only of course you don't have a representative, so I'll have to get you one of those, too. Oh, and while we're on the subject, I hear you're writing a novel, so I suppose you'd like to speak to my literary agent, Rick Ponderosa, who as I'm sure you know is the very best in New York."

"This can't be . . . real."

"Well, it won't be real unless you give me your answer in twelve hours. Which—as you know—is approximately two hours before the results of a certain pee test are due back from a certain laboratory in the San Fernando Valley. Although I suspect that Joey has more urgent problems to deal with, given his current location."

I froze.

"How do you . . . who *told* you . . . ?"

"*Please.* I have my sources. David's waiting for you in the chopper outside. I'm afraid the closest he can get to the hospital is Santa Monica Airport. You can order a cab from there. Remember, Sasha: Twelve hours. *Yes or no.*"

26

Room 709

JOEY PRACTICALLY KEPT an open suite at Mount Cypress Medical Center, ready to take him at a moment's notice. It was one of those running jokes. "Call Cypress!" he'd yell to Mitch whenever something trivial was upsetting him. "Tell 'em to prepare my room. I'm comin' in!" Everyone would laugh. But it didn't seem so funny now.

He'd overdosed, according to Mitch's second text, which had arrived when I was in the air.

It was bad.

After that, no more updates: Mitch had gone offline, wouldn't pick up his phone. So I did as he'd instructed, and made my way to the hospital as quickly as possible. I hardly dared think what might have prompted Mitch's silence: *Was Joey even still alive?* I kept checking the *ShowBiz* website, just in case. There were no dead rock star stories, thank God: Just another page one feature about Sir Harold's German problems, which appeared to be getting worse. "Big Corp implosion buys resurgent *Icon* more time," it read. "Could lucky break save unlucky season thirteen?"

Resurgent? Even *ShowBiz* must have expected last night's ratings to be good.

What a moment for Joey to fall off the wagon.

Three hundred dollars, the lousy cab driver charged me. For a fifteen-minute journey. I guess it was my own fault for calling him in advance, which meant he got to see me arrive at Santa Monica airport in a presidential-grade helicopter. I didn't even argue with his crooked meter, which had raced upward like the jackpot on a one-armed bandit. I just signed the receipt and threw it at him through the hatch. "No wonder everyone buys their own damn car in this city," I said, climbing out.

Security was tight at the hospital: Black-and-whites on the street, armed guards in the lobby. And of course no one wanted to tell me Joey Lovecraft's room number: *"Joey who? I'm afraid there's no Joey-whatever-his-name-is here. You must be mistaken."*

This was precisely why Joey always went to Mount Cypress: The place was built for celebrities in distress, what with the two-thousand-square-foot "recovery suites" and counterpaparazzi squads at every entry and exit point. Not that I'd noticed any telltale blacked-out SUVs on the way in, which suggested no one knew about this yet—or at least no one other than *Nigel Crowther* . . .

Holy crap, tonight had been weird.

I couldn't even *begin* to think about who Crowther's "source" might be—or anything else regarding my time aboard *The Talent and the Glory,* for that matter. With Joey in the hospital, in God knows what condition, it made me feel almost traitorous.

At the reception desk, I tried desperately to remember the fake name Joey had used when booking himself into hotels on the *Project Icon* auditions tour. It was a cartoon character, I knew that much. But which one? *Think, Sash, think.* "I'm here to see Mr. Scooby-Doo," I announced, eventually, to the exhausted-looking and bespectacled African American man behind the counter. "He's in one of the private recovery suites."

"No 'Scooby-Doo' here," he said, without looking up from his paperback.

"Please," I begged, "I can't get through to his manager on the phone. I need to be up there. *It's urgent.*"

The receptionist sighed, put down his book, and shifted uncomfortably on his chair. "Why don't you try again," he said, tapping a key on his computer. "Along the same lines."

"Oh, thank you, *thank you.*"

"Don't thank me, Miss. Just get it right."

I was *sure* it was Scooby-Doo. But there was some kind of twist to it: Something ridiculous.

"Mr. Scooby-Dooby-Doo?" I attempted.

He shook his head.

"Mr. Scooby-Dooby . . . Doo-Wop-Dooby-Doo?"

Handing me a laminated guest pass, he said: "Take the elevator to the fourth floor. Ward three, room 709. Oh . . . and Miss?"

"Yes?"

"Can you please ask Mr. Scooby-Dooby-Doo-Wop-Dooby-Doo to come up with a better name. I've been through this a dozen times already this evening."

"I will. Thank you again. *Thank you so much.*"

I ran.

Mitch was standing outside room 709 with a heavy blanket in his arms. The door was half-open, enough to reveal the shape of Joey's body under starched white bed covers. Next to him was a giant rack of monitoring equipment. It bleeped and pulsed. "They pumped him out pretty good," said Mitch. "It was touch and go a few minutes ago—I had to switch off my phone, sorry—but it looks like he's pulling through. The docs say he should be in okay shape by the morning."

I was so relieved, I threw my arms around Mitch and hugged him, causing the blanket he was holding to twitch and squeal. I jumped back in surprise, almost knocking over a passing nurse. Then I watched in disbelief as two small, pink nostrils emerged from between the folds. They sniffed the air. Then an oink and a grunt.

"Mitch," I said, calmly. "Why do you have a *pig* in that blanket?"

"Oh, uh—Joey got him last week on the advice of his psychiatrist.

He's a 'comfort animal.' Helps reduce depression and anxiety, or so they say. Joey takes him everywhere now."

"Does he have a name?"

"Benjamin Lovecraft the Third, after Joey's great-grandfather."

"Quite a title."

"We call him BLT."

" . . . so what *happened,* Mitch?"

"We just went to the pet store on Melrose. You'd be amazed what you can get for—"

"No, the *overdose,* Mitch. The *overdose.*"

Mitch rubbed his eyes. He looked ragged, spent. "Joey's mom died," he sighed. "Stage-four cancer. He hadn't told anyone about it. That's what caused his relapse, I think. I'm also pretty sure that's why he's been so . . . *unlike himself* recently. He took it really bad. He worshipped her, y'know—probably 'cause his dad was never around. But she was a piece of work, if you ask me. Remember that story he told Ed Rossitto about sitting under the piano while she played? Well, she never *let* him under the piano, it turns out. She'd lock Joey and his brother in their room when she practiced. The only time Joey got under that thing was when he broke out and she wasn't looking. He fell asleep, apparently. Convinced himself she was playing Mozart's Piano Concerto no. 21 in C major as a way of expressing her love. Tragic. He woke up screaming when he felt the boiling water on his legs. Poor kid. He still has the scars to this day. I think that's why he can be so critical of people, y'know. He just does to them what *she* did to him."

I honestly thought I might cry. The way Joey had told the piano story to Ed . . . he must have so badly wanted it to be true. "How could a mother *do* that?" I said.

"I've no idea—I think I'd be shoving pills down my neck, too, if I'd had that kind of upbringing."

"But where did he get the drugs? Did he call a dealer?"

"God, no. When Joey's using, he improvises. I caught him smoking the oregano off a frozen pizza once. So when he got the news about his mom, he just downed whatever was closest to hand, which happened to be a jar of maximum-strength aspirin. Thank God for Mu. She came home a few minutes later. Somehow got him into the Range Rover and drove him here. Then they gave him the pump and the gastric decontamination. Now he's on charcoal tablets."

"Charcoal?"

"Soaks up the drugs. No one knows about this, by the way, and I'm hoping to keep it that way. It might not matter, of course: The pee-test results come back from the lab tomorrow morning. It'll be a miracle if he passes. Here, take this."

Mitch handed me the blanket with BLT still inside. I tried to give it back, but not quickly enough.

"I'm going to get something to eat," said Mitch, who by now was already halfway down the hallway. "It's been a long night. Plus, the canteen in this place has a Michelin star. Oh—there's some milk for BLT in Joey's room. Bottle-feed him when he gets hungry. And call me if he shits himself. That's a two-man emergency."

"Did you switch your phone back on?" I shouted after him.

But he was gone.

With nothing better to do, I walked into Joey's room. It was the size of a large Manhattan apartment, with polished wooden floors, and a north-facing wall made entirely from glass, which supplied a letterbox view over the Hollywood hills and the great terrestrial constellation of the LA grid system below. Facing Joey's bed was a hundred-inch flatscreen mounted on a steel frame, along with what appeared to be every type of gaming console ever invented. Elsewhere I saw basketball hoops, a Ping-Pong table, massage chairs, and an espresso bar.

Groaning from the stress of the day, I fell backward into a deep velvet sofa by the window. BLT nibbled at my cheek. It hurt, but I was too tired to push him away. His breath smelled of . . . whiskey and chocolate. *What the hell had Mitch been feeding him?*

I looked over at Joey. His face was a mass of gurgling plastic tubes. It was doubtful he'd be waking up any time soon. To the left of him, I noticed, was a filing cabinet on wheels — at least ten drawers tall. Written on the side, in black marker: "Lovecraft, Joseph T. — patient history." And then, below that: "Cabinet 14 of 28."

I wanted to laugh but didn't have the energy. Instead, I let my head fall back onto the cushion and closed my eyes — and by the time I realized I was falling asleep, it was too late, or I just didn't care. I was done. For once, everything could wait.

27

Love What You Do

WHEN I AWOKE, there was sunlight on my face. I was still on the sofa, but BLT had gone. Outside: car horns, jackhammers, trucks reversing. "*Twelve hours,*" I murmured. A groggy fumble for my phone. The backlit screen told me it was almost ten o'clock. I'd slept *all night* . . . Jesus, and then some. Now I was late for work. More to the point: I had less than forty minutes to dial the number on the back of the business card in my pocket, and give Nigel Crowther my answer.

An Aston Martin.

A penthouse apartment.

Two hundred thousand dollars a year.

The services of Rick Ponderosa, literary agent.

Yes or no, Sasha. *Yes or no?*

Surely, this wasn't going to take a great deal of thought. And yet . . . everything about Crowther was so wrong. His ego terrified me, for a start. I mean, that was *clearly* what the whole performance with the helicopter and the yacht had been about—pure male ego. Crowther's hubris also explained why he was trying so hard to destroy *Project*

Icon, even after it had rewarded him with global celebrity and a bank account so large he could afford *The Talent and the Glory.* Leaving the panel was understandable. But gloating over *Icon*'s failure, and calling for its cancellation every day in the press? Pure malice. Maybe that's why I couldn't shake the feeling that Crowther had somehow been involved in my pills turning up in Joey's trailer. As an act of sabotage, it was just so . . . perfect. He would have surely known that Joey would be unable to resist; that a relapse of that scale would send him into a spiral of catastrophe . . . turning a bad situation for the show into something even worse.

He couldn't have done it himself, of course. Maybe *Teddy* was acting on his behalf. It made sense. Maybe the two of them had set up some kind of communications back channel, months ago, so *The Talent Machine* could hire Bibi if—or when—*Project Icon* was taken off the air. Maybe Teddy was Crowther's "source." *Maybe Bibi was in on it, too.* Would that really be so strange, so impossible to imagine, after everything that had happened this season? Bibi herself had once threatened to frame me for selling pills to Joey. If she was capable of that, then she was also surely capable of an even grander, even more diabolical conspiracy.

A final reservation about Crowther: If the exploitation of Mia Pelosi had made me so uncomfortable, how would I handle *The Talent Machine?* Crowther had recently admitted to hiring an in-house "psychological counselor" for the first season's contestants, for example. Two Svens had done the same at *Project Icon,* of course—only *his* shrink was brought in to actually *help* the contestants, to stop them going out of their minds from the fame and the weekly threat of elimination. Crowther's shrink, on the other hand, had been given a very different brief. A former psych-ops specialist from Guantánamo Bay, his job was to *break* the contestants, to accelerate and heighten their emotional distress—so the results could be captured on hidden cameras throughout the studio. That was the point of *The Talent Machine:* drama of the lowest, cruelest kind.

Still . . . two hundred thousand dollars was two hundred thousand dollars. A year on that salary, and I'd have enough in the bank to write three novels, nevermind one.

"Have you forgiven me yet, Bungalow Bill?"

Joey's voice — an octave lower than usual — startled me.

I'd almost forgotten he was in the room.

"You've alive," I said, hauling myself upright.

Joey was more than just alive. He was propped up on pillows, a morning feast laid out on a silver tray in front of him. The tubes were out of his nose. Fresh flowers had been placed around the room in tall vases. And in the far corner by the door — which was closed, with the red "privacy please" light switched on — BLT was nosing around in what appeared to be some kind of custom-built piggy playpen.

"You had every right to be mad with me, y'know," he croaked. "It's okay. I get it."

"No, Joey," I sighed. "If I'd have known about your mom . . . that she was sick . . . what she *did to you* . . . I wouldn't have given you such a hard time about the pills. Or, y'know, the other stuff. I'm so sorry this happened. My dad died from cancer, too."

Joey nodded slowly.

"So what's new?" he said, changing the subject. "Apart from me takin' enough aspirin to cure every goddamn headache in China. Shit, man — Joey Dumbass strikes again."

"You were upset."

"My mom . . . she wasn't real emotional, y'know? Some fucked-up Danish thing. Or maybe it was just her, I dunno. Me and my bro, we had a rough time dealin' with it. That ain't an excuse for doin' what I did, 'course. There's *no* excuse for that."

"Look, Joey" I said. "I know this is a bad time, so don't answer this if don't feel like it. But I need to know. When you took my pills, did you *really* find them in my trailer?"

Joey laughed, which seemed to cause him some pain. "You're still busting my ass about that?"

"I don't care if you stole them, Joey. I just need to know."

"They were *right there* in my trailer, man," he said, leaning forward.

"I fuckin' swear! Look at me: I'm done. Game over. Why would I lie to you about that now? They were in the bathroom, on the countertop. When I saw 'em, I was all alone, with the door fuckin' closed. I spent thirty goddamn years on those pills, and another ten getting off 'em. I thought I was hallucinating. I thought the devil himself had come along to tempt me. And I failed, Bill, I failed the test. But I swear to you, *they were in my trailer.* So either you left 'em, or some asshole put 'em there."

I believed him. As much as I felt like a sucker—*never trust an addict*—I really believed him.

"Now let *me* ask *you* something, Bungalow Bill," said Joey, his voice strengthening. "Why are you even doing this job? I mean, you asked me if I cared about *Project Icon* the other night. But what about you, huh? You act like you're too cool for school half the time, like none of this means a goddamn thing."

No one had ever asked me this before. Not directly, anyway. I'd certainly never had to explain it out loud. "Before my dad died," I began, aware how deluded I was going to sound, "he told me to do what I love. And what I love is . . . I love to write, Joey. But the problem is, no one's going to pay me to write a novel when I've never been published before. So I need to save up some money, take some time off, and . . ."—I gave him the spiel about Brock, Hawaii, the whole master plan—" . . . and that's why I took this job. I never even wanted to work in TV. It just came up. Len called me and it seemed like a good idea—"

"What did your old man do?"

"He played the trumpet."

"He made a *living* doing that?"

"Barely. He played in a wedding band."

"So he did what he loved, *and* he made a paycheck."

"Yeah."

"Listen to me, Bungalow Bill. Your daddy was right: You should do what you love. But here's what he didn't tell ya: You've also gotta find a way to *love what you do.* I bet you any money you like, your old man never dreamed of working his ass off—playing two gigs a night, probably—in a fuckin' wedding band. I *know* trumpet players, man: They all wanna be the next Miles fuckin' Davis. That's why most of 'em end up drunks or junkies. Either that, or they give up altogether and go kill their souls in an office somewhere. But not *your* daddy. No, he found a way to love what he HAD to do to pay the rent. Life ain't perfect, Bill. It's easy to complain about the job you've got, how it ain't *exactly* what you want, and this, that, and the other. I used to hear that bullshit from Blade all the time. 'Why are we playin' this shitty little club, now that we're a stadium band? Why are we doin' this stoopid MTV video, when it should be about the music? Why are we doing that commercial, this book deal, that reality TV show?' Well, hey, guess what? No one owes you a living. In the entertainment business, you snap your fingers, your audience has moved on, you've spent your money, and you're back home, livin' with your mom. So you wanna be a writer? Why the FUCK do you need a year on a beach with Mr. Hawaii to do that, man? You're *already* a writer: You ghostwrite for the contestants, dontcha? It ain't *War and Peace*—I'll grant you that—but everyone's gotta start somewhere."

I'd never thought about my job that way before. But it was true—I *did* ghostwrite for the contestants. I wrote those cheesy backstories to the songs they chose every week.

I remembered now what Dad had told me about his old band, Baja Babylonia: Stevie on bass, Jimbo on keys, Fitz on drums. They'd recorded this jazz album—three tracks, each lasting twenty minutes or so—and it had been reviewed by one of the underground listings magazines. A huge deal, in those days. All of a sudden, celebrities were turning up to their gigs. Within a month, they'd been picked up by the same label the Mahavishnu Orchestra were on. And a month after that, they'd been dumped. The album sold a few dozen copies. Stevie, Jimbo, and Fitz couldn't take it. For them, it was a record deal or nothing. For Dad . . . well, he loved the trumpet too much to give up. That's when he joined the wedding band, and gave music lessons at Babylon High when he wasn't touring. He'd always hoped for another break. *But he still got to do what he loved for a living.*

"I just wish I didn't feel like we were taking advantage of the contestants so much," I said. "I mean, that whole thing with Mia's dress. And have you ever seen the contracts that Two Svens makes them sign? They don't even get *paid.*"

"Oh, *honey,*" said Joey, as though my ignorance were endearing. "You ever heard of Brian Epstein?"

"Of course. The Beatles' manager."

"That's right. And d'you know what Epstein told Ed Sullivan when he offered the Fab Four a mountain of fuckin' cash to come on his show in sixty-four?"

"It wasn't enough?"

"Try again."

"I've no idea."

"He didn't *want* the money."

"You're kidding."

"Swear to God, look it up on Googlepedia. Ed Sullivan was offerin' a one-shot deal: one night, three songs, big fuckin' payday. Same thing he'd given Elvis a few years earlier. But Epstein didn't give a shit about the money. He didn't want a one-shot deal—he wanted The Beatles on the show three times in a row, top billing each time And for that, he was happy to take almost nothin' at all. *The Ed Sullivan Show* was a national ad campaign, as far as Brian Epstein was concerned."

"I didn't know that."

"You're ten years old, *how could you?* The point being: Brian Epstein was a smart motherfucker. The Beatles were lucky to have him. Just like those contestants are lucky to have Two Svens. If the greatest band in history was happy to give up a payday to get on prime-time TV, then why can't those kids do the same? Trust me—for the ones with the talent, who can work hard and take the pressure—it's the best deal they'll ever make. And before you tell me *The Ed Sullivan Show* was cooler beans than *Project Icon,* think again, man. Ed Sullivan was a Grade A fuckin' cheeseball. He had ventriloquists' dummies and tap-dancing farm animals and shit on his show. He damn near ruined the Beatles, too. Go watch the tape. He had 'em do a cover of a *show tune*

—and when John Lennon opened his mouth to sing, he put a caption up that said, 'Sorry, girls, he's married.' *Project Icon* is like Shakespeare compared with that goddamn corny bullshit."

Joey slumped back on his pillows. The speech had left him exhausted. Then he leaned forward again. "Tell you what, Bill," he said. "If you wanna write so bad—why don't you write some lines for me in your spare time? I'm sick of that fuckhead Tad Dunkel putting words in Ghetto Barbie's mouth. I'll *pay* you. Whatever Len has got you on right now, I'll give you the same. Double your salary."

I thought I must have misheard. "You mean—"

"A payin' gig. Ain't that what all writers want?"

For the first time in what felt like months, I smiled—a *real* smile, the kind that just arrives on your face, without thought or planning, requiring the use of unfamiliar muscles and sinew. When Joey saw it, he couldn't help but do the same.

"If you suck, though, your ass is fired," he added quickly.

"Okay," I agreed, still unable to stop myself grinning. "It's a deal. Thank you, Joey. *Thank you.*"

So that was it: my future decided.

As long as *Project Icon* remained on the air, which now seemed more likely than not thanks to Sir Harold's bingo problem, I had finally done it; *I had become a writer.*

Okay, so it wasn't precisely the way I had expected my career to turn out. But it was a start. And in terms of subject matter, what could possibly beat The King of Sing, the Devil of Treble, the Holy Cow of Big Wow? Not much. Not much at all. I was delighted—and I guess *relieved.* Not just because of the extra money (which would solve a number of increasingly pressing financial issues), but also because it gave me a legitimate excuse to turn down Nigel Crowther's two hundred thousand dollars a year. It also meant that I could see *Project Icon* through until at least the end of season thirteen, and as horrifically dysfunctional as my colleagues at Greenlit Studios might have been, I'd become fond of many of them: Mitch and Joey, Mu and Sue, the crew guys I went drinking with every so often (all right, a lot). Even Nico DeLuca, the strange-voiced barista, who'd started to leave freshly brewed americanos inside my cubicle at Greenlit Studios every morning, thus sparing me from the green room's 1998-vintage jar of instant coffee. And Len? Sure, he was an asshole, and yet . . . no, actually, he was just an asshole. But that didn't stop me from feeling a certain loyalty to him.

Then I remembered something.

Oh, crap, *how could I have forgotten?* I looked at the time on my phone. Nigel Crowther's deadline had passed, but another was approaching. "Joey," I said, urgently. "*Your pee test.*"

"Huh?" he replied, sounding bored.

"Your pee test. It's due back from the lab this morning."

"Oh."

"Joey, you took my pills. You took the whole bottle. That stuff doesn't leave your system for *months.* You're going to fail. What are you gonna tell Len? He doesn't even know you're here, does he? And what if *ShowBiz—*"

"Will you relax already?" said Joey. "First of all, Len will never know. Doc says I can leave here after lunch, before rehearsal. And the pee test? Seriously, man, not a problem. All you've got to worry about is getting on the phone to Brick or Brack, or whatever the fuck your invisible boyfriend is called, and tell him your plans have changed, and that he needs to get his ass over to LAX. And don't be surprised if he pulls some bullshit excuse. In fact, if he ain't already boning some hula-skirted surf princess with a snatch as tight as a bee's fuckin' asshole, I'll eat my own underwear. No offence. Now, if you don't mind, I'm gonna watch some TV here and play a game of five-knuckle shuffle under the covers. You're welcome to stay for the main event—but if I were you, I'd go make that call."

With that, Joey waved a remote at the TV, and the screen lit up like the scoreboard at the Super Bowl. It was tuned to one of the local Rabbit channels; the kind that employ young and invariably blonde female anchors to wear lipstick and strapless dresses while reading the news at ten a.m. Just what Joey needed.

I grabbed my jacket and got up to leave.

"See you later, Joey," I said. "Enjoy the 'news.'"

I was halfway to the door when I heard the smash and clatter. Joey's breakfast tray had slid off the bed, creating a slick of coffee and orange juice under my feet. A muffin rolled in the direction of BLT, who seemed baffled and yet duly grateful for this unrequested gift from above. When I looked over at Joey, he had the remains of an omelet in his lap and was half out of bed, pointing dementedly.

It was the TV.

The local Rabbit channel was showing live news footage from a helicopter. The camera was pointed at the side of a high-rise building somewhere—but the image wasn't quite in focus. Then it zoomed slightly, and the clarity improved. Through the window—which must have spanned thirty or forty feet—it was now possible to make out the interior of some kind of upscale condominium. In the center of the main room was a huge bed, surrounded by wheeled cabinets of some kind, and a figure sitting up on the mattress, arms outretched. Behind him was another figure, near the door. She had . . . *red hair* and looked . . .

Oh, Jesus, we were on TV.

Joey was now stabbing furiously at the remote, trying to raise the volume.

> " . . . infamously described as 'Joey Dumbass' by President Reagan for his parachute-less jump over Manhattan . . ."

Every phone in the room began to ring. I didn't know which one to answer first, so I just stood there, uselessly, watching myself stand there, uselessly, on the giant screen.

> " . . . troubled history of extreme behavior, resulting in a decade-long visit to the Betty Ford . . ."

Joey was out of bed now, heading for the window. His robe had fallen away, leaving him completely naked—a vision of ruined human anatomy, like one of those cautionary photographs they put on cigarette packs in Europe and South America. Someone had started to bang on the door while at the same time holding down the buzzer. The phones were still ringing.

So much noise.

But I couldn't move.

> " . . . and comes just as *Project Icon* has finally seen the first sign of a turnaround in its ratings, after seeming for months to face certain cancellation. A spokesman for Mr. Lovecraft could not be reached for comment at this hour, although Honeyload bandmate Blade Morgan has taken to Twitter this morning, saying this doesn't come as a . . ."

The news had now cut to a three-way shot. On the left: the anchor, all tight leather and gold jewelry, still talking. Below her, a scrolling caption: "*SHOWBIZ* WEBSITE CLAIMS *ICON* JUDGE HOSPITALIZED — FANS AND COLLEAGUES FEAR DEADLY OVERDOSE. STATEMENT IMMINENT." And to the right, the feed from the helicopter—which, if you looked carefully enough, displayed the outline of a sixty-two-year-old man, unclothed and in an unambiguous state of sexual arousal, screaming from behind tinted glass.

28

Chaz Chipford's Greatest Hits

May

"BILL, MEET DICK."

This was at Greenlit Studios, a few days before the season finale.

Len had just led me into his backstage office, where a tall, heavyset man with a look of barely suppressed rage in his eyes was sitting neatly at a circular table.

"Uh . . . hi, Dick," I said.

Dick blinked twice. Cheap tie, I noticed. Collar too tight. A bull on a leash.

"Dick here is a licensed private investigator," Len revealed. "And yes, before you point out the obvious—that *literally* makes him a private dick." Len laughed at this for—oh—a full minute. Then, turning to Dick: "That *is* your real name, right?"

"Correct," said Dick, unpleasantly.

"Please, Bill—make yourself comfortable," Len resumed, pulling out chairs for both of us. (A worrying sign: Len never wanted me to be comfortable.) "Dick is now going to tell you exactly what kind of *dicking* he's been doing for us over the past few weeks."

Dick stood up.

I'd already guessed the reason for his presence, of course: To investigate the source of all those "*Project Icon* exclusives" that had been appearing on the *ShowBiz* website recently. It had started with the news about Joey's admission to Mount Cypress—resulting in the spectacle of a nude grandfather parading on live TV at ten o'clock in the morning (for which the news channel had been fined for both invasion of privacy and indecency)—and had just gotten worse from there. A new scandal was breaking every day, it seemed. Sometimes *twice* a day. It was a wonder Chaz Chipford's tubby little fingers could type fast enough to keep up.

None of which had harmed us in the ratings, of course. Precisely the opposite. After the first two weeks of revelations, we were back in the top spot across all networks. The week after that, the numbers from the Jefferson Metrics Organization came in at over twenty million for the first time since the season twelve finale. The following week: Twenty-*five* million. And now, well, it was hard not to laugh: We were closing in on the big three-zero. People had even started to *vote* for the contestants again. I mean, okay, so the landline volume was still down. But if you counted text messages, Facebook "likes," and the Rabbit website survey, more Americans had participated in season thirteen of *Project Icon* than in the last two presidential elections combined. It was incredible.

As for Sir Harold: still very much in Germany. Things weren't looking too good over there. Big Corp had practically moved its entire HQ over to Berlin in an effort to get the bingo crisis under control. Meanwhile, all non-bingo-related issues were being left to the divisional chiefs to handle, which in our case meant David Gent and Ed Rossitto—who seemed delighted with the way things were going. They'd even stopped mentioning Nigel Crowther's name every other sentence.

There was no doubt about it: Those "bingo betrügers" over at Rabbit Deutschland—each now facing twenty years in federal prison for their epic scam—had bought *Project Icon* enough time to save the franchise. This wasn't of much comfort to Sir Harold, however. Having caught the fraudsters, the German prosecutors were now going after Big Corp—relentlessly and with overwhelming popular support, thanks largely to the cheerleading of rival news organizations. It was beginning to look as though they wouldn't stop until they'd driven the company out of business, or at least inflicted a lot more damage.

Thankfully, the scandals appearing in *ShowBiz* every day weren't criminal in nature. They were mostly to do with the contestants' personal lives—and, of course, Joey, who never did admit to that overdose. The official explanation was he'd been "overcome by tiredness and emotion" following his mother's death, and therefore—as a precautionary measure—had checked himself into Mount Cypress to spend the night under observation. This spectacular untruth was made a lot easier to maintain when Joey's pee test came back clean. I thought he must have just gotten lucky, or that he'd somehow managed to drown himself in enough Kangen water to fool the lab. It was only when he also sailed through the next test—in spite of having ingested a year's supply of maximum-strength aspirin—that I started to get suspicious. And then of course came Chaz Chipford's story (on which more later), which blew everything apart. By that point it was too late for Joey to get fired, however. Besides, he claimed that it had all been a practical joke, a publicity stunt in the spirit of Honeyload's early days on the road.

"Let's get straight to the point," said Dick, prodding at a remote control barely wider than his thumb. The lights dimmed as a motorized projection screen lowered itself from the ceiling at the far end of the room. To the sound of a tiny fan blowing cool air over hot circuitry, an image wobbled onto the white rectangle in front of us: a stock photograph of a burst pipe, spraying water everywhere.

"As you've probably noticed, Miss King, we have a leak here at *Project Icon,*" announced Dick, nodding with almost fatherly pride at the visual metaphor now being displayed for my benefit. "Someone in this building—someone with the most *intimate* of access to our talent—has been passing along highly sensitive information to members of the press, and by that I mean a certain trumped-up jackass at *ShowBiz* magazine, who writes under the name of Chaz Chipford."

Dick clicked his remote again, and a photograph of Chipford—taken from afar, seemingly without his knowledge—appeared on the screen. He was emerging from a Russian dry cleaner's somewhere, with a curious expression on his face.

"Now, we can only assume that whoever has been providing Mr. Chipford with his information has being doing so in return for monetary compensation," Dick went on. "And this of course would be a gross violation of any *Icon* employee's contract. Make no mistake: Zero Management and the Rabbit network cannot and *will not* tolerate such breaches of confidentiality. That's why they've retained my services to locate this mole. And when I do, Miss King, he—or *she*—will be held accountable, to the maximum-possible extent under the law."

Before I could object to the implicit accusation, Dick had activated the projector again, causing Chipford's face to dissolve into a montage of his recent *ShowBiz* front pages.

I had to admit—it was an impressive body of work:

THIS LITTLE PIGGIE *WENT PEE-PEE-PEE!*—HOW WILDMAN LOVECRAFT BEAT *PROJECT ICON* DRUG TEST
(A CHAZ CHIPFORD EXCLUSIVE)

SORRY GIRLS, HE'S YODEL-*GAY*-HEE-HOO: LI'L NUGG GETS SNUG WITH BIBI'S MYSTERY HUNK DRIVER
(A CHAZ CHIPFORD EXCLUSIVE)

#METHHEADMIA: BAZOOKA-BOOBED DIVA STOLE TV FROM DYING GRANDMA TO BUY "ONE LAST FIX"
(A CHAZ CHIPFORD EXCLUSIVE)

"COMRADE CASSIE" EXPOSED: SHE LIVES ON FOOD STAMPS WHILE DADDY MAKES $200BN A YEAR
(A CHAZ CHIPFORD EXCLUSIVE)

When Dick was sure I'd fully digested Chaz Chipford's greatest hits, he sat back down with a grunt.

"Thank you, Dick, for that insightful presentation," said Len, yawning. "Now, I don't want you to get the wrong idea here, Bill. No one suspects *you* of anything. You're far too tediously honest for that kind of behavior. Nevertheless, I can't ignore what my dick's telling me—so to speak—and he's observed some *lifestyle changes* that need to be explained, so you can be ruled out of our investigation. You took a cab to work today, for example. Highly unusual, as I'm sure you'll agree. After all, we pay you as close to nothing as makes no practical difference. And then there's this issue of your attire. I found myself looking at you this morning and not feeling slightly depressed, Bill. That's unusual. Then it came to me: You're wearing a *dress*—which is frankly nothing short of extraordinary. It's not even one of those hideous tie-dye things you sometimes drag from the swamp of your wardrobe on the hottest days of the year."

"It's a Diane von Furstenberg," I volunteered.

"It's a bloody miracle, that's what it is," said Len. "With some heels and a bit of makeup, there'd be a serious danger of someone finding you attractive."

"You're such an *asshole,* Len."

Len feigned shock. "Finally!" he cried. "*She fights back.* I've been wondering how long that would take. You can't deny it now, Bill: *Something's up with you.* What it is?"

"I'm not your leak."

"But you *know* something, don't you? Yes, you do. Tell us everything, Bill. *Tell us what happened.*"

Silence.

Honestly, I didn't even know where to begin.

When it came to my new wardrobe: Boris was what had happened. Remember that time he'd invited me over for dinner, to taste his grandfather's . . . meatball recipes? Well, when I finally calmed down enough to call him back, I accepted. And guess what? Boris can really cook. Oh, and he can really *kiss,* too. We did that. We did that . . . a lot.

The point being: Boris made me feel so good about myself, I was inspired to go clothes shopping for the first time since moving to LA. Hence the Diane von Furstenberg and a number of other not-usually-my-type-of-thing outfits—all of which had given me enough confidence to stroll right into Nico DeLuca's backstage coffee bar the next morning, and not even be questioned by the two ex–Secret Service guys at the door. They just assumed I belonged there.

Of course, my upgraded look wouldn't have been possible if I hadn't also been moonlighting for Joey as a scriptwriter. This meant I had some money to spend on things other than the rent. Mitch had even fronted my first paycheck as an advance.

I felt *rich,* almost. Plus, it wasn't like I had to save up for a year in Hawaii any more.

Yeah . . . about that. So I called Brock from Mount Cypress, just like Joey had told me to. To make things more difficult, it was a crappy line—or maybe it was the soundtrack to *Apocalypse Now* in the background, provided by the circling newscopters, I don't know—but I pushed on with the conversation anyway. I knew I was essentially breaking up with him. But the ways things had been going, "breaking up" was a technicality. I didn't even expect him to be surprised.

Oh, I had *no idea.*

"Look, Brock," I opened, pacing the hospital lobby, hand over one ear so I wouldn't have to keep asking him to speak louder. "I'm gonna stay out here until the end of the season. I might even stay longer, actually, if we get picked up for another season."

"What the hell, Sash? You said—"

"I got a writing job. This is *real,* Brock. It's not just me sitting on a beach, composing some novel that no one will ever read. It's a paying gig. It could lead to something."

"I thought you hated LA," Brock protested, without actually sounding too upset about it. He seemed to be taking this very well. A delayed-shock thing, maybe.

"Sometimes it's tough here, yeah," I replied, earnestly. "But life isn't perfect, y'know? You can't just complain all the time. You've gotta do what you love—but you've also gotta find a way to *love what you do.*" (For some reason, this didn't sound as good when *I* said it.) "If you never commit to anything because you think you're too good for it, because it isn't *exactly* right, then you'll miss out on all kinds of opportunities, and this is one of those opportunities, Brock. *Joey Lovecraft wants me to write scripts for him.* He's paying me. Why don't you come out here to LA for a weekend—see what it's like? Maybe we could do our plan in reverse?"

"Uh-huh."

A long pause.

"What do you mean . . . 'Uh-huh?'" I said, testily. "That could mean yes or no."

"I mean, uh, yeah . . . right on. Look, Sash, I've gotta—"

"Are you even *listening?*"

"Of course, Sash. Of course."

"Then what do you think about coming to LA?"

"*Me*—go to LA? No can do. I've got stuff going on. And Pete is living on the couch."

"Pete? What is he, *three years old?*" I was beginning to remember how much Brock could irritate me.

"He needs my help, man. He's broke. Look, why don't you come out here, like we said, *like we had planned,* and we can talk? All that hanging around with celebrities—it's like you're not thinking straight, Sash. I'm getting worried about—"

A muffled scrunching noise, like someone had just pulled the phone away from him.

Chaos on the line.

" . . . give it to me . . ."

"Tell her."

"... just gimme the phone ..."

"Fucking *tell* her, Brock."

"... will you stop ..."

"If you're not going to do it yourself, I'll do it for you, dammit. Jesus, you're *pathetic.*"

A female voice—older—addressed me. "Sasha? This is Nadia. I'm Brock's manager at the Hua-Kuwali. Brock's been meaning to tell you: We're fucking. We've been fucking since he arrived in Hawaii, actually, but on a more regular basis recently. We're lying naked in my bedroom at this very moment. Brock is living here with me, Sasha. His bong-brained friend Pete is subletting his apartment. That time he didn't call you back for two days when you were in San Diego? We were on Maui together. We were fucking, Sasha. We're pretty much always fucking, because as you know, Brock here is quite the piece of ass. He's been leading you on, honey. He wants you to come all the way out here, just so he can break up with you in person, which in my opinion is a lot worse than just telling you like this over the phone. But I guess I've just ruined the surprise. *Stay in LA, Sasha.*"

For some reason, I was sure everyone in that hospital lobby knew the line had just gone dead on me. So I stood there for a while longer, hand still over one ear.

"Okay, *love you,* bye," I said, a few seconds later.

Then I walked very calmly to the bathroom, where I bawled my way through half a toilet roll.

I felt much better afterwards. Much, much better.

At least Joey had been wrong about one thing: Nadia wasn't "some hula-skirted surf princess." I'd seen pictures of her on Brock's Facebook page: She was midforties, with a smoker's complexion, and showing evidence of the kind of cosmetic surgery that's intended to repair the damage caused by previous cosmetic surgery. All right, so maybe not *that* bad. But bad enough for me to suspect that Brock had a non-romantic motive, no doubt related to Nadia's salary as the manager of a five-star beachfront hotel. He always liked the good life, Brock. Or more accurately, he liked to be supported, usually via frequent and generous wire transfers from his dad. I wondered how much longer he could get away with living like that.

Then again: *Who gave a fuck?*

Not me.

Boris was sympathetic, as always.

"Dude was a gutless loser, Sash, but I know you wanted to finish your Novel of, uh—Huge Significance?—over there in hula-land. So I'm sorry it didn't work out."

"Immense Profundity, actually. And 'finish' isn't exactly the right word. It's still one sentence long."

"Yeah, but like you said the other day, at least you figured out where to set it."

"Hmm. Guess."

"Have you ever been to a fifteenth-century Norwegian monastery before, by the way?"

"No. But here's the funny thing, Boris: I think I might have already written another book. A totally different kind of book. Without even knowing it."

"What—you've been *sleep-writing* or something?"

"I'm serious. Since I moved to LA, I've been keeping a diary. Just notes on stuff that's been happing at work. Conversations with Joey. Rants about Len. That kind of thing. *You're* in it, too. Not much. But I wrote a few pages about our first date—before I found out about Mrs. Zglagovvcini being your great aunt and everything."

"Look, Sash, she *insisted* I didn't—"

"Let's not get into that again."

"She didn't think you'd agree to—"

"Mrs. Zglagovvcini is *insane,* Boris. No offence to your family or anything. *Insane.* But anyway. *As I was saying:* My novel's been right there, the whole time, staring me in the face—literally—on my laptop. I didn't even realize how much I'd been writing: I've got more than three hundred pages! And I was reading some of it back last night, and it's just . . . the craziest stuff. All I've got to do is change the names and take out that one bit about Wayne—I mean, the whole puppy thing is bad enough—and it's done. My first novel, finished. I even have a title."

"What is it?"

"*A Babylonian Named Bill,*" I said, proudly.

"Ah."

"You like it?"

"Lemme sleep on it. In the meantime, you'd better keep that laptop of yours locked up at night."

"What do you mean?"

"Jesus, Sash—*are you kidding me?* After everything that's happened this season? If Len or Teddy or any of those guys find out you've written a book about them, *they'll go nuts.* It'll be like the Watergate break-ins all over again. Back that thing up, man. Print out the file. E-mail it to yourself. And for God's sake, *don't take it to work.*"

I didn't tell Len any of this, of course. Then again, if Dick had been following me—which wouldn't have come as much of a surprise—he would have known about Boris already. I'd been practically living at his house up on Mulholland Drive. Hence the cabs.

"Look, I don't get it," I said to Len, as the three of us sat there in his office, projector still humming. "Why do you care about the leaks? I mean, okay, it sucked to be Joey when Rabbit found out he'd been using pig pee in his drug tests. And I felt bad for Big Nugg when all that stuff about Jimmy, uh, came out. Mia? well . . . *she* deserved it, to be honest. And Cassie should have known better. But that's not the point. The point is, shouldn't we be thanking Chaz Chipford? Aren't all these headlines the reason why our ratings have been going up every week?"

Len raised his palms as if in surrender.

"As much as I enjoy having a three-hundred-pound dick at my beck and call—no offence, Dick—this wasn't *my* idea," he said. "I got my orders from up on high. The way Big Corp sees it, all this tittle-tattle in *ShowBiz* might be doing us a favor for now, *but what's the next story going to be?* The Germans have put a greased fist up Sir Harold

Killoch's arsehole, Bill. He can't afford another scandal. Besides, he invested a hundred million dollars in *The Talent Machine.* He doesn't want us stealing its glory, which would make it look like the giant fucking pile of ego wank that it is. They're happy to see our numbers improve, yes—but not *too* much. And certainly not if it means giving *ShowBiz* magazine any leverage over us."

"So it's all politics."

"All I care about is catching the mole, getting through the finale next Thursday, then getting on a plane to the farthest point away from Greenlit Studios on Earth, so I can live to see another season—if Sir Legs Eleven gives us that pleasure," said Len. "Now *think,* Bill. How come you're suddenly acting like you're working at *Vogue* magazine, with all these cabs and designer dresses."

There was no point in hiding it any longer. I was amazed Len hadn't figured it out for himself already, in fact. "Okay," I sighed. "So I meant to tell you this a few weeks ago."

"Tell me *what?*" Len looked urgently at Dick, who reached for his notebook.

"It's Joey," I said. "I'm . . . writing scripts for him. Same thing Tad's been doing for Bibi all season, basically. Only I'm doing it at nights and at weekends. Moonlighting."

It was the first time I'd ever seen Len look genuinely surprised. "You mean . . . *you're* the one who . . . ?" He couldn't even get his words out. I noticed something else in Len's face, too. Another first: He was impressed. There was no hiding it.

"Yeah," I confirmed.

"So . . . the joke about the banjo and the cheese stick that got picked up by Letterman the other—"

"Mine. Well, now it's Joey's, technically. Mitch had me assign the copyright."

"Wow, Billy the Kiddo, I had no idea. A scriptwriter. *You.* Well, who would have guessed it? I wanted to be a writer myself, y'know. Always thought I had a novel in me. Mind you, I suppose you could write a hundred novels about this bloody place."

"Am I in trouble?" I asked, expecting the worst, which Len was usually only too happy to deliver.

He leaned back in his chair and put his feet up on the table. Dick looked uncomfortable with the informality and straightened himself, as if to compensate.

"I've given you a hard time on this show," Len declared, with a frankness in his tone that made me nervous. "I remember calling up Bibi not long after you got Bill's job, and telling her to invite you over for lunch when you'd been out drinking until three a.m., just so I could hear how you'd suffered through it. The celery was the best part. Oh, I almost *died.* That was Bibi's idea, by the way. And the fact she kept it going for *seven hours* before you asked to go home. Priceless! They brought out the cheeseburgers and fries the second you were out the front door."

"You mean . . ." A ripple of heat rose up through my chest and into my face. "That was—"

"What I'm *saying* is," Len went on, "I wanted you to quit or commit. There was something about you, Bill: You were good at your job, but you always seemed above it, like you didn't care, like you had some bigger plan." He was looking right at me now, leaving me with no choice but to meet his gaze, when all I really wanted to do was get up and tug at his hair, to see if the Merm could actually be real.

"Let me tell you something, Bill," he continued, changing course. "I was bullied at school. Mercilessly. Head flushed down the toilet twice a day, at ten o'clock and three o'clock, without fail. You could set your fucking watch to the sound of me going under. But it made me a better man, Bill. It made me want to make a living out of what everyone had mocked me for—my love of *pantomime*—and go on to make so much money, fuck so many beautiful women, and buy such an enormous car, that I could come back to Chiswick and laugh in the faces of all those meat-brained arseholes with their shitty houses and ugly wives."

"That's a touching story, Len," I said, squirming. "A modern-day fairy tale."

"I haven't finished yet."

"I think I already know where you're headed."

He pressed on. "So if I've been hard on you, Bill—*it was for your own good,*" he said. "And look at you now: Writing scripts for Joey Lovecraft! I'm glad you found a way to make this job work for you, Bill, and to answer your question, no, you're not in trouble. You have my blessing, as long as this stays off-the-clock. Just don't tell Ed Rossitto, whatever you do. And if I ever find you sitting around in a beret, looking at the flowers for inspiration, you're fired."

"Thank you, Len," I said—and I guess I meant it. For an asshole, he hadn't been as *much* of an asshole as I'd expected. Maybe he wasn't even that bad. Maybe he was just misguided. "For the record," I said, refusing to let his theory of management go unchallenged. "I don't think bullying made you any stronger. I think you would have done well anyway. I think bullying just makes people who are bullied do the same thing to others. It's miserable, Len. A miserable, pointless cycle."

"Agreed," said Dick, unexpectedly.

"Jesus Christ," coughed Len, taking his feet down from the table and glaring at us in turn, disgust in his eyes. "You two should go take a fucking cuddle break."

"I've got a much better idea," Dick suggested, impatiently. "Why don't we get back to business?"

"Yes," agreed Len. "Where were we?"

"Suspicious activity," prompted Dick. He seemed eager to get me out of the room, move on to the next interrogation. Presumably they were working their way through the entire *Project Icon* payroll, in which case, it was going to be a long day.

"Right, yes," said Len, fingers on his temples to focus himself. "So before you go, Bill: I need you to tell us *anything* you've seen or heard at *Project Icon* that's given you cause for concern. Anything. I know you think all this press has been good for the ratings—and it has, yes—but Sir Harold has made his feelings very clear: He wants this leak plugged and the person responsible for it punished. This bingo business has pushed him right to the edge, Bill. Plus, the man's *eighty-two years old.* He's unpredictable. Any excuse, and *bam!* He'll shut us down. And I don't even need to tell you how much pressure Nigel Crowther is putting on the old bugger to give *The Talent Machine* a clear field in September. We're not home free yet, Bill. Not by a very long shot. So think: *Who could be doing this?*"

29

Wingwoman

THE FOLLOWING THURSDAY, when finale night arrived, I was on an airplane.

No kidding: At 4:47 p.m., local time — thirteen minutes until opening credits — I was at five thousand feet, and rising. Only this wasn't a commercial jet, taking me back home to Mom's place in Long Island. No, it was a Beechcraft Super King Air, a rattly old twin turboprop deal, the engines vibrating at precisely the same frequency as my recently formed headache. There'd been a lot of drinking the previous night, after Sir Harold's speech. And who could blame us, really, after everything we'd been through? Still: There I was, in an actually-quite-flattering jumpsuit, with a parachute on my back, and a steel frame over my chest to support a wireless camera unit. Next to me: an instructor and a technician, the latter recalibrating some vital piece of mobile broadcasting equipment.

Oh, and yeah: Joey was right behind me. They had him in the "full James Bond" — tuxedo jacket, white shirt, bow tie, striped pants, cummerbund, spit-polished shoes . . . the works. Not to forget the *Pro-*

ject Icon-branded crash helmet, radio headset with microphone, and —most important of all—matching black parachute.

He grinned and made the triple ring sign.

Joey, being sober, was the only member of the *Project Icon* staff without a skull-crushing hangover—and he'd spent most of the day being insufferable about it: making a high-pitched, nondirectional humming noise during rehearsal, for example. Or mock-vomiting in front of Bibi. (This had backfired somewhat when he actually *did* vomit.)

We kept gaining altitude.

Six thousand feet . . . seven . . . *eight* . . .

In case you're wondering: I told Len and Dick everything. More or less everything, anyhow. When I skimped on details, it was to protect Joey. The details are never kind to Joey.

I started with Milwaukee, and Bibi's threat to set me up. And then I moved on to the part about how my pills had later gone missing—*what a coincidence!*—and reappeared right there in the bathroom of Joey's trailer. Naturally, I lied and said Mitch had discovered them in good time. (There was no need to get into the whole thing about Maison Chelsea, especially with regards to Joey's tongue and my mouth.) I even came clean about Crowther, believe it or not. The helicopter, the yacht . . . the fact that Chaz Chipford himself was *right there,* by the fireplace, drink in hand, those improbably dimensioned women fawning all over him. The only detail I left out was the appearance of Bill. It was irrelevant; and besides, I'd signed that confidentiality agreement, and didn't want to push my luck. As for the climax of my tale: It was Crowther's revelation that he knew about Joey's admission to Mount Cypress Medical Center, *seconds after Mitch had texted me.* I didn't mention the aspirin, of course. "Someone must have tipped him off," I said, hoping they'd suspect, as I did, that it was Bibi.

Or Teddy, of course.

Or both of them, working together: Team Evil.

I was in that room for what seemed like hours, going through all of this. When I was done, Len looked drained of what little color he'd had to begin with. Dick, on the other hand, could barely have smiled any wider. I doubted that he'd ever had a more interesting day. Then the pair of them stood up, thanked me, told me they'd look into it, thanked me again, and hustled me out of the door.

It was over. Done.

Now for the consequences.

I didn't actually see Len again until the day before the finale, when Sir Harold made his "presentation" to the *Project Icon* staff. The Big Corp CEO was supposed to have delivered this in person, of course—it was an annual fixture—but he couldn't, on account of his ever-worsening Bavarian problem. Instead, the crew set-up a video link between Greenlit Studios and his hotel suite in Berlin, and we awaited his address in the seats usually reserved for the audience.

Eventually, Sir Harold's face appeared in triplicate on the stadium-grade monitors.

"Can he see us?" someone whispered.

No one was sure.

"*Guten Abend, Kollegen,*" he began, smiling weakly. He looked every bit as bad as I feared he would: as though every organ in his body were struggling to function. His voice was half-gone, too. All that testimony, no doubt. The Germans had him in court eight hours a day. No life for an octogenarian—even if he *was* a billionaire.

"For those of you who haven't had the pleasure of visiting beautiful Deutschland," he went on—without any discernible sarcasm—"that means, 'Good evening, colleagues.' "

Introduction over, the camera panned out jerkily, to reveal a hunched, scowling figure next to him.

"*Oh, Jesus,*" Len groaned from the front row, not bothering to keep his voice down.

"As some of you over there in Hollywood will know," said Sir Harold, gesturing sideways, "this is Rabbit's Director of Global Advertising, my good friend Bertram Roberts."

"Hello," said Bert, his mouth curled in a way that suggested he was suffering from profound dyspepsia. Given his general posture, this wouldn't have been surprising.

"So, over the past few days, Bert and I have been looking at the Jefferson numbers for season thirteen," revealed Sir Harold, ominously. "And all I can say is—*Wow, what a comeback.* Amazing what the survival instinct can do, eh? Really, very impressive indeed." He mimed applause, reminding me of the time he'd done the same thing in Bibi's movie theater. "Congratulations to you all. And to think, it wasn't so long ago I doubted you'd even make it to the live episodes! Well, now there's hope. I'm delighted to say that Bert and I have put together some projections, run them past accounts, and we're in a position to renew *Project Icon* for a fourteenth season . . ."—the beginnings of a cheer—"as long as the ratings of tomorrow night's finale are enough to raise your *season average* to the number one position. Because number one, as you know, is what Big Corp is all about."

A confused pause: The cheer was on hold.

Without a spreadsheet of the Jefferson numbers for every episode to consult—not to mention a calculator—it was impossible to figure out exactly how many viewers we needed to make up for the show's atrocious performance at the beginning of the season. A lot, obviously. Still, we'd been doing well lately.

Outstandingly well.

Fortunately—or unfortunately—Bert was on hand to provide clarification. "Thirty million," he said, with a tiny, don't-hold-me-to-that shrug. "Should be enough. Thirty-one would be more comfortable, of course. We think it's achievable."

"So there you have it," Sir Harold concluded. "Chins up, everyone. You're almost there."

He reached forward, and the screen went blank.

Muttering in the auditorium. A few groans. But there was hope.

That was when Joey put up his hand and said, "Hey, guys: crazy idea. *How about*—"

• • •

So here's how the opening of the season thirteen finale would go: In a witty reference to the most notorious moment of his career—if not all of rock 'n' roll history—Joey Lovecraft would throw himself out of a light aircraft at ten thousand feet and land on the roof of Greenlit Studios, where a band would be waiting, already grinding out the lustful, swampy, utterly degenerate groove of "Hell on Wheels." And at the precise moment Joey's feet touched down, rockets would burst into the sky, the King of Sing would release the hordes of tortured banshees from his lungs, the band would stop—epic silence!—and a lone guitar, its amp stack set to a volume louder than a Nordic god in a volcano-throwing rage, would begin the riff that had helped conceive a million babies.

Dn.

Dn-nn-nah.

Dn-nn-*nah*-nh! Bleeeowww-neow-neow . . .

Thirty million viewers. Like Bert had said, it was achievable. Or as Joey had put it: "Sometimes you've just gotta grab yourself by the nuts and reach the fuckin' high note, man."

Len hadn't taken any convincing to go along with Joey's plan.

Neither had Ed or David.

It was a go. And because I was the only producer on *Project Icon*'s staff with any skydiving experience—thanks to all those trips to the Keys with Brock—I was appointed Joey's jump mate, or wingwoman, or whatever you wanted to call it. The camera practically welded to my chest would act as backup for the one on Joey's helmet.

Through the plane's windows, Hollywood gleamed. The sun was at that point in the sky where everything turns to molten gold: windows, roofs, street signs, swimming pools . . . The plane banked unevenly. We were circling now. We were ready.

The technician patted me on the arm and held up his right hand: It was 4:55 p.m.

Five minutes to go.

"You okay?" I shouted over to Joey, pushing my headset aside, so I could hear his reply.

"Why?" he yelled back. "*You gonna push me?*"

Before I had a chance to answer: A tone in my ear, like an early-1950s synthesizer. It was my phone. The crew had jury-rigged it to the communications system, so I could stay in touch with Len on the ground. Snapping the foam cups back over my ears, I fumbled for the cord that dangled by my right ear. There was a button on it somewhere that let me take calls. If I could just . . . dah . . . yes, that was it . . .

A click. And then—

"We know who did it," announced Len, his voice so clear, it was as though he were inside my frontal cortex. "Dick is done with his dicking. I just came out of the meeting."

"*The leak?*" I said, looking over at Joey. His eyes were closed and he was singing. Oblivious.

"Well, yeah, we know *that,*" scoffed Len. "We also know who stole your pills."

"Who? I mean, *how*—"

The technician raised his hand again, this time tucking his thumb into his palm.

Four minutes.

"Security footage from Joey's trailer," said Len. "I didn't even know we had a camera in there, to be honest. Turns out Mitch is paranoid. Likes to check up on Joey once in a while. He'd deleted the tapes, of course—but luckily he uploads a copy to a server farm in India. It took Dick a while. But he got it. It's unmissable."

"Len, *just tell me:* Who was it?"

"On the tape, it looks like a bloody cat burglar. Black turtleneck. Leather gloves. Baseball hat, pulled down low. He sneaks in there—your prescription bottle in his hand—fumbles around a bit, then puts it right on the countertop, next to Joey's toothpaste. The poor old fucking junkie didn't stand a chance. We probably wouldn't have been able to make out the guy's face if he hadn't spent so long posing in front of the mirror. Moron. Anyhow, when we zoomed in on the tape—"

Three fingers now.

"WHO?"

"Wayne Shoreline."

"*What?*"

"Oh, it gets better. As soon as he was done, he made a phone call."

"You could trace the call?"

"No, Sherlock: *We had audio.* We just listened to him speak."

"And?"

"He said, 'Nigel, my love, it's me. It's done. See you tonight.' Then Crowther's voice comes on the line, you can hear it almost as clear as if he were on speaker. He goes, 'I'm proud of you, pumpkin,' then hangs up."

"So Wayne *is* gay!" I spluttered.

"No, he's not *gay*, Bill. Jesus, *don't you know anything?*"

"Huh?"

"You don't seriously think Nigel Crowther was born with a penis, do you? *Please.* He's straight. He just likes things a bit . . . twisted. Anyhow: Turns out Wayne is hopelessly in love with Crowther. Totally obsessed. Would do anything to please him. Crowther realized that a while ago and was using him, like he uses everybody. He even promised Wayne a job on *The Talent Machine*—as a judge, this time—if he helped destroy *Project Icon.* But it's all water under the bridge now, I suppose. Stealing prescription drugs is a felony, and we've got videotaped proof. The police should be here in a few minutes. They're going to cuff him after the show."

"Wow," I said, taking a breath.

The technician was showing only two fingers now. He began opening the cargo hatch.

"And the leaks?" I asked, almost forgetting.

"Nico DeLuca," Dick replied. "The in-house barista. Real name: Kevin Smiles. He's a British tabloid journalist—hence the ridiculous accent—who came over to Hollywood in the eighties to set up his own scumbag news agency. Employed by none other than Midas Industries. But it's not what you think. Teddy and Bibi were on *our* side. They'd studied the UK version of *The Talent Machine*—how Crowther trashed his own contestants in the tabloids for the sake of the ratings—

and they wanted Two Svens to do the same thing, to save *Project Icon.* But he refused. The old Swede's too soft. So they just did it themselves —and it worked, obviously. Smiles was selling stories left, right, and bloody center. He even managed to bribe one of Joey's girls, Mu, into giving him the scoop on his relapse. Here's the twist, though: Crowther *also* has Smiles's agency on retainer—he keeps a boatful of his photographers moored alongside *The Talent and the Glory* at all times. Whatever Teddy leaked to Smiles, Crowther immediately found out from the captain of the good ship paparazzi."

One finger. The hatch was now fully open. I could barely hear anything over the wind.

"So Bibi and Teddy *weren't* trying to destroy the show," I said, holding the mic up to my mouth.

"Of course not. If Bibi had wanted a job on *The Talent Machine,* she would have accepted Crowther's offer last summer. As for her threat to you: Coincidence. She and Edouard have been going through a tough time. If you'd have confronted him about the cue cards, he would have thought it had come via Bibi, and it would have made things worse, so she had no choice but try and shut you down. She feels pretty bad now, after what happened with Wayne. She wants to apologize."

Joey put an arm around my shoulder. *He was ready.*

Len got off the line, and his voice was replaced in my ear by the live feed from Greenlit Studios.

Wayne was mid intro.

". . . high above us at this VERY SECOND . . . in an airplane circling the studio . . . we're going LIVE . . ."

Joey winked.

The red light on his helmet cam came on. We were on air.

"Look at me," said Joey, suddenly, grabbing my arm to pull me closer. "Look at my face."

"Joey, I'm okay. Stop it. I've jumped out of a plane before, hundreds of times."

"No, *look at me,* Bungalow Bill," he said. "I want you to remember one thing . . . the golden rule."

"Huh?"

"*RATINGS,*" he yelled, unstrapping his chute in one fluid movement and hurling it out of the open hatch. I screamed and reached out to grab him, but he ducked away.

"*THEY'RE IMPORTANT.*"

That grin.

Then he was gone.

Since the conclusion of Project Icon*'s thirteenth season, two articles regarding the fate of the show have appeared on the front page of* ShowBiz *magazine. They are reprinted here with permission.*

DEATH OF AN ICON

EXCLUSIVE FOR SHOWBIZ

BY CHAZ CHIPFORD

AFTER months of will-he-won't-he speculation, Big Corp honcho Sir Harold Killoch has FINALLY done the deed. As of last night, Project Icon *is no more.*

Dead.

Gone.

An ex-singing competition.

There were bitter tears of regret and humiliation last night at Greenlit Studios, where the long-suffering Rabbit warblefest had just wrapped its unlucky thirteenth season.

Ironically enough, ratings for the two-hour finale are projected to be up by a THIRD over last year, thanks largely to a near-fatal stunt by celebrity judge Joey Lovecraft. The Honeyload wildman had been scheduled to open the show with a well-rehearsed skydive over Hollywood, but changed the plan at the last minute, tearing off his parachute and throwing it from the cargo hatch of the Beechcraft Super King Air as it circled Greenlit Studios at ten thousand feet. Mr. Lovecraft then appeared to leap to his death—prompting a record 924,391 calls to 911 in the Greater Los Angeles area (and a small explosion at Rabbit's call processing facility in Eagle Rock, CA)—only to pull the cord at the last moment on a backup 'chute, concealed within his tux. The producers' shock turned to anger when Mr. Lovecraft veered badly off course, ending up just south of downtown in the LA River—from which he had to be fished, sans hairpiece, and with a broken toe. The incident brought to mind Mr. Lovecraft's infamous parachute-less jump over Manhattan in '83, which prompted President Reagan to name him "Joey Dumbass" during a Rose Garden speech.

Result? The show's opening number of "Hell on Wheels"—which Mr. Lovecraft had been due to perform on the roof of Greenlit Studios alongside the L.A. Philharmonic and a returning choir of Nepalese lentil famine refugees—had to be substituted in haste. Jimmy Nugget did the honors by yodeling his way heroically through the Tom Waits classic "Downtown Train," and was later rewarded for his efforts by winning the season. Meanwhile, a junior-level Project Icon *employee who had accompanied Mr. Lovecraft on his stunt above Hollywood had to be rushed to Mount Cypress Medical Center upon landing.*

"Having not seen Mr. Lovecraft's second 'chute open, she believed he had committed suicide," said a spokesman for the LAFD, whose paramedics were first at the scene.

In the end, however, neither this chaotic opening spectacle, nor the extraordinary succession of scandals that have rocked Greenlit Studios of late, were enough to make up for Project Icon*'s abject early-to-mid season performance—during which it temporarily lost the title of "America's most-watched TV show" to* Bet You Can't Juggle That! *(in spite of the tragic alligator mishap that halted work on the latter show for ten days). Indeed, Sir Harold—whose Big Corp empire counts the Rabbit network among its more profitable subsidiaries—had warned* Icon *staffers in advance that if the finale didn't grab a large enough audience to give the franchise a season-long* AVERAGE *in the top position across all networks, then it would face immediate cancellation.*

As ShowBiz *can exclusively reveal: Old Harry made good on that threat last night.*

"Last night's finale was your elimination night," begins a message

from Sir Harold that will land in the inboxes of Project Icon's *cast and crew this morning (an advance copy was seen by* ShowBiz*). "You gave it your best shot—and for that I congratulate you—but your best wasn't good enough. This is the end of the road for you. You should be proud of all you've achieved; of the history you've made. And I hope you will all join me in wishing Nigel Crowther and his team at* The Talent Machine *all the very best as they go about the hard work of reinvigorating this genre for a new generation of Rabbit viewers."*

The official ratings for the Project Icon *finale, due out from the Jefferson Metrics Organization early this morning, are expected to show that it prevented the franchise from meeting its season-average target by a mere eighth of a percentage point—a fact that will only heighten the anguish of* Icon *staffers being laid off. No matter how close, however:* ShowBiz *has been assured that Sir Harold's mind is made up. He is said to be looking forward to a "fresh start in Rabbit prime time" when he returns to the United States this week from Germany, where he and a team of senior Big Corp executives have been assisting the Bundestag with an investigation into televised bingo irregularities. A settlement in that case is now expected within days—finally putting an end to the bizarre and costly scandal that has distracted Sir Harold for several months.*

As for those dejected souls at Project Icon: *They will be issued their pink slips before noon today—a humbling end to twelve years of pop-culture domination. Reached on his cell phone last night, supervising producer Leonard Braithwaite could utter only grotesque personal insults directed at the writer of this article. Meanwhile, a cooler-headed response to the death of the once-untouchable franchise was supplied by Mr. Crowther, who is currently relaxing off the coast of Malibu aboard his fifty-million-dollar superyacht,* The Talent and the Glory.

"For me, this decision is so overdue, it isn't even a case of 'rest in peace,'" he said, laughing heartily. "More like, 'Goodbye and good bloody riddance.'"

Mr. Crowther's The Talent Machine *will air in the fall.*

ANNOUNCEMENT

FROM THE EDITORIAL BOARD

OF SHOWBIZ *MAGAZINE*

With great regret, ShowBiz *announces today that Executive News Editor Chaz Chipford is leaving the magazine. The mutually agreed upon decision follows an internal investigation into Mr. Chipford's "exclusive" story regarding the cancellation of top-rated reality TV franchise* Project Icon, *which appeared on the front page of this magazine three months ago under the headline, "Death of an Icon." Once again,* ShowBiz *apologizes without reservation for this article, and any distress it may have caused, especially to the cast and crew of that show.*

An internal report produced by the editorial board of ShowBiz *has established that Mr. Chipford filed the story in question with a personal guarantee of its veracity. Given this publication's trust in Mr. Chipford, not to mention his storied fifteen-year career as an award-winning entertainment correspondent, it was sent to press only minutes after* Project Icon*'s season thirteen finale aired, while simultaneously breaking on our website and Twitter feed. Alas, barely an hour later, an extraordinary turn of events proved Mr. Chipford's report both premature and wildly inaccurate: News emerged from Germany that Sir Harold Killoch, proprietor of the Rabbit network—home of* Project Icon *since its debut—had been arrested and imprisoned in Berlin, without bail, on charges related to the manipulation of televised bingo games in that country.*

As our readers will be aware, the arrest triggered a succession plan at Rabbit's parent company, Big Corp, and at an emergency board meeting in Los Angeles, Sir Harold's estranged brother, George Killoch, was appointed new Chairman and CEO of the family-controlled media conglomerate. It came as little surprise in Hollywood when Mr. Killoch chose immediately to renew Project Icon *for another season, with an option over five more. After all, Mr. Killoch was the first to discover the show's format on Belgian television, and had worked tirelessly to overcome his elder brother's resistance to commissioning a pilot.*

Mr. Chipford's departure comes several weeks after he was placed on administrative leave. Meanwhile, ShowBiz *has appointed Kevin*

Smiles, a British-born editor and former agency owner, in a new role as Supervising News Editor. Mr. Smiles will take responsibility for covering Project Icon's *fourteenth season, and the circumstances surrounding the cancellation of* The Talent Machine *after just one episode and a reported hundred million dollar loss by Rabbit. The much-vaunted show, created by former* Project Icon *judge Nigel Crowther, attracted only five million viewers — a quarter of what Crowther himself had once claimed was necessary to avoid a franchise being "put out of its misery".*

His theory was proved correct.

UPDATE

A trial date of early January is now likely for Sir Harold Killoch, in the sensational bingo scandal that has gripped Germany and sent Big Corp's stock price reeling on Wall Street. Meanwhile, prosecutors in Berlin are soon expected to outline their case against the Big Corp mogul, with reports suggesting the evidence may rest on a "smoking gun e-mail," sent to all senior Rabbit network executives, ordering them to "double-delete electronic files" related to Rabbit Deutschland's bingo-related operations. Among those who allegedly received the order: Nigel Crowther, who currently has plenty of his own financial problems, following the repossession last week of his yacht, The Talent and the Glory.

Leaked details of the e-mail indicate it was written in code, with Sir Harold using his mother's native tongue — a tribal language from the South African region of Nbdala — to maintain secrecy. It remains a mystery how anyone outside Big Corp's inner circle could have intercepted — or indeed translated — such a message. There have been persistent rumors, however, that Big Corp was infiltrated by at least one intelligence officer working for the Bundesnachrichtendienst (BND), Germany's foreign intelligence agency. The BND has neither confirmed nor denied these rumors, but one popular German website says it has confirmed the undercover agent's cryptic, single-letter call sign: "Z."